Fury

Book One of The Cure

Omnibus Edition

Charlotte McConaghy

First published by Momentum in 2014
This edition published in 2014 by Momentum
Pan Macmillan Australia Pty Ltd
1 Market Street, Sydney 2000

A CIP record for this book is available at the National Library of Australia

Fury: Book One of The Cure (Omnibus Edition)

EPUB format: 9781760080822
Mobi format: 9781760080839
Print on Demand format: 9781760080921

Cover design by Matt O'Keefe
Edited by Deonie Fiford
Proofread by Laurie Ormond

Macmillan Digital Australia: www.macmillandigital.com.au

To report a typographical error, please visit momentumbooks.com.au/contact/

Visit www.momentumbooks.com.au to read more about all our books and to buy books
online. You will also find features, author interviews and news of any author events.

Charlotte grew up with her nose in a book and her head in the clouds. At fourteen, her English teacher told her that the short story she'd submitted was wildly romantic, so she decided to write a novel. Thus began her foray into epic fantasy and dystopian sci-fi, with sweeping romances, heroic adventures, and as much juicy drama as she could possibly squeeze in.

Her first novel, *Arrival*, was published at age seventeen, and was followed by *Descent*, which launched The Strangers of Paragor series, an adventure fantasy for teenagers.

She then wrote her first adult fantasy novel, *Avery*, the prologue of which came to her in a very vivid dream. Her second adult novel, *Fury*, is the first in a romantic science-fiction series called The Cure, set in a dystopian future.

Charlotte currently lives in Sydney, having just finished a Masters in Screenwriting from the Australian Film, Television & Radio School. With her television pilot script, she won the Australian Writer's Guild Award for Best Unproduced Screenplay of 2013. She will, however, always be a novelist at heart, still unable to get her nose out of the books.

For my brother Liam

Chapter One

Josephine

I am a flame of fury. The last flickering flame in a world long since burned out. I have rage threaded through my skin, whispering against my ears, tied tightly around each one of my bones. My eyes, one brown and one blue, leak with it.

Most of the time this frightens me.

But sometimes I like it.

*

"When did it happen to you?"

He appears to be reading something but I figured out a while ago that he sits there and stares at a blank clipboard. God only knows why. Maybe he thinks it makes him seem smarter, or more aloof. I roll my eyes and turn them to the sky outside the window. A hint of dark gray is edging across the blue, and I can feel the static of a rising storm across my skin. I imagine being inside it, right in the heart of it, wild and out of control, but I only imagine this for the briefest of moments, because otherwise it starts to hurt too much.

"What?" Anthony asks. I know full well that he heard me perfectly the first time, so I don't repeat myself. After a pause he says, "Nine years ago."

"So you were ... what—twelve?"

"Hilarious."

"How old *are* you?" I sit up and face him.

"None of your business."

"You're in a friendly mood today. Aren't you supposed to support every word I say?"

He shoots me a look that says *at this point I couldn't care less what I'm supposed to be doing with you.* He is so tired. I can see it in his blue eyes and in the set of his mouth. I feel a moment of pity but it doesn't last long because he wrecks it by saying, "Have you been taking your pills?"

"No. I seduced all the nurses on staff so that they skip me when it's time for rounds."

He actually looks alarmed, which is amusing.

"Yes, I take them. And they don't do anything, like I've told you a thousand times."

"That remains to be seen," he says sternly. What a dick.

"You don't look that much older than me, but you act like you're eighty, Doc."

He looks at me blankly and I grin. Antagonising Anthony Harwood is undoubtedly the only fun I have left in my life.

"Let's talk about Luke," he suggests.

The grin is wiped clean from my face. "No."

"Why not?"

"Because I don't want to."

"Why don't you want to?"

I lick my lips and then meet his eyes. "For the same reason I've requested a new therapist. You don't understand, Anthony. You don't understand anything."

He looks pale as he glances down at his clipboard, as though searching for an answer. He's on the small side of medium height and medium build, and he's pretty much the definition of the word average. Except he does have nice eyes when he smiles. I only worked that out recently, because he's smiled all of three times in the entire year. His dark hair is prematurely graying at the temples, which he probably loves. Despite this, I would still put him at about twenty-seven, twenty-eight.

"What don't I understand, Josephine?" he asks me.

"You're a drone. You have no concept of humanity any-more—which is why you're no good to me as a therapist, and why the very thought of talking to you about something as private as Luke makes my skin crawl."

He sighs. "Who else do you think you'll get?" He folds his arms, starting to get impatient. "There's no one left who hasn't been cured. Everyone is a 'drone'."

Ain't that the truth.

I sink back against the comfy window seat, depressed.

"The only people left who feel anger are the Bloods."

"And me, apparently."

"Allegedly," he reminds me pointedly.

"Yeah, *allegedly*. So to sum up—Luke isn't on the agenda, today or any day."

"Is the real reason because you made him up?"

"Oh, Lord." I laugh. "We really are back to Basic Therapy 101. Imaginary friends. You've outdone yourself today, Doc. Did you buy your degree off the net?"

"Luke has never come to visit you and yet you say he loves you."

"I would never expect you to understand the simple concept of complexity," I say sweetly.

"You speak in paradoxes."

"And it feels wonderful." I smile. "If only you could appreciate it."

He frowns and drops his clipboard onto the desk in what seems a rather petty manner to me. There are still forty-five minutes of our session to go, but he has that stubborn look on his face that tells me he won't be the first to break the silence.

We've been doing this—sitting here in this room—every day for almost an entire year. Each time he diagnoses me with some new disorder, I get to try a new type of pill that inevitably fails, and we have to go back to the drawing board. I don't mind the drugs that make me sleepy, because they make the time pass faster, but I do not enjoy the hallucinogens. Not. At. All. I'd sooner gouge my eyes out than go through those kinds of visions again. I get enough of them in my sleep as it is.

At the moment Anthony is convinced I have schizophrenia.

I would love to have schizophrenia. I'd *love* it.

Because the truth—a truth I've been trying to convince Anthony of for almost twelve months—is much worse.

"So nine years ago, eh?" I murmur, running my fingers across the glass of the window. It's not cold enough outside for there to be any condensation—in fact the air is warm and humid. The wind is picking up, but I don't want to close the window—fresh air is a rarity in this place, and it's one of the only things that makes me feel halfway sane. "Do you remember your life before you were cured?"

"Of course."

"Is it ... different?"

He tilts his head and then gives a sigh that says *fine, I'll indulge you because I'm infinitely patient and good and you are just a silly, erratic child I feel sorry for.* "Yes, it's different. It's like there's a wall in my head between then and now. Everything on the far side of the wall is wild, chaotic and exhausting. Everything here is calm, beautiful and healthy."

I get what he's saying. I understand the ache of the before, because I've never had the after. I've lived every moment of my life within the full spectrum of human emotion, and he's right—it *is* exhausting. But I can't imagine ever being tired enough of life to want to cut half of it away.

"Were you happy to get the injection?" I press.

He grimaces uncomfortably, taking a pen and pretending to write in his notepad. I stole a look at that pad once and it was covered in doodles of birds. I wait for him to quit stalling and answer, but he remains silent.

"Some people look forward to it, don't they?"

I shudder.

"A great deal of people." Anthony sits forward and searches my face. "Josephine, why are you so against the cure? It helps people. It makes things safer and happier."

The futility of trying to explain something to the brainwashed is not lost on me. I have tried many times and it hasn't made a lick of difference. But I simply cannot bring myself to give up.

"My fury belongs to me, and only me," I say as calmly as I can manage. "No one can take it from me—no one has a right to it."

"Even if it hurts people?"

"Tell me how I'm supposed to have any sense of who I am if I don't have access to how I feel? It's like punishing a crime before it's even been committed—like punishing the *idea* of a crime. Where does our freedom go then? We all have a right to be as angry as we want, just as we have a right to be trusted."

"Give me an example."

Is he serious? "All right. I'm pretty damn angry with you right now, but I'm not going to lunge across the room and strangle you to death. I have restraint, and a logical awareness of consequences."

"That remains to be seen."

"Oh, shut up."

"Why do you *want* to be angry?" Anthony asks. "It doesn't help anyone."

"Want has nothing to do with anything. Have you heard the rumours, Doc?"

"What rumours?"

I smile coldly. "Don't play dumb. Even I've heard them and I'm locked in an asylum. They've cured the human population of anger, and everyone knows that soon sadness will be next. *Sadness.* Can you imagine never being able to feel sad? What value will happiness have? And what will be next? Fear? Jealousy? Vanity? We'll cure ourselves of our humanity."

"Perhaps you should try to calm down, Josephine."

"It's called passion. When was the last time you felt passionate about anything?"

"I don't know—there are pills for it."

It takes me a moment to realize that he's made a joke. My jaw drops open in astonishment. The corners of his mouth twitch and I laugh abruptly. Our eyes meet and a moment later he gains control of himself, looking embarrassed at his outrageous behavior. He will probably go home tonight and school himself not to be so *wild*. Wind is starting to keen through the trees outside. It sounds like screaming and makes the hairs on my arms stand on end. I am reminded of the nightmare in my head, replaying itself over and over and over.

"Do you know what the date is?" I ask softly without looking at him.

"I do."

"Have you made any preparations?"

"What preparations do you suggest I make, Josephine?"

"I've told you a thousand times, and I've watched you pretend to write it all down a thousand times. I'm tired of repeating myself."

"Hallelujah," he says.

My jaw clenches and it hurts to breathe; I can feel the tide creeping up. I am too tired to say another word. We sit together and yet not together—I haven't had a 'together' in a year. Instead I've had lots and lots of 'alones'. We sit alone together until the hour runs out, and then he stands and leaves the room before me.

He has never left the room before me. It's nothing, nothing at all, and yet it leaves me feeling lost. Even though I hate routine, in this place I need it.

Doyle comes to collect me, taking hold of my arm with that alarmingly tight grip of his. I don't know how long I will have to be here without misbehaving before he will loosen that grip. He is unlike any of the other nurses in the facility. His face is scarred, his nose crooked as though it has been broken and, if I didn't know better, I would think he was an angry man. He doesn't want to be here—that much is obvious, and I always wonder why he is.

Doyle jerks me out of Anthony's office and starts walking me down the halls. The lights in this building are fluorescent and flicker just enough to make you go steadily insane, if you aren't already.

Screams follow us down the halls. Screams and sobs and mutters. They make me cold, all the way through, even now. Even after a year.

As we reach my room I flash Doyle a smile. "Thanks, Doyle. One of these days you and I are going to have a really meaningful conversation, you'll see."

Doyle, true to fashion, doesn't respond. He throws me into my room roughly and locks the door behind me. I turn and inspect the view, hoping that maybe my eyes will spot something new this time. What a surprise: they don't.

There is my empty steel desk, bolted to the ground. There is my tiny steel bed, bolted to the ground. There is my uncomfortable steel chair, bolted to the ground. And there is my Maria, mute and asleep and stationary like she's bolted to the ground. I also have four windowless walls, and one large calendar, so large that I suspect it may have been made for the vision impaired. I hate that calendar as much as I need it.

Circled in black is one date. A date that falls in this month. And this week.

Time is running out.

It won't be me who suffers under the blood moon.

It will be Maria. And Doyle. And Anthony. And every other person in the lunatic asylum on top of the hill.

SEPTEMBER 12TH, 2065

Anthony

I don't know how it happened, but at some point in the last year my life has become about Josephine Luquet. I can hate her for it, but I can't seem to do a thing to change it. Every hour of the day is like torture, except for her hour. Josephine's hour.

As she sits there, within the tiny room but miles away from me, I can feel my body start to tremble as though it wants to be angry with her but can't remember how.

Anger is a foreign concept to me. I am still frustrated—endlessly, it sometimes seems—and I am still impatient, but these feelings are dull, shades of what they once were.

I want to make Josephine listen to me but doing that may as well be like trying to force her into a tiny box she is far too big to fit within.

I don't know why Josephine is how she is. Why she wasn't cured like everyone else in the world was. And I don't know why she has such violent delusions.

The only thing I do know is that she is one of a kind. An anomaly. A monster with strange blue and brown eyes, and a smile too cold for words.

Yesterday's session was bad. There's no getting around it. I failed to contain her anger, which is my main job, and I failed to convince her to speak of Luke. But last night an idea occurred to me. Today I am keen to broach it.

"Why hasn't he called you?" I ask as she enters my office.

She blinks, her eyes dripping with scorn. I can't bear that scorn. It's the worst thing about her.

Or maybe it's the worst thing about me, that she has so much to be scornful of.

"Well hello to you too."

"Don't avoid the question, Josephine."

"Oh, Anthony," she sighs. "You suck the fun right out of this."

I don't know who told her that therapy for a mental illness is supposed to be fun, but I shrug apologetically anyway.

"I don't know why he hasn't called."

"Have you tried to contact him?"

Her eyebrows arch. "Would that be via morse code, or with a homing pigeon?"

"Don't they give you phone privileges?"

"Don't *who* give me phone privileges?" she snaps. "Doyle, the barrel-of-laughs nurse who manhandles me constantly? Maria, my semi-comatose roommate? Or my ever-distracted, uninterested therapist who dashes from the room the second our hour is finished? Because the three of you are just about the only people I have contact with."

I find myself speechless. Distracted? *Uninterested*? I must be a better actor than I thought, because those are two of the last things I am with her. I belatedly realize how sad her life must be. She hasn't spoken to anyone except two virtual mutes and *me* all year. "All right, how about I organize for you to make a phone call?"

She doesn't say anything, and to my surprise I see a faint pink blush creep up her neck. She crosses the room and sinks into her usual spot, twisting her face to the window as she always does. The rain has been falling all day and the sky is streaked through with white veins of lightning.

"What's wrong? Don't you want to call him?"

"I don't … know how to reach him. His old number was disconnected."

"I could find a new one for you."

"I don't even know where he is anymore."

"Where did he work?"

"He was a state prosecutor." Josephine pauses, frowning. "Still is, I guess. I forget that the world keeps turning beyond these walls."

"There you go. Shouldn't be too hard to find a contact number somewhere."

Her face lights up and for a moment she is utterly unburdened by the heavy dark veil that usually clouds her.

"On one condition."

Josephine's shoulders slump and she rolls her eyes in that way of hers. "I should have known. You really don't give a shit about me."

"Of course I do," I say firmly, but she won't meet my eyes.

"What's the condition then?"

"Tell me about Luke. All of it, every single detail from the time you met up until the day you arrived here."

Her strange eyes flash dangerously. "What happened to privacy, Doc?"

"That doesn't exist anymore. Not for you, and not in this room."

"Why?" she demands. "Who gets to decide that?"

"I do, because you've tried to kill yourself three times."

There is a slow-burning silence. A clap of thunder finds the right moment to startle us both.

I stand up from my desk, but can't manage to move from behind it. It feels safe behind the desk. "Josephine," I murmur. "I need to figure out what's inside you."

The truth is I already know—an abused child can respond to being hurt in a number of different ways, and Josephine's hallucinations are a perfect example of that. But I need her to speak about it. She never *speaks*, not in the ways I want her to. Without words we'll get nowhere together.

She smiles and there's ice in my veins. "You could have just asked, Doc. It's simple. There's an inferno."

SEPTEMBER 17TH, 2063

Josephine

I'm on fire; everything in my entire body feels alight. Even though my ears are pounding, I need noise, loud enough to drown out the screaming I hear when I blink, and I need darkness dark enough to black out every horrific image I imagine myself to have committed last night. I go into the first place I find, the pounding bass reverberating all the way out into the street. I push my way through a loud crowd, feeling every accidental touch against my skin. I manage to find a seat on a couch and slump down onto it, closing my eyes. Nobody comes near me—nobody even looks in my direction. I'm not sure why this is, but it's always been the same. No matter where I go or what I do, I'm ignored.

I sit for a while and sink into the noise around me. Pain lances through every muscle, every bone. My mind whirls, entranced, dazed. The music helps to keep me here in the room, as does eavesdropping on other people's conversations. There are two girls behind me who won't stop talking about the benefits of wearing primer under their foundation. "*I'd die without it,"* and *"Where do you get yours from?"* and *"Thank god they make travel-sized bottles!"* I had thought primer was something you painted a house with, but I've clearly been labouring under a misapprehension and might die unless I get myself some fast.

"Hello, beautiful."

It's a deep, rough voice. I don't look at him straight away. Instead I roll my eyes. I don't get hit on much, but when I do it pisses me off. Opening with "hello, beautiful" is uninspired. At best.

"Hello," I start to say, but as I turn I forget the second half of the word. He's looking at me. Like, *really* looking at me. And he's beautiful. Despite the fact that he looks like he might not have slept in a month, he has incredibly bright green eyes. There are dark bags beneath them, and they're bloodshot as hell, but damn they're green. He has short dark hair and stubble over his square jaw, and even as he sits there, completely still, there is an undeniable sense of movement in his long limbs. I can't work it out, but he's sort of ... animal.

In all my life I can't remember seeing anyone with a gaze like his.

"It's rude to eavesdrop," he points out, cocking his head to listen to the girls.

"It's rude to point out when something's rude," I mumble.

"What's primer?" he asks me while wincing at a shriek of their laughter.

"No idea."

He gives up on listening to the girls' growing hysteria and looks at me directly. "You looked really lonely."

I pull myself together and give him a bleak stare. "How do I look now?"

He smiles slowly. "You look good."

Yes, he's gorgeous, and yes, he's got possibly the most delicious smile I've ever seen, but in one line he's just reverted into every idiot drone who doesn't have a clue. I feel so tired—and angry, too angry. I want to tear this whole place to pieces so they won't all be so *happy*. Their lives are just … easy. This man sitting before me is easy. I want to run and scream and cry and shut it all out, except that then I would be left alone with the blood moon.

"Just go away," I sigh. I regret coming here. It was stupid. I am almost too tired to get up and leave. I consider what might happen if I curl up on this couch and go to sleep. Would they leave me here? I can't imagine anyone touching me for long enough to move me. I can't imagine anyone even realizing that I am here.

"I can't," the man says. At a guess he's early twenties. He's a boy, really. Or, he'd look like a boy if he weren't wearing that expression. He would have received the cure at fifteen, like everyone else, which means he didn't get much time. He didn't get many years of freedom before they stole his personality.

"What do you mean you can't?"

He shrugs. "I mean I can't before I make sure you're all right."

I eye him suspiciously.

"So are you?" he presses.

"I'm fine."

We stare at each other. "You can toddle off and feel really good about yourself now," I murmur coldly.

"I'm not trying to pick you up," he says.

"I didn't say you were."

"You're the saddest girl I've ever seen."

"So why didn't you run the other way?"

"Because if sadness goes next, I want to remember what it looks like."

And just like that, I am made of sand and sinking through the cracks in the floor. I have an absurd desire to have his skin against mine, to see what it feels like, to see if it burns as hot as mine does. I am a long way from words, but he doesn't grow awkward, he simply waits for me to come back.

"What does sadness look like?" I eventually ask in a soft, rasping voice.

He tilts his head and eyes me critically. "It's cold blue and warm brown. It's blurry edges and stillness. It's unnerving," he says, "and beautiful."

After a while he adds, "I'm Luke," and holds out a hand for me to shake. I don't, because there is still blood on mine, and even though he won't be able to see it, I'll know it's there. I haven't touched or been touched by anyone in years, except for the occasional brushing of a shoulder.

"Josephine Luquet."

"All right, Miss Luquet. If I asked you why you're so sad, would I be the first?"

"That's presumptuous."

"Probably. Would I be?"

I shrug, unwilling to admit that he would be. "Are you going to ask me?"

"Yes. But not tonight. Right now I'm going to walk you home because you look like one touch might send you to dust. Come on."

I follow him outside, blinking to rid myself of the haze I'm trapped in. He feels like a dream. My teeth ache. And my fingernails.

He lights a cigarette and I look at him properly. In the spill of light from inside he looks pale. His white t-shirt is dirty and full of holes, as are his jeans, which sit low on his hips. He's wearing ratty old flip-flops, and I can't believe he got into the club dressed like that. On the other hand, he is undeniably attractive, and men probably spend hours trying to make themselves look as careless as Luke does. He's tall and lean like he might be a little underweight, but he's no less muscled for it. The strength through his arms and chest is real—it's the type that comes from hard work, not from muscle enhancers.

His cigarette smoke makes me feel like I might throw up. My head is pounding and I realize I must get home immediately or I'll be in danger of collapsing in the gutter with a strange and eloquent man named Luke for company. I take off down the street and he follows, uninvited.

"Should we get a cab?" he asks.

I ignore him. He doesn't actually think he's coming home with me, does he? I stumble slightly and he's there to catch me by the elbow, but his hands on me cause my heart to lurch with fear and I pull away. This is too strange. No one even *looks* at me, let alone… this. "Don't touch me."

"Sorry. You were about to eat concrete."

"Are you following me?"

"I'm escorting you home, like a gentleman."

It's becoming too much. I can't breathe. Just last night I … Oh, Jesus, I can't face that—not yet. But there was a *last night*, and now I can't have … this. I can't have him looking at me and saying nice things to me and being a gentleman. I'm not a girl who understands those things—not today, on the 17th. Today I am a wraith. A shadow.

I am covered in the blood of the moon, and I'm the only one left who can feel angry about it.

We reach my block of apartments and I face him. No way is he finding out which number I live in. "Okay. Bye."

"Josephine," Luke says quickly. The moonlight makes his eyes look greener.

"What?"

"It'll be all right."

I smile, and even I can feel the chill of it. "You're a silly boy."

He searches my face with a look of his own. I suspect that among people who know him this look must be famous. It is very assured and direct. It says *you don't frighten me because I am more than I look.* "I'll be back in the morning." I think this is supposed to be a promise, but it feels more like a threat.

"No you won't."

"I have a question to ask."

"Luke." I lick my lips and try to give my next words weight. "If you come back and ask that question, I don't know why but I think I might answer it. And the truth is, if that happens, we're both going to regret it."

Luke

I watch her go into her apartment with the hopeless aware-ness that my life has changed. She's different—so alarmingly different that I knew it the first time I caught sight of her. Under the calm, she's rabid. And I've been waiting a long time to find someone like her.

The world is a sea of ghosts. When the plague annihilated us there were riots in the streets. Buildings came down in a flood of dry rubble. A fury made of fear was born, and the world grew dangerous. Nine years ago the government—every government—built walls around the re-maining cities and started administering the cures. No more anger for humanity. No more aggression. The fight went out of us; we were malleable, controllable drones. But with one emotion gone, the other parts of us grew skewed and out of shape. Now everything is distorted—our perceptions of the world are damaged. A woman cheats on her husband and he can't manage to care. A house is burgled and the occupants think it's funny. A child is lost and nobody understands the importance of this except the Bloods. These aren't rational responses—they are the reactions of damaged psyches, brains that are scrambling to connect pieces of pictures that have been pulled apart.

It is rumored that in three years the first of the sadness cures are scheduled to be administered. And what will the world be made of then?

Society has gone mad. I've been suffocating—until tonight, until she looked at me. I'm not sure what she is, or what she means, but I must ask that question, even if it will make her hate me forever.

Chapter Two

SEPTEMBER 18TH, 2063

Josephine

I am inspecting my bruises in front of the bathroom mirror when I hear the first knock at the door. I ignore it, sure it must be someone trying to sell me something, or worse—the land-lord asking where last month's rent is.

My body is covered in dark blue, purple and yellow. The worst of it is on my right hip and down the length of my spine. My muscles feel stretched and sore, like I've just battled karate black belts or laid under a train. There is a long thin cut along my thigh that looks like it might be getting infected.

Yesterday was a trance of horror. Today is worse. Today is clear and real, and so glary my eyes hurt.

The knocking sounds again, more persistent this time. A foolish thought occurs to me—could it be the Bloods?

My momentary hope flounders when a voice floats through the door.

"Josephine! I know you're in there! Open the door!"

Last night comes back to me in a rush. It's him. The strange man from the club who followed me home. Jesus fucking Christ. He can't be serious, can he?

Pissed off, I grab a dressing-gown from the bathroom. I can't believe he thinks it's okay to turn up at my door.

"Josi!" he shouts. "Come on, open up."

Did he just call me Josi? I open the door a crack but keep the chain in place so he can't push his way inside. "What the hell are you doing here?"

"I told you I'd be back." He smiles disarmingly. He has a wide mouth full of straight white teeth, and the expression is so gorgeous I can barely believe it.

"How did you know which apartment I live in?" I demand.

"I watched you go inside last night. Come on, let me in."

"No way," I all but snarl. "Are you out of your mind?"

"Why not?"

"Because you're clearly a sociopathic stalker. Insanity has risen a lot since the cure, you know."

He grins as though I've said something funny. "Come outside for a walk then. It's a beautiful day."

"Luke—it's Luke, right? I can't deal with this right now. I haven't even had a coffee—"

"Great, there's a café around the corner. Get dressed and let's go."

He bounds down the stairs, whistling something ludicrously cheerful as he goes. I want to strangle him. Instead I shut the door and go back to bed. My body hurts, and my head hurts, and I'm too tired for his smiles.

SEPTEMBER 19TH, 2063

Josephine

I wake to pounding on my door. Disoriented, I lie in bed and try to blink myself awake and into reality. I've got no idea what time it is, or what day. But this feels like déjà vu. Is it Luke again?

As consciousness returns I become aware that my throat is raw and shredded.

Then I hear, "Ma'am? It's the police!"

My heart lurches in my chest with wild terror and hope. Could it be that someone has finally found a clue? A piece of evidence?

Have they come to take me to jail?

I stumble out of bed and pull on some clothes before running to the door. There are two men standing in the dingy hallway. To my disappointment, they're not Bloods, but just normal, low-ranking cops. One of them holds his hat in his hands, twirling it over and over. The other is leaning against the opposite wall looking bored.

"Yes?" I ask breathlessly.

"We had a call early this morning, ma'am."

"Yes?" Nobody is getting any handcuffs out. They're not reading me my rights.

"From a concerned neighbor. Says she heard a woman's screams coming from your apartment. Says she could hear it for most of the night. Are you all right? Are you the only one living at this residence?"

I stare at him and feel all my hope seep away through my pores. There's no proof, no evidence. These men are not here to arrest me.

"Yes, it's just me," I sigh. "I'm fine. I have night terrors."

The man leaning against the wall snorts derisively.

"Oh," says the front officer. "Good then. Glad you're okay. We'll be on our way. You have a nice day, ma'am."

I watch them leave, and that's when I spot Luke sitting on the stairs leading upstairs. He's just watched the whole exchange. I consider calling the cops back and telling them to arrest this stalker.

I feel a storm coming over me and try to breathe through it. What is he *doing*? "Leave me alone," I order through clenched teeth.

He's not smiling this morning. He looks like an entirely different man. A dangerous man. Shadows fall across his eyes. "I heard the screaming too," he says bluntly. "When I got here this morning."

I don't know what he wants me to say. He's got absolutely no idea what he's hovering at the edge of, and it almost makes me laugh to imagine how he'd react if he discovered the truth of me.

"You heard—I have night terrors."

"You sure do," he agrees.

I stare at him and then spread my hands. "What do you want?"

He stands and walks past me. "Come," he orders, and this time there's no nonsense in his tone. It sounds like he's someone who is used to being obeyed. I'm about to slam the door again when he pauses and adds, "If you don't come and get a coffee with me, I'll be back tomorrow morning, and the one after that, and the one after that, until you agree. I might even start coming at night, too. So it'll save us both some time and pain if you just get your skinny butt out here now."

My mouth opens in fury but no words come out. What a *prick*! My mind whirls, trying to figure out how to respond. I could call the cops on him. I could have him thrown in prison for harassment. And stalking. I could move—I'm due to find somewhere new anyway. I'll probably get kicked out pretty soon. I could just out-wait him—I bet I can ignore him for longer than he can be bothered to keep coming back.

I don't trust him for one single second, but I have a disastrous flaw called curiosity. I have no idea what his interest in me is, but I find myself wanting to find out. And wanting, if I must admit it, to understand the look he keeps levelling me with, because it's one I certainly haven't been looked at with before.

I plod back inside and pull on some ratty old jeans and a long-sleeved tee that will cover the bulk of my bruises. I don't bother brushing my hair because this meeting might be a good opportunity to repulse him. Shouldn't be too difficult.

Outside, he's smoking again. And he seems to be back in his cheerful mood. When he sees me he grins and winks. "Good girl."

Condescending wanker.

I roll my eyes and storm past him, headed for the nearest café. I push inside, head straight for the counter, order myself a black coffee and then cram myself into a table in the corner, all without looking at Luke. I hate being around so many drones—they make me deeply uncomfortable.

Luke arrives at the table some time later with arched eyebrows. "No need to order for me," he mutters.

I smile sweetly and then turn my eyes away from him.

"So these night terrors …" he starts.

"Don't even think about it," I snap.

"Clearly you're not a morning person."

"I'm just not a 'have coffee with my stalker' person."

He snorts with laughter. "I'm a nice guy, I promise. Well, maybe not nice, but I certainly won't hurt you."

"What's the purpose of this? Are you trying to sell me something?"

"I just want to… you know—talk. If you still want me to piss off after a coffee, I will."

I stare, too suspicious to believe this could be the real reason.

Luke shrugs. "Haven't you ever just wanted to get to know someone?"

Well, sure. But no one's ever wanted to get to know me.

Our coffees arrive and I blow on mine before taking a big long gulp. Thank god for caffeine. I can't drink it on the other side of the moon—it makes my nerves shatter. But on this side it practically saves my life, calming me right down.

I'm enjoying a moment of blissful quiet when he says, "You haven't been cured, have you?"

I almost drop my cup. The rest of the café disappears, and Luke is the only other person left in the world. I turn slowly to meet his eyes. "What?"

He doesn't repeat himself. He just gives me this calm look, like he's daring me to deny it. Is this the real reason he brought me here?

"Of course I have," I say faintly.

There is no sound except for our breathing, no color except for his eyes.

"Don't be scared," he tells me.

"I'm not," I snap.

He searches my face. "I won't tell anyone. Ever. I'm just curious."

"How did you ... How do you know?" My voice breaks.

Luke is bleak and full of hard edges. "It was obvious from the moment I saw you."

"No one else has ever ..."

"I'm sure they noticed," he says. "But they were too uncomfortable to let themselves really *see*."

"But you saw."

He shrugs. "I don't know why. Maybe it's a glitch in my cure. Maybe it's an incorrect response from my damaged brain: to want to be near someone who could hurt me."

My heart starts beating fast. He doesn't know how close he has come to the truth. "Maybe it is. Maybe you should fight that urge."

"Josephine," he says impatiently. "Don't tell me you're the last woman alive who hasn't been brainwashed, but you believe the propaganda anyway. Because that would just be heartbreaking."

I don't know what to say. Here is a man who understands. He has been cured, but he still manages to see through the bullshit. When was the last time I heard anyone call it propaganda or brainwashing? I try to remember, then realize it was in the riots of '53. Nobody protests anymore—that all stopped when the protesters were cured.

"I don't believe the propaganda," I tell him. "I don't believe people are dangerous just because they can get angry. But in my case … things are different. I'm not … normal."

"I know that—you're the only person I've ever met who isn't cured."

"Not that. Not just that. I'm dangerous."

He frowns. "Why?"

I shake my head and take another gulp of coffee. He needs to stop pulling at this thread. He's not going to like what he unravels.

"How did you escape it?" he presses. "It's impossible to avoid the cure."

I shrug, aware that we are surrounded by drones who could alert the Bloods at any moment if they even suspect I'm uncured. "None of your business." Truth is, I have no idea how I escaped it. Sometimes I feel like a shadow, or a memory—a creature invisible to the rest of the world. How else can I explain being ignored so thoroughly, even when it comes to the mandated injection that every citizen must receive?

"Fine. What do you do for work?" he asks, voice abruptly light. All the noise returns to the café and we are no longer the only two people in the world. We are surrounded by busy, bustling drones going about their calm, happy lives. Luke is one of those drones, I need to remind myself. Just because he knows he's been brainwashed, doesn't mean he's free of it.

"Not much," I reply. "I have a fake ID so I can do bar work here and there. Coffee shops. My last job was in a bookshop. That was nice."

"Why so many jobs?"

"I get fired a lot."

He smiles. "Right. Because you're a crazed maniac who might lose her temper at the drop of a hat."

My lips twitch. "They don't know that. I'm just a crap employee."

Luke grins.

"What do you do?" I ask.

"I'm a lawyer."

"What kind of lawyer?"

He shrugs. "State prosecutor."

I sit up straight. "Then you work with the Bloods?"

"Sometimes."

One of my secrets: I envy the Bloods. I envy them their freedom, but I hate what they choose to do with it. "What are they like?" I ask.

Luke considers carefully, absently stirring more sugar into his coffee. Lots of sugar. I watch, the action seeming out of place but I'm unsure why. "They're colder than you'd expect," he finally admits. "More ... detached. They have all their emotions, but sometimes I think they're more like drones than the drones are."

"Why?"

"Because of what they see, I guess. Terrible things."

"You must see those things too."

"Not really. I see the aftermath. The fractured way society tries to deal with crime. But I don't see what the Bloods do."

They must be like me—they *must*.

"I'll tell you a secret," Luke says, suddenly bleak. "The cure was designed to stop the riots. All the violence after the economy collapsed. But crime has doubled in the last few years. We're building more jails than public housing. The media is strictly controlled. Nobody can know the truth."

I swallow, my heartbeat jacked right up. "So why are you telling me?"

He smiles without any humour. This isn't the gorgeous smile I saw this morning. This is infinitely dark. There are a thousand secrets behind his eyes, all the ghosts of the things he has seen. "Maybe I'm hoping someone will hear."

My mouth opens. I'm having trouble looking away from his eyes. "And raise the alarm?"

That smile again. The twisted one. "It might be fun to run. Really run."

"And when they catch you?"

"They wouldn't."

"Of course they would." I realize abruptly what is happening here: we are testing each other. In a way, I have been running for most of my life and I have never been caught.

"Not if I don't stop running," he answers, as though he has read my thoughts.

I shake my head, glancing around. It occurs to me that I might be in danger. It's lunacy to talk like this out in the open. "There's nowhere the Bloods won't find you."

"I could go west."

I snort. He's so blasé, so careless with his words, as if it doesn't mean anything at all to just announce that he will go west. "There is no west," I say flatly. "Have you forgotten about the drought that wiped everyone out? The disease that followed it? The west is a wasteland."

He doesn't react, just watches me through hooded eyes. "This city is a wasteland."

"You're being ridiculous," I say, lowering my voice. "You'll get yourself thrown in jail if anyone hears you talking like this."

"You like it," he tells me bluntly, leaning forward. "I can see it in your face. You love the danger."

I stare at him for a long moment, and then I let a slow smile curl my lips. "If this is your idea of danger, Luke, then I feel sorry for you."

There is a beat of silence, and then he grins wolfishly, leaning back in his chair and lighting up a cigarette.

"You can't smoke inside," I tell him.

"Watch me."

I reach over and yank the cigarette out of his mouth. "I don't know if you're an arrogant prick, or if you're just pretending to be one, but either way I've had enough."

He looks at the cigarette in my hand, considering me. Then he slowly produces another one and lifts it to his lips, watching me the whole time.

I stand up and walk toward the door. He doesn't stop me. I feel enraged, my heart beating like a timpani drum. I don't need a bratty child in my life. I don't need to spend time with an asshole drone.

Something smashes nearby, startling me. I turn to see that on the other side of the café there are two young men standing over the prone figure of a waitress. A pile of plates and food is smashed beneath her and she's weeping, but the boys are smiling cruelly at her. The eyes of other patrons glance their way and then slide on, unmoved by the sight. I feel a wave of fury too deep to contain. I want to tear down the walls of this world we live in, I want to make people see that this is sick and wrong—nobody cares for each other anymore, nobody has any compassion, any sense of connection. I see things like this every day, but today I hate those boys like I've never hated anything, because within them is the kind of apathy that has destroyed the world.

I start moving, unsure what I will do. If I show anger, the Bloods will come, and I cannot risk getting captured and cured. But I've started moving beyond that thought, way beyond it. The waitress is sobbing and bleeding—I can see a shard of crockery protruding from her arm. One of the boys kicks the mess of food into her face and then crows with amusement. I know it isn't his fault—this is something that has been done to him, stolen from him—and yet I want to hurt him badly. I want to force some perspective into him.

I have almost reached them when someone else moves first. It's Luke. He appears behind the boys, taking them by the ears and wrenching them out the door of the café. Everyone watches silently as he dumps them on the ground. I don't hear what he says to them, but it is spoken with quiet calm. The boys leave in a hurry, smiles gone from their faces. Luke returns, walking straight past me to the waitress. I watch, transfixed, as he helps the girl up and sits her down in a chair. He pulls the piece of plate out of her arm, wraps the wound in a dishcloth and then tells her to go to a hospital. Then he motions for one of the other waiters to clean up the mess, takes me by the elbow and calmly steers me back to my seat opposite him. All without even the hint of an expression on his face.

I stare at him, heart still thumping. My anger's gone, replaced by a deep, curling thrill in my stomach. I have never, ever seen a drone help a stranger. I've never seen a drone admonish another drone. What is it about him that seems so different? I can't put my finger on it, searching his face for a clue.

Nobody else in the café seems bothered by any of it. They've already gone back to their conversations.

"Why did you do that?" I ask softly.

He doesn't look at me as he says, "So you wouldn't." And then, without an apology, he pulls out his packet of cigarettes and drops them into our jug of water. I watch the packet sink to the bottom.

I meet Luke's eyes. "I don't like to be tested."

"I know that now. It's why the smokes are wet."

I hold his gaze for another moment, and then I pick up my menu.

*

We don't talk for quite a while. We peruse the menus, and I don't know what he's thinking, but I can't focus on a single item I read. Luke waves his hand like some English monarch and a waiter arrives at a run. "Bacon and eggs, chorizo, hash browns and spinach," he says. "And mushrooms. And maybe some baked beans. And more coffee. Josi, what do you want?"

"If there's any food left in the world after that I'll just have an omelette," I mutter, my mind miles away. Several screens on the wall depict a primary school fair and another shows a flower festival, both full of smiling, happy people and bright colors.

"You know they film that shit in their studios," Luke says lightly, eyes moving between the screens. I nod. Everyone knows that. But nobody cares. The news programs show people things that make them feel safe and happy, so they accept without questioning. I watch the children in the image flying a kite and laughing. In a few years those children will have their innocence stolen, their freedom torn out of their brains, but nobody ever sees images of that. Nobody ever asks the children if they want to be cured, if they'd rather have passion than calm.

An advertisement for enhancement drugs comes on screen. "Dream like savages, live like humans."

I turn my eyes away, feeling sick. Once someone has been cured they don't dream anymore. New drugs are being developed to create artificial dreams—dreams that have been cleared for safety, dreams that aren't too stimulating—but the fact is: brains have been dulled.

"Would you take those?" I ask Luke.

"Dream stimulants? Fuck no."

I search his face while he is distracted by the holograms. It comes to me with a jerking sensation. "You swear," I exclaim. "Drones hardly ever swear. And you put sugar in your coffee. Drones don't care about taste."

"That's a myth," he replies mildly, still not looking at me. "An old one. Why would they put sugar on the table if no one wants it?"

Good point. "What about the swearing?"

Luke shrugs. "I must be a rebel." Then he smiles and I can't help laughing.

I try to stop, reminding myself I know nothing about this guy. Haven't I longed for someone to talk to though? Haven't I yearned for decent conversation? Wished for a friend?

Jesus, how pathetic am I? I can't have friends if everyone in the world is a drone, because I can't be friends with people I hate. I just need to keep reminding myself of that, or else Luke is going to continue with that smile and that gaze, and all the lonely, stupid pieces of me will respond with an eagerness that could get us both killed.

I finish my coffee and run my finger around the lip of the mug. I regret sitting in the corner—I feel trapped. There aren't many places to look except at Luke. He's not watching me, thankfully. He's sitting back in his seat, long limbs lazily taking up all the space, reading a paper. A frown line appears on his forehead, right between his eyes. It's quite possibly the most adorable thing I've ever seen. I hate him for it.

"Want a section?" he asks absently without looking up.

Get up. Just get up and leave. You know better than this.

But I don't get up. I ask, "The crossword?"

He retrieves the back section and passes it to me. Then he grabs a waitress and pinches her pen in an extremely charming way that makes her melt into the floor. Passing me the pen, he promptly goes back to reading the sport section, apparently oblivious that he's just made the girl fall a little in love with him.

We sit quietly until our food comes, both intent on our papers. As our plates arrive, Luke glances at my crossword and his eyes widen. "Holy shit. You've nearly finished it!"

I flash him a sly smile. "Not just a pretty face, pal."

"I'm becoming aware of that. Oh, baby, I love chorizo."

He inhales his food with a look of delight. I have no appetite, but try to eat anyway, because I can't remember the last time someone bought me a meal. For some reason, despite still having no idea why we're here together, I find myself simply appreciating the company. If I want to continue appreciating his company, however, I'm going to have to make sure he never finds out the truth. The fact that he knows I'm uncured is bad enough.

"How old are you?" I ask him.

"How old do I look?"

I shrug.

"Twenty-six. How old are you?"

"Eighteen."

He spits out his coffee. It's extremely amusing. "*Eighteen?* Good god."

My lips curl into a smile. "Why should that be a problem, Mr I'm Not Trying To Hit On You?"

"All right, clever girl," he laughs, leaning forward. "I was twenty percent hitting on you, eighty percent worried about you."

"And now?"

"You're a teenager, Josi. You're not ready to get hit on by me."

I roll my eyes. "If you say so." I'm somewhat relieved, somewhat confused. If he doesn't want to hook up with me, then why is he here? What does he get out of this exchange? Because I haven't been particularly nice, that's for sure.

"So cynical," he sighs.

"I am not!"

"Right now you're sitting there wondering why I'm here, assuming that nobody does anything nice without wanting something in return."

"Anything nice?" I repeat slowly. Suddenly I'm angry. I stand up. "I don't know what you think of me, or what you've assumed, but I'm not a fucking charity case. You think you're doing something nice, but you're just making a fool of yourself."

I storm out of the café, tripping over his long, sprawled out legs. He reaches for me but I snake around him and run.

Luke

I'm the stupidest man on the planet. I pay the bill and run after her, but she's damn quick. She's already locked the door behind her, but I bang on it and shout at her until my throat is hoarse. Finally I take my tools out of my pocket and pick the lock on her door.

I know.

But I'm losing my mind, standing out here in the disgusting hallway, imagining her behind the locked door. I can't seem to do anything to stop my hands as they break into her home. The apartment block is so old that it doesn't even have a touch lock modulated to her fingerprints, just an ancient metal tumble lock.

The door finally swings open and I stop dead. She's curled up on her bed with the pillow over her head so she won't hear me shout for her. The studio apartment is the tiniest, most revolting place I've ever seen. Although the term 'studio apartment' is a loose one. Her home could more aptly be described as a rat-infested, falling-to-pieces, unfurnished hovel. The walls are water marked, the carpet is filthy, her mattress doubles as a couch and the kitchen is more of a sink situation. She doesn't seem to own anything except a suitcase stuffed full of clothes. My heart aches at the scene laid out before me. She looks so small, lying there like that.

It takes her a moment to realize I've gotten inside. She jumps up in alarm, and I can see the fear in her eyes as she faces me. She glances around for a weapon, but I hold up my hands quickly.

"Don't—it's all right. I'm sorry."

"What the *fuck*?" she hisses. "How did you get in?"

"Picked the lock."

"*What?* Who knows how to pick a lock, for Christ's sake? You're a psychopath!"

"I'm sorry, I don't know why I did that. I just … I freaked out. For some reason I thought you were in here doing something to yourself …"

Her gaze sharpens. "Like what?"

I take a step forward and try to explain. "You're just … You're leaking with guilt and regret. I can feel tides of it pouring from your skin, and in your eyes there's so much sorrow. It scares me. I want to understand and I want to fix it."

"You can't fix it," she whispers. She's so beautiful. I've known it all along, but it strikes me now, abruptly. Tall and slim and delicate. Her features are fine, her lips small and red. Her eyes are the loveliest thing about her; her very own sun and moon, light and dark. Her hair is an incredibly long mess of black.

"Can't I at least try?" I ask. "I never try for anything anymore. I've let so much slip by me. So much is gone from our lives now. I couldn't … look at a girl like you, with *life* in her face, and just walk away from that."

Josephine Luquet crosses the room to stand before me, and then she does something that makes my heart stop. She reaches out and places her hands on either side of my face, and in her eyes there are tears, and in her voice there's broken glass. "Listen to me. You can't fix me. I kill people."

Chapter Three

Anthony

"You told him? Just blurted it out like that?"

"Yep," she smiles. "Just like that."

"What did he say?"

She laughs softly, her fingers pulling at the edge of the window seat. "Nothing. For a really long time."

"So what happened?" I can imagine this man in my mind—he's already starting to get bigger and take up space. Not as much as she does—not nearly as much. He is her shadow, but he exists now, since she started speaking.

I think I truly believed he was imaginary. I suppose he still could be, but her story is so rich with shape and color that I find it hard to believe she could have made it up.

"Our time's up, Doc," she reminds me.

I jerk upright and look at the clock. Ten past five. Grabbing my empty briefcase, I stride for the door.

"Anthony?" she calls and I pause. "Will you call him?"

"You haven't finished your story yet."

"Time's running out."

I glance over my shoulder at her. She is painfully deluded. I leave quickly.

*

At home I run my hand over the lock and the light turns green before admitting me. I press the food button and wait for my meal to arrive. Every night I press the same button and eat the same thing—frozen and packaged food that has been rehydrated to look fresh. And every night I think about all that Josephine has told me about her life. About the squalor she grew up in, the kinds of places she has lived, all the moving and running and going hungry. We have all read about how it was in the past—several classes of wealth, most of which got by just fine. Now there are only two classes—the poor and the rich. The poor are desperately, heartbreakingly poor. The rich are obscenely rich.

I can order any meal I want and it will arrive within minutes. It won't be real, fresh food—the drought and disease killed all the crops so that now fresh food is such a rarity that it's practically black market—but I'll get the best imitation that money can buy. I will never run out of funds. I have already accumulated enough credits to outlast four lifetimes. That's what they think you deserve when you work with the criminally insane. I can't share my wealth with anyone except my biological children. Only my fingerprints can activate it.

This is what I tell myself every night when I think about Josephine's poverty. I *can't* share my money with her. I'm not allowed to. I don't know *why* I'm not allowed to, but I'm not. And I am not a man who questions. So I shouldn't feel so guilty about what I have earned.

I eat at the kitchen table with my case files open on several tablets before me. I try to read, but my eyes keep glancing over the words without properly seeing them. After a while I just switch the damn things off. I look at the photos of Marley on the fridge. I don't have many—just three. I look at them every night for ten minutes.

And then glumly I go to bed and dream of birds.

SEPTEMBER 13TH, 2065

Josephine

I have no idea what time it is or where I am when the crying wakes me. It takes me a second, and then I am up out of bed and crossing the small room. On her tiny bed Maria is sobbing violently, just as she does every night. I touch her warily—past experience has taught me to be careful of her thrashing limbs—and narrowly avoid getting whacked in the face.

"Maria," I repeat until she wakes. Her crying changes as the nightmare stops and reality sets in. This crying is less frightened, but much sadder. I sink down onto the bed beside her and pull her into my arms, stroking her hair as I imagine a mother might do. Since I've been in the asylum I haven't spent an entire night in my own bed. I don't know what's happened to Maria or why she's so frightened all the time—too frightened to speak. But I know that it helps to have someone hold you when the night terrors come, so every night I sleep in her bed with her.

*

Doyle is rougher than usual with me today. His hands around my arms are so tight that I can feel the pain of it long after he dumps me in the doc's office.

I stumble slightly as he lets go of me. This must be enough to get Anthony's attention because he jumps up from his desk with a bewildered look on his face. "You mustn't hurt her," he says with an odd confusion.

Doyle looks at him impatiently.

"You mustn't hurt her," Anthony repeats, like it's a rule he's memorised. "It's not right."

"So?" Doyle asks with a slight lisp. "She's an animal."

"I could have you fired," Anthony says quietly. He's not angry, but he seems to know what he should say, which is more than can be said for most drones.

"No you couldn't," Doyle says with such certainty that we both stare at him. He smirks and leaves.

I open the window and curl up on the window seat. "This rain has been going on forever," I comment.

"Does he always hurt you like that?"

I wonder what will happen if I tell him the truth. That my body's covered in bruises from Doyle. Probably nothing. "It's fine," I say calmly.

Anthony moves slowly to sit behind his desk. He doesn't bother with his outdated pen and paper. He just places his hands in his lap and looks at me expectantly.

I sigh and put my head on a cushion. "Luke and I started working together to—"

"Wait, what happened after you told him you'd killed people?" he interrupts.

"We don't have time—"

"I want every detail, remember. I only call Luke if you talk. And if you're really stressed about time we can go for longer than the hour today."

I blink. He's never let us go for more than two seconds over the hour, except for last night when he lost track of time. This is totally bizarre to me. Anthony feels like a completely different person, like he's actually engaging with me for the first time, and really listening to what I'm saying. It's good, but I wish he'd listen to my other words, my *warnings*. If he can help me get Luke here at least I'd know someone would take me seriously. Make sure I'm locked up before the blood moon comes.

"Why do you care so much about this?" I ask.

"How else am I supposed to figure you out, Josephine?" he says. "You're a vault. We haven't made a single breakthrough in all this time, because I can't work out what you care about, aside from anarchism."

I snort at that, but he adds, "Now I know. The moment you started speaking yesterday, I realized—you care about Luke."

SEPTEMBER 19TH, 2063

Josephine

We stand utterly still for a painfully long time. His eyes have searched every inch of my face and probed deep into my gaze. He is trying to understand. Trying to work out if he believes me, trying to figure out if there's anything else I could possibly mean when I say "I kill people."

"Luke?" I ask eventually. "You okay?"

"Huh?"

"You kinda look like you might have gone into shock."

"I'm not in shock," he replies too quickly. "I just don't ... understand."

I never meant to tell Luke this. It erupted out of me like a volcano. And now he's going to think I'm crazy, and then he'll be gone, and I'll be ... well, the same as I've always been, probably. Absolutely, completely fine.

"Can I sit?" he asks abruptly.

"Sure. I don't have any chairs, but go for it."

He sinks onto my mattress, his back to the wall. It seems overly intimate that he's on my bed. "Okay, Miss Luquet. Explain."

I sigh. "Honestly, Luke. It's probably best if you just go home and forget you ever met me. This next part is the part where I look like a lunatic."

"You're too pretty to be crazy," he says. It's so absurd that I laugh, loudly and wildly. The sound shocks him and he stares at me until I fall quiet.

"Fine," I say eventually. I start to pace, not looking at him, searching for words that could make this sound believable. "As far as I can tell, I seem to be fairly normal for most of the year. I mean, you know—relatively speaking. But for one day, on the 16th of September—"

"The night of the blood moon."

"—yes, the night of the blood moon, I become someone else. I disappear and she comes out to hunt." I lick my lips, starting to feel sick. "When I wake up the next day, I remember nothing. I'm naked and freezing and some place really weird. My body hurts like I'm no longer human and there's dread in my gut. Slowly, over the next year, the truth starts to come back in little pieces, little whispers of violence and death. I've tried to find proof, but there's none. And if I hand myself in they'll cure me. That's not something I can... I just can't."

"If there's no proof ..." Luke trails off apologetically.

"I know," I forestall. "I thought I was crazy for years. I thought they were dreams. But over time it started to get worse. Much worse. I'd wake up covered in blood not my own. I knew the visions were memories. I can feel the truth of them, Luke, the truth of all the people I've hurt. I know what I've done. I know what I'll do again. And I have no way to stop myself."

Luke draws in a long breath, then he bends over and rests his head in his hands. "Jesus," he mutters. "So this was only a couple of nights ago? Was that why when we met you were ..." He searches for a word and ends up with, "Lost?"

I nod.

"It had happened again?"

Another nod.

We're silent for a long while. I wait for him to leave; to look at me with disgust or pity or fear. But when he looks up, his eyes hold something else entirely. "We have to find a way to make it stop."

I'm completely lost for words.

"We've got to figure out what's making you do this, and make it stop."

I turn and walk the two steps it takes to get into the 'kitchen'. I pour myself a glass of water and drink the whole thing, then have another glass, stalling for time. Finally I look at him. "There's no 'we'."

He rolls his eyes. "Don't start."

"Why would there be a 'we'?" I demand.

"I want to help."

"Why?"

"I don't know."

"Well, you can't. There's no way to stop it, and I'm not dragging you into this."

"I can't think of any place I'd rather be dragged."

I stare at him. "Do you have mental problems? I just told you I'm a dangerous murderer, and you want to hang around?" Why is he doing this? Is he an adrenalin junkie? Does he think I'm some kind of experiment? A problem he can solve? A poor soul in need of saving? I don't like any of the reasons I can come up with.

Luke stands. "Tell you what. How about I hang around every day except the 16th. Would that make you feel better?"

He's trying to make light of it. I shake my head. "I don't need you."

"Well then what?" he asks suddenly. "You want to keep dealing with this on your own? Want to live in tiny shitholes for the rest of your life, going from crap job to crap job and feeling like death every damn day? Do you *want* to be completely alone without a single friend to talk to about all of this? Because that's where you're headed with this 'I don't need anyone' bullshit."

I can feel a headache coming on, a slow pounding in the back of my skull.

"Or," Luke goes on more softly, "we could face this together."

And it occurs to me suddenly. The real reason beneath his words. He's just as lonely as I am.

I swallow. "I don't know who you are."

"I'll teach you. That's the fun bit."

My eyes are hurting, and my teeth. The glare of the room is too bright and I squint against it. I can barely make Luke out anymore, just his silhouette, swaying eerily before me. "Whatever," I mutter. "I just … need to have a rest."

I make my way to the bed, the blood rushing in my ears. As I sink down onto the mattress, the contact hurts my skin and my muscles and my bones. I feel a thousand years old, like a skeleton that has long since decayed. I try not to make a sound but I'm not sure if I've managed.

"Josi?" His voice is loud and makes me wince.

"I'll just sleep a while," I tell him. I think I tell him. I'm not sure if I've opened my mouth. My jaw is aching and I can taste blood. I can always taste blood. It never goes away, never leaves me for one second. I'm so tired.

Luke

It comes over her so fast. She sort of sways on her feet, and then all the color drains from her face. She makes it to the bed, but only barely. I touch her shoulder and she flinches; I speak her name and it seems to hurt her.

I stand and stare at her as she drifts to sleep. I don't know what to do. I can only imagine that this is some aftereffect of the episodes she has. I will call them 'episodes' because that makes it sound like she has no control, and I have to believe she has no control. My brain wars with words and ideas and possibilities as I watch her sleep uncomfortably. Despite what I told her, I have seen a lot of bad things. A lot of violence, a lot of death. It's not much of a shock to me anymore. Perhaps this is why I'm not freaking out. Why I'm not running. I can't think of any other reason—I *should* be running. Josephine is the last person I should be spending time with.

But I can't leave. Not now, while she's passed out and clearly in so much pain. I can't just leave her alone in this awful place after she's told me such a terrible thing. The idea of it seems simply too cruel.

Carefully I pull a blanket over her, but then I take it straight back off as I feel how hot she is. Shit, it must be a fever. I look around the apartment for anything I can use to cool her off. Eventually I grab one of the t-shirts out of her suitcase and wet it under the faucet. She makes a sound, like a soft whimper, as I place the cold cloth against her burning forehead. She's grinding her teeth badly—the sound makes me shudder.

In her bathroom I search for something to give her—paracetamol breaks fevers, doesn't it? She's got a shit-load of prescription pills. I read some of the labels and have no idea what any of them mean. I finally find a packet of strong pain medication.

Getting her to take the tablets is no easy feat. I stroke her hair for a minute, trying to wake her up enough for her to swallow, but she just moans. I climb behind her, lifting her as gently as I can until she's propped up against me. She's so fucking hot it scares me. Her skin against mine is like a flame. I pry open her mouth—her jaw is locked—and put the pills right into her throat. Then I stroke her throat like you do with an animal—I have no idea if this is right, but it's the only thing I can think of. She eventually swallows the pills and I sigh with relief.

I start to move out from under her but she moans in pain and I freeze. It's a god awful sound. After a moment I decide to stay put. I keep stroking her hair and soon she relaxes in my arms.

I am scared.

There's no two ways around it. I can't remember the last time I felt fear—probably around the start of my job—but I am definitely afraid right now. She feels hotter and hotter with every second that passes. I can't take her to the hospital—I don't want anyone to find out that she's uncured.

I have to do something. Gently, I lift her up. She weighs next to nothing in my arms, a creature so fragile I find it impossible to imagine her hurting anyone. She whimpers and trembles as I carry her into the tiny bathroom. She doesn't have a bath, so I turn on the cold faucet of the shower and step into the recess with Josi still in my arms. It's freezing and sudden, but even as I wince I feel her cool off.

The water lasts for five minutes and then the legally required timer switches the faucet off. I consider overriding the controls to get her some more water, but then realize she's now so cold that she's shivering. Her lips are blue and her teeth chatter. Her two-colored eyes open drowsily and I can see the delirium that racks her.

"So funny ..." she mumbles. "It's so funny."

"What is?" I ask, propping her against the tiled wall and wiping the wet hair from her face.

"They break so easily. They just snap. Like twigs."

I don't think I want to know what she's talking about. "Let's get you dry," I suggest. I feel like a fucking retard, trying to look after someone when I can barely look after myself. I've never dealt with a sick person before.

Her temperature seems better now though. I grab her only towel and carefully wipe her dry. Her head lolls onto her chin with a loud clack of her teeth. Her clothes are wet, but I think this might help to keep the fever down. I carry her back to the bed and lie her down. Then I get her a glass of water and sit it beside the bed.

She's got a couple of books scattered around—old paperbacks from what look to be the Bronze Ages. It's rare to find real books these days, and I wonder how she managed to acquire these. I pick up her copy of Douglas Adams and cheer myself up with a bit of hitchhiking through the galaxy.

I'm sprawled across the floor and deeply involved when I hear, "You need reading glasses."

Josephine is lying in bed, watching me sleepily. Her color is a lot better and I sigh in relief. "You're alive."

"I don't feel particularly alive," she mutters. "Why am I all wet?"

"We took a little dip. You were about to spontaneously combust."

She presses her face into the pillow.

"Is this normal?" I ask, dog-earring my page. "Do you always burn a thousand degrees?"

"Around this time of year."

"What else?" I crawl over to the bed.

"Nothing else."

Her shirt has ridden up and I catch sight of a strip of skin. Her lower back is blue and purple. "Shit, Josi!" I reach out to lift her shirt up but she recoils, scurrying away so that her back is against the wall. She looks at me like I've just tried to attack her.

"Sorry. You're really badly bruised," I tell her slowly, hands up to placate her. "Why?"

She doesn't answer. I realize she doesn't *know* why.

"All right. Well, do you have any food? You'll need to eat after that fever. And drink lots of water."

"I can look after myself. Can you go home so I can have some privacy? I don't even want to think about how many intimacy levels we skipped today."

I stand up and fold my arms. "Okay, fine. Where's your phone?"

"Why?"

"Because, Miss Suspicious, I'm going to give you my number."

"Why would I want your number?"

I roll my eyes.

"I don't have one," she admits.

"You don't have a phone," I repeat skeptically. "Fine. I'll write it down for you."

"I don't have a pen either." Her lips twitch at my expression.

"Are you just trying to avoid getting my number?"

"Just tell it to me," she laughs. "I'll remember it."

"No you won't."

"I will—I have a photographic memory."

"Bullshit."

"It's true."

I shake my head, but she starts speaking, and then I catch her say, "*...an utterly insignificant little blue green planet whose ape-descended life forms are so amazingly primitive ...*"

As she continues, I stare at her, slowly realizing that this is the opening paragraph of *The Hitchhiker's Guide To The*

Galaxy, and I only know this because I was reading it twenty minutes ago. "You could have just memorized that first part," I argue weakly.

"Okay, give me a page number. Any will do."

"Uh ... One hundred and fourteen."

"*In those days spirits were brave, the stakes were—*"

"—Holy shit."

Josephine smirks. I've never seen anyone look as sexy as she does wearing that smirk.

"The periodic table—go!"

"Hydrogen, Helium, Lithium, Beryllium, Boron, Carbon, Nitrogen—"

"Too easy—do it backwards."

"Lawrencium, Nobelium, Mendelevium, Fermium, Einsteinium—"

"*Einsteinium*? That is *not* real."

"Number 99. It's an Actinides, which is a metal—an inner transition metal to be precise." We stare at each other and she starts laughing. "You will have to learn not to underestimate me."

"I'm officially intimidated," I mutter as I head for the door. "Oh—210418993421." I say it as fast as I can. "Got that?"

"Easy."

"I expect you to call first thing tomorrow. And I know you won't forget."

I'm out the door and down the steps before I hear her call my name. She's still damp, her clothes clinging to her body as she runs after me in bare feet. "Wait."

"You okay?"

"Yeah, I ..." She stops, flushed. I'm not sure if her pink cheeks are from her fever or because she's embarrassed. She drops her eyes to the ground and says, "Thank you. For ... the shower, and ... you know ... the rest."

For the first time all day I feel a real smile consume me. She looks up at that precise moment and flashes me the glimpse of a grin, then turns and runs back up the stairs. It's when I know I'm in trouble.

SEPTEMBER 13TH, 2065

Josephine

"I was sick with embarrassment after that," I tell Anthony. "I couldn't stop thinking about how he'd just … watched me while I was delirious. It was weird."

"You don't trust Luke?" Anthony asks.

"I do *now*. But that was, like, the second day we'd met or something. I didn't trust anyone back then."

"That's a completely normal response, given you'd had no one in your life you had previously been able to trust."

"Don't shrink me." I roll my eyes. "I realized pretty soon that what he did wasn't creepy—it was the nicest thing anyone's ever done for me."

Anthony looks unconvinced, so I sit forward. "Really, it was. He didn't know me. I was a strange kid who told him I'd killed people and then fainted. He stayed for *hours* to make sure I was all right, and that apartment wasn't exactly the Ritz. He looked after me." My voice falters and I hesitate before shrugging, "No one's ever looked after me except Luke."

"Do you feel you need to be looked after?"

"No, Doc," I reply, my voice growing hard. "I don't. But it was nice, for the first time in my life, to have someone want to."

He nods and pretends to write this down.

"Can you organize a solitary room for me?" I ask him.

He meets my eyes but doesn't say anything.

"Or move Maria. Find her somewhere else to stay for a couple of days."

"I believe we are at full capacity," he says, dropping his gaze. "There are no other rooms available."

"What? That's bullshit!"

He shrugs like he doesn't care if I believe him or not. I feel sick, thinking about poor Maria, trapped in that tiny room with me. No windows to escape through, no way to override the locks on the door. "I don't care where you put her, just make sure she's not in that room with me."

"You suggest I remove a dangerous criminal from her confines and have her out in the open for days at a time?"

"Well you didn't mind shutting her in with *me*."

This doesn't get a reply.

"What did she do, anyway?"

"That's confidential patient information."

"So I have to live with her, but I'm not allowed to know why she's dangerous? That seems like great safety protocol." I shake my head. "Whatever. If anything happens to her—and it will—it's on your hands."

"Of course. I'll take responsibility for that. Will that allow you to feel better? More relaxed?" He's actually asking as though this is a reasonable question.

"No, you dickhead. It won't. Just protect your goddamn patients!"

Anthony winces at the sound of my voice like he's forgotten what rage is, which he has. I can see in his face that my words and tone don't make sense to him anymore. I am an irrational monster and he can't relate to me at all.

"Let's get back on track," he says.

I'm going to have to come up with some other plan. Otherwise Maria's a goner. Then there's my therapy time to take into account, when Doyle will open my door and let me out, and then everyone not locked within a cell is a goner. All the staff—the security guards, the doctors and the nurses. The patients in the common area. All goners. There's no telling how long the change will last, but I'm pretty sure it's been at least twelve hours before, and I think it's getting longer each year.

"Tranquilizers," I say. "Could you give me some of those? The highest dosage you've got?"

"That would kill you."

"Trust me—I'm not sure it will even hinder the woman I become. She's not like me, and she's certainly not like you."

"She's superhuman now, is she?"

"Not superhuman. Just … more than we are. Stronger. Faster. She doesn't seem to feel pain."

"I thought we'd moved past referring to this part of yourself as a separate person," Anthony says. "You did a hell of a job convincing me that you don't have split personality disorder, but we can go back to that diagnosis if you'd like."

"Fine. *I'm* stronger and faster. *I* don't feel pain—not until the next day, anyway. Then it's a whole bundle of laughs."

"What do you mean? Are you physically hurt after these episodes?"

A tiny spark of hope comes to life in my chest—he has never asked me about the aftermath. I suppose he's never wanted to indulge me in the idea of it. "I'm a zombie after the episodes. Dead flesh and delirious moaning and all."

"What causes this?"

"You tell me."

"Well, at a guess, Josephine, I'd say you're harming yourself due to your condition, and then your mind is blacking out the trauma of it."

"Perhaps you should stop guessing and actually find out if that's true or not."

"I will on the 16th."

"No, on the 16th you'll be dead."

There is silence in the room. The rain has finally started to slow. The air outside is exhausted and flat. The smell of rain on grass has filled the room—I concentrate on it rather than thinking about what I said to Anthony.

The doc rests his elbows on the desk and peers at me. "I find it quite astonishing that you can say something like that, and then turn around and argue against the cure. You say that rage doesn't cause crime, but you're the only uncured person I know, and you're also the only person who threatens my life."

"I'm not threatening you," I say woodenly. "I'm trying to warn you. My anger and the blood moon have nothing to do with each other. It's not my anger that makes me kill. It's something much darker and much colder."

"Let's take a look at the handbook, shall we?" he suggests, tapping a few things on his tablet.

"Oh yes, why don't we!"

In a moment, the first medical journal on anger is projected onto the wall behind him. In heavy black letters, it says:

'What was once known as a normal human emotion can now be categorized differently—namely, as a disease that is contracted upon the development of the brain in early childhood.

Anger's symptoms include:

- Irrationality
- Violence
- Aggression
- Malice
- Intent to harm
- Loss of appetite
- Breathing irregularities
- Heart conditions
- Death

Humanity, as a race, would function at a far superior level, both physically and socially, if this disease could be cured.'

"Phew," I sigh. "I feel a lot better now, thank you."

He shoots me an exasperated look.

That damn journal has become like a bible to people over the last ten years. Every household has several copies, so that they can quickly check a symptom and make sure they haven't been 're-infected'. As far as I know re-infection is impossible, but there are always warnings popping up for people to get regular checkups and to monitor themselves in case they need a second dosage of the cure. I can just imagine people rushing to the journal and shrieking 'I'm not hungry! I must be turning into a rabid monster!' And to say that anger causes death just makes me want to punch the guy who wrote that article and prove that I can walk away perfectly unscathed.

It's all a big joke, but everyone's forgotten how to laugh.

"Well if you won't take note of the truth, then—"

"Actually, Doctor," I say, "that journal was written by Harold Connolly who has a PhD in philosophy, not a medical doctorate. So it's all personal conjecture, with no scientific basis. What makes anger a disease if happiness and love are not as well?" I smile at Anthony and add, "Doctor Harold Connolly was also a religious fanatic—something that causes *far* more irrational thought than an emotion could. So how about we both refrain from calling this piece of dribble the truth?"

He stares at me. It takes him a while to recover his composure, and then he's apparently desperate to find something hidden within his desk drawers. Eventually he just says, "Do you want me to call Luke or not? Continue with the story."

*

My window faces west. West, where everybody died. I imagine what's out there a lot. I dream about walking through scorched earth and running my fingers over the diseased trees.

Sometimes I wonder if this would be better than the hell I am living now, in a prison of dull wretchedness. I think perhaps the living are dead, too.

I imagine Luke in the west. Walking, walking, impervious to his surrounds, walking until he reaches the sea, where he could be free. I imagine him entering the swelling ocean, clean of any poisons, and swimming out and out and out. I keep imagining this, because it makes my heart swell.

Chapter Four

SEPTEMBER 20TH, 2063

Josephine

When he knocks on my door I am surprised by my reaction.

"You didn't call!" he accuses the second he sees me.

I look him over. He's wearing a black V-necked cardigan and faded black jeans. He looks a lot nicer, although his flip-flops kind of wreck the outfit. He also looks healthier, like maybe he finally got a good night's sleep. His eyes are clear and his skin isn't as pale. On the whole, I am slightly outraged by how gorgeous he is. I am also thoroughly amused at his words. I smile slowly and allow myself to savor the moment. "Did we, or did we not, have a conversation just yesterday about the fact that I don't own a phone? How, therefore, do you propose I should have called you?"

Luke stares at me and starts to laugh. "You might have pointed that out last night."

"The time you sat at home waiting for my call earned me a few extra hours of peace and quiet."

He rolls his eyes. And damn if the bastard doesn't do it as well as I do. "Diabolical," he mutters, motioning for me to follow.

"Where are we going?" I ask, grabbing my old red jumper and pulling it on over my jeans. I can't really criticize Luke for not putting effort into his appearance, since my own clothes are full of tears and holes and I still haven't bothered to brush my hair.

"To my place."

My feet falter. He sees this and grins. "*You're* the murderer, remember?"

"Yeah, thanks," I mutter. "And by all means, be flippant about the fact."

He doesn't answer, just waits.

"So this is actually happening?" I ask. "We're forming a crime-stopping duo?"

"It sounds fun when you put it that way. Come on."

I sigh, following him. "Okay then. On your head be it."

His car is expensive. We strap in and Luke scans his thumbprint before pressing a button that presumably navigates the car to his place. He then turns to me. "How are you feeling today?"

"Effervescent."

He shoots me a sideways look that seems to beg me not to be sarcastic twenty-four hours a day.

I take pity on him. "No delirium, you'll be pleased to hear."

"That does please me. Any fever?"

"No, Mom."

"Well, I went home and did some thinking."

"New for you?"

"I have a list of questions to ask you."

My shoulders slump. This is not my idea of a pleasant outing. I do *not* want to think about any of my 'episodes', and I really don't want to talk about any of it—especially with

Luke—but I have to keep reminding myself that the more I face it now, the more likely it is that we'll find an answer. I'm not going to hold my breath though—I've spent a lot of time looking for answers to my condition, but it's hard to find anything that isn't appallingly biased against any kind of aggression. There's also the problem that I don't know much about what it actually is that affects me.

The car pulls itself to a smooth stop and we climb out. We're outside an enormous block of apartments; Luke is obviously a man with wealth. A *lot* of wealth. I start to feel nervous as he leads me inside, into an elevator and up to the top floor. Great. He lives in the penthouse.

The security is good—Luke not only has a fingerprint scanner, but a retinal scanner as well.

Inside, I freeze. I feel like I've just walked into a page from an interior design catalogue. The space is huge, the ceilings high. Everything is white, black and silver. He has beautiful, clean furniture, white floors and marble benchtops. There is artwork on the walls, but it's minimal and stark. There are no possessions anywhere—no pieces of Luke lying about. I can't see any shoes on the floor, or jumpers thrown off, I can see no junk or trash or clues to who he is. I have no more idea now than I did the first night I met him.

"Wow. How long have you lived here?"

"A few years. Why?"

"Do you have OCD? Or mysophobia?"

"What's mysophobia?"

"Fear of germs."

Luke smiles. "I'm not really home much. I don't have time to mess up the place. I guess it is kind of sterile, isn't it?"

"Like an eighty-year-old man."

"Well I've taken my annual leave," he laughs. "So I'll be home for the next month to get the place nice and filthy. You can help me, since I've witnessed how good you are at it."

"Thanks, smartass."

Luke potters in the kitchen while I explore. The living room has huge white leather couches, upon which you could probably fall into a coma from relaxation. A shiny screen covers one entire wall, and I wonder if it's a hologram or just a normal TV. I snoop through a few drawers but find nothing of any interest. He has no books, but that's not really a surprise.

I pad barefoot down the long hallway, peering into the rooms. There are at least two guest bedrooms that look like they belong in a hotel. Luke's master bedroom has a double king—I've never seen a bed so big. I could lie lengthwise across it with my hands stretched high, and still I wouldn't be able to reach the edges. His clothes are inside a massive walk-in wardrobe that lights up when I walk in. He has suits—at least fifty of them—on racks that spin. Fifty. I can't picture him in a suit at all, but he must wear them for work. There are a lot of other clothes, all much nicer than the ratty shirts and jeans he's been wearing for the last few days. And his shoes! Dozens of pairs—dress shoes, work shoes, sandals and *sneakers*, so many sneakers! I stand there in the brilliant false light, staring at the sea of footwear, and I begin to feel uncomfortable. It puts into perspective my own abysmal collection of attire. I own two pairs of shoes, and I'd thought it was excessive to buy the second pair because they're black heeled boots and I can't wear them during the day.

"Having a good snoop?" Luke asks from the doorway and I spin to face him. He must see something in my expression because his smile disappears and he looks just as uncomfortable as I feel. "It's disgusting, I know," he says softly. "Work pays for it. I don't get much of a choice about any of this—they bought my apartment, furnished it and then paid for my wardrobe to be stocked." Luke walks further into the closet, running his large hands along the fabrics. "Sometimes I want to burn the whole place down. I wouldn't miss a single thing in it. Isn't that stupid?"

I shrug. I have no idea what to say.

"Come on. I'm making breakfast."

"I'll be there in a minute. I want to snoop some more."

He leaves me to it. I look at the wardrobe for another minute, then find my way to the bathroom. Along the way I realize that he has no photos. Nothing framed on desks or walls. It seems like an odd absence. I don't have any photos either, but I've never had anything to take a picture of, nor have I ever owned a camera or a house like this, one that's begging for a few memories and a bit of life.

The bathroom has a glorious tub set into the floor. It's deep and wide and I can see spa nozzles. It's right up against the window, and the view from up this high is dizzying. Lying in that bath you'd be able to see the sky. His cabinet holds tooth-paste, aftershave, deodorant and—condoms. I feel a blush creep up my neck as I survey just how many he has. Like four whole boxes of the things! I shut the cabinet with distaste, feeling even more uncomfortable. What the hell am I doing in the apartment of a 26-year-old man who I don't know from a bar of soap? A man who is an adult with a real job, lots of money and a raging sex life? It's about as far from where I thought I'd be four days ago as I can imagine. I am an unedu-cated, inexperienced child who's never even had a *friend*, let alone a boyfriend.

I walk out of the marble bathroom and into the marble kitchen. Luke is intent on his cooking, and he seems pretty good at it. He has the practiced air of someone who is at ease with food. Expensive implements are whirling, things are sizz-ling on the frying pan and the smell is so delectable that my mouth waters. I am intimately acquainted with hunger. Jobs at restaurants or cafés have been good because they usually come with free food. So sitting here and having him cook for me is a luxury without compare.

Sitting on a bench stool I say, "You have enough condoms to supply a nation of sex addicts."

He stops chopping and looks into my eyes. Slowly he smiles. "Well at least you can't say I'm irresponsible."

I snort. "I don't feel any less grossed out by you, that's for sure."

"Music," he says, but not to me. "Blue and white."

Music starts to play from speakers, something I've never heard that's fun and lively. "Blue and White?" I ask, assuming this must be the name of the band.

"I'm synesthetic," he explains. "Means I remember things in color and shape and texture. Blue and white music for me is upbeat, something with a lot of bass, stuff that makes you want to dance. I programmed my sound system to understand color cues."

I feel thrilled by this insight. My eidetic memory is rare, but so is Luke's synesthesia. The percentage of people who have true synesthesia is roughly 0.05.

"You know apparently everyone was once synesthetic?" I tell him. "Back when the various parts of our brains were all connected. Now our brains are essentially separate, so you're really rare. It means your brain will have to work harder to make connections, but I imagine it must be beautiful in that head of yours."

Luke smiles. He watches me, lost in thought.

"What color am I?" I ask. If he says red, I might die.

"Sort of ... bluey greeny, with darker edges. Smooth and clear."

I think about that and find that I like it. "What other things have color?"

"Everything. It's how I remember names, places, streets ... everything. Your color might change if my thoughts of you change, but I highly doubt they will."

I'm not sure what this means. I decide not to ask, unsure if it would be worse if his thoughts about me were positive or negative. I peer around the kitchen and spot a spectacular collection of wine, rows and rows and rows. I jump off the stool and inspect it, running my fingers along the bottles. At the end of the Wall of Wine is the pantry. This is as big as his oversized wardrobe. I wander inside and am met by a wave of smell. Spices and herbs line an entire shelf. Bottles and jars and containers full of bright colors and various textured items. He has so much fresh food, and it is this, finally, that makes me understand how rich he must be. Even with the apartment, the car, the furniture—he still could have been a normal, middle-class citizen. It is the food that's truly rare.

It's different, too. It seems to me that where the clothes and the furnishings are decided for him, and endured because he doesn't really know what he wants, the food is something that he is careful with, selective and precise. There is reverence, here in these shelves. And that is forgivable. I can allow him this gross excess in the face of all the starvation in the world, simply because I am a girl who loves it when people *love*.

I backtrack to the entrance of the pantry and lean against the doorway, watching him. He's lost in the food and the music. I realize I want to play for him, and I have never wanted to play in front of anyone, not since I first started teaching myself. "What are you making?" I ask softly.

"Poison," he replies. After a moment he smiles. "That's what Mom always used to reply when we asked her what she was cooking."

My nose crinkles but I am suddenly immersed in imagining his family. He has a lovely mother, I bet. Perfect. She scolds him and encourages him, and cooks him anything he wants. She doesn't let him stay up too late, because he has school in the morning, and she helps him with his homework, and watches all of his sports games. He probably has a big family.

Two brothers and a sister they all adore. His father is a strong man who works hard—maybe he was a prosecutor before Luke, perhaps it's a family business. They sit down to dinner together every night and laugh over inside jokes.

"Tell me about them—about your family," I implore.

And just like that he is cold and unreachable. "They're not worth mentioning."

I draw a breath, wishing I could go back to when he had a happy, perfect family. Now I know it can't be true—not with an expression like that one. I watch him dish up the food and take it to the big glass dining table. He glances at me and gives a crooked smile. "Sorry, but really, they're not. Come and eat."

I sit down and dig in, and good god—it's the best meal I've ever had. "Luke! Delicious poison!"

"Pesto baked eggs, prosciutto and asparagus, baked peaches with mint yoghurt and chocolate crepes to finish. Plus a really good cup of coffee."

"I might have to move in if you cook like this every meal."

"I intend on it."

I look up, unsure if he's serious. He's looking at me calmly. "Luke …"

"Josi. I have two spare bedrooms. I have too much space to deal with. I have no one to cook for. All I want is a room-mate, no strings attached."

I get back to my breakfast so that I don't have to reply. His words have made me yearn. And I have never known an element of yearning that has not ended in disappointment. I have to stop my mind from going to the place where I live a life with delicious food and deep baths and music that comes on when you say a color. That life is too absurd, too wonderful.

"So what are your questions?" I ask. Jeez, it must be bad if I seek out questions about the blood moon to avoid another topic.

Luke jumps up and jogs over to a bench. He presses a few buttons and then the contents of his tablet are flashed across a massive white wall. I am suddenly faced with a larger-than-life list of questions.

"Jesus. Did you have to write them all down? I feel like I'm being interrogated."

"Sorry. I just didn't want to forget. I don't have to ask them if you don't want."

I sigh and gesture for him to go ahead.

"Have you tried any medications to stop the transformation?"

The word transformation makes me think of lycanthropy. That would be fun. I wish I were a werewolf. "Yep. Loads. Each year I try something different, usually a lot stronger. Never makes a difference. I can be knocked out and semi-comatose and I'll still wake up and go on a rampage."

"Okay. Could this have anything to do with the fact that you haven't had the cure?"

"I don't see how. Unless we believe the propaganda."

"I reckon we should look into it. Do you know why you were never cured?"

"Nope."

"Definitely worth finding out. How old were you when this started?"

"I can't remember exactly. In the beginning I'd feel really aggressive all day, and I'd have memory loss after, but over the years I started forgetting entire chunks of time. The first years I can remember feeling really bad were probably around ten years ago."

"So you were about eight. Okay ..." Luke taps the tablet and images appear beneath the glass. He starts to make notes about what I'm saying. "The next thing we need to do is make a timeline. I need you to tell me what crimes you've committed, what the year for each was, and the location of them. I'll jot it all down."

He really does sound like a prosecutor now, and I feel awash with weariness. My memories of the nights when the moon turns red are like fragments, hazy dreamlike things—probably how normal people remember everything. Usually my memories are crystal clear pictures. But the blood moon memories are unnerving half images and fractured pieces.

Suddenly I feel a touch on my hand. I'm still holding my fork, but Luke places his fingers over my knuckles, gently pressing on them until I release my tight grip and relax my hand. I look up and meet his green gaze.

"This is work," he says softly. "It's unemotional, clinical work. You don't need to relive anything. All you need to do is recount the pictures you see. Understand?"

I breathe out and nod, feeling his words reach somewhere inside and calm me. I start from the beginning, doing as he says and recounting pictures. This is what I've done my entire life. Everything in my world is a picture, an image I recall in finite detail. This is the same. Separating the two parts of my brain, I start to speak, trusting that he can keep up with me.

I sort through the images, starting from all those years ago when I woke up naked and shivering and nearly dead for the first time. The days after that were the worst of my life. I had no idea what to expect—I was experiencing the sickness, the bruising, the fevers and aches and bleeding all for the first time. Afterwards I became aware, in future years I made preparations, but in the beginning it was a vivid, impossible nightmare of horror.

I become possessed by the pictures of what I've done. I tell him everything I can see, all the pieces I can pull out of my head. I try to stay separate from them.

Afterwards he starts to ask questions. Hundreds of them. He is so thorough, so precise. He wants details even I have never considered, and I am amazed by him, even as I'm sickened by the activity. I assume he must be good with details because of his work—he is writing everything down, storing it in his tablet. For the first time in my life, I have given someone the pictures in my head, and he has kept them in a way that makes them real.

*

I feel mortified. Dirty. "Can I have a bath?" I ask abruptly. It is late afternoon and we've been talking for hours.

Luke nods, distracted and still focused on the notes he's taken. He has that line in the middle of his eyebrows. He gets it when he's concentrating, I've learned. He jogs to the bathroom and starts the water running, then comes back and heads for the kitchen once more. He chops and prepares food, and all the while he frowns, miles away and utterly lost in the words I've spoken.

I watch his broad shoulders and note the tense shape of them. "What are you thinking?"

He looks up, his expression clear and calm. "I'm thinking we need to go to these crime scenes and find our proof."

And this, I think, is more frightening than anything either of us has said all day.

The bath is as spectacular as I hoped. My aching body sinks into the hot water with a strange agony of delight. It's so hot that it burns, but I like it; I like the thought that it's scalding everything away. The lights beyond the window twinkle and I stare at them, letting my eyes go blurry so the colors dance and sway. I wonder if this is how Luke sees the world—colorful and bright and sparkling. I want to get inside his head and see how it works, see what he thinks and feels and hides. I want to see myself through his eyes, and I want to see his family and his cooking and his job. I don't know him at all, but I want to, and that makes me nervous.

He's so calm about all of this because of his cure. His brain isn't functioning in the correct way anymore, so it's wrongly interpreting meeting a murderer as something that's not too bad. Perhaps his fear receptors have short-circuited, or his logic centers. The thought is a sad and disappointing one. I wonder what he'd be like if he was normal. I also wonder what he'd do if I punched him in the face for no reason. Because he certainly wouldn't get angry. He wouldn't get annoyed, or want to hurt me back. He doesn't have a fight response anymore—only a flight one.

I know all of this. I remind myself every day. It's why I never get attached to anyone—how could I possibly respect a drone, or trust their emotions?

It's just that ... Luke's different, somehow. He's sort of ... more normal than anyone else I've met. Does any of this mean I could stand to live with him? Normal or not, he is still a drone and I am still a monster.

But, but... *baths*. And *food*.

Once I've blissed out in the bath for a super long time and the water's getting cold, I climb out and look around for a towel. There's not one in sight, not even Luke's towel.

Opening the door a crack, I peer out. "Luke?"

"Towels are in the cupboard, Josi," he calls from the kitchen.

"Which cupboard? I can't see any ..."

"It's just inside the door there."

"There are no cupboards—trust me, I'm looking."

Luke jogs to the bathroom and I jerk back inside. "There's a cupboard right in front of you. You just have to press the wall and it swings open."

I start pressing the wall in random places but nothing happens. "It's not working!"

"Smartest chick I know and she can't even open a cupboard. I'm coming in."

"No!" I shriek. "Don't you dare!"

"Do you want a towel or not?"

"Not that badly! I'll stand here until I drip dry."

I hear him laugh and the door starts to open. "Stay to the left and I won't look, I promise."

"If you do, I'll kill you." I stand to the left and he walks straight into me. "Luke!" I scream in hot shame. He jerks around so that his back is to me, but I did not miss the moment of wide-eyed shock as he walked straight into my naked body. He bursts out laughing.

"You said *left*!" I hiss.

"I meant *my* left, not your left."

"You're an asshole. You did that on purpose, didn't you?"

"No!" he protests, but he can't stop laughing.

No one has seen me naked before. I mean, I can only assume people saw me naked as a baby, but not since then. *I've* barely seen me naked, since looking at my body makes me kind of ashamed.

My gut feels heavy. "Are you laughing because ... because my body is ... funny or stupid or something?"

"What?" Luke freezes, laughter cut off immediately. He looks like he's itching to turn around and look at me, but I'm so mortified that I can only shrink back against the wall, as far from him as possible. "Josi, *no*," he says firmly. "I caught a half-second look, and I didn't see much, but what I did see was ... You're ... I mean, you look ..."

"Okay, don't say it!" I interrupt. "Just get me the damn towel."

He places a finger on a completely unremarkable piece of marble wall and a door swings open. He holds the towel out behind him and I grab it awkwardly. I wait for him to leave, but he pauses another moment and admits, "I was only laughing because I think I was nervous."

Once he's gone, I contemplate how pathetic my life is—that awkward, accidental moment was probably one of the most intimate of my life.

Luke

After the bathroom debacle, she stands outside on the balcony. I consider joining her, but decide to give her a few moments alone. That balcony is cathartic, and she may need that after today.

I concentrate on cooking, but for once it's not enough to stop my mind from wandering. Specifically to Josephine's naked body. I actually believe that I will think about that body for the rest of my goddamn life. I mean, she's thin and covered in bruises, but ... Christ. I can't think straight. I should be ashamed—she's a *child*, for god's sake. She didn't look like one though. And she doesn't act like one.

I turn off the stove and open the door to the balcony. Outside it's a calm night. An inky black sky is splashed through with stars that are dim compared to the brilliant lights of the thousands of buildings around us. She was in the tub for so long that she missed the sunset.

"What are we having for dinner?" she asks softly. She smells like soap and something prettier, something that is just her.

"Poison."

"Again? Jeez, use your imagination." After a moment she says, "It's nice out here."

"Does that mean you'll move in?" I don't know why I'm pressing this—she clearly doesn't want to, and I would probably go crazy thinking about her in the bath every day, but I just can't stand the thought of her going back to that bubonic plague-infested shithole.

"I don't know," she sighs, leaning forward to rest her elbows on the railing. She looks at all the windows around us. "So many people. Every one of those lights is another life. And all of them broken."

"That's life though, isn't it?" I mutter.

She doesn't reply.

"Do you wish I wasn't cured?"

Josephine shrugs. "I don't wish anything at all about you, Luke."

"No need to be blunt."

Her mouth quirks. "Okay, I guess I wish you weren't so stubborn. Does that make you feel better?"

"Over the moon," I reply wryly and she gives me a real smile this time. Damn, it's a good smile.

"What do you think they're doing out there?" she asks me.

"Who?"

"Anyone."

I crack my knuckles. "Making wishes."

*

Josephine is a good dinner guest. She oohs and ahs and says everything is delicious. It makes me want to cook for her all the time. Once she's finished eating she says she wants to pick something up from her house.

"Like what?"

"Just ... something. I don't have much, Luke, but if I'm going to move in, then I need my meager belongings."

I stand up. "Really?"

"Yes, really." She rolls her eyes. "But don't get all weird. I just like your bath."

Despite her prickly exterior, it's pretty easy to see that she's desperate for the company.

I drive her home and wait for her to grab her stuff. She's not in there long, but when she comes out she's carrying a big black bag in an odd shape—a musical instrument case. She puts it carefully in the back seat and then won't answer any questions about it until we get home. Dumping her bag in the bedroom furthest from mine, she comes back into the living room and looks at me.

"There need to be some ground rules if I'm going to live here. Firstly, I'll pay rent. Secondly, we share the chores. Thirdly, if anything starts to get weird then I'm gone, and you don't get to ask any questions."

"What would get weird?"

Her eyebrows arch pointedly. "*My* left, not yours?"

"That won't happen again," I promise with a grin. "We're just going to work together and share an apartment, like friends."

"Like friends, but not friends?"

I roll my eyes. "What's in the bag?"

Josephine retrieves the case and unzips it to reveal a beautiful old cello.

"Just when I thought you couldn't get any more interesting, you show me a thing like this."

Musical instruments have become more and more uncommon, which means they're expensive. This is the last thing I ever expected Josephine to own. She looks at it fondly for a moment then starts to zip it up again.

"You have to play something!" I protest quickly.

"No way."

"Stop zipping that bag," I order so firmly that she freezes. "I have a rule of my own. Your rent is payable only in music. Every night you sleep here costs a song. Sometimes more, depending on how difficult you're being."

She stares at me, her mouth open slightly.

"You'd better get started or it's a long walk home."

Josephine looks outraged, and frowns while she deliberates. "Fine," she eventually snaps, then sits down on the edge of the couch. "But I might play badly just to annoy you."

She plucks a few strings to hear if it's in tune. I get comfortable on the opposite couch and watch as she prepares herself. Then her face gets this faraway look, and all of a sudden my house is filled with deep, wonderful notes that resonate through my bones and my mind, and make me understand, at last, the nature of loneliness.

I don't think I knew how much was missing from my life until I met this strange, impossible girl and heard her play the cello.

Chapter Five

Josephine

The lights of the casino are so glary and false that they make my eyes throb. There's no way to get away from the noise. Nowhere to hide except the ladies' room, but I'm only allowed two bathroom breaks per shift.

I carry drinks to rich businessmen who leer at the other waitresses, but not at me. None of them look at me, nor do they tip me. I am safe because when people look at me they see someone strange. I don't want to work in a place where you only get tipped because you dress like a tramp, or a place with so many drones, but I will not live at Luke's house without contributing rent money, and this is the only job I've been able to get with my fake ID.

I place a tray of shots that burn with a blue fire in the middle of a large table. These men are in the middle of a poker game, and by the looks of the tally screen, they are bidding in the thousands. They're drunk and careless and crude, which is why I offered to serve them, since they'd be groping at the other waitresses in their short skirts.

Once the drinks have been delivered, I turn to leave but feel a large, meaty hand grab my arm and pinch. My head whips around in shock and I jerk my arm away from the man who touched me. He is a huge beast, overweight and balding, with expensive glasses and a beautiful suit. "Your eyes," he says to me.

I stare, shocked at the fact that he noticed me, let alone touched me.

"They're creepy."

I try not to frown. "Excuse me, sir."

"Wait," he grunts, playing his hand and laughing with a wheeze as he wins. "Wait. I want to look at you."

Edging away, I cover my revulsion with a bland smile. "I need to get back to work, sir." I turn and hurry back toward the bar. I feel sorry for the girls who have to put up with this crap every night.

I'm waiting for Jen to pour my next order of drinks when I feel the same huge hand descend onto my shoulder.

"Why don't you take your break now?" He smiles lecherously.

"I can't. Excuse me," I say more firmly. He's disgusting, with his red cheeks and wheezy breathing. I quickly flee to the bathroom and splash some water onto my face. I can't wait to get home.

I check the phone in my pocket—the one that Luke forced me to buy. There's a text message waiting. *You should leave work sick. I just made the best Peking Duck anyone has ever made.* I smile, shaking my head. He hates that I have a job. He seems to just want me to lie around on the couch all day long and do nothing. Actually, he did imply that I should be going to college, but I ignored that, since he has no concept of how much it costs and how easily my lack of brain-altering cures would be discovered there.

I'm just about to head back out when the door to the ladies' bathroom swings open and the fat businessman enters. I freeze. "Sir, you shouldn't be in here."

"You shouldn't have ignored me. You're an employee—I could buy you three times over with the change in my pocket."

"How charming, but I'm not a whore," I tell him crisply. "Now get out before I call security."

He doesn't go anywhere. He smiles and beneath the glasses I see that his eyes are dead. I try to get past him, feeling repulsed and furious, but he grabs me by the shoulder and pushes me against the wall.

"What are you doing?" I ask quickly. I try to think of something that will get through to a drone, but I can see in his face that he's lost any sense of rational behavior, overcome by a dark and violent lust. I push against him, but he's strong—a lot of his substantial bulk must come from muscle.

This is bad. My mind is going to places I don't let it go anymore. Places that have existed all my life, from before even the blood moon, before I became a monster myself. Nightmare places, nightmare memories. But it has been years since I've let myself get hurt. I'm stronger now. I can solve this.

Except that his hands are so strong, and he has me pinned roughly against the wall, a hand around my throat, long feminine fingernails dragging through my skin and I'm struggling wildly but I can't get free I can barely move or breathe and there's a sickness rising up from my stomach threading my veins with a tremble of terror I need to get free I must get free—

A scream of rage tears from my mouth and I twist my head to bite down on his fleshy hand. He yelps, loosening his hold enough that I can pull free and dash for the door. Pain knifes through my skull as he grabs my hair and yanks me backwards, clutching me around the throat and slamming me onto the ground. The air is sucked from me and panic bursts to life in my chest—it's much harder to get free from the ground; he has all of his weight on me. I stop struggling and he grins with triumph, reaching down to my thighs and pressing them apart. I use his momentary distraction to jam a knee into his groin and he shrieks, doubling over in pain.

The sound alerts one of the other waitresses and she pokes her head in curiously. She stares at the scene before her with mild interest.

"Help!" I cry, scrabbling to my feet. She leaves without a word. It was foolish to hope she would help. The man's hand is around my ankle and I turn and kick him savagely in the face. "You piece of shit," I yell. "*How dare you?*"

He is squinting at me in shock and I realize I must run.

*

I walk through a square of concrete that was once a child's park, but is now a crack den. My feet pick up speed as a group of men catch sight of me. One of them heads my way and I burst into a sprint, dashing out of the square before they can be bothered to follow. I feel sick to my stomach. I should have called Luke to pick me up but I can't manage the sight of him tonight, knowing that he is just another drone and has the capacity to lose it like that at any moment. I don't know why I'm stupid enough to live with him—the idea, in this moment, is terrifying.

My skin crawls and my head is full of vile memories as I walk through the night. I feel like weeping but I don't. I don't cry, not ever. I will never give myself permission for self-pity.

When I get home it is late enough that I hope Luke is asleep.

He's not. He's lying on the couch watching a movie. There's a larger than life couple kissing in the middle of the room. "Hey," he says. "I thought you were going to call me for a ride when you finished."

I don't speak because I can't. I kick off my shoes and sink into the couch beside him.

"How was work?"

The onscreen couple pulls apart and they smile at each other, speaking words I'm too distracted to hear.

"Josi?" Luke leans forward suddenly. "What the fuck happened to your neck? That's a scratch mark!"

I flinch away, putting my hand over the wounds. "I'm fine."

"Who did that to you?" he asks, and his voice has a sudden chilling quality to it.

"No one! Leave me alone."

"Tell me what happened."

"A psycho drone, all right?" I hiss. "That's what happened. I handled it, so drop it, Luke."

"Was it at the casino?" he asks, still in that same creepy monotone. "Describe him."

"Let it go!"

Luke stares at me strangely. Eventually he heads for the bathroom and returns with a first-aid box, gently slathering my neck with disinfectant and covering it with a white bandage. Once this is done he grabs his jacket and heads out without a word.

I sit alone in the dark and watch as the man and woman onscreen pretend they still have the ability to understand what love is.

OCTOBER 16TH, 2063

Josephine

Luke and I are walking down the street when I see it. There on the side of a building is a news bulletin about someone getting arrested. It's an unusual bulletin—the government doesn't want its citizens to think about crime, not after all of their futile attempts at ceasing it, so they don't normally show this sort of thing. The drones around us seem to think the same, as many stop to watch the bulletin as we have done. A few of them are, weirdly, laughing. One man weeps as if he himself is being arrested.

I freeze when I see the real criminal's face. When I see his ruddy red cheeks and steel-rimmed glasses. His huge girth and beady dead eyes. He is being led out of his office building and into a Blood vehicle, hands cuffed, contained by the terrifying men in black. There are tears coursing down his face, and dark bruises around both his eyes and mouth.

Luke stares at the bulletin with me. He is expressionless. I think of him disappearing that night after he put the bandage on my neck. I touch the white pad again now. He's been changing it for me twice a day since.

"Did you ... I didn't even ..."

Luke looks at me but he doesn't say anything. He watches my eyes, waiting for my response, like he so often does. I feel like he makes so many decisions based on the severity of my reactions to things. In this moment he is waiting to see if I'll work it out, but I don't know what to say, how to ask.

Eventually I just say, "Did you make this happen?" It's an absurd question. There is no possible way he could have, and yet it's there in the air between us, reminding me of how little I know about him.

"I don't know what you're talking about," Luke Townsend replies with careful delicacy. And then he walks on.

OCTOBER 24TH, 2063

Josephine

"Why green?"

I shrug. "Why not green?" The paint's a beautiful shade of jungle green, but now that we've started painting I think it might be too dark. My eyes move from the paint to Luke's hand as it slides back and forth, painting along the bottom of the cornice. He's so tall he hardly needs to stand on the stool. It's only natural that my eyes move down his arm, along the strong forearm and over his hard bicep and shoulder ... I can see every line and every muscle because he's only dressed in a singlet.

"I don't hear much painting happening," he comments.

I jump, startled out of my daze, and walk straight into a can of paint, spilling it all over the floor.

Luke peers over his shoulder and laughs in disbelief. "Good god. Do you have *any* hand–eye coordination?"

I blush. The truth is, Luke makes me uncomfortable. I've never spent any time with a guy like him, or any guy. And when I look at him like this, imagining things I shouldn't ... I can't help but think about a lot of other things, awful things, things that include my recent encounter with an incarcerated politician, for one.

I don't know where to put these thoughts. I hate them.

"You're cleaning that up," he tells me. I don't say anything so he sighs and mutters, "Fine, I'll clean it up."

I climb into the bath. "I'm sick of this now."

"We've only done one wall! And *you* did about a two per-cent portion of it."

"Maybe it could be a feature wall." I feel tired, suddenly. Really tired. Lying in the bath is nice; the ceramic is cool and smooth against my skin.

"If you want," Luke is saying. "I was starting to think it might end up too dark anyway …"

I close my eyes, too exhausted to keep them open any longer. Luke keeps talking, and the sound of his voice is soothing, like a breeze against my skin.

*

I open my eyes to the familiar walls of the guest bedroom. My bedroom. There's a cup of tea next to the bed, and by the looks of the steam rising off the top it was put there recently. I sit up and take the cup between my hands, using it to warm the chill in the air. I'm on top of the covers but a soft blanket has been spread over my legs. I have no idea what time it is, but I feel heavy and groggy so after a while I go back to sleep.

OCTOBER 25TH, 2063

Josephine

There's a warm hand stroking my hair. A big hand. I wake slowly, wary of this hand. I have never woken to a gentle touch before.

"She wakes," a deep voice says by my ear. I twist my head around and it all comes back to me. Luke.

I sigh sleepily, rubbing my eyes.

"You need to eat something, Josi," he tells me. "I brought you some toast."

"I might just go back to sleep for a while."

"No, you need to wake up and eat something." There's a firm edge to his voice.

I roll away from him. "Can you get off the bed?" I don't like having him so close. I've got no space, no room to breathe.

Luke stands and walks around to the bedside table where he's put the toast.

"I'm not hungry."

"Force it down then."

I glare at the plate because I want to glare at Luke but can't quite bring myself to meet his eyes. "Just because I moved in doesn't make you responsible for me."

He leans back against the far wall, watching me over crossed arms. "How long have you had this kind of depression?"

"I don't have depression. I'm fine."

"It's not fine to sleep for a day without eating or drinking."

"You've got no idea what you're talking about."

"I've seen it before," he says flatly. "We need to do something."

"No!" I exclaim loudly. "You don't get anything, do you? I'm *uncured*, Luke! If I go to a doctor they'll fry my brain and turn me into a zombie!"

"I didn't say anything about a doctor. We're just going for a walk, so hop up."

I shake my head, furious with him. "I'm not going outside." Where all the drones are. I'm sick of them, so unbelievably sick of the dead-eyed gazes and vacant words. Among them I feel myself starting to disappear.

"Yes you are." Luke is always so flat and calm and I hate it. I want him to roar with primal humanity, because then I'll know that he's alive and that I'm alive too.

I sink into the bed but he pulls the covers off me and hauls me into his arms. I go limp, trying to make my body as heavy as possible, but this only makes him laugh. "You are such a brat, Josephine Luquet. Will the day ever come when you listen to me?"

"Doubtful."

His smile changes and I see something real in his eyes, something alive, something hot and frantic and flickering.

"Put me down," I demand. "I'll walk."

He puts me down. I consider climbing back into bed just to piss him off, and because it would be a huge relief; my body is exhausted, my head sinking into a heavy fog. But getting back into bed would spur another fight and I am too tired for resistance, so I pull on my sneakers and follow Luke out the front door.

All my muscles feel squishy and soft like they haven't been used in decades and the light of the afternoon is glary against my sore eyes. I zip up my jumper and pull the hood over my head, sinking as far into it as possible. Luke glances at me once, expression unreadable, and then strides ahead at a cracking pace. I spend my time swearing at him and praying for him to trip over and hurt himself.

I am beginning to regret this whole venture. Not just the walk, but the moving in with him and agreeing to solve the mystery. What could have possessed me to live with a drone?

I sink onto a seat at a bus stop and pull my hood further over my eyes. Before I know it he's lifting me to my feet and tugging me along with him. "Get off me," I snap, wrenching my arm from his grip. He puts his hand on my back and propels me forward.

"We're just taking a *walk*, for Christ's sake," Luke says.

"In zombieland," I point out grumpily. "Any moment now these people could turn on us."

"Which people?" he asks, gesturing to the empty street we're walking down.

"*You* could turn crazy any time."

"If you keep acting like this I might," he mutters.

I have an idea, a cruel, bitter idea. "I'll show you something. Come this way." I head off, turning onto a main street. We hurry down steps and into the train station, past a woman who is staring at the wall and crying, past people shooting up in a corner, past a man screaming at the top of his lungs about the rapture. I can't bear to look at any of them, so I start to run, moving my legs to the rhythm of the screams, just in time to jump onto a train as the doors are sliding shut. In the quiet of the moving carriage I suck air into my lungs and look at Luke. His eyes are darting up and down the train, checking for something, and I wonder what he's looking for.

I'm about to sit when he says, "Don't. Stay on your feet by the door." I glance at him, surprised by the sharp tone. I follow his eyes to the end of our carriage and see that there are four men lurking. They are dressed strangely, their clothes ragged but functional, and even from here I can see that they're armed with knives and guns. My heart lurches.

"Stand very still and keep your eyes trained on the wall," Luke tells me, and it seems the day has come when I will listen to him after all. I do as he says, heart beating frantically. I've never seen people like that—they are sort of savage looking, and something about them makes the hairs on my arms stand on end. I'm not sure if I'm frightened or excited. They are, very clearly, uncured. I don't know how I know, but I do.

"Who are they?" I ask in a whisper, but Luke doesn't respond, watching the men closely.

As the train starts sliding to a stop, the men approach the door I am standing before. Luke takes my hand and gives it a squeeze.

"Step aside," one of the men orders crisply. Luke and I move aside and watch as the four men line up in front of the door, drawing their guns and aiming out of the doors. Jesus Christ—what the hell are they doing? The gunman standing closest to us turns and meets my eyes. He's young. "Best get out of the way, love," he tells me softly. I am frozen in my spot because there is something deeply human in him, something so utterly present that I feel an ache for what has been lost from the world.

Too stunned to move, I stare at the men until the train stops and the doors open. Streaming down through the entrance tunnels of the station are dozens of men dressed in black. The Bloods, I realize with a chill. Countless of them, like machines flooding the subway.

The four men at the train door start firing their guns, loud explosions that rock the train and my bones. Luke shoves me behind him, pressing me against the far wall, but I can still see beneath his arms as the men are taken down in a flurry of violence by the Bloods. The man who spoke to me has his neck snapped by a huge Blood; another of the four gets shot in the head; the third is riddled with bullets to the chest and the last of the men is thrown onto the tracks and crushed as the train moves forward once more.

And all of a sudden, as if none of it ever happened, there is silence in the train, and the black walls of the tunnel all around. My eyes are wide and I can feel myself tremble—it was so quick, so terribly fast. I blinked and the men were dead. There is blood on the windows of the train and I can't stop looking at it.

Luke presses his palm against my cheek. "You okay?" There's something bleak in his expression, but he isn't shocked by what's just happened.

I nod and manage to whisper, "What was that? Were they... *resisters*?" It's the only possible explanation I can come up with.

Luke's jaw tightens but he doesn't reply. He searches my eyes and his hard gaze softens. With a long sigh, he shakes his head and leads me to sit down. We stare at the passing walls silently, and I'm so lost in my thoughts that I almost miss our stop.

Luke may not believe that the men were resisters, but I do. I know it. There are no legal weapons anymore—only the Bloods have access to guns or knives. But those men carried them as though they were comfortable with their weapons and trained in using them. And yet. And yet—they still got killed in the barest blink of an eye, like their lives weren't even worth a struggle, weren't even worth the effort it took to kill them. It fills me with despair.

"Let's go," I mutter, leading Luke off the train and searching warily for any more gun massacres. A part of me wants a gun of my own, so I can shoot every Blood in the world. Another part of me wishes I'd been gunned down too, or even thrown under a train. In this life you are one or the other—the shooter or the shot.

Luke takes my hand again, and I let him, because I can barely feel it. I lead him up onto the street—it is peak hour now and the crowds flow home like a wave of water, impossible to move against. All these people are expressionless, moving as one without a conscious thought to the alternative.

I know it's dangerous and stupid but I can't stop myself from plowing into the oncoming rush of bodies and pushing through them, elbowing and kicking to forge a path, striding forward with raging determination and pulling Luke along with me. People look at me as though I am crazy, as though I've threatened them in some way, when the truth is all I'm doing is walking in the opposite direction.

Luke wrenches me out of the path of the streaming mass, pressing me against the steel wall of a building. "Are you trying to get yourself shot?"

"Why—would that make you angry?"

He blinks slowly. "It would confuse me," he says, but he doesn't seem confused. He seems to understand perfectly, given the way he's looking at me. Kind of sad, almost.

I shake my head and set off once more, letting Luke decide if he wants to follow me or not. I take him around behind a huge building to where the fire escape hugs the brick wall. It's not lowered all the way so I have to climb onto a trash bin and try to reach the base of it.

Luke peers at me, then takes pity and hoists himself up beside me. His movements are nothing like my jerky, weak ones—he has an odd animal quality to the way his muscles work, swinging up with all the grace of a gymnast. Without asking why, he grabs the fire escape and pulls it down so that we can climb all the way to the top of it. I jump onto the roof and head around to the northern side, where I crouch low and motion for Luke to do the same. He appears at my side, utterly soundless, his eyes scanning the area below. The light has turned golden with the approach of sunset, and something about it makes his skin glow beautifully, all the hard lines of his face further defined to make him even more severe and handsome.

Before us is another building, and from this height we can see directly down through its windows. There are young children playing quietly with trucks and blocks, and drawing at tables. We watch them for a moment before I motion for Luke to follow me across the roof to where we can see the backyard. Here there's a small area of stone and a metal slide. A few older kids run around the colorless playground, making do with the limited area.

"Foster kids," I explain unnecessarily.

"Did you live here?"

"Now and then, in between homes."

"Doesn't look too bad, I guess," he murmurs, watching the kids chasing each other.

"This isn't what I wanted to show you." I head for the stairwell—this building's been abandoned for years—and follow it down two floors, despite the danger all of this puts us in. We are allowed to be in our homes, our places of work, some recreational areas and shops. Nowhere else. We cannot gather in other people's homes, as this could be seen as a meeting of dissent. We can't be in groups, nor can we go outside the city without permission.

We certainly can't lurk in a dark, abandoned building right next to where they hold uncured children.

In one of the empty offices I cross to the window—from this level we can see into the basement of the foster facility. I point, feeling my throat tighten. "See that? The fourteen-year-olds."

Through the barred windows we can clearly see several children shackled to their beds, restrained so tightly they can barely move.

"They're drugged, too," I say softly. "They can barely think, let alone escape."

At fifteen we are cured. So at fourteen we are imprisoned. I want to scream and scream and scream.

Luke is staring at them, at these poor children, and although I never know what he's thinking, I can see that his knuckles have turned white as his hands grip the windowsill with all the strength in his body. It is this—these white knuckles—that make me realize something about Luke, and about myself.

"I want to break them out," I tell him, something I have longed to do for years. I have never been able to figure out how, not on my own, but if Luke will help me, perhaps—

"Let me show you something," he says softly, moving behind me and pointing along my eye level. "See that?" He points to a small black shape. "Security cameras at every window. And there? That's an armed guard, and there are bound to be more at every entrance."

On some level I must have known—I've spotted the cameras and the guards before—but I never really let myself contemplate that it might be impossible.

"So, what—you're saying it can't be done? I don't accept that."

"I'm saying it can't be done by us at this point in time," he says, sounding like a politician. "Our focus is getting you better. If we survive that, then we can look into helping others."

"Nice attitude, Luke," I snap. "Very compassionate of you."

He turns and faces me, spreading his hands. "What do you propose, Josi? That we smash in there right now and get ourselves shot to smithereens like the poor bastards on the train? Because that would be a certainty—neither of us would walk out alive, and then who can we help?"

The rationality of it makes me furious.

Something in his face softens. "You've had a shock," he says gently, a light in his eyes that wasn't there before, something vast and seductive. "I know the attack at the casino sent you into a bad place—"

"Don't."

"Listen to me—I know it sent you somewhere bad, that you want to scream and fight and tear things apart, but you don't get out of that place by being reckless."

"How do you get out of it?" I demand, not expecting him to have an answer. The sun has dipped below the buildings and everything is gray, sapping all the color away.

Luke smiles without any humour; a dangerous smile. "With cunning."

I feel a shiver race over my skin, lifting the hairs and sending my pulse into overdrive. I want to kiss him. Desperately. He leans in like he might want to do the same and my body tenses; I can feel his breath against my face and our eyes are locked together. I can see a thousand shades of green in his deep gaze, and all the rest disappears, my nightmarish life goes floating away on a breath and all that is left is the unyielding certainty that this man is going to change the world with the power in his beautiful face. I don't know who he is, but I know that he is more than a drone, a follower—or he could be, one day. If he can be convinced to fight.

We are standing like this, locked in a weird, too-long pause, when Luke's entire body jerks up, his head cocking to the side as though he's been alerted to something. With the spell broken, I blink to clear the fog from my mind and look around.

"What—?"

"Shh!" he hisses, all of his muscles tense. I watch his face, my heart thumping, and then I finally hear what he does. Sounds from below. *Inside* this building.

"Shit," I whisper, mind whirling. "Back to the roof!"

He grabs my arm in a grip so tight it hurts. "Don't move," he orders in a low growl that sends shivers along my spine. "They're above and below."

I feel cold. "Who? Police? *Bloods*?"

We might have a slim chance of escaping if it's the police. A very slim chance. But if it's the Bloods we are dead. No doubt about it. In my mind, I see the four men from the train blown to pieces over and over again, their red blood splashing against the train windows. I can't stop seeing them, imagining how they got there, to a moment in time when all four of them ceased to be. Who knew and loved those men? Who will remember them, now that they are gone?

Who will remember me when I am gunned down within minutes?

Luke might have, but he will be dead too.

"It's the Bloods, isn't it?" I whisper.

Luke turns his head slowly to look at me. "No. Not the Bloods."

My heart leaps with hope. "Then who?"

At first he doesn't say anything, even with the muffled noises growing slowly closer. My hope dies as I watch him—in Luke there is no fear, no panic, but something in him has turned to granite. "Listen," he murmurs urgently. "There's no order to how they move. No stealth. They sound like ..." He meets my eyes. "It's the Furies."

My first thought is disbelief that he could make a joke at such a time. Then I blink, realizing he's serious. Dread settles at the bottom of my stomach and starts to claw its way up through my insides, tearing and ripping as it goes. "No," I whisper. "That's impossible. They're not real. They're a stupid children's story." I'm babbling with panic.

Luke shakes his head, turning to the window. He inspects the edges, running his fingers along them with quick efficiency. When he can't get it open, he uses his elbow to make a crack in the glass, then pushes the pieces out carefully enough to catch each one and place them quietly on the floor.

I don't know what he's doing but I wish he'd hurry up. The Furies are every child's nightmare—actually they're the stuff of adult nightmares, too. Everyone in the world is terrified of the very idea of such creatures, savages with no access to any thought or feeling that isn't fury. Every once in a while a whisper will be heard about the monsters in the wild, men and women who crave the taste of human flesh and will go to any lengths to get it. It is said that this is what would become of us if we weren't given the cure. But it's just the government's way of scaring people; everyone knows it has no basis in reality.

Luke has all the glass out of the window now, but the awful noises are growing closer quickly. He sticks his head out and peers around. We're on the third storey, and the drop to the ground is dizzying.

"Okay, here's the plan," he says briskly. "You're going to hop onto my back and I'll climb out the window over to that power line there. Then I'll swing along it to the foster facility, from where I can probably reach that old scaffolding and make it to the ground."

"What?" An explosion of laughter erupts from me and Luke crams his hand over my mouth. "Are you completely out of your mind?" I gasp through his fingers. "That's absurd!"

"Well what's your idea then?"

I shake my head. "If by some miracle we make it to the other building, won't we set off the alarms there?"

"That's what we want. If the Bloods come, they can deal with the Furies for us, because it sounds like there are a lot of them."

"Why are they here?"

"Because we are, I'd say. They must have smelled us."

"Oh my god," I groan, closing my eyes. I can hear them more clearly now. They're shrieking with laughter and violence. Things are smashing and breaking and grunting and hissing. The sounds send a deep chill into my blood. "You really think you can make that climb with me on your back?"

"I'll have to."

"Let's do it then." Perversely, as soon as the decision has been made, I feel a wash of excitement flood me. Despite my depression, every ounce of adrenalin I have is flooding my system and calling to my survival instinct. It awakens and I grin.

Luke sees my expression and pauses momentarily. "You're a lunatic," he says softly, but in the gray light of the sinking sun's absence I can see an echoing smile at his lips. He turns around and I climb onto his back, wrapping my arms and legs tightly around him. "Whatever you do, don't let go," he warns.

"I won't." It's a promise I know I will keep. Nothing will pry my hands from his body except the safety of the ground.

Bodies burst into the room, scuffling and wrestling wildly. Luke swings out of the window and hangs onto the ledge. I pray they didn't spot us.

The noises pause, and then I hear a low, scratchy voice. "Hold. I smell flesh."

Fear explodes in my chest and Luke starts moving quickly, using the grooves in the bricks to climb sideways. I don't know how he's doing it—he climbs like a professional, finding the slightest grooves for his fingers and toes with quick confidence. It's just as well, because the Furies have spotted us, their heads poking out the window.

One of them tries to follow, but he slips almost immediately and falls all the way to the ground, landing with a horrific smacking, splashing sound. I can't look down, so I look back at the remaining figure in the window. He is dirty and unkempt, hair long and matted, eyes wild and teeth sharp, but he looks human, and that's what's truly disturbing about him. He gives a kind of blood-curdling howl, like I've heard wolves do on television. Within moments the window space is full of the beasts, clambering to get at us. Several more fall to their deaths and I shudder at the thought of the hunger in their bodies, so strong it makes them blind to anything else, even death.

Luke makes it to the power line and is about to touch it.

"Wait!" I exclaim, grabbing his hand and wrenching it away from the line. "Jesus, Luke—one touch and we could be dead! Just wait a minute." I fumble with my boot and manage to get it off. Its sole is made of rubber, so I touch it carefully to the cord to try and de-energize it. If it has too much power running through it, we'll be dead regardless of the rubber, but I'm hoping that since this building has been abandoned for so many years the power line has been dormant for just as long. Nothing happens and I sigh in relief. It's still not safe to touch the cord, so I sit the boot over it, bending it as much as the stiff leather will allow. It should protect against any wayward jolts of power that have remained within the copper wires, but it won't protect us if the power were to suddenly come back on, which is a real possibility, given wires like these can re-energize at any moment.

"You'll have to grab each side," I instruct Luke, who is sweating from the effort of holding us both to the wall. "Hold onto the shoe, but don't touch the power line, okay?"

Luke grabs the shoe, but his hands are so sweaty that he struggles to keep hold of the smooth leather. Meanwhile, the crazy savages are getting more and more frenzied, and I'm pretty sure they'll figure out how to get to us any second now. My mind whirls, and I pray that Luke is wearing a belt with his jeans. Carefully I reach down and find that he is. I undo the buckle and start pulling the leather out of its loops.

"What the hell are you doing?" he exclaims.

I have a mad urge to giggle but swallow it down. With the belt over my shoulder, I take my boot back and tear the rubber sole away from the leather, letting the boot drop to the ground. I place the piece of rubber over the power cord, then loop the belt over the top of this, pulling against it to make sure both will stay in place when holding our weight. This way the rubber will stop the belt from conducting any energy, hopefully protecting us until we can get to the other side.

"Here," I say, gesturing for Luke to grab the ends of the belt. He twists the leather twice around his hands, making sure his grip can't slip, even sweaty as it is.

"Okay hold on again," he orders and I clutch his back tightly as we launch away from the building and fly through the air. Luke's shoulders must be screaming in agony as they are wrenched nearly out of their sockets, but he doesn't make a sound. The wind rushes against my cheeks, cold and sharp, making my eyes stream. The noises of the Furies turn into a distant blur as everything in the world shrinks to contain only the power line, the rubber, the leather and our two bodies. For several long, silent moments, these are all that exist. And then suddenly the wall exists, looming into view just as we are about to crash into it. I brace myself for impact, but Luke manages to throw his feet up and take most of the force in his legs.

I blink, unable to believe we've made it across. We're not safe yet though—we still have to get to the scaffolding, and it's a good eight feet to the right. Luke starts to swing our bodies back and forth, back and forth, gaining momentum with each motion. I hold my breath, terrified of what he's about to try. He unwinds the loops of belt from around his hands and I realize that he is bleeding badly. The leather must have cut into his skin, but he ignores this, hurling himself through the air to grab onto the metal scaffolding.

His hands slip, slick with blood, and my heart lurches with the knowledge that we are about to fall. I lunge forward, grabbing the metal myself, and Luke manages to catch my waist and hang on.

A gasp of pain tears from my throat as I take his weight as well as my own. My vision turns to black dots. I am not, and have never been, physically strong. I'm too thin and I'm even weaker than people my size should be because I have an alter ego who sucks all my strength from me. So this would be a struggle for a normal person—for me it's impossible. Luke is too big, too heavy, I can't hold on any longer and when I let go we will both die. My arms scream and my hands begin to slip.

"Hang on, Josi," Luke grunts, using my body to reach back up to the scaffolding. Hooking one arm around it, he uses the other to slide around my waist and take my weight. I sob in relief, literally all the strength in my arms gone.

"Can you hold onto me?" he asks breathlessly.

I try to loop my arms around his neck again, but they're shaking so badly that I start to slip. Luke tightens his hold on my waist, taking a breath and starting the climb down using only one arm.

I hate how weak I am, how much of a burden I am to him.

Luke shimmies one-handed to the ground and I realize that the alarm is blaring—my own blood rushing in my ears made it impossible for me to hear anything else. Now it seems impossible I could have ignored the blaring racket. We hit the ground running and don't stop running until we're so far away we can't hear the alarm anymore. We may have been spotted on security cameras, but we'll have to hope they didn't get any retina scans.

I know the only reason the Furies haven't followed us is because they have a bigger problem to deal with now. I shudder to imagine the kind of fight that would occur between the Bloods and the Furies. They are contradictory in behaviour—the Bloods cold and controlled, the Furies wild and instinctive—but both are just as violent as the other.

"You okay?" Luke pants as we sag to a halt.

I'm too breathless to speak so I just nod. I take a look at the two of us and all my fear and adrenalin bubbles over into hysterical amusement. I burst into laughter and Luke looks at me like I need to be committed.

"We make a pair, hobbling along like this," I gasp. "Me limping with only one shoe and two dead arms, you struggling to hold your pants up as you run."

Luke starts to laugh too. He shakes his head, taking my hand to lead me home. It surprises me; I think he has forgotten how badly hurt his hands are—warm blood oozes onto my skin. I look at his face—he's miles away, lost in thought, unaware of his wounds.

Suddenly I don't know what I found so funny.

Luke

I know that very soon I will be in a lot of pain. But right now there is adrenalin flooding me, coating my nerves and making them numb, shielding them from what's to come.

Josi and I stumble home and lock the door. We are both strung out and so wired that we can't stop talking, talking, rapid-fire chatter about all we have just seen and done and the miracle of still being alive. We're on a high, a release-of-terror high, blissful to ride, but when we crash it could be bad. I know this from experience, but I don't think Josi does. She paces the apartment, retelling the whole afternoon in vivid detail—I never realized before but she is a born storyteller. Her hand motions are wild, her gestures unhindered by her injuries—these she will feel soon. Her words are full of color and they fill my head, better than the real memories.

What I am frightened of is the possibility of this sending her into another spell of depression.

"How did you climb like that?" she bursts out in the middle of another sentence.

I shrug.

"Come on! That was seriously like something out of a movie!"

Sighing, I shrug again. "Me and my bro used to do a lot of climbing."

"You have a brother!" she exclaims too loudly.

I go into the kitchen and pour us both a finger of whisky.

"Who is he? What's he like? Can I meet him?"

I hand her the glass and shake my head. "No, you can't meet him," I tell her softly.

She looks hurt by this, but nothing can keep her down for long right now. "How did you know the Furies are real?"

I shrug again. "You hear things at work. I took a guess and it was right."

Josi exhales and I can see the quick way her mind has shifted into another direction, another pattern. I see again the way she saved my life with her rubber shoe, then with the belt and again on the other side, when she saved me from falling. I owe her my life, three times over.

As if our thoughts overlap, she looks at me and says, "Luke, I'm so sorry I nearly got us killed."

My mouth drops open. "What?"

"It was my fault we were there in the first place. Plus I'm so weak I nearly dropped you."

"What are you talking about? You saved my life, Josephine." I wrap my hand around her arm, stretching it out and running my fingers along the length of it. "See this? You have practically zero percent muscle mass, and yet you still caught me, and you didn't let go of that bar, and that's because your determination is stronger than any muscle in my body."

We stare at each other—there is a kind of wildfire in her eyes. I become aware that my hand is still around her arm, touching her warm skin, and I'm startled by the intimacy of the moment.

I pull away from her quickly, pacing to the other side of the room and trying to shake the odd feeling from my limbs. I need to be careful. The closeness between us is growing, and it's dangerous. She is a child—I must make sure I don't take advantage of her innocence.

"Luke, I'm not sure I could have held anyone else up. Without you I think I would have let go."

The air gets stuck in my lungs and my body freezes. This is the first nice thing she has ever said to me—the first indication of any kind of feelings she might harbor. She has been so determined to keep me at arm's length, to ensure that she doesn't trust me, or even like me, that this is like a dam wall cracking. It smashes all of my stupid, naïve vows to put my own wall between us and makes me crave everything on the other side of the dam. Words escape me before I can stop them. "You're like a phantom moving through my life. A dream I can hardly hold onto and yet can't shake."

The room is silent. I don't turn around because I don't know what I will see in her eyes.

I don't know what makes a Fury the way it is, but I'm afraid that Josephine's transformations mean she is becoming one. And if I blink she will vanish.

Chapter Six

SEPTEMBER 13TH, 2065

Anthony

I look at my notes. There's only one word written there. *Furies.*

So that she doesn't pick up on my obvious disbelief, I get up and move to the sideboard, preparing us both a cup of tea. As I dunk the teabags in the hot water, I mentally prepare my argument and the medicine I can prescribe for such extreme delusions. It is clear to me now that Luke must be a hallucination too—if one part of her story is, it seems safe to assume that all of it is. Or, if not a hallucination, then a concoction of her mind due to its past trauma.

As I pass Josephine the cup and saucer, I clear my throat. "Furies."

She smiles, too sharp not to hear everything I'm trying to keep hidden. "Yes, Doc. Furies." She smiles again. Her eyes are somewhere distant as she says, "Perhaps you're right. Perhaps I did imagine them. Sometimes I think I must have. I don't know how something so wild could exist within a world like this, one that is so unforgivably void of life."

I don't tell her what's on the tip of my tongue: that this is exactly what I see when I look at her.

NOVEMBER 21ST, 2063

Josephine

The view, at this particular moment, is quite delectable. I'm surrounded by trees, dirt, leaves and bark. But they don't get a second glance, because in front of me is Luke Townsend, shirtless, and *man* is he yummy. He's wearing blue shorts and thick black work boots. Through his shirt I can see that the broad, lean lines of his back are slick with a fine sheen of sweat, and his muscles look taught and strong as he hikes. It's becoming clearer by the day that I may have serious mental problems. I have to stop thinking about him.

I happen to hate hiking; especially in a dull, boring forest. And especially when we're on a fool's errand that will never bear fruit, and if it does, it's the kind that will be utterly rotten.

We're searching for evidence of one of my crimes. Any single one. This is about number five on the nightmare timeline. Not the worst, but not the best either. I woke up near here one morning, drenched in blood and dew, and I had to walk the twenty miles back to civilization, barefoot and naked. Plus I was nauseous, feverish and badly bruised. And the icing on top of the cake? I was fairly sure that for the first time I'd killed someone the night before. That was a great day.

"Luke!" I shout. "Slow down!" He's a maniac, tearing through here, his long legs covering the distance with an athleticism I can only dream of. The excitement in him was there that first night I met him, and every day since. Something wild and strong and unknowable.

"Come on, Josi," he calls impatiently. "We've barely started."

What? We've been traipsing around the wilderness all day! If he actually thinks we're going to comb every inch of this enormous expanse of land then he's got another thing coming.

"I need a drink!" I yell. I see him sigh and reluctantly turn. The pack on his back contains all sorts of things, including a picnic rug that he spreads out. I slump onto it, exhausted. "Urgh. It's *hot*."

"God, you're really fragile, aren't you?"

"I'm not fragile—you're a machine that never slows down! It's weird, Luke. We haven't found anything, so can we please go home?" I guzzle down some water and lie back on the rug, staring up at the canopy of green and brown. Pinpricks of light dance their way through the gently swaying leaves. As my eyes grow lazy and unfocused, the spots of light shimmer and swell until suddenly they're a different color altogether. Blues and blacks and grays. It's night. Someone is breathing loudly and moaning in pain. The heavy, steel scent of blood is in my nose and I'm hungry. The trees move and distort and there's a scream—

I sit up abruptly, dizzy and nauseous. The colors are back to normal—the sun is out and it's day again, but so glary it makes my eyes hurt.

"Woah—Josi? You okay?"

I might vomit.

"Breathe," Luke tells me softly, placing a large, warm hand on my back. It brings me back to reality and calms me. I struggle to draw breath.

"I saw something," I whisper.

"What?"

"I mean, I think I remembered something."

"What was it?" he asks gently, moving his hand in soothing circles over my spine.

"Just … I was here. That night. I was right here, looking
up at these trees. It was dark and quiet, and someone else was
here with me."

"Who was it?"

"I don't know, I—I can't remember." My voice drops. "She
was crying. Screaming. Bleeding. I must have hurt her." I swallow. "Fuck, Luke, I feel sick. I want to go home."

I start to get up but he takes my shoulder and stops me.
"No. This is why we're here. Don't hide from it, or run away.
These are your crimes. Your memories. So own them."

"I don't understand you," I hiss, shaking my head and re-
fusing to cry.

"We're just going to lie here for a while and calm down."

"Why does everything have to be calm?" I snap. "I hate
calm!"

"Not everything has to be. Just this, for a few minutes. If
we leave now you'll be too afraid to go to another one of the
sites."

He's right, but I don't think staying will change that. I sit
back down, furious with him. Luke always thinks he knows
what's best for me, but I'd like the freedom to be able to figure
it out for myself. I want to make him lose his perpetual cool.
I want him to shout or cry or laugh hysterically. I want to see
a hint of the man who climbed out a third storey window and
swung across a power line to get us to safety. The man who was
brave enough to do all of that without batting an eyelid, the
man who didn't shy away from danger. Although, he didn't lose
his cool even then, did he? He was calm in the face of death.

I don't know if that's horribly twisted or completely
amazing.

Luke says, right out of the blue, "Your hair makes me
mental. Why don't you just brush it for once?"

I look over my shoulder at him, indignant.

"Seriously, Josi—there's like fucking rats' nests in here. Look at this!" He holds up a chunk that isn't far from becoming a dreadlock.

I jerk my head out of his reach. "For your information, asshole, my scalp gets really sore so it's hard to put a brush through it."

"Well I'll help you when we get home because I can't look at it for another second."

"Jeez, what's up your butt today?"

Luke looks like he's about to say something and, for just a moment, I think he seems irritated with me. But that's impossible. Unless his cure is malfunctioning. God I hope so. He closes his mouth with a snap and his eyes are completely clear of emotion. Guess not then.

"Nothing. Now that you're sufficiently distracted from the memory, we can get going."

"Ah, so that was your game. Insult me so that I'll think about killing you instead of someone else."

"Worked, didn't it?"

"Yes. But I always think about killing you."

"Great, then let's go home and log today."

I groan. Luke likes to log things. He puts everything in tables and journals and logs, and then stares at it all for hours at a time. Weird details, too. Stuff that I'd never give a second thought. But hey—he must do stuff like this for a living, so I don't question it. Over the past couple of weeks when he's not at work we've been doing a lot of research. Police records, protocol for the cure, digging up dirt on my old foster families and social workers. None of it has helped at all, but Luke insists that it will all come together somehow so he logs it, all of it. He's a bit of a nerd, actually. I think I like it.

SEPTEMBER 13TH, 2065

Anthony

"So this vision …" I start.

"Memory," Josephine interrupts.

I gaze at her sternly. "What you had is called a hallucination."

She rolls her eyes. "I am quite aware of what a hallucination is, doc: *a sensory experience of something that does not exist outside the mind, caused by various physical and mental disorders, or by a reaction to certain toxic substances, and usually manifested as visual or auditory images.*"

"Exactly," I agree, trying to hide my discomfort. It's not a nice feeling to know that your patient is a thousand times smarter than you are. Josephine's IQ is so high that it classifies her as beyond a genius. It's because of her memory, as is often the case in those with eidetic memories. Her knowledge is almost out of her control—her brain simply retains everything she has ever seen or read. Psychological or emotional disorders are perfectly normal responses to such high intelligence. It's my job to ensure she doesn't feel isolated because of her intellect.

"Therefore, by definition, what I experienced was not a hallucination, because it actually happened."

"We have yet to establish that as fact." She gives me such a filthy look that I spread my hands and add, "Give me some proof then."

"I will," she snaps. "If we're both still alive next week I'll make sure it's my first priority to find you some."

NOVEMBER 21ST, 2063

Luke

When we get home from our little romp in the wilderness, Josi heads straight for the shower and I sit down at my computer to log the day's information. I'm creating a timeline of locations and crimes to fit corresponding dates. I want it all laid out with crystal clarity so that Josi can see it all for herself.

So far we have a collage of violence, pretty damn high on the gruesome scale. I have detached the words on the screen from the girl in the shower. I simply can't see Josephine as the woman who committed these crimes, or else I'm likely to lose my mind. I think Josi has had to do the same.

Her memory loss is a mixed blessing. On the one hand, it means we're having trouble proving her crimes because we can't get a good enough insight into what they are. On the other hand, it's saving her sanity. If she had picture-perfect memories of killing people, I'm pretty sure that would make her a deranged serial killer.

If there is any hope—however slim—of preventing the transformations then I need to help her figure out what's causing them.

For the one-thousandth time I hack into the government child protection database and pull up Josephine's information. She was passed around foster homes for the whole first half of her life. This is listed as due to 'behavioral problems and emotional instability'. In other words, the shithouse foster families who took her in solely to get paid for it couldn't handle that she was a passionate, clever child, and bailed on her repeatedly. There is a picture on her file, and it flashes up on the wall when I tap it.

Looming above me, larger than life, is Josi as a five-year-old. She is horribly skinny, her eyes way too big for her face and full of a strange, hollow sharpness. She has a beanie pulled down to her eyelashes and she looks like she wants nothing more than to disappear.

She is angry; even at five, she is angry. She's a hurricane of it, and I know in one glance at this photo that she's been abused. I've seen it repeatedly in children who've been removed by child protection. No less since the cure.

We humans are violent. We're savage, no matter what you do to our brains. No matter how you fiddle around in our heads. There will never be a future in which we don't hurt each other.

And sitting here in the living room of my ridiculous, empty apartment, surrounded by things I don't need or want, staring at a photo of a beautiful little girl, the truth—*my* truth—comes bubbling to the surface, and for a few long minutes I can do nothing to hide it.

I have a secret, one that Josephine can never find out. I must guard it with everything I have, every piece of training I've ever undergone.

It's very simple: sometimes, in moments like these, my whole body is a flame of pure, unadulterated fury.

I was never given the cure, and I'll die before I ever am.

Josephine

When I emerge from my shower Luke is wielding a comb like a weapon. "I'm getting it now while it's wet," he threatens.

"Don't you have things to log?"

"Already done. I'm a whiz."

"Well, we didn't learn much."

"Sure we did—we now know that one of the victims from '59 was a woman and we know exactly where it happened. Makes a difference. No more excuses. Sit down in the living room and hold onto a pillow, 'cause this is gonna hurt."

I reluctantly sit down in front of the couch and brace myself, but it barely hurts at all. Luke sits on the couch behind me and is so careful with the long tendrils of black hair that it doesn't pull against my sore scalp. After a few minutes he relaxes his legs on either side of my body. My heart starts to thump—this is closer than Luke and I have been since the night of the Furies. Ever since then he has kept himself at a clear distance—which has suited me fine, because when he is close I find it difficult to keep my thoughts straight.

Behind me he is big and warm and smells strongly of amazing things like spice and mint, and dirt and soap. He touches my head gently, like a caress, as he untangles each new lock. If I lean back just the slightest bit he'll be holding me, and we'll be like two normal people who touch each other. But I don't, because I know that he'd just push me away and keep brushing my hair.

My stomach flips over in a way I've never felt before. It's pleasant and unpleasant at the same time. I want to get as far from him as possible, or else I want to stay here within the space of his body for the rest of time. I'm confused and aggravated and he's nothing, just calm.

"What else?" he asks softly, leaning close to my ear. "What else hurts?"

I want to tell him the truth. That everything hurts. That nothing hurts. That I can't breathe. Instead I turn my head slightly toward his and say, "The bruises. They hurt the most."

"Show me."

My hands are trembling as I lift my shirt up at the back and lean forward so he can see. I don't know why I'm doing this—the last thing I want is for him to see me like this, damaged and ugly and vulnerable. But I know that with him sitting so close, there's no way I could deny him anything.

"Shit," he breathes out softly when he sees the awful black and purple bruises that have gotten steadily worse over the weeks. Normally by now they'd be starting to fade, but this year they've stayed longer. I don't know why and I don't want to think about why. I feel his large hands against my skin and it makes me start. He runs them all over my back, along the worst of the marks on my spine. It doesn't hurt because his touch is so light, and I feel myself being gentled like a wild horse.

Almost in a trance, I lean back against him, resting my head on his leg. He freezes and I brace myself, but he doesn't push me away. He slides his hands around to my chest and holds me against him, turning his lips to brush along the edge of my hairline. I can feel his heartbeat through his thin cotton T-shirt. It's beating against my back, a steady, strong rhythm. A lot stronger than my own.

"I want to stop you from being hurt like this," he murmurs, frustrated.

"It's not me I'm worried about," I reply sleepily. He must hear that I'm half dozing already, because he pulls me up onto the couch with him and we both lie down, and he's still wrapped around me, and I've never felt safe until this moment.

Luke

Josephine is rude and rash, sarcastic and angry. She is emotionally unstable. She's too young and she's too difficult. She's inexperienced, frightened and loud. At any moment she could fly away. But as I lie on the couch with her sleeping in my arms, I think I'm already in love with her. I think I love every one of these things about her. I think maybe I was in love with her from that first moment I saw her eyes, brown and blue and sad. And I think maybe I made a big mistake, talking to her in that bar.

*

I don't sleep. I listen to Josi breathing slowly and I think about how badly I've fucked up as I wait for her to wake.

In the beginning I didn't care about lying. It came as easily to me as breathing. I could convince anyone of anything, no matter how absurd. Now it's all I think about.

It's around three in the morning when she finally stirs. She wriggles a bit and yawns, then rolls over so that our faces are less than an inch apart.

"I haven't had any night terrors since I've been living here."

I start to speak then have to clear my throat. "That's good."

"What time is it?"

"Not sure. Late. Are you hungry?"

"Starving."

"What do you feel like? Name your desire. Lobster? Steak? Pâté?"

She smiles. Up close her lips look perfect. "What would you say if I asked for a grilled cheese sandwich?"

"I'd say thank god," I laugh. "If I tried to make lobster we wouldn't be eating until sunrise."

In the kitchen, Josi sits on the bench and dangles her legs while I make us both cheese sandwiches. I sit beside her to eat them. Melted cheese dribbles all over her chin so I reach out to wipe it off for her. She freezes, and I freeze, and our eyes meet.

Abruptly she says, "I think maybe I should move out."

"Why?" I can't help but feel panicked, my hand dropping away.

"You know why."

"I won't touch you again. I'm sorry. I didn't mean anything by it."

"I know you didn't. It's not you, it's me."

"Good line. Did you come up with it yourself?"

"Luke, listen to me." She searches my face and says heavily, "I feel weird. I feel … different to how I should feel."

"What are you talking about?"

"I'm talking about you. How I feel for you. And you don't … I mean, we can't … I just have to move out, all right? I can't live in a house with you. It's too hard, and it's only going to get harder."

"Josi, what—hard in what way?"

She slides off the bench and faces me. She looks sleepy and bedraggled, but her hair is long and smooth and clean, and her eyes are as beautiful as they always are. "Luke, I want you, okay? I want you all the time. I want to kiss you and touch you and be with you, and that makes me feel sick because I shouldn't ever think about anyone like that... And a drone? I absolutely can't ever want a drone, okay? Is that clear enough?"

I stare at her, stunned.

"That's why I have to move out."

My mind is scrabbling. She can't move out.

"I—"

"I know," she quickly forestalls. "I'm too young, and it's not like that for you anyway. It's good, Luke. I'm a lunatic for even thinking it, for *so* many reasons."

"What reasons?"

"I'm a monster. I'd never drag anyone into that sort of mess."

"I'm already in that mess."

"No you're not. We're friends, and even that's too much. The closer we get the worse it'll be when …"

"When what?"

She drops her eyes to the ground. It makes me nervous. "When *what*, Josi?"

"When I kill myself."

The floor drops away and I'm falling into pitch black. All color is gone. I can't believe I've heard her right. She couldn't possibly ...

"I've tried before," she admits so softly I barely hear her. "Before the moon. But whatever my curse is, it healed all the drugs in my system."

"You tried to overdose?"

Josephine nods. "But I timed it wrong. This time I'll do it sooner."

Oh god, I feel sick. She's eerily matter-of-fact, and I think I might throw up. "Josi ..."

"Don't get me wrong. I don't want to die. But I can't hurt anyone else. It's ... worse than being dead."

"So you're saying that if we don't fix this before the next blood moon, you'll just commit suicide?"

She looks at me funny and I realize I need to get control of myself. I close my eyes and try to breathe through my rage. When I look at her again I have a firm grip on the emotions blazing under my skin. I am calm and deadpan. "I don't ever want to hear you say anything like that again."

Her eyes flash dangerously. "Oh? And I do exactly as you say, do I?"

"When I say things like that you do."

Josephine slaps me hard across the face. "You don't control me," she snarls. "You don't get to control when I die. It's the only choice I have left, and no one will take that from me."

And then she goes into her room and locks the door, and even though I bang on it and shout at her for hours, she doesn't come back out. I think maybe my bones might be shattering. My perspective is suddenly so clear.

Until now I have been unsure. Unsure what my part in Josephine's life is, unsure how I should be with her and what I should be trying to achieve. I have a life that does not fit with hers. I've lived twenty-six years without her, and I have been perfectly fine.

But now. Now it's simple and clear.

I will find a way to solve this problem. I've never been so sure of something—I realize now that I've never actually been sure of *anything*.

Josephine Luquet is the strongest person I've ever met. She's brave and honest and sweet and kind. She is too caring, too brash, too clever, too talented. Her music makes me imagine a life that's not this one, a life that's not missing pieces, a life with her and without cures. I will save her. I will.

*

Close to sunrise she has her first night terror since she's lived with me. I'm sitting outside her room, leaning against her door and rehearsing what I want to say—a speech that will make her want to live. A loud, horrific shriek comes from her room and I sit up in shock. It's a scream so full of terror that I'm instantly sick with it. It goes on and on, even when I bang on the door and shout her name to try and wake her.

I can't handle it anymore and override the controls to unlock it. I sink onto the bed and try to avoid her violent thrashing. It's so awful seeing her like this. Beyond awful.

"Josi!" I try, then reach out to touch her. She struggles for a moment, screaming and crying and all I can think of to do is to climb into the bed with her and hold her as tightly as I can. She shouts something, jerks in a weird way and then freezes.

I stay as still as I can, unsure what's happening, and then I hear a soft voice whisper, "Luke?"

"I'm here," I murmur into her ear. "It's okay. You're safe."

But if she ever learns the truth she will hate me, and she will be far from safe.

NOVEMBER 22ND, 2063

Josephine

I wake up in Luke's arms for the second time in twenty-four hours. My skin and my bones hurt. I feel stretched and sore and when I realize that he's wrapped around me I feel frightened by how happy it makes me.

I sit up and try to extricate myself without waking him, but he stirs quietly and mumbles, "You okay?"

I'm so tired. I want to lie back down and spend the rest of my life in his arms, but I've got images in my head, dark things that would destroy him like they've done me, and I can't let that happen.

"I'm not happy," I say simply. "I need to leave, and I don't ever want to see you again."

He lies there, and he looks broken. I leave before he can ruin me entirely.

Chapter Seven

SEPTEMBER 13TH, 2065

Josephine

Anthony is staring at me. He hasn't interrupted me once in the last two hours. He has simply watched my face with that expression they all wear, all the drones. I imagine they must be trying very hard to feel the right thing, but I don't think they are ever sure.

"Would you like to take a break?" he asks. And that's when I see the strangeness in his eyes. The softness. He's never looked at me this way before—as if he cares about me.

"No, I'm all right," I say, voice dry. The quicker we get this done the quicker I speak to Luke. Jesus, even thinking about him makes me all crazy. I reach over and try to push the window further open. The sun is setting and the air is cool, but I can smell everything the rain has left behind and it makes the slight trembling in my fingers stop.

"You don't look … all right," Anthony points out quietly.

I decide to tell him the truth, because the trembling is making me afraid. "It's the curse. For days leading up to it, and weeks after, my body fails." I stand and cross to the desk. Briefly I show him the blood coming from my gums and my fingernails.

"Josephine!" he exclaims, standing in his chair. "What's caused this?"

"I just told you."

"We need to get you straight into the nurse's station."

"They won't find any reason for the bleeding," I warn him. "I've been to dozens of doctors. Not one of them could figure it out. They said that my body was behaving like a body does during organ failure, but none of my organs are failing. You've seen my file, right?"

He stares at me worriedly. I know the file he's been working from is a psych evaluation, because according to the doctors I've seen my symptoms have no physical cause and therefore must be caused by mental problems. The best they could do to explain this absurdity to me was to use an analogy about husbands feeling sympathy pains when their wives go into labor. My body apparently sympathizes with my fucked-up head, so if someone can just get some drugs to work on me, then the problem's solved.

Story of our civilization: all problems can be solved with a bucket load of pharmaceuticals.

"I'm okay," I tell Anthony gently. "For now, anyway. Let's keep going."

He loosens his tie, clearly trying to rid himself of the unruly feelings he suddenly seems to be dealing with. He sits down, puts his glasses on and takes them off again, then looks at me and nods.

I cross back to the window. "I moved out."

"That didn't last long," he comments. "Two months?"

"Yeah. Everything with Luke and me was fast. Out of control. I had this sense that nothing could slow the two of us down except making sure there was no 'two of us'. I got out of there and went back to my crap box of an apartment. I got a job at a bar where all the girls got tips if they dressed revealingly. None of the men tried to touch me—none of them even looked at me. I got no tips no matter how I dressed."

"Why?" The doc seems genuinely confused by this.

I level him with a stare. "Tell me the truth, Anthony. If you hadn't been forced to spend an hour a day with me for the last year, how would you respond to me?"

He doesn't reply.

"You barely glanced at me for weeks in the beginning," I remind him. "You knew without needing to be told that there was something different about me. Your instincts were to distance yourself from me, to make sure you didn't make any contact. You have a basic human awareness of danger that has been incorrectly spooked because your cure causes your brain to send the wrong signals at the wrong times." I pause and then shrug with shoulders that ache. "Or maybe your sense of danger is spot-on. Maybe your instincts sense the truth your mind can't believe: that I've spilt a lot of blood."

Anthony hesitates long enough to confirm that this is exactly right. I don't need him to confirm it for me anyway—I've been around the truth my entire life.

"So you left Luke before anything could happen between the two of you," Anthony says. "A response from your childhood."

I don't want to talk about my childhood. I don't want to blame my problems with Luke on the crap that happened to me as a kid. That seems like the easy way out. It seems like the definition of cowardice. "I left to protect him," I say bluntly.

"From what?"

"Me!" I snap. "Protect him from me, you idiot. Are you really that dumb?"

"Let's not get agitated."

"*You* make me agitated."

He obviously doesn't know what to say. "Do you want to continue? Do you need some water?"

"I'm fine." God, sometimes all I want is to punch him in the mouth.

"If you get so annoyed by my calm demeanor, then why didn't you get just as annoyed with Luke?"

I open my mouth but can't think of anything to say. "Sometimes I did. A lot of the time, actually. But he wasn't ... he was different. He wasn't as bad as you." I think for a moment that Anthony is hurt, but quickly realize how stupid that thought is. Nothing I say has any effect on him, except maybe to exasperate him. I swallow and put my hands out the window, turning them this way and that. This slight movement hurts, but I like the fresh air too much to care. Then the blood on my fingernails catches the orange light of the sinking sun and I wrench my hands inside again, squeezing my eyes shut.

She's coming for me. She prowls at the edge of her cage, but soon she'll be strong enough to break free, and I'll be so weak and sick that I won't even have a chance at holding her back. Doors with locks and guards with weapons aren't enough to stop her. I don't know what will ever be enough.

My eyes hurt, so I lean back on the couch and keep them closed while I speak. I picture Luke the whole time, even though it hurts more than my body is starting to.

DECEMBER 21ST, 2063

Josephine

The slaughterhouse stinks of blood. It's cavernous and has been sitting empty for years, by the looks of it. I climb in through a shattered window and wait for my eyes to adjust to the darkness. Huge meat hooks hang from the ceiling, glinting red with rust. Puddles of old liquid dot the floor, and I pick my way gingerly through them, peering around for any sign that I was here once.

Plastic sheets hang against some of the walls, covered in mold, and I push them aside to try and see the layout of the building. There's a set of stairs that leads down into an even darker, creepier room beneath the ground. More meat hooks hang in long rows, attached to chains that run the length of the roof. There's a big green button on the wall and, even though I know my curiosity never leads me anywhere good, I always give into it.

The button is stiff when I press it. The chains creak and jingle alarmingly, and then the tracks in the roof start to move with a long shriek of metal against metal. The meat hooks slowly grind around in a long circle, swinging eerily. My nerves are shot, making my teeth chatter. I can hear something dripping amid the screech of metal, and the *smells*—I can't think about them or I might throw up.

I shove my palm into the green button but it seems to be jammed, and the damn thing won't turn off. Jesus, my hands are starting to shake, I have to get out of here.

I turn and run headlong into someone. A scream is torn from my throat but there are arms taking me by the shoulders and pulling me to a halt.

"Josi! It's me!"

I blink and realize I'm looking up at Luke. His green eyes are the only bright things down in this pit of death. I let out a choked laugh of relief and extricate myself from his hands. "What are you doing here?"

"Apparently the same as you. Picking dates on the list and snooping around."

Our eyes meet for a split second and then I look away. There's a long, awkward moment as the meat hooks swing and creak behind us. The hairs on my arms are standing on end and I can't shake the fear that creeps further into my heart with every beat. I think Luke's presence makes me even more nervous.

A shadow moves against the wall, making me jump in shock.

"A rat," Luke explains the scuffling sound.

I need to get out of here and away from him, but as I turn to leave something appears in the corner of my eye. I freeze. My heart is pounding. I can't bear to look properly, but this is why I came.

These are your crimes, your memories. Own them.

Luke's words echo loudly in my ears and I force myself to turn and look. It's one of the hooks. No longer covered in rust. There is a body dangling from it, impaled on the sharp metal. A man. He is large and strong, his mouth and eyes open wide in shock. His insides are spilling out of him because his rib cage has been torn open and spread wide like a dripping, pink artwork of horror. Bits of his heart cover the hook protruding from his chest.

I stare, too stunned to move. I can hear my pulse beating in my ears, louder and louder. Ice is moving steadily through every single one of my veins. I've never felt so cold in my whole life.

I turn and vomit violently onto the hard concrete ground. My whole stomach comes up and turns me inside out. I heave and heave until my body aches too much to continue, and when I look back at the hook it is empty.

Luke

When I was a boy I liked to pull things apart. Electronics, old car engines, tools, machinery, toys—anything that could be picked into pieces was fascinating to me. I tinkered with things endlessly, always filthy with oil or dirt. I wanted to know how they worked, what they looked like, how they could be broken. I always wondered what it would be like to pick a person apart—I wanted to know how our bodies worked on the inside.

Once I took a kitchen knife and cut open my arm so that I could see my bones and flesh, my arteries and muscles. My curiosity was so strong that it blocked a lot of the pain. It wasn't until later that I realized we can't be taken apart as simply as a machine can. And I realized, too, that it's even more difficult for us to be put back together.

My mother found me in my room, digging around in my arm and she screamed in shock. When I was stitched and back from the hospital she yelled some more, but differently this time. This was in the days when people still yelled. *You tear everything into a thousand pieces but you never put anything back together! One day you will have broken everything in your life, Luke Townsend.*

*

Outside the sun is too bright. Down a gentle hill of yellowish grass is a wide river. I guide Josephine to it, wary of her shaking legs and chalk-white lips. The fresh air is already doing her some good, and I think the sound of the rushing water is calming too.

We sit on the grass and I wait a long time for her to recuperate. I haven't seen her for a month. But I've been to all of these places, these sites that are the essence of what is wrong with her, and I've pretended that she missed me as much as I did her.

Eventually I ask, "What did you see?"

"I killed a man in that slaughterhouse," she says, her voice detached and cold. "I put him on one of the hooks."

I frown. "Those hooks are at least six feet off the ground. You're not tall enough or strong enough to get a man onto one of them."

She shrugs. "What do you want me to say?"

"What was he wearing?"

"Black."

"Any physical identifiers?"

"He was big. Strong. Very short hair. Clean-cut looking. That's all I could see."

"Are there any assumptions you can make about him?" I prompt. This is important, but Josi shakes her head, looking tired and pissed off.

"I'm going to the next site on the list," she says.

"Isn't that a bit much? Don't you want to leave it for another day?"

She stands and starts walking.

"I'll drive you. It's too far to walk."

"I'm not going anywhere with you."

"Please just stop being so fucking stubborn and get in the car."

"You don't tell me what to do, remember?"

"I'm not telling, I'm asking. *Begging*, if you want."

Josephine doesn't look at me. She simply walks silently to my car.

The grass grows more yellow as we reach the outskirts of the city. Wide fields scatter the view on either side of the road, but there's virtually no livestock anywhere. I haven't seen a cow or a sheep in years, not since they were all moved to private organic farms that produce meat too expensive for more than two thirds of the population to afford. If we keep driving in this direction we'll soon reach the wall. But I'm grateful our destination isn't that far; I hate that wall more than I hate anything in this world.

Since the atmosphere in the car is tense at best, I've distracted myself by switching the Jag to manual and concentrating on the drive. Josephine keeps turning the radio to dumb crap that she knows I hate, and I keep turning it back just to get a reaction out of her. Once or twice I'm pretty sure I see her lips twitch, but god forbid she let herself laugh in the same vicinity as me since I'm now apparently the enemy.

I follow the GPS and turn the car down a winding dirt driveway. It leads us around a few hills and through some paddocks, and finally to an old, dilapidated-looking farmhouse. There is an enormous barn off to the side, and it looks like something out of a children's picture book with its bright red door and yellow eaves. Josi climbs out of the car and stares at the barn for ages. I grow impatient and jog up the two steps to the front door of the house. I knock for about ten minutes before anyone appears.

It's a woman holding a small baby. She peers at me through a window to the left, and then reluctantly opens the door. I wonder what's made her so suspicious. The child squirms but the woman only looks at me blankly.

"Hi," I begin, flashing her a smile. "Sorry to bother you, ma'am. My girlfriend and I were just wondering if we could possibly take a look around your property?"

"Why?"

I decide to take a bit of a gamble. "Josephine used to live on this farm, and she wants to show me all her little treasures. You remember what it was like to be a kid—lots of secret places you never shared with anyone. There's this spot out the back where she buried some of her toys and she's really excited about finding them again."

The woman still looks utterly spaced out. She hasn't responded at all to my gentle, soothing babble. I'm not surprised. She's blissed out on emptiness and confusion. The scientists behind the cure must be over the moon to see the more extreme results like this—it's a classic case of a personality that didn't take well to being messed with. Assholes.

"Do you think it would be all right if we took a little look around?" I press carefully, keeping my smile fixed in place. "We won't bother you at all ..."

"She used to live here?" the lady asks abruptly, her eyes squinting against the sun toward Josephine's still profile. "When was that?"

"A long time ago."

"Oh. That's odd. We moved in only a year ago. The house had been abandoned long before that, I believe."

"So you just found it empty?"

"Our realtor found it for us. The property had been given to the state because its occupants disappeared—every single one of them. Left no will." She shrugs, but the story makes a lot of sense to me. I'm suddenly not too sure I want Josephine to remember anything about this place. By the sounds of it, a lot of bad stuff went down. An entire family ...

I turn to suggest we leave, but Josephine is already approaching the barn.

"Don't take too long," the woman warns vaguely. "And don't disrupt anything."

There is patently nothing to disrupt, since the entire property looks to be dead grass, but I nod and thank her before following Josi to the barn. Behind me I hear the woman start to laugh in a low wheeze that makes the hairs on my neck stand on end. I glance back but she's closing the door and her creepy, deranged laughter is cut off.

"Wait outside," Josephine orders me coldly, and there's something scary about her in this moment, so I do as I'm told.

After about thirty seconds she walks straight back out, strides past me and hops back in the car. I'm not sure what to say when I join her. She refuses to look at me, and there's a hard line to her clenched jaw.

"Josi—"

"You can never ask me about that place. Not that one. Do you understand?"

I swallow and then I nod, because I do understand.

*

I pull up outside her apartment block. We sit quietly for a while. She still won't look at me, so I follow suit and stare straight ahead too.

"I'm going to get really drunk tonight," she announces suddenly. "Would you like to be involved?"

My head jerks around. "Uh ... sure." It's quite possibly the best offer I've ever had in my life. Her smell has filled up the car and I feel kind of heady from it. Since she moved out I've been imagining really embarrassing things that I will never admit to. Shit like candlelit dinners and romantic baths, and long walks holding hands. And when I'm not imagining that stuff or doing my research I'm storming around the apartment in a rage. I smashed the best bottle of wine I owned last night. It was worth a fortune and I'd been saving it for a special occasion. I drew it from the rack and felt so resentful that I wasn't allowed to admit to every one of my feelings that I took the bottle out onto my balcony and hurled it straight down onto the street.

"We're going to a party," Josi says.

"Whose?"

"Some guy I met at the bar." She is clearly demanding a fight but I'm tired of pretending I don't want her. I can barely remember my adolescence. Josephine is the same. So maybe it's self-destructive, but maybe we both need to blow off some steam. Maybe all I want to do is enjoy her for five minutes without being reminded that she might be dead in a few months.

So instead of warning her about how dangerous it could be, or pointing out that young men have the least predictable responses to the cure and when mixed with alcohol they can be truly violent, I say, "Good. What time will I pick you up?"

She hesitates a second then shrugs. "Ten."

Josephine

I have no clothes that are suitable, and as I stare at my filthy home, my tiny suitcase and its meager contents, I have a moment of complete despair. I almost start crying, but I don't, because that's not what I do.

Instead I force myself to be proactive and I spread every item of clothing I own over the mattress. I have a pair of ratty old black jeans with holes in the knees; I decide to cut them into shorts. I have no scissors, so I have to rip them as well as I can, then I cuff them twice so that they're quite short. My single pair of stockings have a ladder in them, so I rip them a couple more times, hoping it will look like they're supposed to be like this. My scalp isn't as sore as it was a month ago so I painstakingly brush my long black hair. I keep meaning to cut it short, but can't quite bring myself to do it. I have no idea why—maybe it's simply that I've always had long hair, and cutting it all off would seem a bit like losing the last part of me that was once innocent.

There's one top in the pile that I've never had occasion to wear. It's a deep emerald green, buttoned down the front with no back. I consider what I could wear underneath it, then remember that I'm supposed to be cutting loose tonight and decide to wear nothing under it. My bruises have faded, but tonight I don't really care if people can see them, and this way my tattoos are visible too. Lastly, I add my black leather wristband, a long earring made of a bird feather in one ear and, because I can't find the other one, a black stud in the other. Impatiently I brush on some mascara and red lipstick.

I only have a small cracked mirror in the bathroom, so I take a look at myself in there. I look like a completely different person. I can't find myself anywhere in my reflection, and I like it. I feel dangerous. And even though this is usually the last thing I would ever want to feel, tonight I want to be wild and difficult. And angry.

There's a knock on my door. My stomach lurches but I ignore it. He let me leave, and he made me confused, and I don't need that shit in my life. I told him that I *wanted* him, for god's sake, and he just stood there and didn't say anything! I've never been so humiliated.

There's also the much more important fact that I can't trust myself around him. If I let myself have feelings for him, I might hesitate when the time comes. And that isn't an option—killing myself is a necessity.

Anyway. I only invited Luke tonight because I need a designated driver and because I'm fairly sure no one will talk to me if I don't come with a good-looking friend.

I open the door and we stare at each other. Oh Lord, the man is trying to destroy me. The stupid bastard looks like he hasn't made any effort at all, and yet somehow he looks hotter than he ever has. He's wearing slim-fitting, charcoal-colored suit pants very low on his hips. A pair of suspenders hangs carelessly from the waistband. I can quite clearly see the outline of his muscular chest and arms through his white tee, and he hasn't bothered to shave so there's dark stubble over his square jaw. He leans against the doorframe, and he looks at me with an expression I have never seen him wear before. It's like he's just as dangerous as I am, just as deadly, and he's had enough of the games.

Luke's green eyes travel over my body and I feel flushed. He doesn't smile, but I can see in his eyes that he's pleased. "You look hot."

I turn and grab my black boots, pulling them on. I glance at his feet and see an ancient pair of sneakers. The bottoms of his pants are scuffed. All those fancy new clothes in his wardrobe and he insists on wearing items from the Stone Age. Even so—he can't help but exude lazy sexuality.

"Come on," I mutter as I brush past him. "Did you get any alcohol?"

"Was I meant to, Your Highness?"

"We're going to a party and I told you I want to get drunk so what do you think?" I'm enjoying being snarky. I want to ruffle him, make him angry. I want to push every single one of his buttons. In fact I want to make everyone angry, everyone in this whole damn world.

"You've got a fakey—you can get your own booze," he comments.

We arrive at the warehouse and head inside. It's full already, even this early. The lights are low and there are bodies everywhere, moving and pulsing to the music. Crates full of drink line the walls and we grab a beer each. I also spot a bottle of vodka and manage to pinch the whole thing. I stalk away from Luke, realizing I don't need an escort—nobody cares who arrived with who. There's a carelessness here. Every person in this warehouse has lost something or is missing something from their lives. I can see it in the way they're desperate to forget.

I take a long gulp of the vodka and nearly vomit. It's without a doubt the most disgusting thing I've ever consumed. I don't drink much because drunk people tend to get emotional, and I can't afford to do that. I soon find that if I chase the vodka with the beer it's slightly more bearable. I want to talk to someone, someone who has no idea that I'm a freak.

Three people are standing close by, two guys and a girl. One of the boys is chatting with the girl and making her giggle, but the other guy is staring into the sea of dancing limbs. He looks carefree and quite handsome, with his blond hair and collared black shirt. I approach him and his eyes glance over me. They quickly take stock of me and then keep moving. My feet falter for a moment, but then I'm reminded of the barn and I don't really care about the fact that he won't look at me. I refuse to allow every person in this place to ignore me.

"Hi," I say when I reach his side. This time he manages to hold my eyes for a few seconds before looking away again.

"Hey," he says shortly.

"I'm Josi."

"Chris." He looks me up and down and sort of reconsiders his reluctance. I can see the thoughts crossing his mind as if they're neon-lit signs. He doesn't know why he didn't want to talk to me. I seem perfectly normal. And he probably doesn't get many girls going out of their way to talk to him. Chris swallows and tilts his body more in my direction.

"Having fun?" he asks.

"I only just got here, but yeah, I guess."

"You've certainly got your drink sorted out," he mutters, gesturing at my bottle.

"Do you want some?"

He takes the vodka and has a few gulps. I follow suit and then we look at each other awkwardly.

"So ... are you, like, on something?" he asks. "Your eyes ... They're kind of ... manic, or something."

My eyebrows arch. Is he serious? What was I thinking, coming over here to talk to a stupid child? I let a slow smile curl my lips; it is closer to a sneer. "I'm sorry. I thought you might be interesting. My mistake."

I walk away from him, even though he calls out for me to wait. What a fucking joke. I press into the dancers, but feeling their skin against mine makes me jerk in shock. This isn't the right way to be touched. I push through them, trying to head for the door, trying to find Luke.

At last I make it to the other side of the massive warehouse. A couple moves to the side and I am finally faced with Luke. He's standing beside a girl in a sparkly red dress with amazing breasts and curly blond hair. She's leaning close to him and he's telling her something that requires lazy hand gestures and a mildly interested smile. She laughs, tilting her head back and shaking her tits.

I want to sink into the floor and cease to exist. Instead of dying, couldn't I just stop *being*? That would be really nice.

But that's when Luke's eyes move in a cursory glance about the room. They reach where I'm standing and he stops. His eyes stop, his hands stop, even his mouth stops mid-word. Very slowly he starts to smile.

I hate him and I hate that damn smile. It hits me in the guts and heats my skin to flames.

Luke doesn't even look at the girl as he brushes past her. She says something and then looks devastated that she's been ignored. I barely notice this because my eyes are locked on Luke as he crosses the floor and leans close. "You look really lonely, girl."

I swallow. He's taking up every inch of the world. His presence is always larger than anything else. "This place is full of stupid little boys."

"I hate stupid little boys." He grins, teeth absurdly white. "Am I a stupid little boy?"

"I haven't decided what you are yet."

Luke moves his hand to my cheek and strokes his thumb to the corner of my mouth. "Well you let me know when you do."

I feel sort of breathless. I want to kiss him, but I won't, because I saw things in the barn today, and they make me want to die.

"Are you drunk yet?"

"Sort of."

"And has it made you feel better?" he asks gently.

"Not really."

"Why are we here, Josi?"

"I don't know."

Something loud explodes and shocks me so much that I jump. Luke's hands are already pressing me behind him. It takes my poor, throbbing ears a moment to understand that it was a gunshot. I can't figure out what's going on, but people are starting to scream. A girl shoves into me and nearly knocks me off my feet, but I manage to stay upright.

"Nobody move!" a voice screeches out over the crowd. Someone has stopped the music. I peer around Luke to see that there's a young man—the one who was flirting with the girl, Chris' friend. He's holding the gun high and there's a crazed look in his eyes. He smiles wolfishly, giving an odd trickle of laughter.

His arm is around the girl's neck, a bit like how he might hold her if he wanted to be affectionate. Her eyes have that eerie vacant look about them. She doesn't know what to feel—she looks like she barely knows what's going on.

"Let's play!" the boy announces. There are a few sniggers in the crowd. One man cheers. Someone wolf whistles. Someone is crying. A few girls keep screaming in a really weird, abrupt way. I hear a high voice softly singing a skipping rhyme.

"Come on! Who wants to play?" He fires the gun twice into the roof, causing another eruption of chaos. "Don't you want to see me shoot her?" And with this, the guy lowers the gun and points it into the temple of the girl.

"Stay here," Luke says. He squeezes my hand once, and then he moves toward the boy with the gun. I feel a moment of terror in my stomach. Luke slinks into the empty space around the shooter. I don't know what he's going to do, but the girl needs help too. Quickly I thread my way through the crowd, moving around toward the back of the couple. I keep my eyes on them and Luke.

The stupid boy fires the gun into the ground this time, but the girl still doesn't try to get away. Luke steps out in front of them. "I'll play," he says calmly.

The boy grins and aims his gun straight at Luke. He lets go of the girl and she stumbles sideways. I reach for her and pull her into the crowd. But Luke has the weapon aimed at his chest.

He's edging his way closer and closer to the boy. Sounds are coming from within the crowd—whoops of excitement and jeers of encouragement. They've all lost their damn minds. Well, I wanted dangerous, didn't I? Now I've got it. The static energy in the air is alive with unpredictability.

"I'll play," Luke says again, "but you have to come closer."

The boy giggles and moves closer, pressing the butt of the gun into Luke's sternum. Luke's hand darts forward and swats the gun to the side. As this happens, he steps forward, beside the sounding shot, and into the boy's chest. His fist connects three times with the boy's chin, and somehow he manages to grab the gun and slip it into the back of his pants.

I blink incredulously. The boy is unconscious on the ground and Luke looks perfectly relaxed. He turns to look for me, but by the time he's found me on the other side of the crowd, there's another eruption from the back of the room. A huge fight has broken out and people are fleeing. Police sirens approach from somewhere outside.

Luke grabs my hand and drags me out through the swarming mass. I can hear shouts and screams and even some more gunshots. People are getting crushed by the crowd—one boy goes down and I look away quickly, horror building in my throat at the thought of him getting trampled. Luke keeps his hand locked around mine and deftly makes a path for us to escape through.

I can hear it all throbbing behind us—the chaos of it doesn't fade until we've driven a long way away. I'm reeling from the whole thing, but Luke is still oddly calm. He's the same as those lunatics inside. His calm is a product of his brain damage. It has to be.

Luke

The idiot with the gun has actually done nothing to wreck my mood. I still feel restless, right down in my bones. Josi looks outrageously gorgeous, and I want too much.

Impulsively I turn the car off the road. I've seen a map of this area, and I know that Josephine spent some time in a house out along the river. It's a gamble, bringing her here, because she might loathe the idea of it, but I'm desperate to get her talking.

"Where are we?" she asks suddenly, sitting up to peer at the quickly passing trees. I'm driving too fast. I don't want to slow down. I rip the handbrake and we slide around a corner. "Luke! Slow down, for Christ's sake!"

I glance at her and smile. "It's under control."

"You'll kill us!"

"I thought that's what you wanted."

"I don't want *you* to die, you idiot!" she hisses.

My smile widens. "I can drive in my sleep. No one's dying today."

Eventually, after a fairly harebrained trip through the trees I pull us to a skidding halt. Josephine looks murderous as she flings herself out of the car and slams the door furiously. I climb out but leave the car headlights on to give us some illumination.

"What are we doing here?" she snaps.

I wink at her and walk over to the bank of the river. There's a long wooden boardwalk that protrudes out into the water.

It's shrouded with mangrove trees, their long, gnarled boughs creepy in the dark. The headlights are throwing strange light against them, making them sway and flicker like thin, knobbly fingers reaching out to trace the surface of the moon-lit river. My feet pound against the wood as I follow the planks all the way to the end.

I don't turn around to see if she's following. Sometimes with Josi it's like trying to tempt a small, stubborn child into playing. Or convincing a timid animal that it's safe to eat from my palm. I hear her feet reach the wood and edge hesitantly toward me.

"Do you know where we are?" she asks.

"Yes. Do you?"

"The house I lived in when I was eight is just up that hill. I used to lie on this boardwalk for hours and stare up at the leaves."

I can tell by her voice that she must have loved it here.

"Did you know that when you drove here?"

"Yes," I admit. "I saw it in your file. You were only here for six months."

She edges a little closer.

"Why did you get moved?" I ask carefully. I think I might be frightened of the answer.

Josephine doesn't say anything. Maybe she is frightened too.

JUNE 14TH, 2053

Josephine

I can see the river at the bottom of the hill, glistening silver in the midday sunlight, and I burst into a run. Before I make it something slashes through the edge of my vision and hits me in the face. I yelp and skid to a stop, raising my fingers to my cheek. It's only when I see the blood on them that it starts to hurt. My face stings like crazy and there are surprised tears in my eyes.

I look around and see that it was a rock that hit me. And it was thrown by Lachlan, my foster brother. He's twelve, and a lot bigger than me. He's fat. I hate his chubby fingers and his pink cheeks. I hate the way he chews with his mouth open, and I hate the way his nasty eyes always look for me, no matter where we are.

He smiles as he crosses the grass toward me. He must have been hiding behind a tree or something. I don't say anything, but I make myself stop crying immediately. I don't really understand why he likes to hurt me, but I do understand that I can't show him anything. None of the things I tell the trees. He can't have any of my secrets or my thoughts or my feelings.

"Where are you going, Josy-posy?"

I don't speak to him. I never speak to him. My words are mine too.

"Cat got your tongue?"

I try to move past him but he blocks the way and then grabs my hair. He pulls it so hard that I want to scream, but I don't.

"Say something, you stupid little bitch!" he snarls. I know he got this name for me from his father. Probably everyone else in the house, too. They all call me that name. I don't know why because I've never said anything mean about them. I've never spoken a single word to any of them.

Lachlan wrenches my hair, making me fall to the ground and skin my knees painfully. He sits on my back so I can't move, even though I struggle like a mad thing. He's too fat. I can't get free. I can feel him pulling up my t-shirt. The sound of his pocketknife being opened is an alarm, but even as I squirm I feel the first sharp bite of agony. It's along my hip, and it feels like he's carving into my bone.

"Rude girls deserve punishment," he says happily. His breath is close to my ear and it stinks like the licorice he's just been eating. Then he says, in a funny voice, "You know I love you, Josy-posy. You're my little sis. You belong to me, and it's my job to protect you. All of my things need to be labeled, right? So no one else tries to use them?"

I don't understand what he's saying until he starts to cut me some more, deep slices of my flesh. I don't cry. I bite down on a clump of grass so I won't scream.

"Nearly there," he tells me. "I'm just finishing up the N."

A surge of rage floods my body. I can't feel the small knife anymore. I can't feel anything except a red tremble under my skin. A scream erupts from my mouth and I thrash so wildly that Lachlan is thrown off my back. He sprawls on the ground and before he can get up I lunge at him, grabbing him by the neck and squeezing until his face goes purple.

Next thing I know I'm being hauled off Lachlan by the ear, and it hurts a lot, but not as much as my hip. I try to blink the spots away from my eyes.

"You little psycho!" a woman screams. The woman I'm supposed to call Mom. Is she talking to me? Yes, she is. Of course she is. More feet arrive. "I just found the little brat trying to choke our son!"

"What?" It's the man now. He clubs me over the head, making my vision cloud badly. I close my eyes and enjoy the darkness. I can still hear them shouting and blaming me. Lachlan is crying. Some of his words drift to me, and he seems to be sobbing over how frightened he is. I keep my eyes closed and my mouth shut. I could try to show them my hip with its bloody brand, but I'm too tired and I don't think they'll care anyway.

Maybe this means I'll get a new house.

But that means I have to say goodbye to the river and the trees, and that will be sad, because they're the only ones who've heard my voice.

DECEMBER 21ST, 2063

Josephine

"Luke?"

"Mmm?" He's looking at the water, standing under the trees I loved once upon a time.

"Maybe I'm crazy."

He looks up. "Why do you say that?"

"Maybe that's why I murder people."

Today there was a barn, and inside it there was a pitchfork. And that's how I know that children once lived in that farmhouse.

Isn't there a thing about kids who are treated badly turning into violent offenders themselves? Could that explain any of this?

"Maybe I'm a Fury. Or becoming one." The thought of turning into one of those savages ... It makes me long for death. "Before I moved here I was mute," I tell him softly, the first glimpse I have ever given him of my childhood. "I never spoke a word to anyone. When I came here, I don't know why, but I started speaking to these trees. They know all of my secrets, these branches, these leaves."

He looks up at them and murmurs, "Lucky things."

I shake my head. "I'm crazy. I *must* be."

Luke walks up to me and pushes me straight into the river. The cold of it is sharp and sudden and hits me in the chest. I am momentarily silent and weightless. Breathless. My body doesn't hurt, and my heart beats a steady rhythm. I want to stay below the surface of the world forever. I could drift away on a current and never have to see a single drop of blood again.

After a while my lungs start to really hurt so I launch myself up to the air again.

"Feel better?" Luke asks from the boardwalk.

"You deserve a smack."

"Do you feel better or not?"

I am loath to tell him that I actually do. He must read the truth in my face because the bastard smirks.

"Come on," he laughs, reaching a hand to help me out.

Honestly? How can he not see this coming?

I grab his hand and pull him in. Luke surfaces immediately, coughing and laughing. He splashes me once in the face and then we both swim for the muddy bank. Luke launches himself up onto the grass with an amazingly acrobatic display of upper body strength. I, on the other hand, scramble out looking like a clumsy oaf and get myself covered in mud. He takes one look at me and then laughs again, showing all of his white teeth.

"Instead of laughing you could *help* me," I point out. "You've been really chivalrous tonight—what with scaring me half to death in the car and shoving me into a river."

Luke walks back onto the boards. He wanders under the mangroves and then turns back to face me. In his eyes the twin bulbs of light from the car are reflected. "I just wanted to snap you out of it."

I step out after him. "You can't. Not permanently."

"Then I'll do it again and again, as many times as I have to," Luke says softly. "Forever."

And he walks toward me again, but this time he doesn't push me into the river. This time he touches my cheeks and presses his lips against mine. It shocks me so much that I forget to pull away. I stand there and I think maybe I've ceased to exist except as a pair of lips.

Heart jerking unsteadily, I remember myself and wrench away from him. I run, but he grabs me and holds me, pulling me back into his body. When his mouth finds mine this time I struggle roughly, and I can taste my tears in my mouth and his and somehow my hands are straying to his chest, to the warmth there and the heartbeat.

I can't move or breathe but I can taste and feel and I want him so much that even with him this close it's still not close enough I can't get close enough. "Luke," I try to say, but it comes out as more of a sob because he doesn't understand all the broken pieces and the things I've done. I've told him but he doesn't understand that I'm drowning in an ocean of guilt and regret. I'm haunted and sick and rotten to the core and he's good and bright, the brightest thing in the world.

His kiss is savage like a thunderstorm, like he's desperate and sure.

"I know," he rasps against my mouth. "I know how it hurts. But it's supposed to."

And I realize at last that he does understand, maybe even better than I do.

Chapter Eight

MAY 1ST, 2063

Luke

The secretary—I can't remember her name—smiles in a way that makes me think I must have flirted with her before. Maybe I hooked up with her. I don't know and I don't care. I ignore her and head straight into the office.

Jean is on the phone when I enter, so I gaze out the windows while I wait. We're on the eighty-eighth floor and the ground is so far away I can barely see it. Every person down there is cracked in the head. I'm surrounded by a sea of dimwits. They disgust me.

This whole fucking world disgusts me.

"Luke," Jean says.

I turn and sit before her desk.

"I trust you're feeling better?"

"Chipper," I mutter.

"Your vacation didn't relieve you of your delightful attitude, I see."

I can't be bothered to respond. If I have an attitude it's because she's given me one. The world has given me one.

Jean leans back in her seat and eyes me. If I didn't know better, I'd think she's cured—she's certainly robotic enough. I'm supposed to be like that, but I can never seem to swallow the fury. "What's my next operation?" I ask impatiently.

"You may be a Gray, Luke, but I could easily have you demoted if you don't watch your tone with me."

I fold my arms—it's the only gesture I can muster the energy for. Hopefully she'll think it means I'm taking her seriously. The truth is she would never demote me—she can't afford to, and we both know it.

"Your mission," she tells me. Pressing a few things on her tablet, she projects an image onto the screen between us.

It's a girl. Dark hair, pale skin, possible European heritage. Between fifteen and seventeen. I can't judge her height because she's sitting on a train, gaze cast to the sky outside her window. She has a hat pulled down over her forehead so I can't see her eyes very well. She's skinny and tired.

"The girl?" I question, eyes narrowing.

"Josephine Luquet."

"Is she a threat?" This girl doesn't look like a potential terrorist, but I've come to understand that nobody looks like what they are anymore. I take a closer look, but can't find anything interesting about her. The picture's too static—I'll need to get a look at her in real life before I can make a proper evaluation.

"You are not required to make any judgments on her—all you are to do is set up a full surveillance program and report."

I stare at Jean. She has long athletic limbs, dark chocolate skin and blue contact lenses. She's startling in appearance, unflappable in manner, and when I was fifteen she was the most terrifying person in the world. I feel so far from that boy that I don't even know who he is anymore. I haven't been frightened in years. Quite frankly, I'd love to be frightened. At least it would be something other than angry.

"You've got to be shitting me," I say softly. "A watch op? I'm a *Gray*."

"When you go on vacation, you get left the crap jobs," she says.

"I wasn't on vacation—it was medical leave, because I got shot in the shoulder doing a job for *you*," I remind her. I can feel my temper rising like a dangerous beast.

"This is your next job. Josephine is eighteen, a foster child. Passed around between many different temporary homes because she was diagnosed with clinical aggression at a young age."

"Parents?"

"Nobody knows. She was found on the side of the road when she was two. She ran away from her last foster family when she was fifteen, and she's been living on her own since. I've sent her file to your home office."

"I'm not there anymore."

She seems to understand what this means straight away. "You'll be needing new accommodation then?"

"Looks that way. How long am I supposed to watch the kid?"

"That depends entirely on the information you find on her."

I crack the knuckles in my hands. Slowly I stand up, trying to keep control of myself. "I'm not babysitting some crazy little bitch for the rest of my life so that you can feel like you've locked me in a safe box."

Jean sits forward, holding my eyes like she does when she's trying to intimidate. It works on most people. "Agent Townsend, listen to me very closely. Yes, you are the highest-ranking field agent in the country, but you still work for me, and for the nation. You will do the tasks you are required to, or you will be stripped and cured. Is that clear?"

My jaw clenches.

"I should have ordered it years ago," she adds. "You're arrogant and reckless and ruled entirely by your emotions. By rights you shouldn't make a good agent."

"And yet I do. Funny."

"You do when you behave as you should. The rest of the time is a disaster."

"I have a higher success rate than any other Blood in the world. What more do you want from me? Do you want me to be a lobotomized freak like the rest of society? Because at this point I don't really care anymore, Jean. Go ahead and strip me if you want."

What's the point in surviving if you're completely alone?

I think of all the people in all the zombie movies I've seen. Instead of running around like headless chickens, always trying to escape the inevitable, why don't they just give in and join the zombies? It would be a lot easier. And nobody would want to eat them anymore.

Jean loses patience. "Get the job done. You're dismissed."

I feel like throwing the chair through the window. This is bullshit. As I walk from the office, moving through all the security scans and swabs and X-rays, I consider when my life became so empty. All I can do at the moment is run and fight, and force myself into impossible situations, because if I spend one single moment sitting still I'll go bat-shit.

Dave would take one look at me right now, make some dumb joke and my foul mood would evaporate. But Dave won't be making another dumb joke, and I have the people I work for to blame for that. I'm part of a system I was too cowardly to deny. If only I could have realized it sooner, I might have been able to change something.

*

I'm onto my thirty-fourth cigarette by the time the girl finally gets home. It's close to midnight—she must do bar work or something. Tomorrow I'll have to find out, but for now I need to know the hours that she comes and goes from her apartment. I'm beyond pissed off. Me sitting here in the cold and the dark is entirely the kid's fault.

After my meeting with Jean I went straight to Josephine's address, scoped out the place, figured out where I'd be stationed, set up my equipment and settled in to wait for her. I haven't been to this part of town for years, which is funny, because Dave and I grew up three blocks from here. Maybe it's not so funny, since I spent most of my childhood hating it. I got so wrapped up in hating our poverty that I didn't see how lucky we were to have the rarest of all things: a loving family. Now I have wealth and no family at all. It's not difficult to work out what the lesson is here, kids.

I'm sitting on the roof opposite Josephine's building with my feet propped up on the stone balustrade when my eyes finally spot something on the path below. The street is well lit, so I catch sight of her while she's still a fair distance away. I grab my binoculars and lean over the edge to scope her out.

My first thought is that the hologram I was shown must have been taken several years ago, because she looks noticeably older in reality. Older than eighteen, that's for sure. She's wearing a shabby black jacket, a skirt and ripped stockings, with worn black boots. She looks every inch the homeless kid I was expecting her to be. She's tall and willowy, with long legs and long dark hair.

But when my binoculars find her face, my hands tighten and the air stops moving into my lungs. My first and only thought is simply: *here she is.*

JUNE 1ST, 2063

Luke

My hands hover over the keyboard, unsure. The report of my first month's surveillance is due in ten minutes. I haven't written a word, despite having spent the last thirty days almost sleepless with watching Josephine Luquet in every facet of her life. I'm addicted to her—there's no other way to put it. I'm addicted to the way she reads avidly with this intense expression on her face, and the way she stretches her muscles with a distraction that speaks to how far away her mind must be. I'm addicted to the way she speaks to random drones, with sarcasm and wit, and most of all the way she plays her cello, as if the instrument was invented for her and her alone.

Eventually I crack my knuckles and type.

Subject is, on the whole, emotionally stable. She shows signs, however, of an antisocial disconnect from society and for this reason I strongly advise maintaining surveillance. Resistance sympathies have yet to be ascertained. Nothing else of note to report.

*

My order arrives four hours and twelve minutes later, flashing on my screen. I have to swallow three times before I'm ready to click it open.

Continue surveillance. Remain invisible.

Relief washes through me, but I still have no idea why I'm watching this girl.

SEPTEMBER 17TH, 2063

Luke

There's bass pounding through the bottom of my seat and someone yammering in my ear. The lights are dim and flashing and I feel so tightly strung that I'm convinced I'm about to have a stroke.

The guy who won't shut up has been drowned out by the revoltingly pungent scent of the woman who's just sidled up next to me. I glance at her. Everything about her makes me feel tired. Her platform heels. Her five layers of make-up. The black roots poking through her white blonde hair. Her expression of arrogant, distorted lust. I turn away from her pointedly. She won't be mad. She can't be. It occurred to me a few years ago that the cure did us guys a favor—it made it impossible for us to incur the wrath of a woman scorned, no matter how badly we treat them.

Everything is detached and discolored. I feel dizzy with disconnect.

Except when I look over at where she's sitting, the girl, *my* girl. I followed her into this club fifteen minutes ago. Since then she's been sitting on that couch, by herself, ignored by everyone. Nobody speaks to her, nobody looks at her. None of them will ever realize what they have sitting quietly in their midst.

Last night I saw some horrific things. Life-changing things. Things I've grown used to seeing in my job, but not things I've ever seen a teenage girl do. So much about Josephine Luquet has become achingly clear. I now understand why I'm doing this job, why I was sent to watch her four and a half months ago.

I spent all of today erasing the crime scenes.

Everything I do is done with a measure of precision so exact that it got me recruited for the Bloods when I was still a child. Even at fifteen I knew what I was capable of and so did Jean. I can make it so that no one will ever know what Josephine Luquet has done. Today my attention to detail was more extreme than it's ever been. I don't know why she did the things she did, nor do I understand how she was capable of such actions, but I do know that her life depends on the other Bloods never finding out about it.

When I look at her now I can feel her change color in my head. Until yesterday she'd been blue with innocence and youth. Not naïve or ignorant—I know how sharp she is, how aware. She was never cruel until last night. Never violent. Never frightening.

Now she's green and navy and gold with all the things I don't understand about her. She's red with the things that make me excited.

And she's the clean, stark white of loneliness, above all else.

As the sun rose I watched her wake, naked and scared and clearly unsure of what had happened, and then I watched her make her way home, covering her modesty with surprising ingenuity—suggesting that this was not the first time she'd been through this—and I wasn't allowed to help her at all. I had to watch her struggle alone. And in doing so something changed in me—I knew this morning that I would never regard strength or courage the same way again.

She's in pain—the way she moves, it's like she's been hit by a train. Every inch of her aches. Even sitting here in the club, she's immersed in discomfort. I don't know why she's come here, to a place in which she'll be even more isolated. But I know that I can't watch her like this any longer. I can't watch her sit by herself after a night like last night. I don't understand why she did the things she did, but I can't be this far from her for a single moment longer.

Rule number one: don't ever come into contact with a subject.

Rule number two: don't ever come into contact with a subject.

Rule number three: if you're ever exquisitely stupid enough to come into contact with a subject, abort the mission immediately.

Things are simple in the land of the Bloods.

I finish my beer and come into contact with my subject. I have to: I am already in love with her.

Chapter Nine

SEPTEMBER 13TH, 2065

Anthony

It's dark outside. Well and truly. I feel like my feet are glued to the carpet. There's glue through my whole body, keeping me perfectly still in a prison of my own horror.

Josephine is sitting in the middle of the room today, instead of her usual spot at the window. She's facing away from me, and I can only see her silhouette because neither of us has thought to switch on the light. There's a moon outside the window, and it's tinted with a red hue, as it will be for the whole month.

She's been talking for hours and hours, and her voice has taken on a tired, rough quality, like gravel under a shoe or the scrape of shards of glass. She describes her first weeks with Luke as I imagine she must remember them—with picture-perfect detail. Her words have a musical quality to them and there's longing in her voice.

I knew she loved him, but I didn't *know*. Not until today.

I want to keep listening, but she's too tired and the lumbering hulk of a guard has poked his head in every fifteen minutes, wanting to know what's keeping her.

"Thank you," I say, even though there's a part of me that hates her for having done this to me. I can't stand the fact that she's become a real person—more than a real person. An *uncured* person. And there's a deep, dark tendril of dread that's starting to appear in my head, warning me that maybe an uncured person is a better kind of person.

"Will you call him now?"

"There's still more of the story, isn't there?"

"Yes."

"Then I'll call him tomorrow, if we finish." I don't give her a chance to argue, I just leave my office as quickly as I can. Halfway to my car I realize I've left my briefcase, but it hardly matters, does it? It's empty. Everything I carry around is empty.

*

When I get home something feels wrong. There's no sign that the security coding has malfunctioned, and yet my apartment smells different. It smells foreign. Like … a man.

I hate body odor just as much as I hate mess or uncleanliness. I shower three times a day, and I use a great deal of product to make sure that nothing on my body or in my home smells like anything except soap or disinfectant.

But here in my space there is an undeniably male scent. Like sweat and deodorant that is not mine. I stop and peer around, my skin crawling.

Then I spot it. There, leaning against the wall beside the fridge, is a large black instrument case. My heart starts to pound and somehow I know what it is. It couldn't possibly be anything else, and yet this can't possibly be happening either.

There can't be a cello sitting in my apartment, where nobody can enter except those with my retinas and fingerprints.

Slowly I force myself to walk over and unzip the case. It's a cello.

I feel frightened and excited at the same time. I don't know what to do with it, except that I do.

*

In the morning I get up and go through my daily routine. I make my bed. I clean myself thoroughly, scrubbing every inch of my skin with an exfoliating brush. I wash my hair and brush my teeth. I eat my breakfast and then brush my teeth again. I wipe down the sinks and the surfaces and make sure everything is in its spot. Everything in my house smells normal again, because I've made sure of it. I drive to work at the correct speed limit and I walk into my office at the same exact time of day that I have done for the last six years.

I do everything exactly the same as I always do it, except that nothing makes sense this morning because I'm carrying a cello in my arms.

When she enters my room at the usual time she sees the instrument immediately. I've placed it on the couch where she sits. She stops in her tracks, stares at it, stares at me. And then Josephine bursts into tears, and I wish with a kind of agony that I'd been the one who'd thought to give it to her.

DECEMBER 25TH, 2063

Josephine

"Why can't we go to your parents' house for lunch?" I whine for the one-thousandth time.

Luke ignores me, as he has been doing for most of this morning, because the feast he is preparing is more difficult than a banquet fit for the king of England.

I pout. "I've never had Christmas with a real family. I want to sit around a big dining table and tell stories and laugh with people who make jokes at each other's expense."

"I can make jokes at your expense if you'd like, babe," he mutters distractedly while lighting something on fire. He nearly gets his eyebrows singed off but grins in delight when he sees the result of his explosion.

I can't help but smile as I watch him, even though I'm rather annoyed at having to eat here by ourselves when he has a perfectly good family waiting not far away. It makes no sense to me—he's *wasting* them! Granted, I haven't actually heard much about this family, but I assume they're perfect. They made Luke, didn't they?

There's a bowl of dough sitting beside me on the bench. He's been kneading it carefully for the last twenty minutes and then letting it rest. I've got no idea what it's for, but I'm blessed with a wicked idea. Picking a substantial piece off the edge of the ball, I roll it around in my fingers until it's a nice shape. Then I peg it at Luke's head.

He spins around and looks at me, mystified. "Did you just throw food at me?"

"Yes."

"Why?"

"Because you're annoying me."

Luke blinks. "You brat," he laughs, and then tackles me, lifting me off the bench and onto the floor. In moments he's tickling me mercilessly and I'm trying not to laugh but I can't help it. I'm squirming and close to kneeing him in the groin, but he manages to make me stop with a kiss. Pretty soon we're rolling around on the kitchen floor, and I'm about to lose my mind because since I moved back in two days ago we've still been sleeping in separate bedrooms. Apparently I'm too young for him. He won't sleep with me until after my birthday, which just seems like an arbitrary day to me, but makes him feel more comfortable, I guess.

However at this particular moment he happens to be touching me. A lot. I can feel the press of his body against mine and it burns from the inside out. Maybe he's given up on his own rule.

I reach for his shirt but he sits up. "Don't," he warns.

I roll my eyes.

"And don't roll your eyes at me. It makes me crazy."

I roll my eyes again. He rolls his eyes at me rolling my eyes. We both burst into laughter. Something starts to burn and Luke lurches to his feet. "Shit! Not the salmon!"

He doesn't really have salmon, does he? Salmon is one of the most expensive foods in the world. I try not to think about it. Instead I pick myself up and wander into the living room. I don't like television because it makes my eyes sore, so we don't watch his enormous TV much. He does have an amazing collection of books though, hidden behind a sliding door where I didn't spot them when I first moved in. I peruse them while I wait for him to finish cooking.

My life has become a constant war between my head and my heart. The last couple of days have filled me with so much anxiety and so much happiness that I'm practically nauseous with both. I know what I should do—get as far away from Luke as possible. I don't deserve him, and I certainly don't want to hurt him. Nor do I want him to have to deal with my death. But, selfish though it may be, I can't leave him. He has found a way to turn the dark thoughts in my head into threads of shimmering gold, pretty and light and ready to float away.

Our lunch is truly incredible. Flavours I've never tasted burst in my mouth and I get so overwhelmed that I have to pause and take a break. I can't eat much at a time because my stomach has never consumed much, so we sit for hours, picking and grazing and talking and laughing. We tell each other stories and we argue and we joke at each other's expense. It is too close to perfect to be believable. This apartment was empty when I first moved in, but we have filled it with words, thousands and thousands of words, so that now the walls heave with the effort of containing them all.

As the sun starts to sink I have a moment of clarity. I don't need Luke's family because *he* is my family.

"I'm going to give you my present now," he tells me once we're stuffed full and ready to burst. "You can give me yours later."

I freeze. All the food feels like it's about to come back up. "Luke—you've already done so much … This meal, and letting me live here, and …"

"It's just a small present," he says. "It's not as good as the one you're giving me."

Shit. The truth is I haven't bought Luke anything. I haven't worked much this week, so I haven't had any money, and to be honest I've never actually had a Christmas with presents before.

Luke smiles slowly like he can read exactly what I'm thinking. "I'll go first and then you can go."

"Okay," I reply feebly.

He places a small wrapped package on the table. I'm dismayed to find that my fingers tremble as I unwrap it. This is too much. I don't want gifts from him—he's given me *so* much. I don't have any money to pay him back for all that he's done, and I can't accept anything more from him.

I get the wrapping open and stare at the little cardboard box. It's a travel-sized container of primer.

I meet his eyes and burst into laughter. I double over and hold my stomach while I laugh. Luke pulls his chair so that it's next to mine, putting his hands in my hair and brushing his lips against my ear, jaw, cheek. I can feel the smile in his body and he's laughing as he kisses me. "Since neither of us knew what it was, I figured we should find out."

"I—" The words are almost out before I can stop them. My laughter is cut off and I'm frozen in horror. That was way too close—without thinking I nearly said *I love you*. And that would be unbearable.

It is unbearable that I even feel it in the first place, and the shock of realizing it makes me feel abruptly cut loose; spinning out into orbit with nothing to tether me.

But Luke's smile doesn't change, none-the-wiser, and as I look at that smile, really look at it, I realize that if I can find the courage to let him, he will be my tether.

*

When we've loaded everything into the dishwasher and it's rumbling softly, Luke motions for me to stay where I am. He's on the other side of the kitchen and we look at each other.

"You can give me your present in a minute, but first I need to tell you something."

His voice makes me worried. He sounds too serious.

"We couldn't go to my parents' house today because I didn't want to. I can't be around them at this time of year, or any time of year, really. Seven years ago on Christmas day my older brother Dave killed himself."

My heart lurches to a shuddering stop. Luke's face is within a shadow. I can't see his expression very well. But I can hear it.

"He hated the cure. He was a protester. One of the last. Made it through the riots without getting killed or caught, but then they got his girlfriend—she was a protester too. Livvy had a bad reaction to the drug they inject. She had to be institutionalized. There was nothing left of her personality. Severe psychosis. Dave lost it. He was so angry—impossibly angry. I think his anger became the heart of his personality, of how he saw himself. So when they finally took it away from him he lost all sense of who he was. The only way he could see out of the nightmare was to die."

"Oh, god," I whisper. "Luke." I don't know what to do, how to help him. I want to take this away for him, but I know better than anyone that grief like this can't be erased. He has a right to it, a right to mourn his brother. The true horror of what I've told him hits me. My own suicide pact now seems unbearably cruel, and I'd give anything to take back the night I admitted to it.

"Can I have your present now?" he asks, and he sounds like a frightened little boy.

There's a lump in my throat and I just want to sink into the floor. Before I can explain that I'm a callous girl who forgot to get him one, he walks from the kitchen. Worriedly I follow him into the spare room—my room. He crosses to the window and picks up my cello case.

"You left this here when you moved out," he says. I know I did—I was a hollow shell without it. Luke opens the case and pokes his hands in. It isn't until he pulls out the two sheets of old, tattered paper that I realize. "I found these," he admits, and god he looks so sad it's breaking my heart.

The pages are covered in sheet music I've written, at the top of which is the title 'Luke's Song'.

"Could you play this for me now?" he asks, voice breaking.

I nod and dash tears from my cheeks. I cross the room and kiss him on the lips, as gently as I can manage. I feel him trembling against me. "Of course." I take the cello but not the pages—these I know by heart—and then I play for him in the spill of moonlight from the window. I play for Luke, and I play for Dave and Livvy, and for every single person who has been robbed by the world and its madness. I play the love song I wrote Luke before I even knew I loved him.

And as I play I realize I can only do so because I am alive. I can only love him because I have the privilege.

I am alive, and I must fight this blood moon and the monster inside me, if only to save the man I love from having to grieve for me.

Chapter Ten

JANUARY 14TH, 2064

Josephine

He wants to wait for my birthday but I'm tired of waiting. I have been waiting since the day I was born for my life to begin. My real life. Not this pretend life.

I feel like a half person. Someone sketched in outline but not yet filled in.

How am I supposed to be more? I imagine him touching me and making love to me, and I imagine that under his touches I'll be more, whole, a real and finished person. It's the only way I can think of to stop this endless, unceasing ache beneath my skin.

I knock on his door quietly.

"Josi?"

Pushing in, I see his outline in the moonlight from the window. He's on one side of his enormous bed, blinking quickly.

"You okay?"

I can't speak. I move towards him. When I reach the bed I take off my dressing-gown and show him my naked body. He goes still, the expression on his face different. It gives me a quick thrill, and I think: this is normal. This is how people are supposed to be. I'm supposed to desire my boyfriend and make love to him. And I'm supposed to like it when his eyes fill with lust like that.

I'm not supposed to be frightened or ashamed.

Angry with myself, I sink down onto the edge of the bed.

"What's going on?" Luke asks me.

But I don't know how to answer, and I think he can see that. I lean down and kiss him. But I can't feel it. I feel nothing.

And I feel nothing when his hand moves to my stomach, brushing softly against my skin.

I feel nothing I feel nothing I feel nothing—

Another hand is on my skin, but this one is delicate and covered in blood. I peer down to realize that it's my own hand in the dark. Another version of my hand. And when I look up, I see my own face staring back at me, but my eyes are red, the blood vessels burst, and I look ancient and cold, like something has stolen my soul.

This part of me, this woman—she turns and starts to tear at Luke, devouring him, and there's so much blood that it becomes like an ocean—

"*Josi!*"

His voice slices into my head and when I blink I see that we are alone, and there's no monster in the room with us, and no blood, but a sound is reverberating around the walls and I slowly realize that it's me, it's my scream, not highpitched but low and throaty and tearing. It goes on and on and I can't stop and then Luke is grabbing me in his arms and using all of his strength to squeeze and squeeze until I can barely breathe and the screaming finally stops and we're silent and he's holding me so tight that it's done the impossible and managed to put me back together and keep me that way and then everything fades and stops and drifts away.

And now I know. In this silence. A touch won't be enough to make me more. Not even Luke's touch. It will have to be me. If I don't want to spend my life as a half person, unfinished, then I must find a way to shed my past from my skin and be more than it.

Luke

Tonight I spend my first night in bed with Josephine. I don't sleep. I'm too frightened of the nightmares filling her up to even close my eyes. Instead I watch the rise and fall of her chest as she breathes, and the flickering of her eyelids, the clenching of her jaw as she grinds her teeth and the curling of her fingers and toes.

I watch these things and I don't know how I am going to do this. How I'm going to be enough for this, equal to the magnitude of the damage done to her. I haven't lived enough life, experienced enough truth. I feel like a child in bed beside her, and for the first time in many years I want to call my mother and ask her what to do.

MARCH 3RD, 2064

Josephine

I wake on my nineteenth birthday to a sick feeling in my stomach. Dressing quickly, I pull on my boots and head for the front door. Luke is in the kitchen as I breeze past.

"Happy birthday!" he announces, but I don't look at him. "Josi?"

I head for the subway and jump on a train. It's not the same station or line, but I think of them of course. The four uncured fighters.

The train takes me all the way to the edge of the city, to where I can see the mighty, looming wall. Beyond that wall is a wasteland. Diseased and dead. Within it we're kept like rats in a lab.

At the end of a street is a steel factory. As I walk towards it, I run my fingers over the knife in my pocket.

Inside I ask for a man by name, telling the receptionist that his sister is here. I say there's been an emergency and I'll need to speak with him privately, so she shows me to a small office where I can wait for him.

I feel overwhelmingly nauseous, and keep a very good grip on my knife.

It takes about ten minutes for Lachlan to arrive. My foster brother. He is still fat, but a lot of his girth seems to be muscle now, too. He's handsome, sort of. A big, robust man of twenty-two.

He is confused, looking at me curiously as he shuts the door, shutting us in this small room together.

"Hi. They told me you asked for me...?"

I search his face and find nothing that connects him to the boy who tormented me. He just looks like a normal guy.

Our eyes meet and I see recognition cross his gaze. It's the dual color of my eyes that's causing him to recall something so long past. Six months with a mute girl over ten years ago.

"I do know you, don't I?" he asks. "You were one of the kids we took in. What's your name again?"

There is no embarrassment in his expression. No shame, no discomfort, no anger or regret. I don't think he remembers any of the things I remember. He is simply curious.

All of a sudden it is bizarre to me that I have come here. Of all the families I lived with, of all the people who harmed me,

Lachlan is not even close to the worst. Perhaps it's the brand he left on my body that makes him feel more permanent, more present in my life now. Perhaps it's *because* he wasn't the worst that I can come here and face him, as I certainly can't face any of the others.

His name will be on my body until the day I die, but he doesn't even remember what mine is. My fingers let go of the knife and I stand, eclipsed by a sudden understanding of the world and its absurdities.

We face each other, and for the first time in my life I feel wildly powerful. I smile, and then I walk past him without a word. I didn't give him a word when I was eight, and I don't need to give him one now.

I don't need any of this; I have moved so far beyond it that I know, suddenly, how very little it truly means. None of this ugliness will ever take anything from me again. And the realisation has made so much clear to me.

My thoughts are, overwhelmingly, of Luke Townsend, and the things that do have meaning.

On the train it starts to rain. I watch the droplets splatter against the glass window. It's late by the time I finally get home. Heavy clouds cover the moon and stars, blacking out the sky, shrouding the whole world in darkness. The apartment is empty, not a single light lit. My heart hammers—Luke must be out.

I have to find him. There's something I need to tell him. Right now. I turn for the door again before remembering my phone. Hurrying to my room, I leave a trail of wet puddles on the marble floor. I have no missed calls, so I find Luke and dial his number.

A soft ringing sound comes from the next bedroom, his. But after following it, I find his phone alone. I swallow, a sense of urgency rising painfully inside me. He had plans for the whole day. He wanted it to be so special, wanted to give me the first birthday I could enjoy and remember forever. But I left without a word of explanation, and I missed the whole day.

I'm breathing very fast as I run for the door. But as I pass the living room I catch a glimpse of something and skid to a halt.

There he is. Standing outside on the balcony, in the pouring rain.

I stop for a long moment, watching him, thinking and feeling a million things at once. Finally I take a deep breath and walk outside. The rain immediately seeps into me, drenching me.

Luke hears me and turns. In the dark his eyes search and find mine. Water runs over the hard lines of his face, the heavy brow, high cheekbones, sharp jaw. I watch droplets slide over his nose and onto his lips, set in a hard line.

The lights of the buildings around us are reflected in his eyes.

"Are you all right?" he asks, his voice deep and rough as if he hasn't used it all day.

I feel overwhelmed by the answer, managing only to nod. I can feel everything building inside me, a shiver across every nerve ending. A sudden, miraculous certainty. I have never felt so sure, or so whole.

"I'm so sorry," I utter. "I had to do something. But now I know."

He tilts his head. Frowns. I must have put him through a lot today. "What do you know?"

"That I'm ready. Really ready. For everything. For you. For us. To trust…" I'm not explaining myself properly because it's all a rush now, a rush to come out and to make him understand. Does he know that it's momentous for me, simply to trust someone? He is my first, my only.

My hands are trembling as I hold his eyes. "I love you, Luke. Desperately."

His eyes sharpen and I see the shock freeze him still. A slice of lightning lights him up, cutting over his green gaze, and I realise that the droplets on his cheeks are not only rain, but tears too.

"Don't," he whispers. "Don't do that."

I reach for him, but he takes my wrists to stop me.

"Why?"

"I don't ... I don't deserve it, Josi."

I shake my head, an ache inside me, all the way through me, a lightning storm of love. "No," I say, and then again, so firmly there is no arguing. "No." Pulling out of his grip, I place my hands on his cheeks and run my thumbs over his lips. "You've saved my whole life," I tell him fiercely. "You've remade me, because you're the only good thing in this whole world. You're a bright thing, the only bright thing I've ever seen, and even though they've tried to dull you, I can see all that courage and generosity, and *kindness* in everything you do." He is listening to me now; I can see everything behind his eyes. I say it again, so he'll really hear it. "I love you."

And then I kiss him, my lips brushing the water from his skin, his cheeks, eyelids, and lips.

As my mouth finds his, I feel him respond at last, like the tide has crashed through a brick wall, one as mighty as the wall around this city. His hands grip me, my back, my hips, pulling me against him. Our mouths open, tasting each other, and my heart is hammering in my chest, because for the first time I'm not frightened of these touches—I am hungry.

I reach for his T-shirt and lift it over his head. My lips find his chest, the startling heat there. His hands, when they unbutton my shirt, are trembling. His breath is against my ear, my cheek, my mouth and I can feel something prickly and stirring inside me, spreading flame throughout my body.

Wildly my heart flutters, a heart of raven's wings.

Luke's mouth burns a path over my jaw, down my neck and along my collarbone. Then it ducks again, to circle my breast. I feel his tongue dart out to trace my nipple, and I'm unprepared for the sound that leaves me. Something erupts in me, something I was completely unaware existed in the world.

Who could imagine that a body could give pleasure as well as pain?

I feel the same sense of urgency in him, in his hands, his mouth; I can feel him trying to hold it back, trying not to scare me, but I want it, I'm desperate for it, for the passion I can feel beneath his surface.

He's coming alive in my hands, and for the first time since we met I forget that he's a drone. I allow myself to forget.

His mouth drops again, down over my stomach and then lower, and I feel a moment of terrified exhilaration before I feel his tongue slip inside me and I gasp aloud as sensation bursts to life within. It overwhelms me, too much, too intense, I can barely stand it and I think I'm breaking or dying or falling.

My hands thread through his hair as I pull him away.

Luke looks up at me and I can see a wildness in his eyes, too. "Let go," he breathes. "Just let go."

"Not without you."

I push him to the ground, sliding over him until I can acutely feel the precise places we are touching. It makes it hard to breathe; he makes it hard to breathe. Everywhere we touch is like its own brand on my skin and when he gives in to the tidal wave that has picked us up and swept us away with it I feel him move inside me and begin to make love to me, and it's a trembling, taut revelation of all the things I thought must be make-believe. He finds my eyes, keeping me with him the whole time, and he still has those lights in his gaze, golden orbs that pull me inside him so I can live within his bones and muscles and veins.

I can feel it all building inside me, burning and aching, and when he starts to move more quickly inside me, against me, I know I can't hold on any longer. Amidst the storm, rain against our skin, lightning in our eyes and a thousand lives in the buildings around us, Luke and I burst and shatter and let go together.

As all the pieces of me fall from the sky to clink softly against the ground like the tiniest shards of crystal, I feel my mind disappear. It drifts up and away, out of my body with all its raw nerve endings.

I spend a moment wishing I could stay this way forever. Weightless and empty and full.

But it's his deep voice that brings me back. "Josi?"

"I'm here," I whisper, looking into his eyes. "I'm here."

The truth is simple. Loving someone, and caring about them more than you care about yourself, is the only thing strong enough to set a soul free from its prison.

Luke

I carry her inside to my bed. I feel buoyed up to impossible heights and grounded deep in the warm earth at the same time. I feel happier and more devastated than I have in my whole life.

Placing her on top of the sheet, I gaze down at her naked body, drinking it in, unable to believe that I'm allowed to do this now, that I am exquisitely fortunate enough to have Josephine Luquet stare at me with those inferno eyes and *want* me to look at her like this.

I can't help it—I duck my face to kiss along the line of her rib. There's something impossible about how she tastes, about having her salt skin against my tongue.

A sense assails me suddenly—like a slap—of this moment being too perfect, like a bubble that must pop, a stone thrown that must fall back down again. It fills me with a strange melancholy, and the love inside me grows weary of constantly being tempered, contained. It wants out, wants free. It wants no caveat, no conditions; only truth.

"You've ruined me for every other person on this planet," I tell her softly, unable to articulate better the tragedy of what we have done and will do to each other.

"There *are* no other people on this planet," she replies.

I smile, and in this moment the truth of that envelops me and becomes everything. A perfect, lonely world, shared by two who make each other not, in fact, lonely at all.

I thought it when I first saw her, and I think it again now. *Here she is.*

Chapter Eleven

JULY 21ST, 2064

Josephine

"You know what's weird?" I ask suddenly.

Luke looks up from the images we've been studying. We're sitting in bed, projecting our timeline of crime scenes onto the opposite wall and undertaking our usual session of 'stare at a picture that has no meaning for hours while your mind daydreams about other things and pretend you're making progress'. Only this time I think I actually have thought of something.

"Why hasn't anyone noticed these deaths? Or at least the disappearances?" I knead the tight muscles in my hand while I mull it over. "I mean, if you got murdered, I'd report you missing, right?"

"I wouldn't want you to put yourself out, darling."

He is cutting a mango into slices on a board, and I consider warning him that juice is running onto the bed before realizing I don't care and turning back to my epiphany.

"So we need to prove that all of these victims are real people with names and families. How do we do that?"

He smiles like he's been waiting for me to reach this point. There is mango caught in his teeth, and it makes me grin. "We have to steal the missing persons reports from the police."

"Excuse me?" Like that, my grin's gone.

*

We're standing two blocks away from the biggest police station in the city. I'm freaking out; Luke is calm. What a surprise. These are our perpetual states of being. Maybe we balance each other out.

"Wait!" I hiss. "Can we go over our cover story one more time?"

His eyebrows arch in disbelief. "We're brother and sister. Our mother has gone missing. That's it. It's not particularly complex, baby."

"Should we have back stories?" I ask, wringing my hands worriedly. "What's my motivation?"

He seems amused by this. "Your motivation is that you want to find your mother."

"Right. Yeah, okay. That seems plausible. What else? Do I have any personality quirks? What's my job? What's our family like? What—"

"No, nothing else, Josi," he interrupts. "Just keep it simple. In fact you don't have to talk at all. Just look sad." Then he adds, "Won't be too difficult for you, Sad Eyes."

"I don't have sad eyes!"

"Trust me, you do. Let's go." Luke leads the way into the station and I focus on getting into character. I'm sad. My darling mother is gone. I'm not remotely attracted to my brother.

Inside the station it's a rather chaotic mess. Every wall is a screen full of constantly changing information. Officers are everywhere, chatting and calling out to each other, or ordering other people to get a move on. There's a row of criminals sitting handcuffed to their chairs, which seems really weird to me—shouldn't they be kept out of the way of the innocent public? I give a choked, somewhat hysterical laugh—I just considered myself an innocent. Luke shoots me a warning glare over his shoulder and I swallow.

He walks straight up to a desk in the middle of the room. The woman sitting behind it looks up and actually does a double take when she sees Luke. I roll my eyes.

"Hello, gorgeous," he says smoothly. "You brighten a rough day with those peepers."

Jesus, what a sleaze! I go ahead and assume that treating a woman like a disrespected 1950s housewife isn't the best way to go, but it seems to work on the girl, so what do I know. She smiles and blushes.

"Where can my sister and I go to file a missing person's report?"

"Oh, that's at the front desk there ..."

"Thank you," he says, letting his voice drop off a bit as though he's struggling to contain his grief. "It's just ... Could we maybe speak to the officer who'll be handling the case? I'd really like to convey the details myself."

"Once twenty-four hours have passed a detective will find you and question you—"

"It's my mother," Luke whispers. "She's not well. If she's left the house, then I fear the worst. I can't bear it, knowing she's out there on her own, scared and cold. Night's coming on. And she was making threats."

He's certainly laying it on thick. The young female officer gives a quick nod. "Of course. Follow me—I'll take you to Detective Webb who handles the missing persons."

"Thank you so much," Luke sighs, flashing her a smile that's so delicious I'm surprised the girl doesn't melt straight into the damn floor.

Quite frankly, I'm amazed and a little bit disgusted. It's disconcerting how good an actor Luke is. We follow the young woman to the back of the station and into a quieter area. She pauses at the door and speaks through an intercom. After a terse response from within, she places her thumbprint on the scanner and admits us.

Luke and I enter a large office with a window that looks out onto a parking lot. There's a huge screen on the back wall, and a professionally dressed woman is standing in front of it, moving pieces here and there, tapping images and muttering to herself under her breath. As soon as she hears us enter she claps her hands and the whole screen turns into an image of a tropical fish tank. It's unnervingly real, even though the fish are too big to be comforting or cute. They kind of look like massive sharks gliding around the room. Not exactly the most relaxing environment in which to work.

The woman's eyes travel over our faces. She reads Luke first, eyes softening appreciatively, but when her gaze finds me her eyes narrow uncertainly. I grow uncomfortable, horrified that she could somehow guess the truth—she seems to be searching me with a hawk's keen eyes, aware that I'm unusual.

"Sergeant Landers brought you to see me," she states briskly. "Why?"

"Forgive the interruption," Luke says, taking a few steps forward so that Webb is forced to look at him instead of me. "We have a crime to confess."

Detective Webb motions for us to sit in front of the desk. She remains standing behind the chair, clearly to intimidate us. "And what crime would that be?"

"We're responsible for an old woman's disappearance."

Webb's expression doesn't change. "You'd better explain."

"Laurel—our mother—needs constant care. Lately, she's been talking about wanting to get revenge for what 'they' did to us, but I have no idea who 'they' are. In any case, she got out of the house yesterday. She'd been ranting on and on about some man named Ben Collingsworth and then she smashed the window to go after whoever that is. Josephine and I waited the twenty-four hours, but now we need help. She might try to hurt someone, or herself."

"Ben Collingsworth," Webb repeats. Her eyes are shrewd, calculating. She's watching Luke closely, but his mask and story are flawless. If I didn't know better I'd believe every word out of his mouth. "Do you know who Ben Collingsworth is, Mr ...?"

"Bates."

"Mr Bates."

"No, ma'am, I don't believe I do. But it hardly matters anyway, right? Whoever he is, or whatever Ma is trying to do, we need to find her and get her back on her medication."

Doctor Ben Collingsworth is none other than the scientist who first developed the cure and successfully introduced it into the world. I really wish Luke had warned me that he was going to go into this much detail. I have no idea what he's doing here, dropping a name like that and tying it to our fictional mother.

His plan becomes clear very quickly.

Detective Webb walks for the door. "Stay here. We have protocols for a threat like this."

"Threat?" Luke asks in alarm. "There's no threat—she's just an old woman—"

Webb closes the door behind her and we both hear the locks deploy, sealing us inside. Luke immediately grins and launches himself over to the screen.

"We're trapped in here!" I hiss.

Luke raises a hand sharply. I go still in fear. He points one of his fingers to his ear and then to his lips, and I realize he's warning me that someone is listening to us. He starts pressing the screen, his fingers moving with startling speed. Colors, pictures and files appear, moving around the screen at Luke's bidding. I can't follow what he's doing—it's too quick for me to make out any of the words. I do see a flashing red icon popping up in the middle a few times, but after only a moment it turns green and Luke smiles once more.

"Okay, you can rant at me all you want now—I've disabled all the bugs."

"She locked the door!"

"All part of the plan," he says mildly.

"What the hell is going on? Why did you say that stuff about Collingsworth?"

"There are certain alarm words that police use to identify levels of threat. It's a whole business around terror. Collingsworth's name is one of those. Some years ago he was the most hunted man alive—the protesters and rebels had a movement against him, and there were countless attempts on his life."

"In '55 he was put in hospital with stab wounds," I agree faintly, remembering the pictures I saw plastered all over the city. For months—years, actually—every surface of every building was covered in moving media centered on the Collingsworth riots. Pictures of him in hospital were even splashed across buses. For a while there, everywhere you looked was the man who started all of this mess, alongside slogans like *"Even our savior isn't safe from the infection"*.

"Right. So lovely officer Webb has gone to inform the necessary channels that they have a threat that could turn into a new terrorist movement."

"It's an elderly woman!"

"Doesn't matter—they have to treat every person on the planet as a potential threat."

"There have been terrorist movements?" I ask, amazed.

"Sure have. Never got very far, but they tried—gotta give them that."

"Do you think they're still out there?"

"I don't know, babe."

"But, wait—why would we want her to alert the channels that there's a threat?"

"So she leaves us alone in this room." He focuses more closely on what he's doing and starts typing in a whole lot of coding script that I don't have a hope of understanding.

"And how are we supposed to get out?"

"I have it covered."

"Right." I swallow a wave of irritation. If he's being intentionally mysterious in order to show off I'm going to be pissed. "What are you doing now?" I inquire.

"I'm pulling up the locked records and sending them to our computer at home. Then I'll have to break their firewalls and ensure I can't be traced."

"How the hell do you know how to do that?"

"Did I not mention?" he grins. "I'm rather good with computers."

Holy shit. My boyfriend is some sort of hacker. "What about when they ask for your prints and stuff?"

He shrugs. "There are ways around that."

Not in this world. There was a technology created ten years ago called PRD that is famous for being completely and utterly unbreakable—it's used on all the locks on every door, in every piece of security in the world, and it can't be faked, either. It stands for prints, retina scans and DNA samples, and to everyone's knowledge it has never been tricked or overridden. And Luke is standing there calmly finding 'ways around it'.

"Who *are* you?" I ask incredulously.

He doesn't reply. After a few minutes he punches his fist in the air. "Done! Let's get the hell out of here." Luke jogs to the door, grabbing my hand and pulling me with him.

"How will we get out?"

"Quickly," he winks. I'd really rather he didn't have such a condescending streak to his personality. He is busy doing something with the security system so he doesn't see my look. I prepare myself for the alarm that is undoubtedly about to go off, but miraculously the door clicks green and then opens!

We are halfway through the huge front room when Webb's cold voice rings out over the chaos. "*Stop those two!*"

Luke's face falls—I guess he expected to reach the door before Webb cottoned on to anything. He doesn't let go of my hand, pulling me forward into a headlong sprint for the front doors. There are about a thousand cops in this place, but it takes them all a few moments to figure out who the detective is talking about. Pretty soon they're diving at us from every angle.

We're definitely going to jail. Worse: I'm going to wind up cured.

Except that somehow, even though I'm his biggest fan, I still keep underestimating Luke Townsend. He dives beneath cops and jumps over flying chairs, and he drags me along with him, never letting go of my hand even though I'm slowing him way down.

He palms off a policeman with a casual jab of his left hand that breaks the man's nose. He does this a few more times until someone finally manages to sever the hold Luke has on me. An officer dives into me, flinging me to the floor. I skid across the carpet and it burns the skin on my thighs. As I try to free myself from the hands that have grabbed me by the shoulder and neck, Luke launches himself back toward me. He has to jump over a large wooden desk to reach me, and as I watch, feeling a bit like this whole thing is happening in slow motion, a huge, burly cop flies toward him and connects with Luke midair. The two of them crash like a ton of bricks onto the table, which buckles and splinters impressively.

A scream erupts from amid the wreckage and my stomach twists before I realize gratefully that it was the policeman who made the awful sound. He has a piece of wood through his calf and he's whimpering in pain. Luke is already up, armed with one of the desk legs. He holds it in one relaxed hand, and his eyes flash dangerously, taking in every person in the room. He gets this same look when he's solving a problem.

Everyone is watching him warily now that he has a weapon of sorts. Most policemen are approaching slowly; a few are shouting at him to drop the wood, their own guns raised. Jesus, I'm surprised he hasn't been shot down already.

Luke turns back for me, but a policewoman's strong hands are around my wrists, holding them tightly behind my back so I can't get free.

"Go," I tell Luke.

He rolls his eyes. And here's me thinking it was a heroic declaration of love and selflessness. The stupid idiot doesn't even appreciate it.

Luke launches himself over the broken table and wounded cop, moving too fast for anyone to stop him. He lands behind my captor, and even though I can't see him anymore, I can hear the swish of the table leg and I feel the impact it has on the woman's body as she gasps and slumps on top of me. Jesus Christ. I'm instantly queasy, but the adrenalin's still pumping through my body, making it possible for me to function. Luke grabs my arm and hauls me to my feet. We almost make it to the door before we're stopped—properly this time.

The police have made a wall before the door, and they have their guns aimed straight at us. There are at least a dozen of them.

"Stop there," Detective Webb orders coldly. Her gun is pointed at Luke's head.

"We haven't committed any crimes," Luke says calmly.

"You got out of my office somehow. Explain."

"Must not have locked it properly." He shrugs.

"You reported a threat and then you escaped confinement," Webb murmurs. "You then proceeded to attack and injure several of my officers. That's assault. Put the weapon down."

Luke holds up his bit of wood and looks confused. "This is a desk leg," he points out slowly. I have a mad urge to laugh, probably caused by my complete terror.

"*Put it down.*"

"Of course," Luke says softly, holding Webb's eyes. "Whatever you wish, Detective."

My heart picks up just as the atmosphere in the room changes. I can feel the energy freeze and then shift, quick as lightning, but not as fast as Luke is. He places the wood on the floor slowly, but instead of straightening, he twists down and in, moving with more speed than I've ever seen in a human. The policeman closest to him doesn't stand a chance. Shots go off, but I don't think they hit anything.

My eyes are locked on Luke. I thought I had at least a bit of a hold on who he is, but watching him now, I'm not so sure. His right fist moves up and into the cop's chin, causing the man's head and neck to snap back. His hold on the gun drops, and Luke is there to relieve him of his weapon, dropping to the ground and rolling back up behind me.

Before anyone has a clue what's happened, my boyfriend is holding a gun to my head. "Nobody move," he orders, and there's death in his voice.

Every police officer in the room is a statue. Webb's face is finally starting to show some concern. She's watching Luke with that hawk gaze, and I think that maybe there's even a bit of admiration in there somewhere. "Don't do anything stupid," she says.

Luke smiles; I can hear it in his voice. "I won't if you won't, sweetheart."

"Put the gun down, Mr Bates."

"My name's not Mr Bates," he informs her mildly. "Here's what's going to happen, Detective. You're going to order your officers to stand down and let us leave, or I blow the pretty girl's brains out."

I feel cold all the way through. There's something so terribly cruel in his voice. A hard edge of violence, a hint of the insanity brought on by his cure. I can't tell if it's real or not.

"You wouldn't hurt your sister," Webb says, but she doesn't sound very sure.

"This isn't my sister," Luke says with a sneer. "I haven't got a damn clue who this girl is. I'm quite happy for her to become collateral. Are you, Detective?"

I don't have to fake the whimper of fear that escapes me. My knees wobble but Luke steadies me. "Careful," he orders me, and it doesn't sound like Luke at all. I feel a bit like I'm trapped in my worst nightmare—I have always been terrified that one day he would lose his rational thought and act like all the other drones do in situations of stress. I know Luke well, but I don't know *drone* Luke—unpredictable Luke. The reality is that he could turn on a blink—he could be anyone and do anything.

Detective Webb is thinking quickly. Her eyes are darting between Luke and me. I force myself to meet her eyes and beg for her help. "Please," I blubber.

She makes a soft noise of helplessness and then nods. "Stand down." Her officers lower their weapons and Luke pulls me straight out the door.

"Run, and don't slow down until I tell you to," he orders crisply. So I run. I run as fast as I can, pushing and stretching my muscles until they scream, and then I run some more.

Luke leads me toward his car, but he takes a long and difficult route, hiding for long stretches and doubling back to avoid pursuit. He's extremely thorough and patient, timing

how long we have to wait in certain places, somehow knowing when feet are about to approach the mouth of an alley or
turn a corner past where we're hiding. Eventually we reach
the car and hop in. He sets it to manual and drives us a few
miles, then stops in a car park. He hops out of his car and
promptly slides into another vehicle that's just been sitting
there waiting for his fingerprints to activate it. I compartment-
alize all of this shock and confusion and follow him into the
second car. He drives this one for a while in silence until we
arrive at another seemingly normal car park, where we switch
cars again.

We don't go home. Luke drives us to the other side of the
city and rents a room in a small motel. This seems stupid
to me, since we'll have to pay for the room with our prints,
and these can be traced back to Luke's override of the police
station locks. I don't say anything though, because Luke has
shut down entirely, and I'm freaking out that he's going to
turn into the crazy guy with the gun at the warehouse party. If
I had somewhere else to go, I might. But I might not. I might
follow him anyway, even knowing how dangerous he could
be, because he's been doing the same for me all along.

It occurs to me that if he does suddenly snap and lose his
mind, I'll have no way of defending myself. I've just seen him
take on an entire room full of armed police officers and come
out on top. I don't know the extent of what he's capable of,
but I know it's frightening. And here's me, five foot seven and
bony, not a single ounce of muscle on me and no idea how to
fight.

Luke locks the door behind us with his thumb, then flicks
on the lights. I look at him, searching for the man I know. I
just need a sign or a hint, anything to let me know that he's
still here with me.

He's facing away, so I can only see his tall profile. He's
beautiful, his strong features even sharper from the side.

Standing like this, still and strong, he makes me think of something ancient and powerful. I can't find him. All I can see is how big he is, how overwhelming. At six foot four, he towers over me, and the thick cords of muscle in his arms and back have taken on new meaning for me after today. I've never been sure how he acquired the body that he has, or the scars on his knuckles. Now it seems obvious—he got it all from fighting. Who or why I don't know.

I want to say something to bring him back, but I'm too scared that it won't work. With the cure, even if Luke knows me, he could still hurt me. He might not even see it as wrong.

Moments stretch out, and then he turns to look at me. His eyes find mine, and they're so green, as always. At last he speaks, and there's something young and sweet in the rough tones of his voice. "You okay, baby?"

I feel all the sharp edges inside me melt away. My shoulders sag in sheer, gut-wrenching relief. He's here again, my Luke, just as he's always been. I cross the room and hug him as tightly as I can, pressing my lips against his cheek in an almost savage way.

"It's okay," he says softly against my hair, hands stroking calm circles against my back. "I'm sorry, Josi. I didn't mean to frighten you. I had to get us out."

I nod, and Christ—it's so obvious now. Of course he was just pretending, doing whatever he had to, to keep us safe. I feel like an irrational fool for having jumped to such awful conclusions, and worse than that—I feel ashamed of how easily my mind betrayed him. "I know," I tell him, kissing him a hundred times, a thousand, trying to make sure there's no doubt.

Luke pulls back a few inches and cups my face in his hands. He looks into my eyes. "You were so afraid," he says, almost like an accusation.

"Of the police."

"No, of me."

I move out of his reach, staring at him. "I thought—I was worried that maybe you'd ... changed."

"Like the other drones?"

I don't reply. Does he really want to do this? Surely the answer should be obvious.

"Don't you trust me?" Luke presses.

"Of course I trust you. I just don't trust what's been done to you."

His hands drop to his sides as though he's being confronted by something huge. "Josi ... that was all me. It wasn't the cure. You get that, right?"

I lick my lips. "You hit a woman with a piece of wood."

He grimaces and I can see his teeth. "To get you free."

"Is she ... was she badly hurt?"

Luke cracks the knuckles in his fingers. "I hit her between the third and fourth ribs. She was winded, but she'll be fine. I didn't even break anything."

"How did you know how to do that? How do you know so much about fighting?"

"What does it matter? She's fine, and we're fine."

I swallow, moving back another step. "What if she'd been hurt?"

He spreads his hands. "Is there a question in there somewhere?"

"What if you'd killed her? What if you'd had to?"

Luke knows exactly what I'm saying—I can see it in his face. He watches me through hooded eyes, and then he says very clearly, "I would have killed her. I would have killed every person in there if it meant saving you. Even now, I could go back in there and destroy them all. You don't understand what I could be, if it came down to it."

My breath catches in my lungs.

"You're scaring me," I tell him. "I don't know if you're serious or not."

"Yes you do."

Didn't I prepare myself to do what I had to? But what is the difference between fighting for freedom and committing wanton violence? When do we stop 'doing what it takes'? When does it become too much? I guess in the scheme of things we haven't really done much—not when I think about the men on the train.

"There's a war raging inside you," Luke tells me quietly. "She's stronger than we are, which means we'll have to fight a lot harder than she does. I'll do whatever I must."

My heart is like a drum being pounded again and again.

I tell him, "So will I."

Luke crosses the room and kisses me fiercely, and he's here, every part of him is here with me, like I know it will be until the day we're robbed of everything—even our ability to love.

Luke

I don't sleep anymore. I lie awake, waiting for her screams to start. This is my penance. The agony of listening to her fear is the price I pay for all the lies I've told her. I feel like a ghost, but I love her. I love her.

I won't sleep for the rest of my life if that's what it takes. I'll wait through all the hours of night until she starts to thrash and cry and shriek with all the things hidden in her mind, and I'll hold her as tightly as I can until there's no strength left in my muscles.

I don't know what else to do.

One day she will hate me; of this I am certain.

Chapter Twelve

JULY 22ND, 2064

Josephine

The sharp, tangy scent of rusted steel is in my nose. Bales of hay are bright yellow, like spun gold, shimmering in the light of the fire. And more yellow—long tendrils of hair that belong to a child. I can smell her, can smell her fear.

It makes me hungry.

It's not rusted steel I smell after all—it's blood.

*

I wake, gasping for air. There's a deep, rough voice speaking to me, and even though mentally it takes me a moment to interpret it, instinctively I know it's him, deep down in my bones.

"It's okay, Josi," Luke tells me.

I pull myself to a thorough halt. I'm still and calm. Under the spell of the moon it all seeps into my consciousness, but when I wake I push it all back to where I won't find it. In my dreams my memories rebuild themselves, but vanish like fog between my fingertips when I try to hold onto them. Some part of me must be saying *no—these will ruin you. Leave them be.*

Luke's warm body is big beside me, his large, square hands drumming a steady rhythm against my spine.

"Hey," I sigh. "Did you sleep?"

"Yep." He's lying—I can see the exhaustion settled beneath his eyes. The hollows there are dark like bruises. I reach for his cheek and brush my hand over it gently.

"Poor darling," I murmur sleepily.

"I'm fine," he argues, sinking further down beside me. We rest our heads on the pillows and look at each other. His hand finds mine and threads its way through my fingers.

"I was scared yesterday," I admit. "Of you."

"I know."

"Because of your cure. Because no matter how close we are or how well we know each other, there will always be the possibility that some switch in your head could flip."

Luke nods as though he's been thinking the same thing. "I can show you how to protect yourself."

"What, like fighting?"

"Self-defense."

"No *way*, Luke. I need to be making myself *less* dangerous, not more."

"It's a moot point because we're going to stop your curse."

"In less than two months?" I snort.

"We have the missing person reports now. They'll help." His tone is flat, but I can see an edge of desperation in his eyes. I realize that he's more frightened of the blood moon than I am.

"Okay," I agree gently. "Let's go home and take a look."

*

Luke's standing with his face nearly pressed up against the screen on the wall. He's reading down the list of names and dates.

"Luke, I'm telling you—you need glasses."

"I'm fine," he replies distractedly.

"Hey—how come you know how to fight? And hack computers?"

"Huh? Fighting is 'cause of Dad and my brother. They just loved it, I guess. And the computer stuff is all for work." I can tell he's too focused on the screen to pay my questions much attention. "What's this one? There's an entry on the 19th of September 2060, but there's no name beside it."

"Click on it."

Luke presses the date, but it just takes us into a blank file.

"Weird," I comment, moving a bit closer. "See if there are any more like it."

He starts to scroll down through the missing persons, and we find several more dates without names, all between the 17th and 20th of September.

"It's them!" I breathe excitedly. "It has to be! If we can just find out who these people are—"

"Josi, it doesn't matter who they are," Luke cuts in. "You're looking at this the wrong way. What's the question you should really be asking?"

I stare at him, and then my eyes shift to the dates on the wall. I feel like an idiot for not having thought of it—it's so obvious now. Swallowing, I ask quietly, "Who deleted these from the police database? Who would have enough power, and why would they want to?"

JULY 25TH, 2064

Luke

Josi is seriously on edge, which means that I am too. She's started grinding her teeth without realizing it, and she gets these awful headaches and sore muscles. She's warned me about what will happen to her as we get closer to September, but she already seems worse than when I was watching her last year. It means the change is having more of an effect on her body. We have to make it stop. That's the only answer.

She's doing a pretty damn good job of pretending she's fine though. As we drive, Josi sings along to the radio, her off-key alto voice kind of like screeching baboons. It makes me laugh and reminds me of all the things we still have.

"Where is this place?" she asks curiously, peering around at the chaos of the inner city. On every surface there are bright HD pictures or videos, advertisements of every kind, moving and flashing, attacking your senses. I hate the city for this very reason, and I can see that Josi does too. All the visuals probably can't be doing much to help her headache. Everything is a button away—every thought, every action, every word or wish or want. I don't know when we became so obsessed with easy. Everything in the world is designed to create ease.

Even the cure. The funny thing is that the cure has done the opposite. People are just too stupid to see.

"Not too much further," I assure her. "He's set up in a fairly dodgy area, for obvious reasons."

Once I've parked we head toward the back alleys. For the last few days since the police station, Josi's jumped at every sound and neither of us have been able to get any sleep. I'm still on alert. Honestly—the stunt at the station was pretty stupid, even for me. The whole charade of it was ridiculous. I could have used my security clearance to download the files, but I couldn't let Jean know I had them, and I also needed to procure them without Josi questioning how. Hence involving her in the steal. I won't make the same mistake again—with that little catastrophe I've given away a substantial clue about my skills, and I'm pretty sure she won't buy the explanations I gave her for long.

When I think about this whole mess I realise what a complete web of lies I've created for myself. Lying to Jean about my continued and distant surveillance of my subject. Making her believe I'm still a loyal Blood agent ignorant of the truth about Josi. Lying to Josi about who I am, what I can feel, and taking her on this wild goose chase to help her discover the truth for herself, without giving away what I know about her in the process. It's just lies upon lies and I can't stand it.

Down some steps there's a door with metal caging over it. I bang on it as loudly as I can, knowing Harley will no doubt be listening to his music full blast despite the fact that he knows I'm on my way. After about ten minutes of continuous pounding, he eventually opens the door, looking shell-shocked at any evidence of the sun.

"Luke, pal, how are you? You're looking as pretty as ever."

"Hey, man," I grin. "Off with the fairies again?"

"I've never been off with the fairies in my life." He winks and gestures me inside, but stops dead when he spots Josephine. "Well hello," he says slowly. "Aren't you lovely?"

Josephine's eyebrows arch. She's unimpressed and it makes my grin widen. Harley is an odd-looking guy. In his thirties, he has wild blond hair and a crooked nose. The glasses he wears for his work are magnifying lenses, and make his blue eyes look huge. He's forgotten to take them off, as usual, so he's probably trying to figure out why we look giant and disproportionate.

"Come on, let's get off the street," I suggest as I usher them both inside. The den is almost pitch black except for the eerie blue glow of several beautiful computer monitors. There's an icon made of shimmering gold, flapping like gossamer wings through one screen and onto the next. Harley's hacker ID is Wasp. He's obsessed with them; at the back of the room there's a large glass container full of wasps. Josephine moves closer to the glass, transfixed by the soft and graceful buzz of the creatures' yellow, brown and black wings.

I let her disappear into her thoughts and turn to Harley. He's staring at Josephine, just as enthralled with her as she is with the wasps.

"Is she ...?" he asks softly. "She's not, is she?"

I don't reply. Although I'd trust Harley with my life, I'm not about to trust him with Josephine's. The less people who know that she's uncured, the better. He's the only civilian apart from my parents who knows I'm a Blood.

"I have a job for you, man," I tell him. He blinks and finally turns to look at me.

"Sure, Luke. Whatever you want."

"It'll be hard."

"Don't insult me."

I smile and pull out my hard drive. He connects it to his monitors and the saved police data pops up. I've been staring at it for the last three days, but I need a new perspective.

Harley's quick eyes glance over the information. He whistles slowly. "How did you get this, kid?"

"It's amazing what people will do for a smile."

"Maybe *your* smile," he concedes. "So what do you need? The missing entries?"

I shouldn't be surprised that he's spotted them so quickly, but I am. "No—I want to know who erased them."

Harley's eyebrows pull together as he stares at me. "Well I can tell you right now that it would take an extremely high classification. Even higher than your—"

I hold up my hand quickly and he stops mid-sentence. I gesture to Josephine, who's too distracted to have heard, but Harley gets my meaning, eyes widening and nodding quickly. "Sorry. Anyway, once information has been entered into these programs, it can't be removed—it can only get reclassified. If a case is solved, it'll be filed, but it won't disappear. These names haven't been erased—they've just been moved."

"So can you find them?"

"Don't you know me at all?"

"You're right. But can you find the people who moved them?"

Harley rubs his chin and starts tapping things on his screens. He's coding and recoding and breaking patterns quicker than anyone else could. His cyber crimes are too long and too complicated to list. If he wanted to, he could make the stock market crash and take us into another recession. Or he could steal every cent from all the biggest banks and smash the economy. I can't think of anything he couldn't do, but after a few minutes he turns back to me and frowns.

"Luke, this shit is heavy. Whoever we're looking for is dangerous. The levels of security and firewalls in place would take a long time to crack, and I'd have to do it without getting traced myself." He leans closer and whispers, "You could get this information through work, man. Why do you need me?"

"This is off the books. Work can't know I'm interested."

He leans back and rubs his eyes. "I can try, but—"

"I can pay you, Harls," I say softly. "Whatever you ask for."

"Luke, that's not it," he replies, sounding wounded. "I don't give a shit about money. I'm just making sure you know what you're getting yourself involved in."

"I know."

"Right then. I'm in." He claps his hands together excitedly. "What a wonderful age to live in."

My eyebrows arch and he grins sheepishly. "Well, technology wise, anyway. Does your girl there know about any of this?"

"The girl knows," Josephine replies, moving to stand beside me. She's watching Harley closely, as if she hasn't decided whether or not to trust him.

I've known Harley my whole life. I knew he was a hacker before I became a Blood, and had to make him a vow never to tell a soul at work about him. It's a vow I'd protect with my life. Friends aren't easy to come by in this world. Especially ones who've managed to retain a fair amount of their personality, even after having been given the cure.

Harley grins at Josephine. "I like you. You're feisty and you've got great eyes."

Her expression doesn't change one bit. I try not to smile.

"How long will this take?" she asks bluntly.

Harley rubs his chin again. "Not sure. Could be six months, could be a year. Or several. I won't know until I start."

"A year," she repeats.

"Man, we need it in a month," I say.

Harley chokes on his own laugh. "Christ, Luke—I'm flattered by the assumption, but you've got no idea what you're asking for here."

"I know exactly what I'm asking."

Harley sighs and presses his palms into his eyes. "Look, all I can say is that I'll try, but don't hold your breath."

I nod and clap him on the shoulder. "Thanks, Harls. You're a life saver. Literally."

I walk to the door only to find that Josephine is staring at the wasps again. Harley approaches and stands beside her, and I watch them for a moment in the dim blue light. In the corner of my eye, the golden wasp has resumed its exploration of the six monitors.

"Are you with them?" Harley asks her.

"With who?"

"The resistance."

Josephine looks at him slowly. "Resistance?"

Harley shakes his head quickly. "Did I say resistance? I meant something else entirely."

Josi rolls her eyes in her most cutting manner. "You're an idiot."

Harley chuckles. "That I am."

I'm about to call out for her when she asks abruptly, "Why wasps?"

Harley folds his arms and smiles. "They don't die when they sting."

*

It's silent in the car as I wait for her to say it. I know her too well to expect her not to bring it up.

"You heard him too, right?"

"Yeah, I heard him."

"A resistance." She sounds wistful and delighted and disbelieving all at the same time. "I *told* you that's who the men on the train were."

"Could just be a rumor," I warn her. "Harley's a bit of a wacko."

"How do you know him?"

"He's an old uni friend."

"Who also happens to be a world class computer hacker."

"Right."

She sits back in her seat and I can see her brain starting to whirl. She's piecing it all together—I can see it. Something in my own heart ratchets up—something like fear but also like excitement.

Josephine

A resistance. I wished for it, and assumed it must exist, but I didn't know until now. I feel like crying with an insane hope I can barely contain. The idea of other uncured people gives everything a new sense of meaning, of possibility. The world doesn't seem so cold or so lonely anymore.

I don't know where they could be hiding, or how they've survived, but I want to find them. Right now, it's all I want.

JULY 30TH, 2064

Josephine

I wake in the middle of the night to find myself alone. Blinking in the darkness, I pull on my dressing gown and pad into the living room. I can see Luke standing outside on the balcony, the glass doors closed behind him. He's on the phone, and the side of his face looks tense. I watch him for a moment, curious. His hand jerks in an odd way, his brow heavy over his eyes.

I go back to bed and wait for him to return. He doesn't come for a long while, and when he does he slides back under the covers and runs a hand over my hair. I don't know why, but I pretend to be asleep and eventually I hear his breathing deepen.

I lie awake, his hand gesture from the balcony replaying itself over and over in my mind. I can't put my finger on what's so strange about it. I don't even know why I think it's strange.

And then, near to dawn, it finally occurs to me.

In that simple hand movement, Luke looked angry.

SEPTEMBER 14TH, 2065

Anthony

"So did Harley ever get to the bottom of it?" I ask. I have to try and infuse a certain level of disbelief into my tone so that she doesn't feel too encouraged to keep spinning this fantasy, but the truth is I'm getting sucked into the story.

"Does it look like he got to the bottom of it?" Josephine snaps, and the suddenness of her temper is a kick to the teeth. I forget, every single time, how swiftly it can come upon her, seemingly triggered by nothing.

She sits up and licks her lips like she does when she's preparing herself. "Have you called Luke yet? There's only a day or so left."

"Not yet. I will."

"Have you made preparations for me? For Maria?"

"I told you, there are no other rooms available."

Josephine closes her eyes and I can see the rise and fall of her chest. When she looks at me again, her strange eyes are blazing with fury and impotency. "You're such a coward," she whispers. "Sometimes I hate you more than I've ever hated anyone."

My heart falters.

"I've tried," Josephine says. "I've tried every day for the past year to convince you of something, but you refuse to listen. I thought coming here was a good idea—I thought it would keep people safe, but it seems I was wrong. The blood I spill will be on your hands, Anthony. I can't do anything more."

I don't know what to say. I feel sick and ashamed, even though my rational brain is ordering me not to give in to emotion. She is a mentally damaged patient, for god's sake. She is not a woman who understands the truth of reality. She is not someone who can manipulate me with a story she made up.

"I need to leave," she adds flatly. "I can't stay here anymore if you refuse to isolate me."

I clear my throat. "Leaving won't be possible, Josephine. Not at this juncture."

"I came here of my own free will!" she protests. "I can leave whenever I want!"

"Actually, that's not the case. Because you have professed aggressive thoughts and feelings, you are now required to remain in our care until we can effectively treat you."

Her mouth falls open. "You mean I'm a prisoner?" She stands up, her limbs shaking. "This is ... You can't ..." She turns white with fury. In all my years as a doctor, I've never seen anyone so out of control. She crosses to where her cello is standing against the wall. This is the cello she wept over, the cello she has been playing without pause until I reluctantly forced her to continue her story. This is the cello she believes Luke somehow delivered to my apartment, because he knows how much it means to her.

And this is the cello she now lifts into the air and smashes again and again onto the ground, screaming in despair and rage.

I hold myself very still, alarmed and terrified of all that she is, of all that she's turning me into. I want to go to her and hold her. I want to make this better for her, but I don't know how.

When at long last she stops battering the poor, ruined instrument, she stands amid the wreckage of it and stares at me. There are tears in her eyes, and I know it's bad if she's let herself cry. No matter what we've talked about all year, through all the horror stories of her supposed crimes, all the nightmare tales of her childhood, she has never once shed a tear, except in the moment she first saw this cello.

"I can't do this again," she whispers. "I need to make it stop." And without waiting for me to dismiss her or call for her escort, Josephine strides from the room.

*

I sit and stare at the broken cello for what feels like hours. I should up her dosage of meds. That's what I should do after an episode like that. It's the rational response. Instead all I feel like doing is everything she asks me.

The pieces of her story are turning themselves over and over in my head. They've awakened something in me, an awareness of a puzzle that needs to be solved. I get up and walk in a trance to my car. Inside I don't turn the engine on. I stare up at the tree I'm parked under. It's huge, its smooth branches stretching out in every direction. Pinpricks of light dance through the green leaves, shrouding me in dappled shade.

How old was Josephine when she first started having her delusions? Eight or nine, I think. Which would make it about twelve years ago. The first of the cures started being administered nine years ago. Is there something there? My heart's beating very fast. I can feel the clue building itself in my mind.

A sound, loud like an explosion, bursts into the car and something smashes into the windscreen. Glass cracks out in every direction. I've never had a moment of such shock; it is physical pain as the gasp is torn from me. A dead crow is lodged in the windscreen. Its beak pokes through, only inches from my face. I can see one of its beady black eyes. It seems to be staring straight at me, vacant and detached. It reminds me of myself.

People are running to the car, calling to me through the windows, asking me if I'm all right. They're pointing and gesturing and yammering away, but I don't look at any of them. I look only at the bird. I've drawn it a thousand times without even meaning to. I've dreamed of it for years.

I spend the night on the phone, calling in every favor I've ever accrued, coaxing information from every angle I can possibly think of. I trawl the net for news bulletins and articles from twelve years ago. I save every single piece of information I can manage.

SEPTEMBER 15TH, 2065

Anthony

I work until the sun is rising. I've forgotten to shower, and the realization makes me feel sick. I push myself through the hot water, scrubbing more quickly than usual, and then head out the door, armed with everything I've discovered.

My heart won't slow—there are moments when I feel giddy from the speed of my blood.

As soon as I'm in my office, I send a nurse to fetch Josephine Luquet. Then I nervously drum my fingers against the table. I feel sharp as a knife. Everything is too raw to interpret properly—I haven't felt much of anything in nine years and now I'm a set of nerve endings.

Doyle hauls Josephine into my office with a cold, affronted look—honestly, the guy has no idea of the extremely low status he holds in this facility. If he looks at me like that one more time I'm going to have him fired. I dismiss him with a flick of my wrist and turn to my patient.

She looks wary. "What is it?" And then she adds, changing my whole life, "Are you all right, Anthony?" As if she is worried about me. As if her first thought when being called early into my office is for *my* wellbeing instead of her own.

"I've figured it out," I breathe.

"Figured what out?"

I'm so excited my hands are trembling as I load my drive into the tablet. Behind me on the wall the screen lights up and loads. I tap my icon and a handful of pages pop up.

"What is this, Anthony?" Josephine sounds nervous now.

I take a breath, trying to order my thoughts. Along with the shock of what I've concluded, there is also the fear of what it means, and the gut-wrenching guilt of my own inability to see it earlier. Christ, all this time she *tried* to tell me and I didn't listen. I didn't even entertain the thought. It makes me ashamed.

"You're right," I say. "Josi, you've been right all along. I thought you were having severe delusions and hallucinations because of the abuse in your childhood, but after yesterday, I started thinking. Why weren't you cured? And the police records you found?"

She's looking at me so closely that it distracts me, so I turn to the screen and start to explain. "Here's my idea. I could be wrong—there's no proof here, just lots of ideas being pulled together. In the beginning, when you first develop a new technology or drug, you have to test it, right? But you need a raw test subject. With something like the cure, you need a brain that hasn't developed completely, because if it won't work on the malleable mind of a child, then it certainly won't work on a mature mind."

I move some of the articles into the middle of the screen. "In 2054, a family sued the medical research center H&S for experimenting on their child. The boy had been taken in because he had anger issues and they wanted to see if he could be medicated to stop the aggression. The experimentations harmed him irreparably, but the family didn't win the case because they'd agreed to the experiments in the first place. There are a couple of other cases just like this—five that were documented. Each was a child who'd been diagnosed with behavioral disorders—some of them even had IED—intermittent explosive disorder. I looked into each of the five children's names and found that over the last twelve years they've all died of unexplained medical conditions."

"H&S are owned by the government," Josi says slowly. "They're the company that first developed the cure." Her hands are clenching and unclenching with quick tension.

"Correct," I agree eagerly, bouncing on the balls of my feet. "So what does it make you think? That the first tests of the cure failed and children were irrevocably altered. If a company makes a huge mistake, killing children in the process, that's not something they'd ever want the public to know about, right? It could compromise the company's reputation—especially any plans to inject the whole world with a drug of theirs. So they covered it up."

"And they got rid of the names of all my victims to cover up the fact that there was a problem at all!" Josephine says. "They created a monster and then cleaned up all the mess. Holy shit. This is huge, Anthony."

I nod, turning around to look at her face. She's staring at the articles on the screen. "In a way, your abuse *was* the cause of all this."

She looks at me sharply. "Not that again, Anthony."

"When you were eight, you were taken by your foster family to H&S because you had anger problems. It was reported that you attacked your foster brother. You were the perfect candidate for the first round of experiments."

"But if I went wrong, and they turned me into some sort of maniac, then why did they just let me go nuts and kill people?"

"I can't answer things like that without speaking to someone involved."

"Is that even possible?"

"I doubt it. They've guarded their secret closely. I'm assuming that even the fact that I've guessed the truth could put me in a lot of danger."

Josephine looks at me for a long moment. Her brown and blue eyes are studying my face, and I'm not sure what she'll see. Suddenly she crosses the room and takes me in her arms, hugging me fiercely. "How did you work it out?" she asks against my shoulder.

"A bird," I reply faintly. "It was because of a bird."

She laughs in disbelief. "I'm going to get your bird tattooed all over my body so that I never forget that you were the one who figured it out, Anthony. I'll never be able to thank you enough."

I pull away and look into her beautiful face. "Don't thank me. I should have worked this out in the beginning."

"Don't worry." She smiles. "You're programmed not to understand, Doc. But you worked it out anyway. You're a bit of a rebel, really." And then she kisses me on the cheek and I've never loved anyone as much in my whole life.

"Did you call Luke?" she asks expectantly.

"I will. Right now. Go back to your room and I'll sort things out."

"You mean ...?"

"Everything. I'll get you into a private room, with a sedative and handcuffs if I have to."

"Anthony ..." Josephine swallows, and she's holding my eyes, looking at me in a way no woman has ever looked at me. I imagine for a moment that I'm Luke, that I'm the one she loves. When she looks at me this way it's an easy thing to imagine. "I've studied this puzzle for about ten years now," she admits softly. "I've looked at it every way I can, and I've had Luke examine it every way he can, and neither of us came to this conclusion. I don't know why that is. Only that you're the one who did. Do you know what that means?"

Mutely I shake my head.

"I never knew ... if I was just crazy. I never knew if it was real." She touches my cheek gently. "I can die now, or I can go to jail, or whatever. I've killed people. I really have now—it's not a dream or a kind of madness. It's real. But at least I know. And knowing is the freedom you've given me—the only freedom I've ever had a right to hope for."

I swallow, feeling frightened. "Josephine, you're not going to die or go to jail."

She smiles and it's pained. "You do understand what you've just uncovered, right? We're talking government conspiracy here. And who works at the top? The Bloods. No one can deny them. No one can fight them. As soon as they know that I understand, they'll kill me. There's nowhere in the world to hide from a Blood."

I feel cold, knowing she's right. The Bloods are like ghosts, doing as they please, controlling the world, deadly and impossible. If a Blood wants you dead, the only question is when. I feel a sharp awareness of fear.

She squeezes my shoulder and her smile changes into something soft and genuine. "No matter what happens, Doc, you've saved me, and I'll love you forever for that."

I feel myself blush like a child, and I'm so dumbfounded that I can't think of anything to say before Doyle arrives to take her back to her room. I don't know who he thinks he is, deciding when patients are supposed to be in their rooms, but I'm too distracted by something Josi said to argue with the oversized lump of meat.

Numbly I sit alone at my desk, trying to work out what it was that caught my attention.

I've looked at it every way I can, and I've had Luke examine it every way he can.

Luke is a state prosecutor. He was best friends with a computer hacker, and had skills in hacking himself. He would have had access to the same information that I did—more, in fact. He looked repeatedly into Josephine's child protection files, and he knew enough about hacking computers to be able to get in and out of a police station. Except that it's supposed to be impossible to override the PRD system. So maybe he didn't hack anything at all.

Maybe ... maybe he didn't discover the truth because he already knew it.

I can feel a tingling sensation in my fingers. I sit up straight, my mind whirling with possibilities for the thousandth time today. Before I convince myself out of it, I race from my office, using my prints to get me through several layers of security, down many hallways that all look exactly the same, and finally to Josephine's room in the East Wing. I've never been here before. In all this time, I've never once come to see where she spends all of her time.

Doyle is standing at the door, looking intimidating. "No access," he says.

"I'm her doctor," I say. "I have full access to every room in this facility."

He studies me skeptically and then reluctantly stands aside.

I place my print on the scanner and the door opens for a five second window to let me in. Josephine is lying on her tiny bed, staring at the ceiling. The room is small and sparse, the only other thing worthy of note being her roommate, a woman who is not a patient of mine, but who Josephine has described as near catatonic. Maria is curled in a ball, snapping her teeth repeatedly.

As I enter Josi sits up in alarm. "What's wrong? Am I being moved?"

"I've just been thinking. I need to ask you some things, if it's all right."

"Yeah, sure," she replies, making room for me on the bed. "Is something wrong?"

"No. I don't think so." I grip my hands together, unsure how to start. Now that I'm here, I haven't got a clue how I'm supposed to ask these questions. I take a breath and tell myself to treat this like any normal patient—I'm confident and in charge. This is for her health and safety.

"Josi ... Can you tell me about Luke's apartment?"

"What do you mean?"

"Did it feel lived in? Did he have a lot of possessions? Personal items? Photos?"

Josi stares at me as though I've said something bad. Her eyes narrow cautiously. "He's wealthy. His apartment wasn't his choice. He didn't like it."

"That's not what I'm asking."

"Okay, well no I guess he didn't have much stuff. He was a bit like that—neat and tidy."

"You were together for almost a year, right? Did you ever meet his family?"

"They were estranged. He had a bad relationship with them, so he didn't see them."

"Did you ever go to his workplace?"

"No."

"Did you ever feel like he was lying to you? Like he was hiding something?"

She looks at me for a long moment and then says softly, "No."

"Did he ever actually tell you he loved you? Did he say the words?"

Josi opens her mouth but nothing comes out. She looks like she's starting to unravel, so I steer the questions in another direction. "Did you ever see him grow aggravated or angry?"

"He's cured, Anthony. So no—never."

"What about friends? Did you ever meet any of them? Or anyone at all who knew him?"

"What are you asking?"

I steel myself for the next question. "Did you and he ever get ... intimate?"

"What?"

"Did he make love to you?"

Her eyes widen in disbelief and I can see the storm brewing inside her. She stands up. "Get out."

"It's an important question, Josephine. Did the two of you—"

"Get the fuck out of my room. *Now*."

I get up helplessly. "I'm not trying to hurt you—"

"Get out!" she shouts. I flinch, so unused to rage. I don't know what else to do except leave, but even though I've upset her, I think I have my answer.

AUGUST 19TH, 2064

Josephine

Luke's phone is ringing *again*. It's been ringing every day for the last week, and always at really weird hours. He's in the shower, but his phone is on the bedside table, and it won't shut up. I click my tongue and reach over to answer it.

The caller ID reads *Lou*. I've seen Lou's name on his phone several times before.

"Hello?"

There's a pause on the other end of the line. "I'm looking for Luke. Do I have the wrong number?" It's a woman.

"He's in the shower. Can I take a message?"

"Who is this?" the woman asks.

"It's … Josephine." For some reason my skin prickles at the idea of telling my name to a strange woman on the end of Luke's phone, but I'm not sure why I should lie.

"Right. Well, Josephine, would you kindly tell him that Louise phoned? And get him to call me back, would you?"

"Sure."

Louise hangs up and I stare at the phone. I'm tempted to scroll through and see if he has any photos in here.

Luke emerges from the shower with a towel wrapped around his waist. He looks slick and gorgeous, his dark hair wet, his chest and arms covered in a faint sheen of perspiration that defines his long, lean muscles.

"I need to ask you some things," I tell him.

He looks over his shoulder and smiles. "Sure, sweetheart."

"Explain to me why I'm here in this house with you. Because as I understand it, you saw a random girl in a club, decided to help her, invited her to move in and made your entire life about solving her problem. It's a stretch, Luke."

He frowns. "Are you serious?"

"Very."

Luke breathes out in a puff. He walks to his side of the bed and sits down, running a hand through his damp hair. "Okay. You want the truth? I saw you and felt bizarrely connected to you. You were the only still thing in a world of agitated speed. You were lonely and pitiful, and I was inexplicably worried about you. I was also deeply attracted to you, and I'd like to say that I'm not controlled by my desires, but that would be a lie. At least a part of me is. We met. We talked. I liked you a lot, right from the start. I recognized in you someone who understood the things that I did. Someone who hated the way the world is as much as I did. I was excited by your obvious fury. I wanted to be close to you. I wanted to be with you. I can't explain it any better than that. It's all I have."

His words take me back to that first night. He appeared like a dream, speaking in his deep, comforting tone. A part of me must have loved him from the very beginning, in that stupid club, even without knowing it.

I slide over the covers so that I'm sitting behind him, threading my arms around his shoulders and neck. "I love you," I murmur against his ear, "but sometimes I feel like I don't know you. Before we met, what did you want, Luke? What did you fear? What did your life contain?"

I can feel his lungs fill with air as he breathes. I move my right hand to rest over his heartbeat. The smell of him is so familiar it makes me ache. I love him so much that I actually *miss* him, even when he's sitting within the space of my arms.

"I didn't fear or want anything," he says softly. "That's what's so scary, Josi. I was a ghost. I lived for work, moving through my life like I was underwater. I was a drone."

"And now?"

"Now I'm alive again, sweetheart. You woke me up."

"A cure for the cure?"

He smiles and turns his face toward mine, catching my lips in a kiss. My mouth opens with a sigh and I feel his tongue slide across my lip. He tastes sweet and lovely. He tastes like freedom.

"Who's Louise?" I ask softly.

Luke stiffens. He pulls away, staring at my face. "What?"

"She just phoned you." I glance at the clock. "At one in the morning."

"My boss," he sighs. "She's hounding me."

"Why?"

"Guess I've been letting things slip at work."

I consider this. The woman on the phone didn't sound like a professional figure—she sounded worried and jealous. Plus she phoned in the middle of the night. But the cure makes people behave weirdly. "Okay, well maybe you should focus more. Leave me to worry about myself."

"The blood moon is less than a month away."

I flop back onto the pillow and throw an arm over my eyes melodramatically. "Do you know what I'd like to think about?" I sit up and grin. "The resistance."

Luke's expression doesn't change. He watches my eyes closely.

"Don't you want to find them?"

He cracks his knuckles. "You know who else wants to find them? The Bloods."

I roll my eyes.

"Don't," he says suddenly. "Don't make that face like it doesn't matter. You've got no idea who the Bloods are, Josi. You don't know how dangerous they are."

"And you do?"

"Actually, I do," he says.

"So tell me about them."

He stands up and walks to the window. Golden lights from outside dance across his skin and flicker in his eyes. "You don't have to be given the cure to be a robot."

I'm not sure that I know what he means, but I stay quiet, hoping he'll keep talking. Getting Luke to talk about anything other than my curse is becoming almost impossible. Morsels of his life are so rare that if I had to live on them I'd be long dead. He disappears for several hours a day, but he never talks about his job, despite how many questions I pound him with each time he comes home. Legally he's not allowed to speak about his cases—I'm just surprised at how strictly he follows that law. I understand what it means never to want to speak about your past—I loathe the very idea of even mentioning my childhood. But the fact that he seems to feel the same way makes me think he must have his own fair share of darkness, instead of the perfect life I used to imagine him having. Perhaps when he goes there in his head he's met with his brother. I can't imagine grieving for a sibling—it is too vast a sorrow.

He doesn't seem to want to go on, so I prod at him, hoping for some kind of reaction. "What if the Bloods did come and find us? Wouldn't that be better than this?"

"What's *this*?"

"This land of drones."

"You'd rather be dead than live here with me?" he demands.

"That's not what I'm saying. I've been hoping all along that the Bloods would come for me, but they never do. They seem to be the only ones who can stop me now."

"By torturing you for information and then slaughtering you?" Luke turns around, and I've never seen him look so cold. "You're a child."

"And you're a coward," I tell him softly, trying to hide how much his words hurt me. "You're too frightened to fight. We could leave right now. We could find the resistance and join them. We could face whoever comes for us."

"Do you know what the reality of that kind of life is?" he asks. "It's isolation. It's having no friends, no family. It's living your life in fear, never having a place to call home."

"As opposed to how we live now?" I cry. "This isn't a home—it's cold and empty. We spend our lives searching for something that doesn't exist, and we dread the moon. Why couldn't we do the same in a place where we could actually try to make a difference?"

"You idealize it."

"I don't idealize shit," I snarl, standing up. I spread my hands. "My whole goddamn life has been a waste. Did you know that until I met you, no one had ever *touched* me, except to harm me? I've lived with more instability, more isolation than you could ever imagine. I don't have any friends or family to leave. I know how to take care of myself. And what's more—you know all of this about me. Which makes me think that *you're* the one who doesn't understand, Luke. *You're* the one who couldn't live on the outside." And then I tell him again, "You're a coward."

He just stands there, looking wounded.

"Fight back!" I yell suddenly. "I can't bear that you won't fight back! Yell at me! Shout and scream and get *angry*!"

"Would you like me to pretend?"

I scream in frustration and storm out, locking myself in the bathroom. I turn the faucets on and start filling the bath. While I wait I can't help pacing back and forward. Doesn't he get it? If anyone in the world has the ability to reverse the cure, then it's the resistance—they are the only ones who won't have been given it in the first place. And no matter how much I love Luke, I don't know how much longer I can be with a drone.

*

The boiling hot water loosens my muscles. I feel like a cigarette, even though I've never smoked one in my life. I consider calling out for Luke to get me one, but I'm not quite sure what the response would be, or if I'm relaxed enough not to scream at him again. I honestly don't understand—if there's even a hope that somewhere out there are other people like me, then isn't it our responsibility to at least search? If it's possible, wouldn't he want his personality back?

That thought stops me short for a moment. It's never occurred to me before that Luke might not be who he once was. And if he had the cure reversed, then who would he become? Is it possible that's he's an entirely different person? One I don't know at all?

"Josi," Luke says from behind the door, "I'm coming in."

He opens the door, wearing cotton boxer shorts and nothing else. Without looking at me, he sits with his back against the tub, hands laced over his raised knees. "After the blood moon," he says quietly, so quiet I almost think I've imagined it.

I hold my breath. I don't need his permission—the truth is I could go on my own, but the thought of leaving him behind is too painful to entertain. "After the blood moon what?"

"We can look for them. If it's really what you want."

I run my hand through his hair, wetting it. He leans his head back against the lip of the bath, closing his eyes and enjoying the feel of my fingers. "You'd leave your job?" I ask softly. "Your family?"

204

He doesn't reply. After a while he gets up and climbs into the bath with me, underwear and all. "Fuck it," he announces wildly. "*Fuck it!* None of it matters anyway—everything in this whole goddamn world is bullshit. Everything except this."

"This?"

"You." He splashes me in the face. "You and me. So let's fly away and join the fairies. Why the hell not?"

It's kind of lame, but that's the most romantic thing he's ever said to me.

I kiss him. He smiles against my lips, threading his hands through my hair. "But first," I add, smile fading, "We have to survive the moon."

Chapter Thirteen

SEPTEMBER 15TH, 2064

Luke

"Your reports have become less and less detailed," Jean tells me. "It's unlike you."

"There's not much to report, Jean. Watching the girl is as dull as watching paint dry."

"Then why do you continuously recommend that she needs to be surveyed? It's been almost a year and a half, and you've given us nothing."

"Like I said, I have yet to ascertain where her loyalties lie."

Jean laces her fingers together on the desk. She's gearing up for something big here, and I unconsciously brace myself. "Agent Townsend. I'm going to tell you something very interesting. Josephine Luquet has a unique condition. Once a year, she is overcome with aggression. This causes her to be violent—or at least, it has in the past. For the last four years, we've had various agents watching her, all of whom have reported her behavior to be extremely dangerous. On the last blood moon you were the agent sent to monitor her. You were unaware that we also sent three other Bloods to watch the girl. Those three Bloods never returned from the op. But you reported the next day that nothing of any interest had occurred."

My heart beats a little too fast. Jean leaves her words to pollute the air between us. I keep my expression empty.

"You're my only Gray, Luke. I've waited patiently, trying to give you the benefit of the doubt. Hoping you'd come to me."

"Why wasn't I informed of her condition?" I ask softly.

"You didn't need to be," Jean snaps. She sits back. "Either you neglected to inform us that the girl murdered three of our finest agents, or she didn't in fact have an outburst like she has had in previous years. Which is it, Luke?"

My mind starts working quickly. Obviously, this is a trap. The latter explanation is utterly stupid, and she knows it. If Josi didn't do it, then what happened to the three agents? There's no way out of this.

"Fine. I have something to admit," I tell her. "On the day of the 16th the girl was acting strangely. I thought she was sick—she collapsed—so I broke into her apartment to see if she needed to be taken to the hospital. Next thing I knew she was attacking me. I don't remember anything else. I woke up hours later, alone in her apartment. I didn't report it because I was embarrassed that some kid managed to get the drop on me."

"So you let three of our agents die without explanation?"

"I didn't know about the other agents. You never told me about them."

We stare at each other. It's clear she doesn't believe me, but I don't really give a shit what she thinks, since she can't actually prove that my words are false.

"All right. You might be able to explain something else to me."

"My pleasure."

"Why it is that you are living with your surveillance subject?"

I freeze. Every muscle in my body goes still as my mind launches ahead and moves faster than it has ever done. It was always a possibility they'd know we were living together, I just thought I'd have more warning than this.

"I changed her status from surveillance. I got sick of your secrecy, and being treated like an amateur. Watching her was delivering nothing. I decided to intensify the information I was acquiring so I upped her to contact status and got close to her. I figured you might want her as an asset, if she turned out to be working for the resistance."

Jean smiles without any humour. "Really. Townsend, you do amuse me. There'll be severe punishment for this breach in conduct. Did you manage to learn anything with your reckless activities?"

"Nope. She's clueless about herself."

"Very well," Jean says. "Your new mission has been sent through. It's very simple."

There's something in her voice that makes me wary. There's no way I'm getting away with what I've done that easily. I don't move a muscle. Jean opens some files and displays them on the wall. It's a new photo of Josephine—one that I took last week.

"Josephine Luquet has become too difficult to contain. Her crimes are too extensive to disguise. She must be brought in."

I don't move—I can't move. Somewhere inside me I knew that this would come one day, but I'm not ready for it. I haven't figured out a plan. I've been wasting time, trying to help Josi figure it all out on her own, when I should have just fucking told her. I'm a coward. I'm the worst damn kind of coward, because I put my own happiness before her safety.

Bringing her in means one of two things. Either she'll be cured, or executed. I don't know which is worse.

"What's the first rule we learn when we're recruited into the Bloods, Luke?" Jean asks me softly.

I don't reply—I can't.

"Never make contact with a subject. Not even the novices could get that one wrong." Jean stands up and it's obvious she doesn't expect me to answer. "Get it done before she changes tomorrow, or she won't be the only one who gets brought in. You're dismissed."

*

I swerve my car to the side of the road, open the door and vomit into the gutter. Everything inside me comes tearing to the surface, shredding my organs as it goes. When I finally stop there's a song playing on the car radio, its tinny electronic voice drifting over the quiet of the afternoon air. It seems to be about a man who's forgotten his wife's name.

I am so weary of people who forget.

I squeeze my eyes shut and rest my forehead against the steering wheel. Jean knows my secret. I would rather die than be given the cure. The very idea of it makes me sick with loathing.

My phone is ringing. Over and over and over—whoever it is won't give up.

Filled with despair, I answer it without looking at the caller ID.

"Luke!" It's Louise. "Where are you? I've been trying to reach you for days!"

"Why?" I snap.

"Because you're my boyfriend!"

I climb out of the car and breathe in the smell of the grass under my feet. I'm not sure where I am—I seem to be standing beside a park. On the other side of it there's a playground with children climbing over brightly colored objects.

"We've been broken up for a year, Lou," I tell her, forcing myself to stay calm.

"We're not broken up!" she moans.

"We have this same conversation every time we speak," I tell her as patiently as I can. "You don't seem to be able to understand, so I'll tell you again and again until you do. I don't love you, Louise. You're everything I can't stand about the world."

"It's because of Dave, isn't it? You changed when he died."

Is this supposed to be a surprise? Would it be strange for a man to change when his brother kills himself? I want to scream at her, but I can't. Eleven years of being a Blood—of rage—seethes under my surface, but I can never let it out or they will take it from me.

"If that's easier for you to process, then yes," I say flatly.

"Have you had an affair?"

"I haven't had an affair, because you and I aren't together."

"Who was that woman on the phone?"

"Louise, I have to go. Don't call me again. Do you understand?"

She doesn't say anything, but I can hear her breathing. She's trying to work out how to feel, but she can't get there. After a moment she starts to giggle. I hang up the phone.

*

The house I park in front of is small and run down. I haven't been here for years. I don't know why I'm here now—a sick kind of self-punishment. Trance-like, I walk to the front door and knock.

My mother opens it and stares at me. Her hair is almost entirely silver, but she wears it with an innate grace she's always had, even after they damaged her brain and she lost her oldest son. Her eyes are my eyes, but lighter. Slowly they fill with tears and she throws herself into my arms. She's tiny. I get my stature from my father, who's a hulk of a man. My mother has never felt so frail though, like she might crumble to dust at any moment.

I feel a desperate kind of sadness. Here in the powerful hold of her limbs is the physical proof of a notion we can never quite understand. It is a real, tangible manifestation of love, this hug, these tears. I feel my own eyes prickle because there is nothing so profound as the way she is, in this moment, forgiving me.

"I'm sorry," I whisper. She's stroking my hair over and over like she did when I was a kid. "I'm sorry, I'm sorry, I'm sorry."

"Come inside, my darling," she tells me, taking my hand and leading me into the house where I grew up. The smell of it is intense—a wash of memories and feelings I thought I'd forgotten. And Dave. God, Dave is here in every inch of this place, and it hurts so damn much I feel like my chest is being cracked open.

There are his trophies on the mantel. There are his photos on the wall. His guitar in the corner. A painting he did as a child on the fridge. I thought I would never see these again—I wanted never to see them again. But now that I am here, in among it all, it's a perfect, sweet kind of agony.

A question with no answer.

My mom—Claire—wipes her eyes and bustles around in the kitchen, making a pot of tea. I sit down at the kitchen table and clear my throat. "Where's Dad?"

"At work. He'll be home this evening—if you could wait?" There's such longing in her voice that it nearly makes me start crying again. Jesus, I've got to get a grip on myself. I can't stay that long—I have to figure out what to do about Josephine—but I can't bring myself to tell Mom, so I sit quietly and she goes back to the tea.

When she's brought it to me she sits and we look at each other.

"Mom ... I should have come back. I should have visited."
She reaches out and places her hand over mine.

"I don't know what to do," I whisper. "I've really made a mess."

"Okay, darling. Start by telling me the truth and we'll go from there."

So I do. Mom and Dad know I'm a Blood. They were the ones who sent my test scores to be analyzed. They wanted security for me. Wealth, status, a nice place to live. They didn't understand—and neither did I, in the beginning—what it would mean to have such a job. What I would have to do. What I'd be made to watch. They don't get it, even now. All they know is that I work for the good guys, and Dave died trying to fight them. That kind of confused grief is enough to send anyone mad.

I tell Mom about getting shot, and about how when I returned from sick leave I was given a low-level job as punishment. I tell her about how I watched Josephine, how I started to lose my mind to obsession. How I lost forty pounds and stopped sleeping. I tell her about the night I first spoke to Josi, even though I knew it could get us both killed or worse—cured. I tell her about how we've been living together and I've been trying to help her figure out the truth. And I tell my mom how I was ordered this afternoon to kill my girl-friend before she murders any more innocent people.

"You love this girl," she states.

I stare into my cup.

"And if you don't take her in you'll lose your job?" she asks faintly.

I feel the air leave my lungs in a gust. I feel sick. I should have known this would be her response. All she has ever cared about is making sure I'm not poor. Once upon a time that's all I cared about too. When my brother went to protests and riots in the street, I went to work, knowing I had to keep my job to keep my money. I couldn't afford to have any ideals, any opinions. I was a body for hire, and I was good at what I did.

Then my brother died and I realized there was a different reason to be a Blood now. I didn't care about anything, not one single thing except the anger. The anger was mine, all mine, and it would only be mine if I remained uncured.

"I don't care about my job," I tell her. "It will be my life. They'll cure me and turn me into a mindless drone."

Her eyes drop to the table and I feel instantly bad. "Mom, I'm sorry—I didn't mean to insult you ..."

"I know it's true," she says. "Your father hasn't laughed in years. Even before Dave. I feel plagued by the thought that I might not be missing my son enough. I can't ... feel *anything* enough."

I close my eyes.

"You can't let yourself become like this," she goes on. "Not ever, Luke. I don't grieve for my dead son. I don't love him. It's like living through a waking nightmare. You wouldn't ... I'm not sure you would survive it."

"So you're telling me I have to have her killed then," I say, voice breaking. "That's the only other choice and you're telling me to take it."

My mother stands up and gestures for me to follow her. She takes me down the hall to where Dave's bedroom sits. I pause outside the door, not wanting to go in. My heart is pounding like the panicked flutter of a bird's wings. I can't go in. I *can't*.

"It's just our Dave," my mother says softly. "He's nothing to be frightened of."

So I follow her into my brother's bedroom and I sit down on the bed, looking around at all the shades of Dave, and I know that she's right—he isn't frightening. It's the idea that he was right all along that scares me to my bones.

Mom walks to the desk. There is an old-fashioned white-board against the wall, covered in pictures and ticket stubs. In the middle Dave has pinned up a quote, and as I read the words I feel everything shift.

"Your father and I always thought he was foolish and headstrong," Mom says softly, running her fingers over the photo of Dave and Livvy on the desk. "But he was the smartest one of us all, wasn't he? He knew about life, *real* life, and he knew how to live it big and fast, and full."

I can't help it now—I start to cry. I close my eyes and the tears slip out onto my cheeks.

"You have more than two choices, my love," she tells me gently. "You have a third. You can stop behaving like a child, and become a man. You can fight. For yourself, and for the woman you love. Because there's nothing else left."

And then she reads aloud the words that defined my brother's life, and as she does I come to understand that maybe I'm not so different.

"All that is necessary for the triumph of evil is that good men do nothing."

*

At home she's gone. The only trace of her is a note, written in lipstick on the fridge.

I won't put us before the lives of others. You don't need me to fight—you're brave enough to do it on your own. I love you.

I go cold with terror, and I start running.

Chapter Fourteen

SEPTEMBER 16TH, 2064

Josephine

I'm the cracked bed of a drought-ridden river. I'm dry and parched and sore and falling into thousands of tiny pieces.

I want to claw out my eyes and my hair. I want to yank the teeth from my mouth and tear the fingernails from my hands. I want to die.

I've been walking all night and all morning. Now the sun is high in the sky, so hot it's making beads of sweat trickle down my aching spine. I know that what I'm looking for must be out here somewhere, but my eyes are unfocused and I'm having trouble staying upright.

Something is wrong with my body. Parts of me feel like they're shutting down. But I have to reach my end before the curse takes over. I wish I'd had the courage to leave earlier. I should have done this days ago, so that there would be no doubt at all.

Finally I recognize the photo I saw on the news three months ago. This is the entrance to the site where they were building a new shopping center, but had to stop because of building restrictions. There's a massive canyon out here that's unsafe to have people working near.

I am a long way from where anyone lives. Surrounding me in every direction is rough wilderness. In the far distance I can see the smudge of the wall towering into the sky. And before me, as I stumble toward it, is the hole in the ground, deep enough to destroy even a curse-ravaged body.

I duck beneath the safety partition and stand at the edge. The drop is dizzying—I can barely see the bottom from this height. A crater gouged from the red earth as if with the fingernails of a mighty hand.

I look up into the sky, my vision blinded by the pure light. With my eyes stinging, I think of my parents, whoever they are. I think of the world we've been left to and I imagine a life outside this one, in a place where no one can take anything of yours. I imagine what a world without sadness would be like, and I think I'm quite happy not to see it.

I think of Luke's brother and I wish I could have met him. He sounds brave.

I don't think about Luke.

I don't.

I close my eyes and take a breath. I *must* do this. I must. What will I be if I wake tomorrow and learn that I've killed again? I'll barely be human anymore. My toes curl over the edge.

And that's when I hear a sound from behind me. I freeze, disbelieving. It's a car. I have to do this now. I can't be around people so close to nightfall.

"Josephine!" a voice shouts. My heart lurches. How did he find me? I shake my head. There's no possible way he could have followed me, *so how did he know?*

"Don't you dare!" Luke yells. "Get away from the edge!"

I swallow. I can't let him distract me. I have to do this now, before he creeps inside my head.

"If you jump I'll hate you forever," he tells me.

My mouth falls open and the breath catches in my chest. I look over my shoulder, which is definitely a mistake. He's standing at the partition. He could reach me if he tried to. His green eyes are brighter than I've ever seen them. There's something different about him, something frenetic and excited. Something real.

"You don't understand," I whisper. "You couldn't possibly. Something like this … it could almost be forgivable. No control, no memory, no concept of the damage being done. But I know what it's like to be hurt, to be attacked. It goes back so far I can't even remember a life without it. I mean, Christ—when I was four they made me sleep outside in the rain because I didn't finish my dinner. I got pneumonia from that. I've been hit and kicked and whipped and beaten in just about every way you could imagine. And it's okay, but it's not something I will ever forgive myself for doing to another person."

He closes his eyes for a brief second. "If you die, you'll be doing it to me."

"This isn't about you," I utter. "My life's not worth more than anyone else's."

"Yes it is," he says loudly. "Don't you get it? It is worth more because you're the only one left with enough fury to fight!"

"This is… I'm trying to fight her," I whisper. "This is the only way I know how."

His jaw clenches. "I'm not talking about that anymore. It's not just about fighting the moon and the transformation—it's about fighting the cure itself, and the Bloods, and this wall that's locking everyone in. The world needs you, Josephine Luquet. You're going to help me find a way to stop all of this madness. I can't do it without you. I won't."

I realize with a start that this is it—this is the difference. Luke has only ever wanted to fight my transformation. He never wanted to find the resistance—he wanted to coast along and live beneath the radar. He wanted to hide and survive. Now the wildness I saw in him from the start is making its way to the surface. He's vicious and savage and he wants to fight the entire ruined world.

"Give me your hand, sweetheart," Luke says.

I feel a thrill of excitement slam into my chest. I turn toward him, but something in my head hurts, and then it's black and I'm falling over the edge.

Luke

She turns around and I see the moment that I get her. The spirit is back in her eyes. In that moment—that millisecond of time—I see our future stretch out before us. I see the two of us taking a stand. I see us together, for the rest of our lives, living in passion and joy, fury and love.

It's a stupid thought, because it doesn't take into account two things. First, that I'm the asshole who has lied to her repeatedly, and that she'll loathe me until the day she dies when she finds out. Secondly, that there is still a kind of poison in her veins, turning her into a monster, and that we have no way of stopping it.

"Give me your hand, sweetheart," I tell her, reaching out. She lifts her hand, but something comes over her, like a dizzy spell. Her eyes glaze over and she starts to fall backwards.

I launch myself over the partition, hooking my feet over it. Stretching myself to my full length, I catch her by the elbow, my hand gripping fast. She's unconscious, which means she's all dead weight, and she nearly pulls my shoulder out of its socket. Groaning with effort, I stretch out to take her other hand. Since my legs are hooked and the rest of me is dangling over the cliff, I have nothing to use as leverage and no way to climb back up. Breathing heavily, I think it through. I can't last much longer like this. I'll have to swing her up to the top. I start moving her from side to side, which has the unfortunate result of loosening my grip and scaring the shit out of me, but pretty soon I have her picking up momentum. Praying that it won't hurt her too much, I haul her up to the side where she plonks down on the hard ground and makes a moaning sound. Using the cliff edge, I push myself backwards bit by bit, until enough of me is on solid ground to maneuver myself to safety.

I crawl to where Josephine is lying and check that she's breathing. My hands brush her face and she opens her eyes.

They are red.

I jerk backwards in shock. All the blood vessels in her eyes have burst, and she looks like some sort of bloodthirsty demon. This didn't happen last year. I'm sure of it.

"Josi?" I whisper. But she's gone. There's nothing human behind her eyes. Only a depth of cold such as I've never seen before.

She sits up slowly, her red eyes locked on me, vacant and terrifying.

"Josephine, it's me—Luke," I try desperately. I don't know why I'm even bothering—nothing will bring her back now. I need to run.

The noise of an engine sounds close by and, before I know it, there's a sleek black car exactly like mine rounding the corner and pulling up beside us. There are three men dressed in black within it—Bloods.

One of them I've met before but I don't remember his name. I'm not supposed to—all I need to know is that he's a Blue, the other two are just Reds, like the Blood Josi impaled on the meat hook in the factory. I outrank all three of them by a lot.

"What are you doing here?" I snap coldly. I keep one eye on Josephine—she's staring at the newcomers with an eerie fixation.

"We came to make sure you did your job."

"How did you find me?"

"Isn't it obvious?"

So Jean had me tracked. I shouldn't be surprised. It's ironic, really, since I put a tracker on Josephine last week and that's how I found her today.

"Go home," I order. "This is under control."

"We're here to help you," one of the Reds says mechanically.

We are standing around talking, when what we should be doing is running as fast as we possibly can. My heart is thumping painfully and adrenalin is pumping through my body. These boys are highly trained and dangerous, but they don't understand the threat standing three feet from us.

Another noise interrupts us. It is further away, the sound of a much larger engine. We all stare in concern at the mouth of the road, and pretty soon a huge fire truck rumbles into view.

"You've got to be kidding me," I mutter in horror. "What is that doing here?"

The other Bloods share a glance—they still don't get it. "Must be here for something to do with the construction."

"Well get it out of here!" I snarl. "Or every person in that vehicle is dead."

The Blue looks at Josephine skeptically. She doesn't look dangerous. In fact she's standing quietly, looking well behaved. But for her red eyes, you could almost believe she's perfectly normal.

I'm not fooled. I know something's going on inside that head, something sinister. The cells in her body are rearranging themselves to make her stronger and faster, fuelled by the white-hot flame of fury only she can feel.

The Reds move over to the fire truck, but they're too slow—half a dozen men are already pouring out of it and approaching us. I start toward them, raising my hands to forestall them, but that's when Josephine moves.

In this state she is faster than I am. Much faster. She moves past me with a fluid, animal grace, straight into the path of the first firefighter. He doesn't even have time to react to her approach before she snaps his neck.

Everyone in the dirt clearing freezes. There's not a single sound, for one impossibly long moment.

"*Ray?*" one of the firemen gasps, his voice strangled with sheer disbelief. It doesn't make any sense.

Another fireman starts whistling. His brain can't interpret the right response to what he's seen. Neither can mine, actually—I don't know what the right response is for this. I don't know that there is one.

I force myself into the state of calm I use when I work. I can't get emotional right now, or I'll never save the rest of these men.

"Get back in your truck," I order softly, my eyes locked on Josi. She's staring down at the body of the man she's killed. She kneels beside it and lifts the fireman's head, letting it drop back down. She looks like a child playing with a doll, unable to understand that the man is dead. She does this again, lifting his head and watching it flop onto the ground. It chills me.

Nobody is moving. They're too shocked. "Get back in the truck!" I roar. The sound of my voice gets Josephine's attention. Her eyes jerk up to me, blazing savagely. I hold her gaze, wanting to give the men a chance to get away.

Two of them get into the truck quickly, but three of them start toward Josephine, wanting to fight I suppose. The Bloods move quickly to cut them off, but Josi senses all the movement behind her and she lunges toward the Blue while his back is turned. She grabs his elbow, kind of like I grabbed hers to save her life. Josi pulls him backward with a jolt of strength that makes him lose his footing.

I have no doubt that if this man had seen her coming, he could have fought her and maybe survived for a little while—he's a soldier. But the speed at which Josi now moves is undeniable. Before the Blue has even finished stumbling, she snaps his arm with a ferocious twist. He screams briefly, then cuts himself off because he's trained to manage pain.

It's pretty much a free-for-all now. The two Reds plus the three firemen attack her all at once. I race around to the back of the fire truck, searching for something I can use to dispel the situation. My eyes alight on the huge hose.

Climbing up to the reel, I unwind it and place it on the ground. It's a monster of a thing, extremely heavy. I've got no idea if I'll be able to aim it once there's water bursting through it, but I have to try. I grit my teeth and wrench the wheel around—it takes all the strength in my arms to loosen it on my own.

Water explodes out of the nozzle, and I scramble down to catch the wildly bucking hose. From behind the truck I hear gunshots and my heart skips a beat. Wrestling the hose into tremulous obedience, I point it toward where the fight has been raging, but when I round the corner it is to see that all the men—every single one—have been torn into pieces. There is a pile of body parts and a pool of blood seeping toward my feet.

Woozy shock pummels me—it's the most appalling thing I've ever seen, this macabre arrangement of human bits. But I don't think about it—I can't, not yet. I have to find Josephine.

That's when I feel it. Someone watching me.

Whirling around, I see Josephine lunging at me and I manage to aim the hose just in time. A mighty rush of water hits her in the chest and knocks her backwards off her feet. She is washed toward the edge of the cliff and a strangled gasp leaves my mouth. Thankfully she crashes into the partition and stops in a rumpled heap. I drop the hose and approach slowly.

I can barely breathe. She isn't moving, so I take another step closer. My teeth are clenched so firmly they feel as though they'll shatter.

Josi makes a soft sound, causing me to jump in alarm. She rolls onto her back, but I remain cautious, watching closely.

Another muffled cry escapes her, and then I hear the word, "Luke?"

I am flooded with relief as I scramble toward her, skidding my knees on the hard earth at her side. "Josi?"

"What happened?" she asks woozily. Her eyes are still red, but there's a person behind them now, someone kind and gentle, funny and clever.

"You started to change. It was only about ten minutes ago. I … does it normally happen like this? That you turn back so quickly?"

She shakes her head, wincing in pain. "I'll change again when the moon is high. And when that happens it will last until sunrise. This was just …"

"A preview," I breathe. Jesus, I feel nauseous.

"What happened?" she asks again. Her eyes narrow suddenly and she tries to sit up. I'm not sure what alerts her, but it's clear that she knows something is wrong.

"Don't look!" I order, moving in front of her. Josi stares at me, her breathing shallow. "You don't need to see."

She licks her lips. She's dripping wet and shivering, but I think it's more from shock than from cold. "Yes I do."

I search her gaze, knowing that if she sees what's behind me, she could very well throw herself straight over the cliff.

"They're my crimes," she whispers. "I have to own them, remember?"

Closing my eyes, I step aside.

Josephine looks at the nine dead men and she goes so pale that it looks as though there's not a drop of blood left in her body. Her lips are like chalk.

I expect her to break down. To start crying or lose her mind. But she doesn't. She stands up, and there's iron around her spine, holding it in place. "I won't forget this," she whispers; not to me, but to the men, I think. "I will never forget again."

Then she looks at me and says, "You need to get away from me, Luke."

"Wait. Just wait." My brain's working a mile a minute, eyes scanning our surrounds to stop at the canyon. "I've got an idea."

Josephine

Luke uses all the lengths of hose on the truck, tying them together at the ends, to lower me into the canyon. It's not long enough, so I untie myself and drop the rest of the way. The impact hurts, but not as much as it should—the curse spends weeks ruining my body, both before and after, but for one day of the year I am nearly invincible.

The length of hose starts to disappear into the sky, and I know Luke will be dealing with the bodies up above. Once he has buried them somewhere, he will get in his car and drive as far away as he can. That's what he promised me, anyway. I hope he does it, because I'm not sure if even the chasm will be enough to stop me.

I lie in the dirt, burrowing my hands and feet beneath it. In the sky there are clouds, but I've never been able to make them into shapes, even as a child. The moon is rising—I can feel it. Or maybe that's just the beast inside me. Maybe all I can feel is her. Maybe I won't change back this time. Maybe she'll take over forever. It feels a bit like she could, if I let her.

And I'm so tired. The idea of trying to fight her is almost too much.

Down in this hole I am alone. I can't fight her on my own. I can't.

I start to shake badly, and I bite my tongue. My mouth is flooded with the steely taste of blood and it makes me want to retch in revulsion.

I'm always alone. No matter where I go or whom I meet, I will always be alone. Even before the curse I was alone, and now I can't escape it. I start to panic. I can't be down in this hole anymore. I need to get out. I can't be alone down here.

There's a strange noise surrounding me and I look around in fear before I realize that it's my own breathing growing more and more hysterical. I can't be down here. I have to get out right now. Right now right now right now. I'm going mad. I can't I can't I can't I can't—

Something drops from the sky to land a few feet away from me. I blink, the sight freeing me from my head. I slither through the dirt like a creature until I can see what it is. A piece of paper, scrunched into a ball. With trembling hands I smooth it out and look at the words typed over it. My eyes are blurry, so it takes me a moment to understand.

It's a page from one of my books. *The Hitchhiker's Guide To The Galaxy.* One of the pages I quoted to Luke when he didn't believe I had a photographic memory. I stare at it, bewildered.

Another ball of paper falls down to land nearby, and I crawl over to unfurl it. It's the next page in sequence, and my eyes scan the words I already know.

A few minutes later, another page falls. I don't understand, until suddenly—I do.

He's too far away for me to hear, so he's sending me a message.

He's not leaving me.

The pages fall for hours, and they're the only things that keep me from going mad. They fall all afternoon until the sky darkens, and then they keep falling into the night. They are the last thing I see before everything goes black, and my body is no longer my own.

Chapter Fifteen

SEPTEMBER 15TH, 2065

Anthony

I am holding in my hands the formal request for a single room in which to lock Josephine. It feels like a triumph. I'm going to do it—I'm going to keep her from hurting herself or anyone else. I'm going to solve this problem and save Josephine.

She won't be able to think of me as a drone then. She'll have to see me as a real person. And maybe once I tell her the truth about Luke, she'll realize that she fell in love with the wrong man.

I stride purposefully into my office but stop dead, the door swinging shut behind me with a soft click. Facing the window is a man. He's not wearing the staff uniform, and he's not one of my patients. He's tall—even bigger than that damn nurse who hurts Josephine. This man is leaner than Doyle, but he looks stronger. Even standing still like this, I can see the coiled lengths of his muscles and the way they are tense and ready.

The man turns around. There's something about the way he moves that is almost animal. The room is dark, so I can't see his face, but I know who he is. Instinctively, I know exactly who this man is.

I flick the light switch so the room is flooded with light, and there he stands. Luke Townsend.

He's just as Josephine described him. I can see the confidence in his stature and the arrogance in his eyes that she laughed over. The lines of his face are harsh and unforgiving, and his eyes are a brighter shade than she could have ever explained.

"I understand you are Josephine Luquet's doctor," he says softly, his voice deep and rough. Everything about him, even before he's *done* anything, makes me feel emasculated. I hate him. My fingers tingle with it. I feel small and weak.

Doesn't she understand that loving a man because he's big and strong and handsome will result in betrayal?

"I am."

He folds his big arms over his chest. "In that case I'll need you to help me."

"Why would I help *you*?"

Luke's incredibly sharp eyes move over my face. I have no idea what he sees, but after a moment he frowns. "She told you?"

"Of course she did."

"And you believe her?"

I swallow, feeling myself flush. "Of course."

The corner of Luke's mouth twitches in dark humour, and I know he's seen right through me. "Then you'll know I'm here to help her, Doc."

I don't like that he calls me Doc, like Josi does. It makes me uncomfortable. "I've arranged everything. You're not needed, Mr Townsend."

"What have you arranged?"

I consider calling security, but there's something about his gaze that makes me want to tell him. "She'll be moved into a single room. I'll dose her with sedatives. If need be, we can cuff her to the bed."

Luke stares at me and my skin prickles. He steps forward, looming over me. "And when she pulls the bed frame from the ground?"

"Mr Townsend," I splutter, "the frames are made of metal and drilled into the ground. I assure you, no one could pull them out."

"You don't have any idea, Doc. Some of the things I've seen her do under the blood moon chill me to the bone, and I'm not a man who's easily unsettled."

On this I believe him. "Look, Luke—I've got it under control."

"You've got no fucking clue," he says coldly. "I need to get her out of here, or she's going to tear the place down and kill everyone inside. On this you can trust me."

My heart is doing funny things in my chest.

"All I need you to do," he orders me, as if he's in charge, "is bring Josephine to me here."

"Why can't you do it yourself?" I demand, baiting him to admit the truth.

"Because trying to get through any of the security doors with my prints will send an alarm to the Bloods."

"Perhaps I'll simply sound the alarm myself right now."

Luke gives a sudden, wolfish grin. "I bet Josi likes you."

My mouth opens but nothing comes out.

"Anthony," he says firmly. "I'm here to get Josephine out. I'll do it with or without your help, but if you help me I'll have a better chance of hiding her from the other Bloods."

I hesitate, looking at the form in my hand.

"Don't be a dick," he snaps. "Go and get her."

I walk to the door and pause. "She's going to hate you," I warn him. "When you tell her."

"That's my problem."

"You're going to, right? Tell her?"
"Go, Anthony."

NOVEMBER 27TH, 2064

Luke

I'm waiting by the bed when he wakes up. The old man gives a cry of shock when he sees the hooded figure standing in the shadow of his room.

"Easy now," I murmur softly.

"Who are you?" he gasps, sitting up unsteadily. "How did you get in?"

"I'm a Blood."

The man—Ben Collingsworth—goes pale. He looks like he's about seventy, with white wisps of hair and dull eyes.

I move to the bed and help him out of it gently, not wanting him to break a hip.

"What do you want? Have there been more threats?"

"No, I just want to ask you some questions, so I'd appreciate it if we could move into the living room."

"It's the middle of the night!"

"It is indeed."

Ben sits down in what is presumably his favorite chair, since it has a footrest in precisely the right spot for his short legs.

"I'll make some tea," I offer. As I fumble around his kitchen, finding what I need, I keep one eye trained on Ben, just in case he gets any ideas about alerting anyone to my presence.

I carry a tray with two mugs and pot of tea to the coffee table. "Milk? Sugar?"

"A Blood who makes tea," he says softly, shaking his head.

"My mother taught me the importance of a good pot of tea. It's an art form, getting it just right." I let my voice drop to a soothing level to make him more comfortable. If he doesn't feel like he's about to be murdered, he's more likely to open up. If need be, I can resort to threats later.

Once we've each had a sip, I sit back in the chair opposite his and eye him. He's sizing me up just as I am him. He's probably had a lot of dealings with Bloods. They've spent the last ten years protecting him. Doesn't mean he's any less wary of me.

"What are your questions, Blood?"

"My name's Luke," I tell him pointedly, lacing my fingers together.

"Are you a Red or a Blue?"

I meet his eyes. "I'm a Gray."

Ben blanches, spilling some of his tea. He stares at me, awareness dawning in his milky eyes. "Good god," he whispers. "What do you want with me?"

"Like I said, I just need some answers."

"Of course."

"Where's your drive?"

He points to where his hologram projector is mounted on the wall and I slot my USB into it. Images appear in the middle of the room and I navigate through them until there is a girl standing between us. She has long dark hair, so long it reaches the end of her spine. Her clothes are ratty and careless, and there's an unimpressed look in her two-colored eyes. She's sitting on a kitchen bench, arms folded impatiently. I took this photo six months ago, just after I'd made fun of her poor cooking skills.

The sight of Josephine sitting there, so real and vibrant, makes my chest clench painfully. I haven't seen her in over two months, the worst two months of my life. The image is so believable that I feel like I could reach out and touch her.

"Do you know this woman?" I ask Ben softly.

He's gazing at her closely, his brow furrowed. "I don't believe so. Her eyes …"

"Are familiar?" I press.

He nods slowly, still trying to work out where he's seen such a distinctive gaze.

"How about this? Do you know this child?" I slide the image to the side, making room for another photo. This is a child protection file photo of Josephine when she was eight. If I'm right, this would be the year that she met Professor Ben Collingsworth. I watch the man's face as it dawns on him. A breath of air leaves his lungs and he sags in his chair.

"Josephine," he whispers.

In one word he has confirmed everything I've suspected. I've been staying with Harley for the last two months, laying low, helping him uncover as much as we possibly can about the first experiments of the cure. We figured it all out a while back, but we needed to hide any evidence of us being linked to the discovery of the information, and leave a kind of trail of our own, one that will make it easy for people to uncover the truth in future. People like the resistance.

What we haven't been able to learn is the medical side of what's been done to Josi. I know she was experimented on, and I know that the inventor of the cure, Ben Collingsworth, was responsible, but I don't know what that means for her physically.

"What did you do to her?" I ask, my voice dropping.

"Show me the other one again," he pleads quickly. I switch the photos back so that he's looking at the current one. "When was this taken?"

"A few months ago."

"Then she's alive?"

"She is." Barely.

Ben stares at nineteen-year-old Josephine, and to my shock, he drops his head into his hands and starts to cry. I watch as his elderly, weak shoulders shake faintly. When he looks up at her again, I watch the way his eyes fill with longing. "She's so beautiful," he whispers. "I never thought she would ..."

"Survive?" I demand. "You thought she'd die and take your filthy secret with her?"

"No!" Ben exclaims, wiping his eyes.

"Tell me what happened. From the start."

"We were developing a cure for clinical aggression," he says wearily. "We needed subjects to test it on."

"So you experimented on *children*?" I growl.

"We thought ... we thought it would help them. But it had an adverse reaction."

"So why didn't you reverse it?"

"We didn't know what it had done to them!" he protests. "Any symptoms formed gradually. At first there was simply minimal memory loss, so we thought the drug hadn't worked and we moved on to a different formula. It wasn't until later that we realized that the test subjects were ... changing."

"And then? Why didn't you do anything about it then?"

"We did! We found all the children involved in the case and we monitored them to make sure they were safe."

My eyebrows arch in disbelief. "Is that really what you believe?"

Ben looks confused. "That's what happened."

"They were murdered, Ben," I tell him flatly. "The Bloods found and killed every single one of them."

"No," he shakes his head quickly. "I almost wish it was so, because ... Because the truth is worse."

I stare at him, feeling the hairs on my arm stand on end. Something about his tone is frightening me.

"All of the children—except for Josephine—were brought into the labs and held. They exhibited all kinds of antisocial qualities. A kind of rabid violence that occurred every year on the day they were injected with the drug we called

Zemetaphine." Ben sits forward, his hands moving as he speaks. "Zemetaphine is a strand of durable virus. The brain has two main parts—the cerebral cortex, which is responsible for logic and reasoning, and the limbic system, responsible for our emotions. This second part of the brain is more primitive. When we feel angry, the limbic system is working, usually without the help of the cerebral cortex, which is why we become so irrational. We even have a small structure inside the limbic system called the amygdala. This houses our 'fight or flight' response, and when it activates, it can force us to behave entirely without regard for the consequences."

"And Zemetaphine?"

"Zemetaphine attacks the limbic system—specifically, the lobe that houses our anger response. But instead of killing this response, it had the adverse effect of confusing it. Being a Blood, you will understand about the uses of adrenalin?"

I nod. "If you can tap into it, your physical attributes can be heightened."

"Precisely. You have learned to activate your amygdala, flooding your body with the adrenalin of this 'fight or flight' phenomenon, but you use this in perfect synchronicity with your cerebral cortex, allowing you to act rationally. So you're clear-headed, while also stronger and faster, correct?"

I nod again. I'm starting to see where he's going with this, and it's making me nervous. "We have a short shelf life, though. It isn't healthy to have that much adrenalin pumping through us so often. We get burned out."

Ben clasps his hands together. They're trembling, but I'm not sure if this is because he's emotional or just because he's old. "So imagine that your amygdala has taken over your entire brain. Imagine cutting out the cerebral cortex entirely, and living only with this heightened limbic system. You'd be out of control. You'd be wildly aggressive, with nothing rational or reasonable to hold you back. Add to this, extremely heightened physical attributes—the sheer volume of adrenalin is more than our bodies could ever dream of producing on their own, and could make us almost superhuman for a short amount of time. When it wears off, however, our bodies would be ravaged, right?"

"So this is what happens to Josi once a year?"

Ben nods.

"Why doesn't she ever remember?"

"That is purely a self-preserving reaction to such a traumatic event. She blocks it out, instinctively understanding that it could send her mad if she had to relive it. Especially since she has an eidetic memory, and can recall things with more clarity than the rest of us."

I rub my eyes, feeling overwhelmed. "And the other kids?"

"They died, Luke. The virus destroyed their bodies. By the time we understood what was happening, it was too late to think about developing an antidote. I am deeply amazed that Josephine has managed to survive so long. She was the first child we ever tested."

"Why didn't you bring her back into the lab with the others?"

"We couldn't find her. She ran away from the foster family and no one had any idea where she was. When the Bloods finally tracked her down, she was the last living patient, and we decided to monitor her in the real world instead of bringing her in, wanting to understand what made her different. The captivity was the only variable that we could pinpoint—was it her freedom from the lab that kept her alive?"

"Well was it?"

"We don't know. We have no idea what makes her strong enough to survive when the others couldn't."

"All right," I say levelly, swallowing down all the violent rage pounding through my body. "So you'll have to develop the antidote now."

Ben frowns. "Luke, I'm seventy-two years old. I've been retired for years. I haven't been to a lab. I haven't thought about science or cures in just as long."

"Are you honestly going to sit there, after a story like that, and then announce that you won't help save Josephine's life?"

"Luke, I don't believe it's possible," he tells me gently. "Her body will have been shutting down dramatically in the last few years. I fear that if she goes through one more change, it will be the end of her."

"Then she won't have one more change!" I snarl. "We'll fix her before September—it's ten months away!"

He shakes his head helplessly. "It took me years to develop Zemetaphine, and then several more years to develop the strand of it we use as a cure, but you want me to come up with a reversal in *months*?"

"Yes."

Ben shakes his head again.

I'm starting to panic. This isn't what I wanted to hear—not from this man. He is my last hope. He's the only person on the planet who has any chance at saving Josi, and he won't even try.

I stand up, trying to gain control of my emotions. I suck in a breath, but it doesn't help, and before I know it there are words pouring out of my mouth, desperate, aching words. "She's the smartest person I've ever met," I say. "She has this insane desire for knowledge, and she never forgets a single thing she reads. She didn't go to school, because she couldn't, but she's taught herself more than most people learn in a lifetime of study. She's funny as hell, too. She's got this really wry, sarcastic sense of humour, and she laughs at herself, most of all. When you can get her to let her guard down, she's sweet. Sweet and kind and generous. She plays the cello with more heart than I've heard in any music."

"Luke—"

"She has this funny dance that she does when she's trying to distract me, and she has a terrible singing voice that you can't help but laugh at. She's so compassionate. And *brave*. Fuck she's brave. She carries around all this shit that *you* did to her, and she never complains, even when it all gets really bad."

"Luke, I don't—"

"She's going to make the best mother," I exclaim. "She needs to have children, and a family. She deserves a life, Ben. *Please*. You're the only one who can help us, and I—"

"All right!" he interrupts loudly. "All right, Luke. I'll try."

I stop, sagging back into the chair. I close my eyes, faint with relief.

Before I leave, I tell him the rest of the story. About how no one knows I've come to him, and if they did find out, Ben could be killed too. And I leave him with the date. The 16th of September.

"Where is she now?" he asks as I step out the door. The sun is starting to peek its head over the horizon.

"She's waiting for you to save her."

Chapter Sixteen

SEPTEMBER 15TH, 2065

Anthony

I'm shaking with nerves as I walk to Josephine's room. Inside the cell Josi is curled up in bed and I'm surprised to see Maria sitting over her, stroking her hair.

Maria glances vaguely at me and says, "You might have to put her down. We did that with our cat when it was sick."

Repulsed, I move to look at Josephine. She opens her eyes and looks at me, and I've never seen her so tired. "Did you get me another room?" she asks, voice rasping and faint.

I nod, moving to help her stand. She trembles, but manages to stay on her feet. Before I can lead her out, she turns back to Maria. "You'll be okay now, honey."

Maria nods solemnly. Josi reaches out a hand to brush over the other woman's cheek, and then she follows me into the hall. We walk past Doyle, who doesn't say anything, but watches us with hawk eyes.

"Where's the room?" Josi asks through a wince. I wonder which part of her is hurting so badly.

"We're stopping by my office first."

I think about bypassing the office and taking her to the room I had planned for her. I could exclude Luke from this whole thing. But one look at Josephine tells me I have underestimated what is happening to her. Only Luke has been through this before—I'm loath to admit it, but he will know how to help her.

We reach my office and I place my thumb on the scanner. I realize I'm holding my breath as we walk inside.

Luke's back beside the window, but he turns quickly this time. Josephine spots him and freezes. I'm still supporting her, and I feel the jerk of shock in her pulse as it starts to race. Surely this can't be good for her?

But that's the last conscious thought I have, because Josephine drops my hand and then they are moving toward each other, and all I can do is watch as they meet in the middle of the room like magnets that have been drawn undeniably together. Luke wraps her up in his arms, and her hands are on his face, his neck, in his hair, and her lips are against his and on his cheek, his jaw and his ear and he's whispering things to her over and over again, and it isn't Josephine who cries—it is on Luke's face that I see a tear slide, but then it's gone because she has kissed it away.

I feel dizzy and overwhelmed, but I don't look away, and I'm ashamed of myself. It is now, in this moment, that I realize what I am, and what I have been my whole life. I am a voyeur. I watch people and listen to their secrets, and I live my life through theirs. I've even fallen in love with another man's life.

"Sorry I'm late, sweetheart," I hear Luke murmur against Josi's ear.

"You're right on time," she tells him.

"Christ, I've missed you."

She kisses him again, long and slow. I watch their lips and the way their hands are so tender as they hold each other. Have I ever had an embrace as intense as this one? Once in my entire life?

"I've worked a lot of stuff out," he tells her. "I have a plan."

Josephine smiles. "Of course you do. You're an over-achiever just like Anthony is. He worked a lot of stuff out too."

Luke meets my eyes. "I know he did." He turns back to Josephine. His girlfriend. "Okay, time to go."

"Where?"

"I'll explain on the way. Anthony, we'll need you to get past the guards."

I swallow, standing up. "Josephine, leaving might not be the best thing for you."

She smiles again. "Come on, Doc. Live a little."

Luke smiles slightly too, and for a moment I hate them both. "Fine," I sigh. "Let's go."

Josephine

I think I've spent the last year convincing myself that I don't miss Luke, which seems rather ridiculous now that he's here. It's possible I do have some serious mental problems, because even though my body feels like it's being pulled apart piece by piece and I'm terrified of the looming moon, I can't stop smiling.

He looks leaner than when I last saw him—closer to how he was when I first met him. Stress makes him lose weight and sleep. But he's just as handsome as I remember—even more so. His hair is short and he hasn't shaved in weeks. He's holding my hand in his large grip, and we can't stop looking at each other as we follow Anthony toward the exit of the asylum.

I stumble a couple of times, and Luke rights me quickly, murmuring, "Easy, darling."

We reach the front entrance. Doyle is blocking the way, with two other security guards right behind him. "Stop," he orders almost lazily.

Luke gives a sigh of long suffering. He doesn't seem particularly bothered as he gestures for Anthony to take my arm. "Don't let go of her," he orders, then steps in front of us.

"What's your name?"

Doyle's lip curls. "Leave the girl or I'll arrest you."

"Citizen's arrest?" Luke asks with a grin. "You're making me sad, big guy. How many times have you applied to be a Blood? But they just won't let you, will they? Unfortunately I think it's 'cause they require their agents not to be total fucking morons."

Doyle starts to reach for his gun, but Luke makes a sharp noise. "Uh uh. You reach any further for your gun and you'll be dead before you touch it."

He opens his jacket to show Doyle the gun holster over his shoulder and the black weapon sitting against his ribs. "Quick draw. You want to play?"

Jesus Christ—where did Luke get a *gun*? And why is he smiling like this is an everyday occurrence?

Doyle hesitates, clearly unsure.

He reaches for his gun, but Luke is quicker. He has it out of his holster and pointed straight at the security guard. "Hold it," he orders calmly. Doyle stops. "Drop it on the ground." Doyle drops the gun on the ground. The security guards behind him have no idea what to do, so Luke orders them to drop their weapons too. Pretty soon we're through the doors and heading for Anthony's car.

"We need to borrow your Porsche, man," Luke says, looking rather pleased about it.

"It won't run without my print."

"Well then open her up and start the engine for us."

Anthony shakes his head. "I'll drive."

Luke clearly doesn't like the idea of this, but after some deliberation he rolls his eyes and hops in beside me. "Step on it, Doc. Head north toward the highway."

"What's the plan?" I ask.

Luke looks at me across the back seat. "I've made a new friend. His name is Ben Collingsworth."

My mouth falls open and Anthony snorts in disbelief up front. "Bullshit," he says. I think it's the first time I've heard him swear. I like it.

Luke grins. "It seems our favorite scientist has a case of remorse, and wouldn't mind setting a few things right. You know about the tests and the cure and all that?"

I nod. "Anthony worked it out yesterday." I can't help but smile. "So I'm not crazy after all."

"Well," Luke concedes, "You're not *overly* crazy."

I shoot him a look, making him laugh, and he slides over the seat and plants a kiss on my lips. He tastes delicious, like freedom, as he always has. For a minute as he kisses me I forget about how sore I am. I feel alive and tingling and full of desire. I want him so badly I'm in danger of losing my head and undressing him right here and now. Which would not be particularly ladylike, given poor Anthony is chauffeuring us around and might catch an eyeful of something he probably wouldn't want to see. I almost start laughing at the thought.

"Pull in here," Luke orders, pointing to a small roadside motel in the middle of nowhere. When the car is turned off, Luke starts hacking into its central security systems and overriding them so that we can't be traced. Anthony is standing in the parking lot, looking nervous. I walk around the car to stand beside him.

"Thanks, Doc. Really."

He nods.

"You okay?"

"I'm fine. Are you, Josephine?"

I smile. "I'm good, actually. I bet you didn't think he was real, did you?" Anthony flushes and I laugh. "It's okay. I know I sounded like a loon all year. I probably wouldn't have believed me either."

"We've still got a lot of therapy to get through with you, Josephine," he tells me sternly. "You're by no means healthy yet."

"Well don't bowl me over with the vote of confidence," I mutter, giving him a shove. This seems to confuse him, and I wonder, not for the first time, what he was like before he was cured.

"Okay folks," Luke announces, climbing out and locking the car. "We'll spend the night here."

"Why?" I ask worriedly. "We're still so close to the asylum, and tomorrow I'll be starting to change …"

"I know, baby. I'm hoping that by then this will all be over. But if not, I have a contingency plan, and we need the asylum nearby. Come with me and I'll show you what I mean."

Anthony and I follow Luke past the reception desk and up a few flights of stairs. He uses a funny little secret knock before he enters one of the rooms. I enter curiously and am instantly stunned. The dingy motel room has been transformed into some kind of science lab. There are technical-looking instruments everywhere, and boiling liquids in bizarre colors on every surface. There's barely enough room to stand, and in among it all is an old man tinkering away with something under a microscope.

He looks up as we enter. "Did you get her?"

"Josephine Luquet, this is Ben Collingsworth," Luke introduces us. I stare at the man, who is underwhelming, to say the least. He's aged a lot since he retired a few years ago and they stopped splashing his photos everywhere. He looks a lot smaller, a lot frailer. This is the man who ruined my life. A man I don't remember one bit.

We stare at each other, and I'm surprised to realize that I'm not angry. Not as much as I expected to be, anyway. He's too pathetic looking to elicit anything from me other than a bit of pity and maybe some disdain.

"Hello, dear," he says. "You've certainly grown up a lot since I last saw you."

"As I am to understand it, that was over ten years ago," I point out.

Ben nods slowly, looking tired.

"Why did you do it?" I ask.

"To try and help you." He goes on a bit more, talking about adrenalin and brains and anger, about a drug that was supposed to help instead of destroy, and it all makes sense, but I'm not so quick to believe his motivations were entirely pure.

I search his weathered face. "Did you diagnose me with rage?"

"No, that wasn't my job. Your parents informed me of your condition."

"My parents?" I give a cold laugh and lift up my gross hospital shirt. There on my hip are the deep scars gouged into my skin, Lachlan's brand. "The parents who let a cruel little boy do this? The parents who punished me for it?" I shake my head, letting the shirt drop. "You probably should have checked your facts before you rushed in to dose a child up with mind-altering psychostimulants."

All three men are staring at me. Ben and Anthony look horrified, but Luke wears an odd expression, almost like he's proud of me. I keep looking at him until the memory of Lachlan is well and truly out of my head, and when my face clears Luke gives me a small nod.

"I don't know how to apologize," Ben tells me.

"You just say the words."

He hesitates, takes a breath and then says simply, "I'm sorry, Josephine. You are the greatest regret of my life."

And it's such a sudden relief to be given an apology, to be given an answer to the question that has plagued most of my life—for someone to simply take *responsibility* for this mess—that I find myself nodding. "Okay."

Ben seems so startled by my reaction that his eyes fill with tears. He quickly wipes them away and ducks his head back to his work.

"Any progress?" Luke asks. He flings himself onto the bed, which is only partially covered in scientific chaos. I climb over a bunch of instruments on the floor to join him on the mattress. Anthony stays standing right near the door, as though he's going to make a run for it at any moment.

"I need some samples of Josephine's blood before I can give you any answers," Ben says. "Who is that small man by the door?"

Luke tries to cover a laugh, like the childish idiot he is. Anthony blushes.

"This is Doctor Harwood," I offer. "My therapist at the institute."

"Anthony," the Doc says, trying to offer a hand to Ben, but the old man doesn't even look at him.

"Well then Doctor Harwood, can you be trusted to take some of Josephine's blood?"

Anthony nods, looking around for the right equipment. Once he has the tools, he sits on the edge of the bed and rolls up my sleeve. With capable, slender hands, he taps my skin until he finds a vein, and then inserts the needle. Even this tiny prick is enough to make my teeth clench in pain. My skin is so sensitive at the moment that a mere touch makes it ache. The needle feels like a knife.

"Careful!" Luke snaps.

"I am!" Anthony replies indignantly.

"It's not you," I tell Anthony. "It's me. My skin."

Ben takes the vials of blood and smears a few drops onto a clear slide, which he then slots into the microscope. "Would you like to see what's happening to your blood, dear?" he asks me.

I climb over to him and peer into the eyepiece. There are lots of little shapes. They're moving and dividing as I watch. "Should they be changing like that?"

"No. They're mutating as we speak. That's why you're in so much pain. This is a drop of my blood—can you see the difference?"

Ben's blood looks well-behaved compared to mine.

"I'm going to test out a few different things," he mutters distractedly. "It will take me all night, so you three can please yourselves until morning."

"Let us know if you need anything else," Luke reminds him, picking his way through the mess. Once the three of us are outside the locked door, Luke looks at Anthony.

"Up to this point, you could say that I forced you to drive us away. They'd believe you, Doc. But if you stay with us any longer it's going to be hard to avoid getting implicated."

"You should go home," I tell him gently. "You've risked yourself enough."

Anthony meets my eyes. I can't read his expression because it's slightly off. He says, "I'm staying. I won't leave until I know you're safe. And you're going to need as much help as you can get."

I smile, reaching out to squeeze his hand. "You know what, Doc? You do have a bit of passion in that heart of yours."

Anthony smiles too.

"You'll need a room then," Luke tells him. "Don't use your prints to pay for it." He pulls out a big wad of cash from his back pocket.

"I can't pay with cash!" the doc protests. "It's illegal."

"In a place like this they won't mind, especially since you'll be paying three times the rate of the room. Off you go."

Anthony takes the money and plods down the stairs.

"And don't use your real name!" Luke calls after him softly. He then shows me into the room beside Ben's, which is empty except for a backpack I recognize as Luke's.

"You shouldn't patronize him so much," I admonish softly.

"He's a dick."

"He's not! He's just a bit of a ... drone. *You* should be sympathetic to him, being the same and all."

"Well excuse me if I don't buddy up to the guy who ignored you all year."

"It's not his fault my story sounded so stupid."

Luke shrugs, riffling through his backpack. He pulls out my favorite old pair of jeans and one of his T-shirts. "Thought you might like to get changed out of that revolting hospital gear," he says as he offers me the clothes.

"You don't think I look sexy in this?" I ask, tugging on the poo-brown, oversized sack I'm wearing.

"Baby," Luke grins, "You would look sexy in just about anything."

"Except this?"

"Except that," he concedes with a laugh. I smile as I head for the small bathroom. Once I'm alone I turn on the shower and get undressed. I haven't looked in a mirror for a year and I brace myself. My eyes jerk in shock—it's worse than I thought it would be. The sight of my body is deeply alarming—I am covered in black and blue bruises, plus I'm so skinny I can see my ribs and spine jutting out against my skin. My cheekbones are sharp and angular, and my eyes are surrounded by deep, bruised hollows. My hair is greasy and lank and my gums are bleeding. Jesus, I look *awful*. I can't believe Luke has just seen me like this, when he hasn't seen me in a year.

I am humiliated as I step into the shower. I want to close my eyes and stay in here forever. I'm not embarrassed about looking ugly—I can deal with that—it's simply that I appear weak and alien.

My fingers tremble as I try to feel my limbs for any sense of myself. I don't look like me, and I don't feel like me. So what the hell am I? I lean against the wall and slide to the ground, turning my face up to the water. There are billions of people out there who don't feel much of anything, and sometimes it seems like all of their lost emotions have been crammed into my chest and are crowding me out. I wish the water from this showerhead could wash them all away and leave me with a clean slate.

Did I just wish to be a drone?

The bathroom door opens. Quickly I pull my knees to my chest and try to cover myself. The thought of him seeing me like this is too much to bear.

"Luke, don't," I try.

He ignores me, walking to the shower door and sliding it open. I drop my head to my knees in shame. But Luke climbs into the shower and sinks down beside me, pulling me into his arms.

"You're the most gorgeous thing I've seen all year," he says against my hair.

I shake my head, pressing it into his chest. "I'm disgusting. I'm disappearing."

"You're right here—I can feel you perfectly." His hands hold onto me tightly as if to make the point.

The parts of my skin that touch his feel the most like me, the real me, whoever that is. "Luke," I sigh. "You must be so sick of looking after me."

"Not at all. Do you know why?"

"Why?"

"Because you look after me." Luke pulls away and tilts my chin up so that I'm looking into his face. "I should have told you that last year. I should have told you how you've changed me. How you've made me into a better man. It's no burden adoring you, Josephine Luquet. It's a privilege."

There's water trickling down the bridge of his nose and I smile as it falls onto my lips.

Luke

After we've probably used up the entire supply of water for the whole hotel, I leave Josi to dry off and get dressed. There's a building sense of dread in my stomach. How much longer can I let this go on? This one destructive lie? I can't tell her before the change—that seems too cruel somehow. But if not now, then when? What if she doesn't make it through tonight?

I finish getting changed and lie down on the bed, staring at the ceiling. Josi has been in the bathroom for ages. I know she's horrified by how she looks, by how the drug is changing her. She's becoming something she can't identify with, and if I tell her the truth I'll take away the last piece of our lives together. When that is all a lie, all those memories, what will she have left?

The funny thing is, my feelings weren't a lie—not one single piece of them. I don't know how I'll convince her of that.

The last year has gone by too slowly and too quickly. I have been dreading September, which has brought it on with alarming speed, and I have been longing to see Josi, which made it seem as though time stopped. In the room beside us is a man who holds her life in his hands. I feel impotent and frustrated, knowing he's in there and there's nothing I can do to make him work faster. I can hear the steady tick of the world spinning to face the moon. I can feel time rushing away from me like a receding tide carrying Josephine with it. I can't think about the possibility that Ben will fail. Because if he does, I don't have any more ideas.

Josi finally emerges from the bathroom wearing my T-shirt over her undies. Her hair is wet and tangled, and she's frighteningly thin. But she's wearing an expression so strong that I know she can face anything, survive anything. It culminates in my chest and I know what I have to do.

I sit up and open my mouth to tell her the truth. But then she smiles, and all the words vanish. Josi crosses to the bed and climbs on top of me, lying flat along the length of my body. My hands unconsciously move to her back, making small circles, trying to ease some of the discomfort she's in. She weighs nothing at all—it feels like a gust of wind could brush her right off me.

There are words that I've never said, because I wanted to wait until there were no lies between us to say them. I wanted them to mean something to her. They build inside me now, desperately, but won't come. I'm blocked, like there's tar through my arteries. Fear pounds inside me, a sickening, poisonous thing, and it won't let me tell her.

Because if I tell her I love her, when everything gets taken away I'm afraid that not even that will remain.

SEPTEMBER 16TH, 2065

Luke

When the clock strikes midnight, I'm awake. I'm staring at my phone, watching the minutes tick by. Josi is thrashing in bed next to me, shivering and moaning and grinding her teeth. I can't do anything to stop it except try to soothe her. Ben delivered some painkillers a few hours ago, as he'd apparently been disturbed by the noise she was making. I don't think the pills have done much.

Whatever this virus in her system is, it's a fucking tornado.

Why would they make something so strong in the first place? So destructive? I fail to see how anyone could have thought that such a thing would help any part of a child.

"What time is it?" Josephine asks woozily.

"Five past twelve."

She sighs angrily and rolls over. I rub her back and wonder if I'll ever have the guts to tell her the truth.

*

We're both awake when the sun rises.

"My favorite day of the year," she mutters. Her tone actually makes me smile.

"Ben will come through for us."

"I don't care. I don't want to think about it." Josephine reaches for me, running her hands over my chest. It feels like a drug, her touch. I've been craving it every moment of the last year, craving it to the point where I thought it was going to drive me mad. I couldn't go to her in the asylum until we had a cure though, because it could have led the Bloods straight to her. "Luke."

"Mm?"

"Take your clothes off."

I look at her. "What? Josi, we can't—I'll hurt you."

"Then be gentle. I want to make love to my boyfriend," she says. What she doesn't say is: for the last time.

I don't know what to do. I want her, and I want to give her what she wants, but it feels like the worst kind of lie. She will *hate* me when she finds out.

"I can't," I mutter.

Her hand drops away. "Because I'm ... because of how I look? I know I'm hideous at the moment—"

"No!" I exclaim. "Jesus, no. That's not it at all."

"Then tell me why."

I search for words, any words, but they fail me. I stare at her helplessly. She reaches for my face, running her fingers along my lips. "I want to be with you," she says, and I realize I don't have any more fight left—not for this.

"I want to be with you too," I tell her, and then I kiss her. Gently, very gently, I undress her, running my hands over her damaged body. I lean down to kiss her hip, where the scars are. Then I kiss every inch of her, remembering our first time with an aching vividness, hoping that one day she will remember these kisses and these touches, and not all of the lies.

*

Josephine has just disappeared into the bathroom when there's a knock on the front door. I pull my jeans back on and peer through the peephole, spotting Anthony.

Sighing with irritation, I step outside and close the door behind me. "You okay, man?"

"Fine. Have you told her the truth yet?"

I eye him up and down. Anthony is fairly average looking, a bit on the small side. He has neat brown and silver hair and a starched shirt collar. And he has a weird, squirmy quality to him. I realize he must be quite worked up, the way he's wringing his hands in agitation.

"It's not really your business, Doc," I tell him.

"Of course it is—I obviously care more about her wellbeing than you do."

"My whole life is caring about Josephine's wellbeing, so don't you dare tell me you have a clue what that even means." I step forward, bristling with everything pent up inside me. I'm growing weary of holding it in, squashing it down. I'm growing sore with the weight of it, the betrayal of it. It's what I fight for, what I live for, and yet it gets given no voice.

"You're infatuated with her," I say. "But you don't understand the difficulty and the beauty of loving someone so broken."

Anthony takes a step back, brushing against the balcony railing. He says, "You talk like you know the meaning of everything. You're arrogant."

I close the door in his face, but I hear him say, "If you don't tell her I will."

My heart pounds with sudden, unavoidable loss.

Josephine

I'm in the bathroom when he says it.

"I have to tell you a story."

"Okay, baby, can you just wait a minute?"

"No, now." His voice sounds weird. He starts talking before I've even come out. "I grew up over near your apartment. We didn't have any money, and sometimes we didn't eat. I hated how poor we were, because I thought it was something to be ashamed of. When I was fifteen my parents made me take a whole bunch of aptitude tests and then they sent the results to the national agency. The results then got sent to the Bloods, who decided they wanted to recruit me."

My fingers are on the door handle, but I don't open it. I stand still, listening.

"There is a part of this whole story that Anthony didn't explain to you. Several years ago, when Ben's team started realizing the effects of Zemetaphine, they took most of the test children into custody. They were teenagers by then. But they couldn't find you because you'd run away from your foster home and disappeared. The Bloods tracked you down eventually—they followed the trail of your crimes as they got steadily worse. They watched you and hid your condition from the world. I think they wanted to see what you could do before they decided how to act."

He pauses, and I'm not moving at all, not even breathing. It's something about the tone of his voice. It's almost ... dead.

Then he says, softly, "As your crimes got worse, they sent me in to monitor you. I'm classified as a Gray—I'm one of three in the world—so they assumed I'd be able to clean up whatever messes were made. That first year, I watched you for four months before I saw you kill three other Bloods on the night of the blood moon. I covered it up. I didn't tell my commander, but last year I was given the order anyway. To bring you in. To be killed or cured. That was the day before the canyon. After you changed that year, I reported you as dead and, as you know, I took you to the asylum. Then I spent the year in hiding, working with Harley and Ben to come up with a treatment."

He pauses.

I feel cold with shock. I can't move or speak. There are no thoughts in my head.

"There are two more things you don't know. The first is that Louise—the woman you spoke with on the phone—isn't my boss, she's my ex-girlfriend. She can't accept the fact that we aren't together anymore because she's confused by the fact that the deed to her house is in both our names, so she calls and calls. And the second thing you've probably figured out by now. It's that ..." Luke clears his throat. I've never imagined he could sound like this, so unbelievably detached, even calm as he's always been. I haven't figured it out—whatever he's talking about. I haven't figured anything out, but I brace myself because there is something in the air that's telling me that this will be bad.

"I've never been cured," Luke says.

It takes me a moment of complete incomprehension before the words make sense. Then it's an explosion. An attack so savage I feel instantly ruined by it.

"I feel angry all the time," he mutters. "I feel like I'm made of fury and sometimes there's nothing else left. I hate what's been done to you, and I hate the people I worked for, but mostly I hate myself."

He's listing things like he's ticking them off. He's listing lies without any emotion.

I lean over the toilet and vomit. It hurts so badly I think for a second that pieces of my insides have come up and out of my mouth. I stand and wipe my face, looking into the mirror. The man behind that door is a stranger. He made love to me twenty minutes ago, but I have no idea who he is. Anthony's questions make sense now. He figured out that Luke was lying to me without even meeting him. It was that obvious. Memories are flashing before my eyes, all the time we spent living together, sharing things with each other, all the time we spent trying to solve a problem that Luke knew the answer to from the start. Those memories are all false. My head is full of moments I have imagined. Anthony was right all along—I've made the whole thing up. I am a crazy person.

The humiliation is like broken bones. The betrayal is worse.

Luke says my name and I hate him. *I hate him.*

Taking a deep breath, I open the door and walk past him. I don't look at him or listen to him as I pull on my jeans and my ugly hospital shirt—I will not wear anything that belongs to him. He's speaking in a desperate voice, on and on and on, but I don't hear any of the words. I'm blinded by rage and loss and hurt.

I clear my throat. "Of all the deception, the worst is that you could pretend to be cured. All this time, you let me think I was *alone.*"

I take one look at his face, but find that I can't stand it so I run out of the motel room and down the stairs. Luke is following me but it doesn't matter. I get in the car and smile humourlessly at the fact that he reprogrammed it last night to accept any fingerprints. He tries to climb in with me but I lock the doors from the inside. The engine roars to life and then I'm driving, and I don't look back, not once.

Turns out I was wrong after all.

Love and fury can't live in the same place.

Chapter Seventeen

JANUARY 3RD, 2064

Josephine

"Amorous," Luke says.

"That's not a feeling—it's an adjective."

"I know, smartass. I'm veering from the game for a moment. Indulge me."

I watch him closely. We're sitting cross-legged on the floor, facing each other. He dragged the coffee table out of the way so that there's nothing between us except a stack of cards, a bag of chocolates and a big bottle of tequila. Luke's long legs don't cross very well, so he has them thrown out all over the place where they take up an obnoxious amount of space. He's smoking, which I hate, but he's also talking, which I don't hate. We've been together for a few months now, and I've come to understand that Luke talking about himself is an extremely rare occurrence.

"Do amorous," he presses.

"For me? Never."

"Bullshit. Even as a kid? There must have been some time when you were desperately in love with something."

I shake my head. When I was a child I learned how fragile the world is. "Your go."

Luke muses for a moment, getting this distant look on his face. "My mom used to tell me to fall in love with as many things as possible."

This seems like a perfect mom thing to say. "So did you?"

"No. I thought she was fickle. Now I think she was something else entirely."

"She sounds good, your mom."

"She is good."

"So when?" I ask. "When were you most amorous?"

Luke shakes his head. "Nope. You didn't answer, so I'm not going to."

I smile. "Fine then. Have a drink, pal." As he takes a swig, I think of my next word and eventually come up with "Obstinate."

He runs his tongue over his teeth; I'm fascinated by the act. Watching it seems absurdly intimate and I'm quite sure I'm blushing, which is completely weird. Since our brain-aneurism-inducing, impossible-to-ignore kiss by the river, Luke has been super careful around me. Christmas Day was somewhat of a break from all his rigid rules about which bedrooms we sleep in and how much physical contact we have, but after that day he went straight back to being awkward. We're a couple and we live together, and we're great ninety percent of the time, but when it comes to the physical stuff, it's becoming more and more difficult to ignore the fact that there is something building between us. And I don't understand it because I've never experienced anything remotely like it.

I've started to feel nervous and shivery all the damn time. I want kisses and touches and the smell of cinnamon and aftershave and boy sweat. I'm not sure what I want beyond that, but I know it's there, and it's getting harder to ignore. I'm terrified of what's looming, not sure if I'd prefer to keep it at bay forever or just get it over with.

"When Dave tried to make me protest with him," Luke says. "I wouldn't go, and nothing he said would make me even consider it. Now I'd give almost anything in my life to go back to those days and tell him yes. I'd say yes to everything he ever asked me." He takes another drink of tequila then passes it to me.

I feel that a confession like that deserves some discussion, or even just an acknowledgment, but that's not the game. The game is that we never comment on what we divulge, embarrassing as it may be. I lift up my shirt and point briefly to Lachlan. Luke hasn't seen my foster brother's name before—or if he has, he's pretended otherwise. He blinks and stretches forward to clock the ugly red brand. "When I was given this," I tell him.

"How old were you?"

He's not supposed to ask questions, so I don't answer. I have a swig of the revolting alcohol instead.

"What were you obstinate about?" he presses.

I was obstinate about not crying, but I discover I don't want to talk about it anymore, so I pass him the bottle. "Your turn."

"Fine. Curious."

"That first morning you took me out for breakfast."

"When I accidentally bumped into you naked."

I throw a cushion at him to disguise my flaming cheeks. Luke catches it in the face and laughs.

"Embarrassed," I say.

He thinks for a bit and then grins. "I took a piss in the middle of class once."

"*What?*"

"I was in my first year of school," he laughs. "Stuck my hand up to go to the bathroom, trotted off to the toilet block but got cornered by some boys from another class who were mucking around with a ball. I got distracted, played with them for a bit, forgot to wee, went back to class and sat down. It was a good thirty seconds before I remembered that I was busting. The teacher wouldn't let me go again, so I sat there in my seat and pissed."

I stare at him. "Oh my god. That's, like ... too funny to even laugh." But even so, we do laugh, and we laugh a lot. My cheeks are sore by the time we calm down and it's my turn to answer. Sighing, I admit, "When you walked in on me in the bathroom."

"What? That was the most embarrassed you've *ever* been? Bullshit. I barely saw you."

"Well."

"Trust me—you've got *nothing* to be embarrassed about," he assures me, letting his eyes travel over my body. I feel like a heater has just been turned on full blast.

"You can't look at me like that if you won't ... *you know*," I say.

He meets my eyes, looking pained. "We can't do it if you can't even say it."

"I can say it!" I protest.

"Go ahead then."

I swallow, feeling incredibly embarrassed.

"You're not ready, sweetheart," he says gently.

"Then when?" I demand.

"When you can tell me what you want me to do to you without getting embarrassed."

Oh good god. My cheeks flame at the idea of speaking such things aloud. Luke laughs at my expression. "Shall we get back to the game?"

I nod, grateful to change the subject.

"Frightened," he suggests after a thought, and even though he sounds casual, I'm fairly sure he's been saving this one up.

"When I woke up after my first change. I was in the middle of a deserted car park. Every inch of my skin was scraped raw from the concrete ground, and I had no idea where I was, what had happened or how to get home. There was blood under my fingernails. I was frightened because I *knew* I'd done something bad."

He sighs, flopping over onto his stomach. "When you told me you'd kill yourself."

I swallow; don't reply. My last one is "Inspired." I know what my answer will be.

"I don't know," Luke replies.

"Come on—"

"No, really," he interrupts, and he sounds weird. "I honestly don't know."

I watch his face, his bright eyes, and I think this is sad, so I give him mine. Instead of telling him, I play for him, the first piece of cello music I ever heard—*The Swan*.

These are our mosts.

We give them to each other, speaking them aloud, playing this game, because we never want to forget them. These are what make us human.

APRIL 11TH, 2064

Luke

We're walking down the frozen foods section of a small grocery store. It's outrageously overpriced, because it only stocks items you can't order in an average meal package.

Josephine is distracted, but I'm enjoying myself immensely, reading all the labels and getting excited over things I've only ever heard of before. We had to drive two hours to find this place (I had to trick Josi into agreeing) but it's worth it.

"Lost," she says suddenly, and I'm not in the rare food store anymore. It doesn't even exist. This is a bad turn, and I didn't even realize it was sneaking up on us. She gets like this sometimes, drowned in severe depression. I can't do much about it except make sure I'm here while she rides it out.

"When Dave was gone," I offer, because in these spells all she cares about is truth. It's what I'm most afraid of. She reaches for my hand. We keep walking. I don't make her tell me what hers is. "Hopeful," I say.

"I don't even know what that means."

Jesus, this is a bad one. How the fuck did I let us get all the way to this stupid food shop without even realizing? "Mine is when I listen to you play," I tell her with a smile. "I always imagine the weirdest things. Almost like dreams, but more embarrassing."

"Embarrassing?"

"Yesterday when you played I imagined that we lived on a houseboat, way out at sea."

She smiles. "That sounds nice."

"We weren't alone though."

Her eyebrow arches quizzically.

"We had three children and they were beautiful."

Josephine meets my eyes. We stop walking and stand in the middle of the frozen section, with people moving around us like the ebb and flow of the ocean I just spoke of. In this game I always try to tell the truth, and here is one, one truth that comes from the core of me. I don't know if it will be enough to outweigh all the lies, given how many there are. I'm suffocating under them.

At last Josi says again, "That sounds nice," and I can see in her eyes that she means it, *really* means it, and it is no small thing—it is a miracle. It is everything.

These are our mosts.

We do this because maybe one day they will all be gone.

SEPTEMBER 17TH, 2064

Josephine

There's a blanket around me and it is itchy in the most unforgivable way. I sit in the front seat of Luke's car and burst into tears because my blanket is itchy.

"Don't, *please*," he whispers, his voice so broken and haggard I'm surprised he got any sound out at all.

Last night I was a monster and this morning I was alone in a canyon gouged out of the earth. But then he appeared, lowering himself out of the sky along the length of hose that once belonged to the men I killed. During the night he must have found a way to make it longer, because it reached to the bottom now. He was carrying this blanket and he wrapped it around me, and then he put me over his shoulder and climbed all the way back up the hose. It took him hours, but he did it.

There was no trace of any death or violence above. I don't know how he got rid of it all, but something about the absence of it was familiar.

Now we are sitting in his car and I'm crying. I never cry.

"Angry," I say.

"I don't want to play. Not now."

"Tell me! Tell me the moment in your life when you were angriest, Luke Townsend, or all of this is just ... it's just a handful of dead men."

He's not calm exactly, not like he always is, but he is certainly contained, and I can't for the life of me work out how he could be such a thing after a night such as that. "The day before my cure," he says carelessly. I don't believe him, but I don't know why. I turn my eyes to the window. I am a monster, but for a moment he is unforgivable. Luke reaches out and puts his hand in my hair. It hurts my aching head, but it makes sense to me, having him touch me.

"Happy," he says softly.

I don't reply, because I can't remember if such a thing truly exists, or if someone just made up the word to taunt me.

Chapter Eighteen

SEPTEMBER 16TH, 2065

Anthony

The door to my room bursts open as I'm brushing my teeth for the third time.

"Does your car have a tracking device you can access?" Luke asks breathlessly.

I spit out the toothpaste and shake my head. "Not from here. Why?"

"Fuck!" he roars, disappearing like a hurricane of force.

I'm torn between brushing my teeth again and following him. After a moment I remember what an idiot I am and race after Luke. He's in the process of breaking into someone's car, a big four-wheel drive. His fingerprints allow him access to just about anything, so he doesn't have much trouble, it just takes him a few extra minutes to override the tracking devices in the vehicle so we can't be found via satellite.

"What are you doing?"

He grunts. I'm not sure if this is his form of communication, or if he just wants me to shut up.

"Luke," I say in what is hopefully a firm tone.

"She split, okay?" he snarls. "I fucking *knew* now wasn't the time to tell her, but you forced me, and now she's run off to god knows where to get caught by the Bloods, only a few hours before she turns into a maniac. Are you happy, Doc?"

I blanch, panic striking me. No wonder Luke is so out of control—he's not even bothering to hide his anger. "I'm coming," I announce.

"You're a moron," he mutters, but he doesn't lock the door, so I hop in and pretty soon we're zooming nightmarishly fast down the empty highway.

The silence is starting to suffocate me so I remind him, "None of this would have happened if you hadn't lied to her in the first place."

"Would you like to get shoved out of a moving car?"

I close my mouth. Bare, empty fields flash past the window, dotted with tall, dying trees. It's depressing, seeing the way the land is now. My hand is drumming nervously against my thigh, which is bouncing repeatedly. Luke is utterly still, every inch of him tight like a stretched rubber band. His knuckles around the steering wheel are white.

"What did you say to her?" I ask. "It might help to talk."

Luke flashes me a smile, but it's more like a grimace. "You think I need a *shrink* right now?"

I shrug. "Maybe just ... someone to talk to."

He rolls his eyes, and it's every bit as awful as when Josephine does it. These two are made for each other. We're quiet for a long time, and then Luke finally mutters, as if he's been tortured into it, "I told her the truth. Told her the story I kept from her all this time."

"Did you tell her how you feel?"

"No, I told her the facts, Doc. For once I told her the bare facts."

"So she drove off thinking you'd lied to her about liking her?" I ask slowly.

"I don't *like* her," Luke snaps. "She's been my girlfriend for two years, Anthony. I fucking love her."

"Then why didn't you tell her that?"

"I didn't have to—she knows how I feel."

"You're an even bigger moron than I am."

Luke clenches his jaw angrily. "What about you then? Did you ever tell her?"

"Tell her what?"

"That you love her."

"That's nonsense!" I splutter. "Completely absurd. She's my patient."

"Right," he sighs. "Whatever. You better just hope we find her before she starts to change."

We do. We do find her.

My car is wrapped around a tree, metal and bark entwined as though it came out of the ground that way, perfectly seamless and indistinguishable. My heart jerks to a stop and my head is empty of all thoughts. It is Luke who presses the car forward and then spins it off the road, flinging himself out almost before it's stopped. I follow at a dazed stumble, moving around toward the front to where I know she will be, my heart in an agony of terror at the thought of what I will see.

First is a hand. It looks tiny, hanging out of the car like that. Limp but unblemished. As I force myself to keep moving, she comes into view. It reminds me of a puppet show, a marionette with its strings cut, the way she is lying there with her head through a smashed windscreen. Glittering pieces of glass wreath her hair and there is a forest of green leaves inside the car.

The bonnet is smoking, and when it catches alight the whole tree will go up, and with it the car. I stare at the sight, oddly stunned by how beautiful all the shapes and colors are. With the green and the crystal, there is also the blue of my car and the bright, brilliant red of Josephine, trickling onto everything. If it caught alight there would be orange, too, and that would be amazing. I wish I had a camera—people would like to see this.

"Anthony!" Luke says, breaking into my thoughts. He moves to grip my shoulders. "Your brain's tripping out—it's not your fault and I know it's hard to control—but you gotta focus. I need you, man."

"It's so beautiful," I say, confused.

"No," Luke says firmly, looking fiercely into my eyes. "It's not. This is very bad. I need you to help me get her out of the car. Do you understand?"

I nod reluctantly.

"There's a tree branch pinning her in. I'll try and lift it, and when I do I need you to pull her out. Okay?"

Again I nod, moving to Josephine. I'm excited now, my heart picking up speed. I can do this. I can do what Luke needs.

He climbs onto the bonnet, careful about where he places his feet. I can see the branch he's talking about now—it's enormous. He has to wedge his shoulder underneath to have any hope of lifting it. I get ready to pull Josi out, holding her around the waist. She feels hot and feverish in my hands. I imagine what's making her so warm—there's a hissing fire within her body, flickering and licking at her. Luke grunts and heaves, and as he gets the mighty log into the air he gives a scream of exertion and I slide Josi out. At least I try to—something's keeping her in place. I peer over her shoulder to see that her foot is caught under something. The inside of the car has been so badly mangled that there are bits of the engine on top of her leg.

"Is she out?" Luke yells.

I burst out laughing. "She's caught!" I giggle.

Luke swears furiously and lowers the branch back down, trying to move it so it's not on top of Josi anymore. "Anthony, snap out of it! Can you get her free?"

"Maybe," I shrug, poking my head over her shoulder to get a look.

"Focus!" Luke orders.

I swallow and try to focus. My head feels so slippery, and I'm suddenly not sure what I found funny. Okay, if I reach over and try to twist her ankle around, I might be able to slide it under this massive piece of metal … "I got it!" I shout. "But I need a knife or something! Her seatbelt's jammed!"

"I can't put this branch down, man, or it'll crush her now that she's in a different spot," Luke tells me. He's amazingly calm, given he's holding up what has to be a couple of hundred pounds worth of wood and his girlfriend is about to burn alive. *If* she's still alive.

It hits me suddenly. Josi might be dead. This is her body in my arms. I drop her just in time to lean over and vomit onto the ground. The violence all around makes me tremble in fear and shock—I can't get any air, and my stomach is heaving so painfully my head's spinning.

"Come on, Anthony," Luke's deep voice floats down to me. "It's okay. We're going to do this. Just come around behind me and grab the pocketknife off my belt, okay? You can do this. Just take the knife and then we'll go from there."

I stumble around to the other side of the car and reach up to Luke's belt. My hands tremble so much I can't get the clasp off.

"Easy," Luke breathes to me, and his voice is so amazingly gentle that I feel myself calm right down. My hand steadies and I get the knife unhooked.

"Good man. Now go around and cut the seatbelt. Don't think about anything else."

I focus on the task, not the situation, and do as I'm told. It takes a while to saw the small knife through the thick seatbelt, but once I've done it, Josi slumps back onto my chest.

"Support her head!" Luke says quickly, and with the words my own medical training kicks in. I slowly slide her backwards out of the car, careful with her neck, looking for any superficial wounds or the type of bruising that indicates internal bleeding. Her ankle is badly swollen and she has an array of cuts over her face, plus a long gash along her hairline, but apart from that I can't see anything else. She needs a hospital, badly. She could have brain trauma or spinal trauma. I hear Luke dropping the massive branch heavily back onto the car—it caves in a new section of the bonnet and as it connects the whole thing lights up in flames. I gasp, looking for Luke, but I can't see him behind the wall of fire.

I don't know what to do. Josi is heavy on top of me, pinning me to the ground, and I don't want to move her too much in case it jerks her head, but I can't stay where I am either, because if the car blows up then we're both dead. I look for Luke again, but my eyes move instead to the flames. I was right—they are amazing. There's more color inside them than I ever imagined. I've never seen fire before—not in real life. It's always on television, but it never looks like this, dancing eerily across my vision. How could anyone call it dangerous?

"Anthony!" Luke shouts, appearing in front of my face. I jerk in fright. Luke leans down and lifts Josephine into his arms, making it look easy and simple and I'm reminded of how much stronger than me he is. I wonder how he got to be so strong, and this makes me wonder what his job entails, and this—

"Come *on*!" he yells. "Move it, Doc, or you'll fry!"

I launch to my feet and run after him just as the car explodes. A wall of heat pummels into my back, throwing me off my feet, and the noise is like something's burst inside my head. It takes me a moment to blink off the shock and crawl to where the stolen four-wheel drive is parked. Luke has Josi behind it, shielding her from the debris of the explosion, and when he sees me appear he sighs.

"I thought you were dead for a minute there, man."

"Not dead," I say, dazed.

"But not very alive, either," he mutters. "Get in the car, quick."

Luke settles Josephine in the back seat, placing his jacket under her head and strapping her in carefully. He drives for about ten minutes before he pulls the car back onto the side of the road.

"Anthony," he says calmly, "How are you feeling?"

I stare at him.

"Do you feel ... anything too strongly?"

Anything too strongly? I don't understand what he's asking me.

Luke swallows. "I can't drive, man. I ... I'm ... My hands won't stop shaking."

"I can drive," I tell him quickly. "I'm fine, Luke. I can drive."

I go around to the driver's seat, and Luke climbs into the back with Josephine, sliding her head onto his lap, and even though I'm concentrating on the road because there is precious cargo in this car—I can't help but look into the back seat every few minutes. And so I see what I missed yesterday. When he came into my office I hated him for his arrogance and the way he has hurt her. I hated him for his contempt, but now I see that he has none. Now I see what he has done, not *to* her, but *for* her. I see the look in his eyes, and the way that he touches her, and I understand what it was that was missing from my own marriage. I wonder if there is anyone in this entire world for whom I would give up my life like he has done for Josephine Luquet.

And then Luke Townsend looks up at me, and he says, "It's going to be all right, Doc. I promise I'll make it all right. For you and for Josephine." Even though I'm the prick who didn't do his job, who didn't believe her. He says it as though he really cares about me, as though it's his responsibility to fix the mess I've created for myself, and even though it's pretty damn obvious I'm in love with his girlfriend.

I even like that he called me Doc.

Looking into the back seat, I understand something. These two people are real and they are alive. But I am just a drone, who laughs when he sees a woman dying.

Luke

When I lifted my foot the earth was still. In the space of a step it has started to shake and I've lost my balance. She's lying in my arms and she looks like she's asleep, except that there's blood on her face and bruises all over her skin, and the sight of it hurts me more than anything. As I watch her face from above, there are tears on her skin, and too late I understand that they are not hers, because she never cries.

＊

Part of my brain is screaming and screaming and wanting to tear something down, but the other part is hyper aware of everything that's going on. I know that we have been driving for twenty-three minutes when we pull back into the motel, because I have counted every single second. I know that Anthony is doing well, because he's managed to hold it together for the whole drive, despite his mental meltdown at the crash site. I have called Ben and told him to be ready no matter what, and there he stands on the side of the road, arms full of equipment, when we pull over to pick him up.

The old scientist climbs into the front seat and turns around to gaze at Josi. "Is she ...?"

"She's not dead," I reply calmly. Always calm. I am constantly surprised at my own ability to remain calm, even when I feel like lighting a fire that could destroy the whole damn world.

"Car accident," Anthony says. "Where are we going, Luke? Hospital?"

"We're going back to the asylum."

"What? Why?"

"Because there's an emergency aid station there, and it's the only one close enough."

"What about the Bloods?"

"They're chasing us away from there—it'll take them a while to realise we've gone back."

"Yeah, but ..."

"Does the station have everything you'd need to treat Josi?"

"I don't know how badly she's hurt, Luke, I—"

"Her body will be repairing itself at the moment, so any damage done is less harmful than it would be for anyone else," Ben says.

"But ..." Anthony tries.

"We need a place that can be sealed down, with no access from the outside, to give Ben a bit more time to finish his cure for the cure," I say in a measured tone. I am patient and relaxed and I am not going to snap at any moment. I'm gripping the seat very tightly, and I am *not* going to snap.

"There's heavy security at the facility," Anthony warns.

"That's why the three of us are going to be armed," I reply.

"With what?"

I reach over to the backpack I stashed in the four-wheel drive this morning. Inside are two six-inch knives, a tear gas grenade and four guns. Two of the guns go straight into my shoulder holster, sitting snugly against my ribs. I slide the knives into my boots and pass the other two guns to the men in the front. They stare in disbelief at the weapons.

"What the hell is this?" Anthony asks.

"It's a semi-automatic weapon and you're going to use it to defend yourself."

"I don't know how!" he protests in a voice several octaves higher than usual.

"Aim and pull the trigger," I snap. One glance at his face tells me he's starting to panic, so I talk to him in a warm tone, knowing it will help relax him, regardless of what I'm saying. "A semi-automatic weapon doesn't need to be manually chambered for each round, but you have to pull the trigger every time you want to fire—fully automatic is when you just hold your finger down and go nuts, and a weapon like a rifle needs a round loaded every time you fire a shot. Pulling the trigger in this causes the hammer and firing pin to strike and fire the cartridge. A bolt then recoils to extract and load a new cartridge from the magazine, making it ready to fire again. Each magazine for these guns contains ten rounds, so once you've used them all you have to change the magazine by pushing this in ..." as I speak, I press the release button and catch the clip as it falls out. "Then you take the new one and you jam it up in there, nice and hard until you hear it click. Keep the safety on until you need to shoot it. And when you fire bring it up to your eye level and hold it with both hands. Take a deep breath before you pull the trigger 'cause it'll help your aim. It's a small enough weapon that it won't kick, so you should be right just by holding it firm."

I probably should have waited until he'd pulled over, because Anthony is perilously close to hitting another car, so intent on the gun is he. I remember perfectly the first time I held the cool steel in my hands and felt the weight of a weapon like this one. There's something seductive and addictive about it, and I've seen a lot of men and women overcome by the illusion of power in a gun. There's nothing glamorous about something that can kill with the flick of a finger though. To be honest I think it's lazy.

"What kind is this?" Anthony asks, glancing at the gun sitting on his lap.

"That's a Smith & Wesson police pistol—an old one. But don't worry, I keep it nice and clean so it won't blow your head off. Benny boy, you've got a Beretta 3032 Tomcat."

"What about you?"

"I'm a Glock man. This is an Austrian nine-millimeter semi-compact model, and the other one's a basic 17." I holster the two guns again and hand out the extra magazines. Slumping back in my seat, I look down at Josi again, smoothing her dark hair off her forehead. Her eyelids are flickering as if she's having a dream. The odds of it being a good one are slim, but I hope so for her sake anyway. She smells like she always does, and it hits me with a powerful wave of melancholy. I feel perverse and sleazy as I lean down to kiss her gently on the lips. It might be the last time I ever get to do it, even if by some miracle we all survive this day.

*

Anthony pulls into the hospital, which is now oddly quiet. "You two carry Josi between you and I'll cover you," I order. They help me get her out of the car.

"The back entrance will be quieter," Anthony says, so we follow him around to a deserted loading bay. He puts his fingers to the scanner to open the bay. "My prints have been blocked," he sighs.

I was expecting as much. My prints would undoubtedly get us in, but there's only one reason they've been left activated since my operative status was changed to 'rogue', and that's so I can be tracked. Cars and smaller scanners aren't connected into the Blood hub, but a facility like this may be. When I dropped Josi here last year I was sure it was one of the last non-government facilities in the country, but that doesn't mean it's entirely safe.

"What's your alarm system like here?"

"I don't know, it's never gone off," Anthony replies.

I remove my gun from its holster. Instead of aiming it at the lock on the door—a bullet will just ricochet straight off and probably land in my face—I move to the large steel roller door and shoot through the chain at the top of it. Now there's nothing to hold the pressure of the spring-loaded roller system down except the small metal locking device at the bottom. Grabbing one of the knives from my boot, I lie down on the ground to get a good enough angle, and then I set about jimmying the tiny screws loose. Once they're out, it's simple enough to remove the locking device and the door springs up to the roof with a loud screech of rusty metal. Clearly, this is not a facility that has much money.

"Wow," Anthony says. He's obviously not seen much in his life if something as simple as opening a door impresses him. Poor guy.

"The noise will have notified everyone in the whole damn place, so we better hurry."

Ben's having trouble supporting Josi, so I take her weight from him and give the old guy a quick pat on the back. "Thanks, man. I've got her now. Just stay behind me."

Anthony directs us through the asylum. I don't bother to inform him that I've studied a floor plan, and could probably make my way around quicker than he could. Instead I keep my eyes peeled on every doorway and every corner, waiting for the first glimpse that it's all about to fall apart. It will come, sooner or later. Someone will see us and sound an alarm, and then it won't be long before the Bloods are here. We just have to secure ourselves somewhere before that happens.

A young male nurse rounds a corner in front of us and stops dead. He clocks Anthony holding the prostrate form of Josi. I'm about two seconds away from knocking him out when he says, "Doctor Harwood?"

"Jamie," Anthony says quickly. "Good boy. I have a patient who collapsed outside. Could you run and get a gurney for her?"

Jamie nods, about to dash off when he spots the gun in my hand. He stops, mouth falling open. "What's that? I mean, why—"

I sigh. "Take her weight," I order Anthony, then I step forward and knock Jamie's head against the wall. It's barely more than a light tap, but it's in the right spot, so he dozes off pretty quick.

"Luke!" Anthony protests.

"I know," I agree. "A gurney would have been great."

Another few feet along the hallway three men in lab coats emerge from a room. They spot us.

"What the—Anthony, why are you …?"

"Call security," one of them orders coldly. "Harwood's under Blood watch."

Shit. I was hoping they'd yet to work out Anthony's involvement. "Run," I say crisply. As Ben hobbles past with his satchel and poor Anthony hauls Josi on his own, I take a few moments to bundle the three doctors back into the room they'd come from, locking it behind them. Their protests are dull and not particularly forceful—they just toddle into the room and start talking about a golf game. Damn drones.

Security starts streaming toward us, guns raised.

There's a secret few people know: certain security guards and police officers are given a slightly altered version of the cure. It allows them to act without quite as many of the irrational mood swings and sharpens their brains to react with more savagery. It's not anger—it's a survival instinct, the same part of the brain that we Bloods are trained to switch on and off whenever we need to. The amygdala gives only a fight response, with no option for flight.

All of this has never really concerned me much before—I couldn't give a shit who has what weird alterations in their heads. But right now I understand the danger: these men will keep fighting me until they die, not because they care, but because their nut-job brains are flooding them with bravado. I suppose it must be a bit like being on cocaine.

"Left!" I tell Ben and Anthony and they veer down a corridor away from the security guards. It won't take long before the guards have flooded every hallway in this place. I pause at the corner and fire a few quick shots into the fray. I aim only for legs, shoulders and arms, taking down a couple of guards and deterring the rest for a few minutes.

Ben's having trouble breathing so I take his bag from him. The absurdity of doing this with an old asthmatic and a terrified, scrawny shrink instead of my usual team almost makes me laugh.

"Keep going, old man," I tell Ben gently. "You can do it."

"I'm not old, you little shit," he mutters, picking up the pace. I grin.

"You okay, Doc?"

Anthony nods, his face bright red. His footsteps grow more and more dogged with every breath. If I carry Josi I won't be able to shoot at the same time, so he's gonna have to tough it out.

"It's not much further," I reassure them, firing behind us a few times to deter the guards from sneaking around the corner.

We make it through a few more hallways and find ourselves faced with a flight of stairs.

"You've got to be kidding," Anthony gasps. "There's an elevator right there!"

"An elevator's too dangerous. They can just wait at the other end for us. I'll take her for the climb, but get your gun out and concentrate."

Anthony's legs are jelly when he passes Josi over to me. He looks like a newborn foal as he tries to climb the stairs, trembling gun waving wildly. Jesus, he's going to wind up shooting one of us by mistake.

Josephine is over my shoulder—unfortunately we don't have the luxury of looking after her head anymore—if she has a neck injury, then we're screwed and there's nothing I can do about it. With my other arm I support Ben up the stairs—I have a real fear that he's about to have a heart attack and drop dead.

The door to the stairwell opens a few floors below us and suddenly there are two guards racing up. "Doc, shoot them!" I order.

Anthony whimpers, but shoves the gun over the railing and starts firing erratically. There's no chance of him hitting them, but it at least gets them to dive out of the way. We move faster until the door just above us opens and two more men appear. I let go of Ben, draw my left gun and shoot the first man in the chest. He falls straight down on top of Anthony, who crumples under his weight. Swearing under my breath, I lower Josi to the ground, placing her awkwardly on the stairs, and then I launch myself up to where the second man is trying to whack the Doc with his baton.

Holstering my gun, I punch the baton out of the man's hand, then grab him by the neck and throw him over the railing. He hits the ground with an ugly sound. I hoist Anthony out of the tangle of the other dead man, setting him straight and pushing him up to the exit. Then I shoot the two men who are still following behind, taking a bullet through a fine layer of skin on my arm. Once they're dead, I help Ben over the bodies, then lift Josi back over my shoulder and emerge out of the nightmarish stairwell.

The room I've been aiming for is in sight at the end of the hallway. It's a hospital-style nurse's station, but what's great about it is that it works as a panic room. It can be locked off from the outside, with no access at all. Within this sealed-off area is an even smaller patient room with glass walls, and this can also be sealed in case a contamination were to arise. It was also probably designed like that because they have a bunch of psychotic, violent patients to deal with in this place. The security guards don't have a high enough clearance to open the panic room, but I do.

Anthony starts running toward the room.

"Wait, Doc—get behind me!" I call. Anthony ignores me, probably too freaked out to have even heard me. There's a hallway that leads off to the right just before the entrance to the room, and I'd be willing to bet my life that there are security guards waiting for us to rush into their line of sight.

"Anthony!" I boom, and the idiot finally jerks to a stop.

"What? This is it!"

Ben and I catch up to him and I push him against the wall, giving him a rough pat on the cheek. "You need to listen to me, or you'll get yourself killed. Watch." I wave a hand past the opening of the corridor. Within half a second, four guns fire. I jerk my hand back in time, but my heart's racing with dread.

"Fuck," I whisper. Those bullets missed by the breadth of a hair, and not many people have that kind of speed or aim.

"Security beat us."

"No," I mutter. "Those guns belong to Bloods."

"How do you know?"

"I can hear the difference."

"Oh Christ," Anthony wails, starting to panic. "We're dead. We take one step and we're dead."

"Calm down," Ben tells him wheezily. "No use yammering on like a bitch."

This shuts Anthony up immediately. I think I may love Ben Collingsworth.

I get the tear grenade off my belt, my mind working overtime to come up with a plan.

"His print won't work on the door, will it?" Ben clarifies, jutting his thumb toward Anthony.

"No, it'll have to be mine. I'll get across, open the door, then I'll distract the agents so you can carry Josi across."

"They'll just shoot you as soon as they see you!" Anthony hisses.

"I'll be fine."

I crack each of my knuckles, using the familiar movement to calm my heart to a more manageable level. My breathing slows and I can feel the adrenalin coursing through my limbs, making me stronger and faster. It's a good thing—I'll have to be *very* fast to survive this.

Unbelievably, Josephine takes this moment to start waking up. She sucks in a ragged breath and moans loudly, causing my heart to jerk in shock.

"Shit," I breathe. "Keep her still and quiet."

"How?" Anthony demands.

What is wrong with these two? Do I have to spell *every* tiny thing out? "Hold her firmly and cover her mouth if she starts to make too much noise," I say clearly. This is distasteful to the doc, but I don't have time for his stupidity.

I take a few steps back and get ready. If I can get across higher than they're expecting, I'll have a few extra moments while they readjust their trajectory. One last breath, and then I go for it. Launching myself into a sprint as fast I can, I wait until I'm one pace before the hallway and leap into a dive. I press myself as high into the air as I can and tuck my body into a tight ball. I can feel bullets whizzing through the air, but they're too low. The force of my jump sends me forward quickly, and as soon as I'm past the hall I pull myself down into a roll. A bullet has grazed my back, but it's shallow.

I unlock the door and then turn back to see that security guards are approaching from the stairwell we used. Anthony's firing at them repeatedly, and one of the bullets actually hits a guard in the head. This is *not* a good thing. Anthony sees what he's done and freezes in horror. All the color leaves his face and the gun drops from his limp hand. Ben's trying his best to shoot a few rounds, but his aim is even worse, since he looks like he has about a thousand cataracts on his eyes.

I throw my tear grenade into the Bloods and then scream for Anthony and Ben to run. Anthony manages to haul a woozy Josi to her feet, and together he and Ben support her across the opening. Shots are fired, but thankfully the smoke is so thick that none of them connect.

I have the door open and ready for them to bolt through, and at last the four of us are locked inside a somewhat secure room. I don't know how long it will take for the Bloods to break in, and I don't know how long it will take for Ben to finish his antidote.

I also have no idea how long it will be until Josi changes. But the reality hits as the raging guns go quiet and everything within this room falls still.

We're locked inside a room with a ticking time bomb.

She is worse than everything we just escaped.

Chapter Nineteen

SEPTEMBER 16TH, 2065

Anthony

In my head is another head. This second head keeps exploding. Over and over again, a mess of blood and brain and skull. I can't stop seeing it, I can't block it out, I can't take back the jerk of my finger that made this happen.

In the eerie silence of the sterilized lab room I know that I will never stop seeing the man's head exploding. Not until the day I die.

Josephine screams.

Josephine

There's a fire my whole body is on fire it's searing through my skin and my organs and it's cracking all of my bones I can't stand it not for one single moment more but I can't escape it either it's taken over everything and in my head there's no place to escape to there's only the memories all of them at once like a furious hurricane of death and violence and all the things I've spent my life blocking out—

Luke

The sound she makes is straight out of my hell. Somehow she's awake even though her body should be dead, and she's enduring a pain I can't even imagine. A night terror while she's conscious enough to understand it.

I run to her side, but she's thrashing around on the operating table like she's being tortured.

"You're the doctor—*do* something!" I roar at Anthony. He looks at me, still dazed from having killed someone. I wait for him to respond, breath held. If he loses it again like he did at the car wreck, I don't know if I'll have the patience to talk him out of it. I may have to punch him in the face.

Slowly he nods. "There's morphine in here somewhere—look for it while I place an IV in her arm."

Thank god. "What does it look like?"

"There's probably a supply cupboard or fridge. It'll be in a little jar labeled clearly."

Ben is already setting up his stuff at a work bench, so I run around like a lunatic looking for morphine. Once I've got it, Anthony injects it intravenously and then stands back. Watching Josi thrash around is the worst thing I've ever seen. At one point I try to hold her arms down, but she's so strong that she launches me off my feet and onto a steel surgical tray.

It takes about twenty minutes for the morphine to kick in. Anthony's given her an extremely high dose because according to Ben the temperature of her body will be burning it off much more quickly than normal. We'll have to keep her on a steady flow of the stuff because if I never hear her make these sounds again it will be too soon.

Josi's screams stop and she lies still, whimpering slightly. There are tears streaming down her face as I approach slowly. "Sweetheart," I whisper, reaching to touch her cheek very gently.

She swallows once and then opens her eyes. They're clouded with pain, but she's managing. "Luke," she rasps with a shredded voice.

The relief of hearing her say my name is so much that I slump down onto the edge of the bed. "Oh Christ, girl." There are tears in my eyes and I try to blink them away. I don't think I let myself acknowledge how terrified I was until this moment. I really thought she was never going to wake up again, or if she did it would be as a monster. There's air being injected straight into my lungs, like a shot of adrenalin.

"What happened?"

"You were in a car accident, but you're okay."

"It hurts." This seems to slip out before she can stop it, before she can jam her teeth together, pulling that cloak of cold invincibility around her. She's been wearing this cloak every day that I've known her. I've wished for the cloak to disappear so many times, but now I love it. It keeps her strong, strong like iron, strong enough to get through torture.

"I know, baby," I murmur brokenly. "We've given you morphine and we'll keep it coming. Just try to relax." Try to relax? There's a virus moving through her body, determined to steadily destroy her from the inside out, and I'm telling her to relax.

"Where are we?"

"In the asylum with Anthony and Ben."

"Was anyone else in the car with me? Was anyone hurt?"

"No, sweetheart, everyone's fine. You were alone."

This seems to confuse her. "Why? Why would *I* drive anywhere? I don't even know how."

Oh fuck she doesn't remember. We'll have to go through the whole nightmare again. I feel sick, closing my eyes. The walls are closing in around me and I'm unsteady.

Josi makes a soft sighing sound and I see her nod wearily. "I remember."

We look at each other and I don't have a clue what to say.

"Stop touching me," she murmurs. "It hurts."

I swallow, moving my hands from where they rested over hers.

"Get off my bed and explain to me what's going on," Josi orders crisply.

I stand up, clearing my throat. "There are Bloods outside that door, and if they get in they'll kill the four of us. Ben is currently finishing his antidote, hopefully in time to stop you from changing. So we've got nothing to do but wait."

She thinks about this, not looking at me but over at Anthony. "And if by some miracle he does stop me from changing, what then? How do we escape the Bloods?"

I shake my head, feeling exhausted. "We'll figure that part out if we reach it."

Josi makes an impatient sound. "And you? Why are *you* here? Shouldn't you be out there with the rest of your kind?"

I open my mouth but realize I'd rather die than speak a single word aloud right now. I could try to explain, but at this point it feels like sullying the last shreds of pride we both hold. She doesn't deserve excuses or platitudes. I told myself that I would only speak the truth to Josephine from now on—the truth so she would never feel that I lied to her again.

So I turn and walk away, over to the other side of the room. I sit down next to Ben and inspect whatever the hell it is that he's doing. I don't look at Josephine, because if I do I might break down and bawl my eyes out, which would be mortifying. This is a mess I got myself into. I don't deserve tears or apologies or explanations—I deserve guilt, oceans of it.

Anthony sits in my spot by her side, and she doesn't tell him to stop touching her or go away or explain.

"You're still here," she says. It's slightly alarming that every word spoken in this room can be heard like it's hooked up to a microphone.

"Of course."

"You've risked your life to help me, Doc. How do you feel?"

"A bit … nervous, I suppose."

Josi laughs softly. "I'll bet. It's all going to be fine, I promise. Just tell them Luke forced you."

Great, thanks.

"I'm sure he'd love that." Anthony smiles.

"I don't give a shit what he'd love."

I must make some kind of noise, because Ben looks up and gives me a mundane task to do to distract me from eavesdropping.

"He's done a lot … to get us here," the doc says, and my ears prick up in interest. I definitely never thought Anthony Harwood would be the one to stand up for me.

"Like what?"

The shrink lowers his voice, unaware that I can still hear him perfectly. "Well he … Josephine, he saved you from dying at the crash site, and then he got all three of us into this room, at great risk to himself. Without Luke we'd all be dead."

"He's a Blood, isn't he?" she asks coldly. "He's supposed to be good at breaking into places and sneaking around."

I can feel her eyes boring into the back of my head and I feel like sinking into the floor. *Breaking into places and sneaking around.* Yep, that's pretty much it.

"Not just that," Anthony says, but I can't stand being trapped in here with Josephine and her words, and this other man who also loves her. I stride from the room into the outer section. From here I can see them, but I can't hear them unless

I press an audio button—which, despite wanting to escape her voice, I can't help but press. I find another button that turns the glass from clear to reflective. I love this button. It seems to support my complete self-loathing and desire to disappear. I can now see the three of them, but they can't see me. I'll always be a voyeur, it seems. Ben is looking at something through a microscope again—this is all he seems to do. His cheeks are still worryingly flushed, but he seems to be breathing okay. I have a clear view of the complete left side of Anthony, sitting with his shoulders hunched, speaking softly to Josephine. He can't be too much older than thirty, but his temples are graying slightly, and he's got a certain look of refinement about him. He's definitely made of money, and well educated.

It occurs to me that Josephine has spent an entire year with this man. That's as long as she and I were together, so I can't claim to know her any better than he does. I can't claim to care more about her.

I want to smash the glass window to pieces. How could this man know *my* Josephine? How could he love her more than I do? How could anyone?

He has not touched her like I have, kissed her like I have. He has not whispered to her in the dark or held her while she sleeps. He has never cooked for her, played with her, danced her around the top of a dining room table. He has never pushed her into a river or listened to her screaming nightmares. He has never made love to her and felt like the world could be exploding outside and he wouldn't care.

But, in all probability, he has never lied to her either.

Josephine

The morphine feels squishy in my veins. Everything is an aching dullness. It's so strange and disorienting that I almost want to go back to the agony. It seems absurd that the human brain can erase the memory of pain so we're completely unprepared every single time it hits.

Morphine takes its name from the Greek god of dreams, Morpheus. There's a Morpheus in an old 2D movie, too. I can recite the script, just as I can recite the script of any movie I've seen. I am delirious with all the trash stuffed into my brain. It is never ending, and it's confused all the important things. Like being unable to figure out that my boyfriend is a scumbag who doesn't, in fact, love me one little bit.

His hands on my body hurt. I don't know why he can't feel it. Doesn't he hurt too? Doesn't some part of him, some distant part, accept that something huge has dropped out of our lives, leaving a gaping chasm? Can't the part of him that has always been uncured see that there was an enormous love inside me? Can't he try to imagine how it must feel inside my chest right now? Who can take such a thing, *fake* such a thing?

I squeeze my eyes shut tighter, because these are the thoughts of the child I have never been. The child I never had the luxury of being. The truth of the world is that people lie, and they pretend, and they hurt. I know this. It is all I have ever known. Luke Townsend was given a job and he did it. He had to watch me, so he did. He had to learn me, so he talked to me. God only knows what else he had to do.

My foolish, treacherous heart can't help but wonder what's going on inside him now, as he sits there across the room from me. I can't help but imagine what he must think and feel, having undertaken a job of such magnitude, only to have it blow up in his face. I want to talk to him, ask him about it, about his thoughts and feelings, because this is what I did for a year and imagined doing for another one. He is so much a part of my life—my adult understanding of who I am—that at this moment I feel almost like I don't exist anymore.

How utterly pathetic.

Since when, in this broken, shattered life I've survived, have I relied on anyone other than myself?

I made him stop touching me. It's the only way. I'm a burning inferno of fury, and if he touches me I will destroy this whole room.

I don't even realize that Anthony is sitting with me now—my eyes have followed Luke to where he sits with the scientist. Anthony tells me that Luke saved my life and we'd all be dead without him.

The thing is, this doesn't surprise me. It doesn't surprise me that he is capable of something wonderful and brave and skilled—these are the reasons I loved him. I loved him because he could always do the things that seemed impossible; big, courageous things. I know now the reason for those abilities. None of these words can take me back to when I didn't know.

I wonder why my memory hasn't sliced out this piece. It seems to pick pieces that could hurt me and dispose of them, so why not this?

Luke gets up and walks into an adjoining room. I can still see him, sitting behind a glass wall. Moments later the wall turns to reflective mirror, and I can only see myself. It makes me crazy imagining him sitting there—I want him out of my head, out of my body, I want him *gone*. He is a jagged knife, hacking its way through my body, my organs, destroying the rest of me like my brain was destroyed many years ago.

"Would you like to talk?" Anthony asks me. I blink, looking at him. It's so silly that I smile. I reach out and take his hand. Drones don't lie. I'll give them that much. He and I haven't really touched before. It is strange, but also important. All of these touches—I think drones forget about how important they are.

"What do we have to talk about now?" I ask softly. "You're a party to my wacky story."

He smiles awkwardly. His blue eyes are open and honest as always, but he seems troubled by something.

"Would *you* like to talk, Anthony?" I ask. He doesn't answer, so I press, "What's wrong?" Focusing on him helps me to ignore the pain I'm in.

"I shot a man. Outside. I didn't really mean to. I was just aiming … and it hit him in the head. By mistake."

I stare at him. "I'm sorry," I whisper. "I didn't realize it got that bad outside …" I squeeze his hand because there are no words. I know very well that there are no words to fix this kind of mess.

"You're so strong," he says suddenly. "So resilient. I feel fragile all the time. Even before the cure."

"You're not fragile," I tell him. "You're here, and that's brave."

"All those drugs I made you take," he whispers, voice breaking. "And the electro-shock therapy … Jesus, I feel sick."

"It's okay," I tell him quickly. "I'm resilient, remember?"

"But everyone in your life has hurt you so badly …"

I look away, over at the mirror of glass. I wonder if Luke can hear us. I want him not to hear us. I want him to go away and never come back. I want him to come back into the room and climb into bed with me and tell me that none of it matters because he loves me and that not everything was a lie. How could he tell me the truth but not tell me how he feels about it? How could he say: I lied, but not also say: I regret it? How could he still be here, in this room with me, if he did not feel … *something*?

Lying here in this bed, I am faced with a simple, awful reality. I am about to die, one way or another, and I want the man I love to hold my hand and kiss me. That's all. Even if I could have anything in the entire world, all I want is Luke Townsend, even after his betrayal.

The only problem is that I'm not sure Luke Townsend—the Luke Townsend I know—exists. The Blood agent exists. The liar exists. I'm not sure what else is behind that glass because he doesn't seem to want to tell me.

Or perhaps he has told me and I was just too foolish to listen.

"You have a daughter, don't you?" I ask Anthony, pulling myself away from the glass. I heard a nurse ask him how she was, and the idea of him having a child stunned me at the time. Now, knowing him better, it makes more sense.

"Yes."

"What's her name?"

"Marley."

"How old is she?"

A very strange look passes Anthony's face, but he swallows and says, "She's two."

"I bet she's beautiful," I murmur, closing my eyes. I feel so tired. Everything hurts, every tiny movement, every breath, every heartbeat. My body is failing.

"She is," Anthony says. "I wish I knew her better."

"Does she laugh?"

"Yes, I imagine so."

I smile, sharing his imagining of it. "So beautiful. Don't let her get cured. Luke and I will never let our children get cured." I can see a little girl, laughing and crying, playing and kissing me as I brush my lips across her forehead. Her hair is dark and thick and smells sweetly of lavender, soft against my cheek, and her chubby little hands clutch around my fingers stronger than anything I've experienced.

I am stretched with longing for her, *our* her. She'll have his eyes, too green to believe, and she'll have grandparents, his parents whom he loves, people who will cuddle her and give her presents and no one will ever hurt her because I'd die before I let that happen.

"I'm here, baby," he says against my ear and I realize I have been saying his name, and he has come in from behind the glass, and he is lying in bed beside me, holding me, and his touch doesn't hurt anymore—the spots where his fingers rest are the only parts on my body free of pain.

"I hate you," I whisper.

"I know," he says, and I can taste his tears on my lips.

"You keep making me fall in love with you, over and over and over. Even when you do nothing but sit behind a mirror I still fall in love with you."

Maybe it's because he gave me the impossible possibility of this child while we were in the supermarket. He brought her into my heart, along with another two, and these children are something we will share now until we die.

Maybe it's because he remembers things in color, or cooks like it's brain surgery. Maybe it's because he loves old music and deep bathtubs and solving problems and brushing my hair.

Maybe it's just because he's lovely.

"Sweetheart," Luke utters, and then his lips are on mine, and if only I had more energy I might be able to care that it is a betrayal, that *he* is a betrayal, but instead I have only the energy to adore him and pretend we are back in the beginning. Then things were complicated in a simple way, but now they are complicated in a complicated way.

"You need to figure out how to get out of here," I tell him, looking into his eyes and trying to escape this dreadful pit of quicksand. I need to get back to reality, to this room, to the painful fact that I'm about to die and there are things to be done. One of Luke's hands is on my cheek, the other rests along the length of my spine, burning like a column of red-hot iron. "You and Ben and Anthony. Do it now, while you still have a chance."

"Ben hasn't finished what he's doing."

"He won't finish it—not before I change." I lick my dry, cracked lips. "There's no point. I'm dying, Luke. Save yourself."

His hand moves into my hair and, even though it hurts against my sore scalp, I love having it there, having part of him entwined with part of me.

"Josephine Luquet," Luke says in his deep, rough voice. "You are the love of my life. There is nothing else that matters. If you die, I die."

And so he's done it after all. He's come here into the abyss with me, and he's given me the one thing he could never give when under the cover of all the lies. Here is his 'I love you'. Here at the end when it means something.

My hands shake and I can barely get my words out. "Then why did you do this to me? Why did you lie?" I start to cry, hating myself for it.

Luke's lips are against my skin, moving over my tears, and he's holding me so tightly that it's an agony of impossibilities. "I don't know," he whispers. "I saw you and I loved you. That's it—that's the only thing that makes any sense. From there it was this stupid string of wrong decisions. I thought it would be safer for you if I stayed your agent and reported you as non-threatening. I knew that if I reported my feelings for you they would send another Blood who wouldn't care about what happened to you. I needed to keep you safe. I knew it was a mistake to talk to you in that nightclub, but I had to, Josi. I wasn't supposed to but I fucking *had* to. You and I together ... It was like a tidal wave I never even had a chance of denying. I had to keep it from everyone I worked with. I was lying to them just as much as I was to you."

"Why didn't you tell me?" I hiss. "I would have understood, Luke! I would have forgiven you! We could have worked it out together!"

"You would have hated me!" he exclaims. "This thing between us was so fragile for so long—you were suspicious and untrusting. We both worked so hard to create the love between us—it felt like such a triumph, such a beautiful triumph. I was the first person you'd ever trusted, and I couldn't let that fact be the very thing that hurt you. I was desperate to preserve what we had."

"You were a coward."

"Yes," he agrees fervently. "I was. That whole year I was a coward until the moment my mother told me something."

I swallow, a lump in my throat. "What did she tell you?"

"It was something Dave used to say. 'All that is necessary for the triumph of evil is that good men do nothing.'"

There are more tears coming, more than I can manage. This seems perfect in too many ways. "Where is your fury?" I sob. "All this time, where has it been?"

"Rotting my insides," he says flatly, and even now he can't let go, can't raise his voice, can't scream or shout or smash things. I realize that he has such an interminable control over what he feels that it has become the very definition of how he sees himself.

"Where is it now?" I press.

"Don't ask for it," he utters. "Don't ask me to let it out. I'll lose myself completely."

"Or maybe you'll find yourself."

"Through rage?" he demands. "You think all that matters is anger? That's not who we are. It can't be."

"Not anger," I murmur. "Choice." I move my hands to his face, running my fingers over the hard edges of him, the softness of his lips, the strong line of his jaw. "No one can tell you what you're allowed to feel, Luke Townsend. Not ever."

"I'd burn the whole world down if I could," he whispers, his eyes flashing with a bright, exhilarating fever. "I'd make it so that there was no cure, no censorship, no propaganda, nothing but you and I."

And this is when I understand the truth, the one truth that means anything.

They cannot take my fury from me, but I can let it go, because there are more important things in life.

Luke

When she says it, I have to go to her. It's like I am being pulled out from behind the glass.

Luke and I will never let our children get cured.

It's the most wonderful sentence I have ever heard in my life. I don't even think she knows she's saying it—she's delirious and fevered and mumbling through the agony, but it seems to me like the deepest truth she has, and it means only one thing for me: I still have a chance, and I'm going to spend the rest of my life fighting for it.

"Luke," she cries, closing her eyes. "Luke!"

I reach the bed but Anthony tries to stop me. "She doesn't know what she's saying. She's hallucinating."

"I don't give a shit," I snap. "She's asking for me, so I'm here. Get out of the way."

Anthony looks like he might protest further, but he doesn't have much fight in him, so he vacates the bed and I slide in with her.

*

An hour and fourteen minutes have passed when Josi goes very still in my arms.

"You okay?" I ask quickly.

"I'm numb. I can't feel the pain anymore."

I sit up, inwardly freaking, outwardly calm. "How's it coming, Ben?"

"Don't rush me," the scientist snaps.

"It means I'm getting close to the change," Josi warns.

"But just the first one, right? Not the proper change."

"What difference does it make?" she snaps. "I murdered nine people the last time I went through the first change."

I walk over to Ben and look at what he's doing. He shoots me an irritated glance and then harrumphs. "If you're so tense, you can help me. You too, Doctor."

Anthony has been sitting in the corner looking haunted, but now he gets up and joins me at the workbench.

"Heat half of that up," Ben orders, pointing to a small vial of yellow liquid.

"It's not piss, is it?" I ask and receive a cold glare.

"It's Zemetaphine."

"The stuff that started all of this?"

"The last bottle I know of that exists. I'm using it to create an antidote."

I sit down and pour half the liquid into a beaker, swirling it around against the light. "I feel like smashing it on the floor."

"Do that and we all die. Stop gawking at it and heat the damn stuff up."

I look around for a microwave or stove.

"See this metal thing here?" Ben says, tapping a steel faucet. "This is called a Bunsen burner. Did you pass high school science?"

I can't help but laugh at his deadpan manner. "Give me a break. I'm on edge."

While I'm waiting for the liquid to boil, thoughts start colliding in my mind. I look over my shoulder at Josephine, who is staring at the roof. She looks so frail and weak on that hospital bed that it's almost impossible to imagine the way her muscles are knitting together to make themselves stronger. If I hadn't seen the proof of it, there's no way I could believe it.

"Ben," I say slowly. He doesn't look up at me. "What would this drug do to an adult?"

He pauses, milky eyes moving to my face. "Why?"

"Curiosity."

"There's no way to know. It could heighten physical attributes. It could induce rage. It could be instantly fatal." Ben frowns, meeting my eyes. "Or it could cure someone of their fury, like we first hoped it would. In an adult brain, it would be utterly unpredictable. There's only one certainty—it would be extremely dangerous, and would end up killing you, no doubt about it."

Everyone in the room is staring at me now, so I shrug blithely. "Just curious."

*

At one o'clock in the afternoon, Josephine starts pacing the room. I watch her, unable to help Ben any further. Anthony is staring at the wall, oblivious. Outside they're not bothering to try and get in—Jean has no doubt informed them that the safest course of action is to wait for Josi to kill us all and then arrest her in the morning when she's safe again. She doesn't realize that Josi will be dead by then, but it would probably suit her just fine.

I don't ask Josi how she's feeling because we all know.

Anthony starts crying. I close my eyes, willing him to stop. He gets louder and louder until Josi puts her arms around him and holds him tightly. "It's okay," she tells him gently. "It's going to be fine, I promise."

"I killed a man," he weeps.

"I know," she murmurs. "I know."

"Tell us about your daughter," I suggest. Josi releases him and starts pacing again. She's got too much adrenalin in her system to stop. Anthony wipes his eyes and looks at me. He seems hollow and vacant, like a switch has flipped in his head, turning off the wave of sudden emotion he was flooded with only moments ago.

"Marley," he says her name on a breath. "I write her letters. I draw birds on the paper. Hundreds and hundreds of birds. We went to the zoo once and she wouldn't stop watching the birds. They were her favorite."

Something about the way he's speaking makes me go cold. I sit still on my stool, watching him, a part of me shifting to dread.

Josephine has stopped pacing—she can feel the change in the air just as I can.

"I write her a letter every night."

"You don't ..." I clear my throat. "You don't see her, Anthony?"

"Brie and I met six months before we were cured. We scheduled our procedures on the same day so we could be reborn together. But after ... everything was different. We had Marley and I thought it would change things. Make us closer. A family. But Brie was severely depressed. She got hooked on all kinds of prescription medication that I brought her from work. I couldn't see what she needed—I thought she just needed more pills. I thought they'd remind her how to love. I thought they would make her more lovable."

He is speaking in a dead monotone, his eyes locked onto mine but also miles and miles away. The sensation of seeing him but also not seeing him is chilling.

"It didn't work, nothing worked. I moved out. I knew Marley wasn't safe with Brie, not in the state she was in, but I was selfish and obsessed with work. I didn't want to look after a child. I couldn't care about either of them. Brie begged me not to leave. I didn't listen. I went back two weeks later. They were both dead. No one had gone to check on them. Brie had overdosed and left Marley to starve to death."

I feel so cold I'm sure my bones will shatter at any moment. The horror in the room is palpable. Josephine is frozen, her eyes wide. Anthony is still staring straight at me as he says, so softly it's barely more than a whisper, "I stood there and looked at them both for so long. I didn't know what to do. I was just ... blank. I still am. Except that I can't stop drawing birds."

Josi sits down on the end of the bed, her head in her hands.

This is what they take from us when they give us the cure: our humanity.

Chapter Twenty

SEPTEMBER 16TH, 2065

Josephine

At three o'clock I've had enough. I feel powerful. I feel enraged. I can't stop thinking about Marley, and I know what I have to do.

Before it's too late, I walk over to where Luke is sitting, snatch his gun from the holster at his ribs and lift it to my temple.

"*No!*" All three of them shout at once.

"I have to."

"I'm nearly there!" Ben cries, holding up a slide. "I swear, Josephine—I'm nearly there. Just wait, *please.*"

I look at them, the three of them, and I lower the gun.

It's a mistake, as it turns out.

Anthony

Josephine lowers the gun, but as she does so she closes her eyes. I feel a moment of relief until she opens them again. They are red.

I gasp. She looks like a creature out of a nightmare.

"Get behind the glass now!" Luke yells at Ben and me. I grab the things off the bench and run for the door. Josephine lunges at me but Luke pummels into her from the side, knocking her into the bed. It buckles under their weight, and I am momentarily stalled by the sight of Luke being launched into the air and sailing back down on top of the workbench. It reminds me of a bird in flight and my fingers itch for a pen so I can draw it.

"Come on," Ben says, tugging me through the door. He switches the glass so it's not reflective and turns on the sound—I can't think of any reason to do this except to torture ourselves with the sight and sound of Luke being torn to pieces. I stand in the doorway, calling for Luke to hurry up, but he can't get to us. Josi is blocking the way, throwing him into the walls, hitting him with blows strong enough to do serious damage. He's so quick, but she is faster—I've never seen anyone move like she does.

"Luke!" I shout. I can't leave him out there on his own with her. I can't lock this door until he's safe. I *will* not.

"Shut the door, Anthony!" Luke yells at me just before he has his head smashed into the wall. I wince in horror, but he manages to stumble out of the way, dazed and very strong.

"Shut it," Ben echoes but I can't, I can't.

I run back into the lab and grab the gun Josi dropped. It feels heavy in my hands, but I raise it and point it toward her. I'm shaking terribly and can't get good enough aim. She has Luke by the throat, lifting him off the ground and pinning him against the wall. She has her back turned; as I move closer I have a clear shot.

"Don't you dare shoot her!" Luke chokes out. "Don't you dare, Anthony!"

I must. My inaction will never cause another death. I refuse to allow it. I aim the gun at her leg, trying to sight it like Luke told me in the car. That feels like a long time ago now. He's choking to death—I can see it. His face has gone purple and he's not even struggling. Some twisted part of him is determined to let himself be killed just so he doesn't have to hurt her.

I take a deep breath and squeeze the trigger.

Nothing happens. Shit, the fucking safety is on. I fumble with the weapon, clicking the switch, then raise it to aim again. Except that within the tiny space of time it took me to do this, Josephine has dropped Luke—I'm not sure if he's alive—and turned toward me. I raise the gun, shaking like a leaf. A shot is fired—it shocks me so much that I jerk my hand up and accidentally fire a second bullet. Jesus Christ! A third bullet is let loose, purely because I can't stop shaking, and this one actually whizzes right past Josi's ear.

She approaches, baring her teeth like a wild beast. It is truly terrifying to think that her transformation is caused by a drug that's similar to what every person in the world has been given. I can just imagine a planet of rabid animals like this—a world of *Furies*. I wonder what—

"Anthony, *run!*" Luke screams. I blink, coming back to the room.

I forget about the gun. I can't kill Josi, no matter what she's about to do to me. I turn and run back toward the safe zone, but she's much too fast. I feel her hands—small, slender hands—grab the back of my head and wrench a chunk of my hair from my scalp. A shriek of pain escapes me and I stumble backwards, straight into her waiting grip. Josephine has her hands around my neck now—one twist and I will be gone. I feel a rush of euphoria at the idea of this, but there is also a part of my brain that is still functioning well enough to interpret this as a panic response. A response of the cure.

"Josephine!" Luke shouts suddenly. He sounds close. I'm not sure Josi recognizes her name as much as she simply responds to the proximity of the voice, but she spins me around to face Luke. He is holding the gun I discarded, and within the space of a heartbeat, he fires one quick shot, skimming the edge of Josephine's arm. She shoves me away, snarling in fury. The force of her push sends me heavily onto the ground and as I blink once, twice, I am lying on a sea of hot, jagged rocks. My body is alight, my mind is endless and white, I am shattering into a thousand pieces but I have absolutely no idea why.

Coughing, I force myself back to reality—it is too easy to escape with a disjointed mind like mine—to find that I am lying on the cold linoleum floor and I can't seem to move. My back is hot like fire; there's a searing sensation spreading from one point in my spine. I can't move my legs, no matter how hard I struggle.

I look up, searching for Luke. Swallowing the bile in my mouth, I push myself up using just my arms. There are a thousand leaves in my mouth and I cry through the thick taste of them. I can see Luke now. He's on the other side of the workbench, acting quickly, his hands fiddling with something I can't see. Josephine is on the other side of the room, crouched over the ground. I have no idea what she's doing, but something about it is eerie.

"Luke!" I hiss. There seems to be blood in my mouth now—where on Earth would that be coming from? What happened to the leaves?

"Hang in there, man," Luke tells me softly, eyes flicking to mine briefly. He's keeping a close watch on Josi while he does whatever he's doing. "Can you get yourself back behind the glass?"

"Not without you."

And then a miracle: Luke *grins*. "That's touching, but you're not particularly helping me right now. Get behind the glass and I'll follow as soon as I can. I'm gonna need some serious 'shrinking' after all this shit—and you're my man."

In any other person this kind of mirth at a time like this would point to a malfunction in the brain, but for Luke it's just … I think it's courage. He has such spirit. When he smiles he really smiles.

Since I have no feeling in my legs, I have to flip myself onto my stomach and drag my body, inch by painstaking inch, toward the outer room. Something tells me not to look at Josephine as I pass her, but I can't help myself. She's still squatting over the ground, but now I can see what has her so captivated. On the floor is a pool of blood—I don't know if it belongs to her or to Luke. She is running her fingers through it dreamily, making swirling pictures on the ground, smearing it on her skin, in her mouth, sucking her fingers and snarling, snarling.

It's not the worst thing I have ever seen—I am a man who discovered his wife and daughter dead in their beds—but it certainly comes in second. Josephine has become like an animal, but what separates the drones from what she is? Wasn't it me who laughed when he saw a girl dying in a car wreck? Wasn't it me who walked away from my wife as she cried and begged, feeling nothing? How am I more human than this creature before me, smearing blood on her skin?

I reach out for the edge of the door, dragging myself forward. It hurts so much I can't help but weep as my muscles constrict. I don't want to think about why my legs won't work. It's too frightening.

Ben is there, hauling me by the armpits into the room and slamming the door shut. He locks it with a click; I hear the echo of it within the room for what seems like an eternity. He is staring at me, at my back. He wears a look of aghast pity. In his face are the flashing neon words *it's bad, very, very bad.*

"Have you finished it yet?" I ask. More blood in my mouth. I must have swallowed pints of it.

Ben shakes his head.

"Then hurry!" I urge.

Ben ambles back to his small area of desk, clicking his tongue and shaking his head.

I close my eyes, preparing myself. Slowly I reach around to my back, fingers tingling. I don't know what I will find, but I know that it will change everything. I feel something cold and smooth, something hard. I wince, but force myself to keep exploring. It is long and round. And as my fingers follow the shape of it, I realize that it's some sort of pole. A pole embedded in my spine.

Luke

My hands can't move fast enough. I am watching Josephine, crouched on the ground, and I am watching Ben through the glass, and I am watching as poor Anthony drags himself toward the fleeting idea of safety, the metal leg of a stool impaled in his body. I am watching all of these things while my fingers take the vial of yellow liquid, prepare a syringe, fill it with the drug and then move the sharp point of it to the vein in my arm.

Anthony

I am imagining a murder of crows flying through the air when Ben's voice slices into my awareness.

"He has the vial! The Zemetaphine—oh shit, lad—what are you doing?"

My heart stutters to a jerking halt. "Is he ... what's happening?"

"He's using it on himself," Ben whispers.

Luke

I can't see what she's looking at, but I can see the dark tendrils of her hair, and it's enough. It's enough for me to imagine the life we could have led, the days we could have spent together. In the space of a moment, one single moment before I push the end of the syringe and an extremely high dose of virus floods my bloodstream, I experience the freedom of choice, the simplicity of liberation.

For ten years I've feared the cure more than anything. I've always said that I'd die before I let myself be injected.

But here I am, willingly dosing myself with something harsher, more destructive. Something that could make me a drone or a monster before it kills me.

And I couldn't be happier. I am alive with choice, with freedom, with love. I'd inject myself with a thousand cures, because it would be my decision, my *privilege*, to die for someone I love.

Who has ever been as lucky as I?

I see the children, the three children. Two sons and a daughter. I bid them farewell, and I tell them I'm sorry. I'm sorry I don't live in a world where they can exist. I want them, I want them with Josephine. I know they could have been wonderful, everything could have been wonderful, in another life.

But this is the one we have lived, this is the life that is ours, and I will own it, just as I always told Josi to own her crimes.

She stands up and turns around, and in the moment her red eyes find mine, I push the syringe into my vein and inject myself with Zemetaphine.

Josephine

There's a rushing wall of sound approaching, and it hits with a sudden burst of sensory explosion. I feel, I hear, I smell, I taste, I see.

I am.

I am squatting in a puddle of blood. A strangled exclamation of disgust leaves my mouth and I haul myself to my feet, heart beating in panic. I am still in the asylum lab. The light is the same. The smell is different—now there is blood in the air. I turn slowly, terrified of what I will find. Things have been smashed and broken, pieces of the bed are bent and scattered on the ground, along with instruments from the bench. The stools are all broken, legs missing or splayed at odd angles.

And Luke. There is Luke.

He is behind the bench, and he is holding something. His eyes catch me, so green, and then he does something, and I blink, not understanding.

"Luke?" I say softly.

His expression changes. I read surprise, relief, despair. Together our eyes go to what he holds: it is an empty syringe. A tiny bead of blood wells on the soft skin of his arm. My mind is too slow. I don't understand what's happened.

"Did I do something?" I ask. My throat sounds raw and painful, but I can't feel anything. "Where are the others?"

"Behind the glass," he says calmly.

"Was that ... just the start?" I have no sense of time passing—for all I know it could have been weeks.

Luke nods. "It was twelve minutes." He's breathing heavily. His pupils are dilated and his eyes start to dart around the room.

"What's going on?" I burst out. "Are you all right?"

He seems to snap out of some daze, dropping both his arms and nodding resolutely. "I'm fine, sweetheart. Are you okay?"

I nod mutely. I don't know when the next change will happen—it could be hours away, or it could be much sooner.

A voice enters the room. *"Luke. We need you in here. Anthony is ..."*

Luke lurches for the door and I spin around to face the glass wall. I can see behind it now. Ben is in there, but I can't see Anthony. I start to feel frightened. I walk toward the window, trying to prepare myself, but I can't, I can't. Marley is in my head, again and again. I can't seem to wed the idea of the therapist I've spent a year with, with this man who experienced the death of a child. It's a grief too big, too unfathomable. I don't understand how it could fit within the small, contained body of Anthony Harwood.

Perhaps that is the answer: it doesn't. Perhaps he no longer has the ability to grieve.

I peer through the glass. Luke and Ben are bent over something. I don't see it until Ben straightens awkwardly, stretching his stiff back and shaking his head. Luke is speaking, stabbing a finger, face contorted strangely.

And then. And then.

My eyes move down to the body on the ground and I see. Anthony is lying on his stomach, and there is a metal pole cutting through his body. There's blood, a lot of it, but he is still conscious, lying there and looking at Luke. I see his expression with a lurch of comprehension. There's something so perfectly simple about it. Something pure. Something rare for a drone. Something human.

"Let me in!" I shout, banging my fists against the glass. "Please, let me in!"

All three of them look at me, and it is Ben who shuffles over to the door and unlocks it. Even though it is unsafe, even though it could mean the end of them all. I shouldn't be asking for this, but there's a savagery to the need in my chest.

"Just for a moment," I breathe, entering the quiet, cool room. I can taste my tears, slipping down my cheeks. The three of them are staring at me. It is one of the worst moments of my life. It is absolute bewilderment—how could I have done this to a man I care about?

I sink to the floor, hands hovering above the pole. I look at Luke, who is pale and fidgety in a way I have never known him to be. "What do we do?" I whisper.

"If we pull it out, he'll bleed to death," Luke says.

"So then what?" I demand raggedly. "What do we do?" I look at Ben, but he spreads his hands helplessly. I swallow, make a decision. "He needs a hospital. I'll open the door and let them in. They'll take him and fix him."

Luke opens his mouth, but then he breathes out in a puff and nods tiredly. "Yeah. All right." We have been defeated and we all know it.

I'm about to stand when Anthony grabs my hand. "Don't."

I look down at him, at his face. I feel bruised by his eyes, by the sudden passion in them. I've never seen him look so alive, so human.

"If you open that door," he tells me, "I'll never forgive you."

"I have to. Your life's not worth less than ours, Anthony."

He shakes his head. "I feel alive for the first time in years. I want and I imagine and I regret. It's a perfect way to end it."

I start to sob, the pain of this tearing through my body. It's too much. I have committed too much.

"A man who cannot mourn his daughter should not be alive," Anthony says softly. Luke places his hand on Anthony's head. Something intimate passes between them. "Get her out of here," Anthony tells him. "Save her, and save yourself."

"Anthony, no, wait—" I blubber. His eyes shift back to me and he smiles. "You're fine, you're fine," I say. "We can fix this. We just need to—"

"It's okay," he tells me. "You were the best patient I ever had, Josephine Luquet. You changed my life. Now pull the pole out."

I stare at him, distraught. Luke has one hand in my hair, the other is still in Anthony's. "No," I sob. "There's no way ..."

"Luke," he implores. "Please, just pull it out."

Luke's jaw is clenched. He's looking between Anthony and me. Slowly his hand moves to the pole.

"No!" I snarl. "Don't you dare!"

"Please," Anthony begs.

"Get away from him!" I shout. Hands take me by the shoulders—it must be Ben—and pull me backwards. "Don't!" I scream, sobbing so hard my chest is turning inside out. "Please, Luke—*please*!"

Luke looks at me. "He's dead already, Josephine. This isn't … this can't be fixed. I won't let him suffer."

"*No!*" I scream, struggling forward. Ben has his arms around me and I know that I could throw him off and incapacitate Luke, and I could carry Anthony out of here and give him to the Bloods, but the truth hits me, a well of grief—it would simply be prolonging the inevitable. Anthony is ready now.

A moan leaves me, a horrendous sob that racks my body and throws me to the ground. I can barely breathe I'm crying so hard. I want to die, I want to disappear, for all of this to be a terrible nightmare. But it's not, and I cannot disappear—I must live through this, because it is my burden and mine alone.

"I'll do it," I weep. "I'm the one who killed him, so I'll finish it."

"Josi, I—" Luke starts to say.

"I'll do it!" I sob, pulling myself forward. For long minutes I close my eyes and force myself to breathe, to push everything back down to where I can manage it. I reach for the pole, placing trembling fingers around the cold metal. "Hold his hand," I tell Luke.

Luke reaches for Anthony's hand and grips it tightly. I look at Anthony's face.

"It's okay," he tells me softly. There's blood coming out of his mouth. "None of this was your fault, Josephine. I

310

didn't listen to you—I should have. I get to die fighting for something important. I've never fought for anything before."

I nod, touching his face once, stroking it gently, and then I pull the pole from his back.

Chapter Twenty-one

SEPTEMBER 17TH, 2064

Anthony

I don't like impromptu meetings. I don't like things that break my daily routine. But when the chief calls you, you go.

One of the nurses lets me into the medical station.

"Harwood, quick, get in here," the chief tells me distractedly. I enter the observation area of the lab, surprised by his focus. As I move to the glass window, I see what is on the other side. I go quite still, unnerved by the sight.

There is a girl sitting on the gurney, facing us but unable to see us. Her skin is covered in streaks of dirt and blood. Her eyes are completely red. Something about her expression chills me to the core.

I clear my throat. "Who is she?"

"We don't know her name. We don't know anything about her. But she says she's killed people. Lots of people."

My heartbeat quickens and I am unable to look away from her.

"I want you to take her on," the chief tells me.

"I have a full case load already."

The chief turns to me for the first time. "You don't want to know what's inside that head?"

I glance at him, then look back to the girl. I open my mouth to deny it, but find that I can't. I've a red-hot curiosity threading through me. I want to know who she is.

I nod once. "All right. I'll fix her."

Because that's what I do. I've not yet met a patient I can't fix. This girl will be no different.

In the corner of my eye there are birds, a flock of them, wings fluttering across my mind and brushing against my skin. They carry a name with them, a name I hear with every beat of my dull heart.

SEPTEMBER 16TH, 2065

Luke

As Anthony bleeds to death on the cold floor, I'm too agitated to feel anything about the life slipping from the room. It is unforgivable. But this is what I've done to myself.

Josephine won't stop crying; it is odd because tears are so rare for her. I know this but I feel rabid. I want to hurt something, inflict pain or just scream scream scream. I stand up and pace. I recognize the adrenalin flooding my body but I can't control it or focus it. I'm moving too fast, way too fast and I can't do anything about it. I think I might scream scream scream—

"Luke!" Ben says sharply, and I realize he's been trying to get my attention. "You need to run, lad. Get your body moving really hard."

"There's no space in here!" I snarl, furious with the stupidity of his suggestion. Does he think I haven't imagined pressing my body into the fastest sprint of my life? All I want is to run and run but there's no room and I can't breathe, Jesus, I can't breathe—

"Luke?" Josephine's voice slices into my head. She is looking at me from the ground where she's been slumped over Anthony's body. Her bloodied face is streaked through with tear tracks. "What's wrong with you? What did you do?"

I bare my teeth—I know it's weird, but I can't stop myself. It makes her flinch in alarm.

"He took the Zemetaphine," Ben says flatly.

"What?" Josi stands up slowly, horror struck. "What's he talking about, Luke? You didn't, did you? Of course you didn't."

I don't have to say anything—she sees it.

"Oh my god," she whispers. "This is … How could you?" Suddenly she's furious. "*How could you?*"

I snarl. "I did it for you!"

"I would rather you'd died than go through what I have," she whispers, making me cold.

It's too awful for words. I can't speak. My teeth are grinding together. There's too much strength in my body—it feels wrong. I'm a frenetic mess of energy and power and Josephine has just said the worst thing she's ever said to me.

Before either one of us can say more, a screen flashes on. It's on the far wall of the observation deck; I noticed it earlier but thought it must not be functioning.

Jean's face flashes onto the television. Her voice inhabits the room. "Agent Townsend. We have you surrounded. You have two options. You can send the girl out so that she can be erased. Collingsworth, Harwood and yourself will be dealt with leniently. Or you can all stay in there and die before morning."

I want to kill her. I want to tear her limb from limb and make her beg for mercy. I pick up a stool and smash it into the screen. Sparks shower down into the room and Ben ducks his head quickly.

When I turn around Josephine has gone. In her place is the monster. She lunges for me, a shriek of fury leaving her mouth. I duck my head and let myself plow into her as hard as I possibly can. We crash together in a brutal clash of limbs and bones and muscles. I have to get her into the other room, away from Ben. I throw a punch into her side and another to her chest—she feels neither, but they force her back a few steps. We tangle. She is so strong, but I have become more than I was, more than just a man. I make myself faster and tougher than I have ever been; I force her into the other room using every trick I have learned over the years, every piece of brute force and pure stubbornness. I will not let her harm the old man—I will find a way to cure her of this. Even now, when it should be too late, I don't care—I am determination.

A roar leaves my mouth as she smashes my head into the ground, but I learned about pain a long time ago. It's just a series of messages to the brain, easily shut off.

"I've got it!" Ben shouts suddenly.

Thank god, because I don't think I can hold Josephine off for much longer. She has me down on the ground, twisting my arm the wrong way—it's about to snap. I pull on it, jerking her forward. I manage to flip her over so that I'm on top, using all of my weight to hold her down. A shriek leaves her mouth, a ferocious animal sound.

"Quick!" I scream at Ben. "Inject her!"

Ben approaches but just as he's bending forward, Josi gives a mighty scream and launches me off her. I feel myself moving through the air and I brace for the landing, twisting myself into a roll so that my back won't take the force of the fall. I hit the side of the bed and feel my shoulder yank out of its socket. I send my mind away so I won't feel the pain of it—a dislocated shoulder can be particularly painful. Still, even high as a kite and trained to deal with pain, I feel it. I feel the crunch of bone against bone as I push the joint back into its socket. I grunt, spots dancing in front of my eyes. I look for Josephine as I stumble to my feet.

She approaches Ben, slowly like a predator. He is wielding the syringe like a weapon, but we all know she is too fast for him to have a chance at injecting it.

"Josephine!" I shout, but she ignores me. I start running, hauling myself into a dive, hoping I'll catch her before she lunges.

I'm too slow. Her hands dart out, taking the old man by the neck and lifting him off the ground. There must be something primal in her that enjoys the play of it all, else she would have snapped his neck within a heartbeat. Instead she toys with him, letting him dangle.

I plow into her, knocking her sideways, but as I do something sharp slices into my head, a blinding pain that brings me to the ground. I lie still, conscious only of the shallow air moving in and out of my lungs. My last thought before I slip away is, strangely, of Anthony's birds. Ravens. An unkindness of ravens. They lift me up, up, until I can no longer see my Josephine, racked as she is by the virus. She has survived this virus for years and years, the same virus that has destroyed me in minutes.

But then, I always knew she was stronger than me. I like that. Feathers are whispering against my skin, carrying me away.

Josephine

The first thing I'm aware of is a kind of heat unfurling from my elbow. It makes me think I must have it resting in a fire, so intense is the feeling. I look down, but there are no flames. Just floor. I must have cracked one of the bones in my elbow.

Dazed, I look up to see that Luke is on the ground, having a seizure.

His body is rigid and ghastly, jerking uncontrollably, and his eyes have rolled into the back of his head. A sound escapes me, a yelp of fear.

"Don't touch him," Ben warns, and I whip my head around to see him slumped on the ground, holding his chest.

"Ben, what happened? Are you all right? Is Luke ...?"

"He's seizing. He'll either come out of it or he'll die."

A wave of dizziness nearly drops me to the ground.

"I have the antidote," Ben wheezes. His face is red.

"Give it to Luke," I order quickly, crawling to his side to take the syringe.

"If you don't take it, Josephine, you'll kill us all. Luke may yet survive without it."

"But he might not!" I exclaim hysterically. "I can't take that chance!" I can't and I won't.

"You're not listening to me, dear. Take a deep breath and hear my words: you must take the antidote, or you will change and kill him. That's all that matters right now. You *must* take it—quickly now, before you change again."

"Will you make more for him?"

Ben nods faintly. "Of course, dear. Just take it."

I look at Luke, sick to my stomach at the sight of him jerking like that. He looks like he's being electrocuted. The urge to give him the antidote is so strong that for a second I don't think I'll be able to fight it. I edge toward him.

"Take it or Luke dies," Ben says again, and it finally sinks in. He's right. Of course he's right. I can't help Luke if I change again. I place the needle in my left arm, find the vein and push.

It's cold and painful, right away. I feel it move through my body, my whole body, creating a kind of deep freeze. When it reaches my head I black out.

SEPTEMBER 17TH, 2065

Josephine

I can taste blood. My tongue dances over my cracked lips, finding traces of steel. I open my eyes and the light is so bright I have to close them again.

"That's it, dear," Ben's voice floats over to me. He sounds far away. "You're all right now. You'll be all right. It's just taken your body some time to fight the Zemetaphine."

"Did it work?" I rasp, still unable to sit up. "Am I fixed?"

"I don't know, Josephine, but it definitely did something. You've been unconscious for a long time."

"How long?"

"Hours. It's around midnight, I think."

It takes me a moment for this to settle. Deepest joy takes root in my stomach, poking its head out and teasing me. "Wait," I whisper, scarcely daring to believe. "I didn't change again? When it got dark? I didn't change?"

"You didn't."

I'm flooded with music. *The Swan*. It's playing over and over in my head, so loudly that I start to laugh. Tears stream out of my eyes, because I know, I *know*, that I will never change again and there's so much relief, so much joy that I am utterly weightless and floating through the sky.

"Luke!" I call quickly, grinning like an idiot, wanting to share this with him. "Where's Luke?"

"He's ... I don't think ... I can't hear him breathing anymore."

And just like that I'm a thousand miles under the ground, suffocated by the weight pressing down on my chest. I lurch up, ignoring the dizziness that this causes. Luke's lying close by, very still. I remember now—he was having a seizure when I injected myself. I crawl over to him and listen for breathing. I can't find a pulse either. "I should have given him the antidote!" I gasp in deepest horror. "I should have given him—"

"Give him CPR," Ben orders loudly.

My head is a jumbled nightmare for ten long seconds. But then something happens. I close my eyes and I think a very simple thought.

I am calm.

I think it so loud and so bright and so strong that it comes true. I am calm. I will be calm until this is over, until Luke is awake again. No matter what happens until he wakes up, I am calm.

I tilt his head back and blow a burst of air into his mouth, then I pump on his chest swiftly, firmly. I am weak now, weak and in a lot of pain, but I keep pumping, blowing, pumping, blowing.

"Good girl," Ben says faintly.

I glance at him. "Why didn't you do this? Why did you let him stop breathing?"

"I've had a heart attack," he says simply.

"What?" I gasp, then remember that I am calm. "All right. It's going to be fine. As soon as I've got Luke breathing again, I'll come and help you. We can let the Bloods in and they'll get you straight to hospital. You'll be perfectly fine."

"If you let them in they'll capture you and sentence you to death. Both of you."

I don't say anything. I problem solve. While I pump and blow and pump and blow, I look around the room for another way out. There are no doors or windows, of course, but there is an air vent in the roof.

Bingo. As soon as Luke wakes up he can help me get Ben out through that vent and find him some medical attention.

"He's been out for too long," the old scientist tells me softly, but I don't listen. "He's gone, dear."

"No he's not," I say calmly. "He's fine. He just needs a push. He needs to be reminded of why this world is so wonderful."

We forget, don't we? We all forget. Amid Furies and Bloods and cures and drones, we all forget how beautiful life is, how hard we must fight to keep it. I need Luke to wake up so I can tell him this, so that I can tell him how we've been focused on all the wrong things, how we've thought only of the curse but not the blessings we have lived. I want to tell him that my life has been good because of him. That I have known wonder and bliss and excitement and joy because of him. That I have known grief and fury and loss and pain because of him. Who can say that they have given someone so many things? So much *life*?

I start pumping even harder, climbing onto his body and putting every ounce of my strength behind my arms. Luke's lips are tinged with blue as I duck my mouth to his, giving him all the air in my lungs. His skin is clammy, but I keep going. I keep going. I will never stop, not ever. Even if I have to keep pumping his chest for the rest of my life, I will do this gladly. I will never stop.

"Stop, Josephine," Ben says. "It's over. It's been too long."

"No." He doesn't understand Luke. Doesn't understand what kind of man Luke is. I remember back to that night, a thousand years ago, when we were standing in an abandoned building, right before we were attacked by Furies, and I thought a very simple thought: Luke Townsend is going to change the world someday. I know this in my gut, in my skin, my bones, my blood. "He's stronger than anybody I've ever met," I utter as I pump. "He's too strong to die like this." *He will not die like this.* Not after injecting himself with a drug he hates to save my life. That kind of courage deserves recognition—it deserves *life*.

"He's just a man. Nobody can be more than a man," Ben says sadly.

"A woman can. *I* can. I can make him wake up." I hit Luke's chest as hard as I can, knowing, somehow, that it will be enough. It has to be enough.

Luke gives a mighty gasp, sucking air into his lungs and convulsing on the ground. A ragged breath leaves me and I slide off him, laughing in delirious exhaustion.

"God almighty," Ben whispers.

Luke doesn't regain consciousness, but he is breathing on his own now, a steady, strong rhythm. I scramble over to Ben. "We're going out through the vent, okay? Can you stand?"

Ben looks at me. There's something so weary in his expression. "No, dear. I can't move."

"Then I'll carry you."

He shakes his head. "You'll have to carry Luke."

"Luke will wake up any moment now."

"My guess is that Luke's in a coma. That much air loss would have resulted in brain damage. There's no telling when he'll wake up, if ever."

I swallow. I can carry them both. I can—

"You can't, dear," Ben says softly, reading my expression. "You can't carry both of us."

I can't carry them both. I am weak and small—I have made myself weak and small because I thought it would hinder the monster inside me. Now I see how much of a fool I have been. I should have been making myself strong—strong enough to fight her, to carry these two men I cannot leave.

"Take him. Get as far away as you can. They won't come after you until morning."

"What about you?"

"I'll be fine. In the morning when they break in they'll take me to hospital. Now go, Josephine." He puts one hand on my cheek, smiling. "You're a medical marvel, child. You should have died years ago, so live every minute of your life like the miracle that it is."

I open my mouth to speak, but find that I can't. Instead I nod, unable to manage more. Climbing to my feet, I drag the remains of the bed to the wall beneath the vent. It's still not high enough, so I have to place a metal drawer on top. I'll be able to climb up, but getting Luke up there is another problem altogether. He's huge and probably weighs twice as much as me.

Grabbing the leather straps from the gurney, I use them to tie him to my back, a bit like I'm giving him a piggyback. I step forward, testing the weight, and stagger to my knees under his bulk. "Shit," I gasp. "He's a *lot* heavier than he looks."

"Use your thighs," Ben suggests rather unhelpfully. I haul Luke up onto the bed and then onto the drawer, which wobbles precariously. I'm sweating a steady stream by the time I get him up into the vent, and my limbs all feel like jelly. It's no less than a miracle that I have managed to haul him up, but there's something made of granite inside me—something that will not give, not ever. I will lift him into this vent, and I will carry him out of this hospital, and I will keep going forever if I have to. I have a body that has known the furthest reaches of human capability. I don't need a drug—a *virus*—to be strong. I can do that on my own.

I can't help but sob in relief as I pull him into the vent. The fit is tight and it takes even more effort to drag him through the small space. Before I disappear entirely, I pause.

"Goodbye, Ben. Thanks for everything."

"Goodbye, Josephine. Sorry for everything."

And that's all I have time for.

I can barely breathe by the time I find another vent opening. I look down but it's not an area I recognize, so I keep moving, searching for a safe place to emerge. After the fifth unsafe vent, I peer down and realize that I've found my way to Anthony's office. Groaning in relief, I pry the metal screws out and let the vent fall into the office. The next bit is going to be even trickier. I consider untying Luke and dropping him in first, but I don't want him to accidentally land on his head and break his neck or something. Which means leaving him where he is and hoping that I don't snap *my* neck.

"You're gonna owe me big for this, you jerk," I mutter to him and then fling myself down into the room. At the last minute I chicken out and grab onto the edge of the vent, but Luke is so heavy that I don't have a hope of hanging on. We crash to the floor and I'm practically suffocated under his weight. My elbow slams into the ground, sending an impossible agony up my arm. It is definitely broken—if it wasn't before, it is now. I can barely see through the haze of pain, but I drag myself to my knees and pull Luke toward the window. Time is extremely important now. The window is locked, so I kick through the glass, shattering it easily, but unfortunately since I'm not wearing any shoes, I can feel pieces of it slicing into my foot. An alarm sounds from inside and I know they've detected me.

I make sure there are no shards left to cut Luke and then pull him through as quickly as I can. Once we're outside I head straight for the trees in the distance. There's a fence to slow us down, but it's not electric, thankfully, and I manage to bend back the wire at the bottom and drag Luke beneath it. I don't want to think about why he hasn't woken up yet—I refuse to entertain the idea that he's permanently brain damaged and might never wake up. Instead I spend my time cursing his size and weight, and cursing every aspect of him, actually, because it's all right to do that when you know someone will wake up and fight back soon.

On the other side of the fence I try to run, but I'm too weak, so I push myself doggedly forward, step by step; every inch of ground I cover is an agony of triumph. Hours pass and I don't know how far I've gone, but it can't be too great, given the speed at which I'm moving. I can hear people all around.

The alarm is still wailing in the background, and the Bloods are searching through the forest for me. I keep low and quiet as I make my way.

I tread on something sharp and stop in pain. Luke is really starting to hurt my back, so I haltingly undo the straps tying him to me and let him drop to the ground. After stretching my aching muscles, I check that his breathing and pulse are still strong. It's dark and getting colder by the minute.

I think of Anthony, but I don't weep for him. I'm too cold for the vastness of that grief. One day I'll mourn him honestly, and I'll try to atone, but first I must survive this night.

For the first time in my life I am completely free. There are people hunting me, but I am free.

I reach over and stroke Luke's hair, willing him to wake up. "Come on, baby," I whisper against his ear. "I need you to wake up now." I'm so tired I don't know if I can carry him any further. A thought occurs to me and I rummage through his pockets, hoping to find something that might be useful to me while we're lost out here. I shudder to think of how I'll keep him alive if I don't figure out a plan soon.

He has a phone, the rest of the illegal cash, a couple of bobby pins (perhaps for picking locks?), a pocketknife, and a folded piece of paper. This surprises me—paper isn't used much anymore. I unfold it, but it's impossible to see in the dark. Using the light from his phone, I illuminate the paper. I'm looking at some sort of hand-drawn map with a few scrawled words underneath.

West of the asylum. Keep going until you hit the river. On the tree with the arrow, leave your name and wait for dusk.

I read it several times but still can't work it out. It's a set of instructions, but I don't know what will be waiting at the end of it. Was this Luke's plan? Or did he write this for me? Could it be a trap? Thoughts of the Bloods flash through my head. I have no other option but to see what's at the tree with the arrow. I feel sick with weariness at the thought of carrying Luke again, but in the distance there is a shout, the faint flash of torchlight, and I know they're getting closer. My heart lurches in terror and I scramble to my feet. Hoisting Luke onto my back again, I stagger forward, moving as fast as I possibly can. Without the straps it's more difficult, as he keeps slipping.

My elbow is searing and the blood from my foot is no doubt leaving a clear trail, but I can't do anything about it except grit my teeth and hope.

Soon the sounds start to get louder and I realize it is a whole search party, trawling behind me. They will catch me soon—I'm moving too slowly. I refuse to give in though—refuse to stop. My vision starts to go, but I press forward, stumbling blindly.

The Bloods are getting louder and louder. I consider finding some place to hide, but the scent of my wounds will draw them. A new sound reaches me—the blissful gush of what has to be a river. My heart flails around in my chest, a wild animal on its last legs, taking its last breaths, but I tell myself I just have to reach the water, just reach the water.

A shout sounds and I know they have spotted me. I am too late. Too slow.

My legs give way and I slump to the ground.

But then—

A noise pricks my ears, a different noise. Wild and primal. There are people approaching from the other direction. Shapes moving, pounding the ground with heavy footsteps, confident and sure.

I don't know what's going on, but I lower myself against the ground, watching for signs of approach.

And then I see. It's the Furies. Hundreds of them in the distance. They run with a ferocious war cry and plow through the Bloods' gunfire. There are so many of them as they reach the first ranks of the Bloods and start slashing with machetes. I gasp, looking away before more images reach my eyes. I have been given a chance. By some miracle, I have been given a chance at survival where I should have had none. I start crawling forward, staying low, knowing I must keep to the pitch black shadows because I am double my size, covered in Luke's hulking body. I'm a long way from the battle, and in the dark I can't see much, but the sounds are brutally clear. Screams and grunts, moans and the twisted sound of weapons against flesh.

If I survive this night, a day will come when I will have to fight like that, with that much savagery. Even though all I have wanted is to fight, I have never truly understood the reality of it—not until now, in this moment of dark and bloody violence, with human screams echoing in my ears.

I keep crawling until finally the river arrives before me and the sounds of the battle have faded into a distant muffle. I fall flat on my face in the shallows, sobs tearing themselves from my body. With the gray light of dawn creeping into the world, I can see a huge tree with a red arrow gouged out of its bark. It's on the other side of the river.

I can't help but moan in frustration as I wade into the water. It is moving quickly, washing me further and further from the arrow, but I force my tired limbs to kick and stroke, dragging the two of us to the other side. There's water in my mouth and my eyes, and I go under for one horrifyingly long moment, but the thought of Luke not getting any air makes me kick for the surface again. I'm weighed down by a thousand pounds by the time I reach the slippery bank on the other side. I have to perch Luke's limp body against gnarled tree roots poking out of the mud so that I can climb out.

I can hear individual voices now, shouting at each other and giving orders. They have dogs, lights and guns. The battle must be over, and the Bloods have won, even against the superior number of the Furies. They are not crossing the river, but moving along its length. If they come any further south they will see me, so I *must* get out. I must.

I think of Lachlan and the foolish, stubborn fury in my heart gives me enough strength to haul myself up onto the bank. I turn and drag Luke, with everything I have, up onto dry land. He grows heavier with every passing second and my limbs shake wildly. I have to stifle a gasp of exhaustion as I pull him slowly, slowly toward the largest tree I can see. Once I'm behind it I collapse to the ground and hold my breath, praying for the Bloods to keep moving.

Hours pass, and I am too frightened to move. I press myself against Luke's body, trying to stay warm as I listen to the sounds of search parties passing along the river. I don't know why they don't cross. I wait for them to come and find me, I wait for them to kill me, knowing I will not be able to fight or run, not anymore. But they never come, and as I lie staring up at the bright blue sky I look at the clouds above. For the first time in my life, the clouds form pictures. It's a new world.

Chapter Twenty-two

MARCH 3RD, 2064

Josephine

I am nineteen today. And I'm inside the glass, looking out at the balcony to where Luke stands in the rain.

The truth is, my body misses his. I missed him before I even knew him, like my body was carved in the beginning to fit with his. In a world where connection is almost impossible, the two of us have found it.

I imagine the life we will spend together, and I know this is just the beginning. I know that I've survived all that I have—all the beatings and broken bones and torn skin—so that I would learn the opposite. Not only the hurt of a body, but the pleasure of it. The meaning of it.

He thinks I am not ready, and I thought that too. Until today, this moment, realizing that I have been ready from the beginning, from the day we met, and before then, from the first day I knew that I wanted to learn joy instead of fury.

Because that is my right, too.

SEPTEMBER 17TH, 2065

Josephine

It's late afternoon before I move. I haven't heard any sounds for hours, and even though it's tempting to just lie here forever, I must figure out what to do next. Leaving Luke on the ground where's he's been all morning (still breathing, thankfully), I walk back up the hill to where I spotted the large tree with the red arrow. I'm stiff like a thousand-year-old skeleton, and I feel like I might disintegrate at any moment, but I have to make myself move. Peering closely at the arrow, I see that it has been carved into the fine bark and colored with paint. Actually, the more I look at it, the more I think it might not be paint at all.

I have Luke's knife in my hand, and I contemplate scratching his name into the wood. I don't know what it will achieve. I don't know whom it would be for. In fact I think it's fool's hope to sit around here and wait for someone to stumble across it. Who could be out here? Who would wait for a name on a tree? If someone really is out here, won't they see *us* better than they would see a carving? None of it makes any sense.

Plus there's a stinking, smoking battlefield behind me. I can feel it on my skin. No one would come near it.

But then I think about Luke. He does nothing without reason, he would never act without thinking through every implication and weighing the results. If he weren't sure about this, then he never would have written it down on a piece of paper.

I have nothing to lose, so I start carving Luke's name into the bark, right beside the arrow. Once I'm done, I make my way back to Luke and sit by his side again. In my head I make plans. Lists of things I will need to find. First, we need food and water. We will need shelter and warmth before night comes again, because I don't think we can survive another night like the last one. Luke needs medical attention badly; I have no idea why he's not waking up.

I think about the note. West, it said. West where everything has been ravaged by drought and plague. There is nothing for me there. I will have to find some way to infiltrate the city without getting caught. An impossible task. You can't exist without your prints.

Time passes and I feel stupid for waiting. Dusk, the note said. Wait for dusk. But what if I'm just wasting time? The sun starts to sink and I peer through the waning light, hoping for some clue.

"Luke," I say softly, running my hand through his hair. "You have to wake up now. Remember what you said to me? When you brought me to the asylum? Well it's been exactly one year to the day, to the hour. You made me a promise, and now you're breaking it. So wake the hell up."

He doesn't stir. I can't bear it, watching him like this. He's always been so strong, every moment of every day since we met. I have never seen him lose his cool or get upset, never live a moment of doubt. He's never been hurt or sick or un-sure. Even when he was injured, he bore it like he didn't feel a thing. He has been a locked vault, and I have no real idea what's inside. The only clue, I think, was the night he told me about Dave, but even then it was a dull, distant tragedy. Nothing is raw for him, at least nothing that I can see.

And the real miracle here? None of it is because of the cure. This iron-willed, detached weapon of a man is Luke, entirely Luke. He made it so that I can't trust him, but the truth is, he never once trusted *me*, not with any real part of himself.

The question now is: will it ever be possible for us to trust each other?

SEPTEMBER 17TH, 2064

Josephine

"Where are we?" I ask, blinking the sleep out of my eyes and trying to squint against the setting sun. Shadows and light reflect on the windscreen of the car, making it hard to see much more than a huge, looming shape before me.

"We're at an institute."

I look at him, confused. The blanket is still itchy against my naked body. I'm covered in dirt and blood, and every inch of me hurts like I've been beaten with a two by four. "What institute?" It's not like him to be evasive. I can see straight away that he's hiding something from me, that he doesn't want to say his next words.

"A mental health facility."

I stare out at the large stone building. It looks like a creepy old castle, sitting on top of the hill. All of a sudden I know where we are. "The lunatic asylum?" I whisper. This is where they keep the truly dangerous, the nightmare results of the cure.

Luke is looking at me. There's something hard in his eyes, in the line of his sharp jaw, his heavy brow. His large hands rest calmly on his thighs. At first I think he is unfazed, as usual. But when I meet his gaze, I realize it's something else entirely.

It's unflinching belief he's staring at me with. A cold, unyielding faith. "You're going to be fine," he tells me softly in that deep, deep voice of his. I love his voice. It is like being carried away in a soft wash of seawater. "You're stronger than every single person in that building." There's not even the *hint* of doubt in him, not even a trace.

"So then why am I here?" I ask.

"Because they'll look after you. We both know your body is starting to deteriorate. They can give you what you need."

"Drugs?" I whisper. "Cures? I'd rather die."

"This is a non-government facility—the only one left on the whole east coast of the country. They don't have the authority to cure patients—they'll treat you anonymously."

"Luke—wait, we're supposed to be finding the resistance together. That's what we agreed—"

"You're not well enough, Josi."

I swallow, looking up at the building. I can feel the truth of the words in the pain of my body—it has never been this bad before. "But what if they do give me the cure?"

"I won't let them," he says, and somehow I believe him absolutely. It makes no sense that he'd be able to stop them, but something in his voice goes right down into the heart of me and makes me believe.

"I don't want to go in there," I say. I will not plead; I will not let my voice waver. But I can't just go into a place like that—it is my worst nightmare.

"I know you don't," Luke replies, and then he says simply, "That's why you'll have to be very brave."

I draw a breath through my teeth. There is a moment of silence in the car, as I think about this, and about that place. Finally I nod.

"Josephine. Do you trust me?"

I look at him. His green eyes are blazing with that same determination. "Of course."

"Then you'll believe what I say next." Luke leans over the gear stick and cups my face between his big square hands. His skin feels cold against my burning hot fever. Last night I lay in a hole, waiting for him to send me his love letters. Last night I killed nine men.

"I've been weak," Luke says. "But I know now. I know what I have to do to solve this mess."

"I don't understand—"

"While you're here I'm going to find something."

"What?"

"I'll tell you if I find it. For now, you're going to walk into that asylum and you're going to tell them that you've tried to kill yourself, and you'll tell them the truth about the curse, and they won't believe you, so they'll keep you in there, and they might try to drug you, but you will be strong, and you'll withstand it all, because you'll know that I believe you, and one year from now, from today, from this very moment, you will be fixed, and I will take you in my arms and I'll kiss you like the first time I ever kissed you. That's a promise."

SEPTEMBER 17TH, 2065

Josephine

"You promised," I whisper again, trying to shake him awake. "You don't get to die, Luke Townsend. I haven't forgiven you, and I haven't even gotten to punish you. It's been one year exactly. I'm here, and I'm fixed, but you haven't kissed me. So you damn well don't get to die."

*

Another hour passes and I'm about to leave. I prepare the leather cords that will tie Luke to my back once more and wrap the strip of hospital gown more tightly around my bleeding foot.

And that's when I hear it. The snap of twigs, exactly like a footstep.

I freeze, heart shuddering to a halt.

I can't see anything, but I can hear more footsteps approaching. They are further upstream, but they are definitely on my side of the river.

Very softly floats a voice. A young woman's voice. "A girl, right? Dash said a girl?"

Then a deeper voice, a boy's voice. "Why would a girl be using Luke's name?"

"Who cares—we just gotta find her," says a third voice, a younger boy.

I listen as they move through the trees, headed the other way. This is it then. Time to choose. I have no idea who they are or why I'm here. I could take Luke and head back toward civilization. It seems more sensible. My instincts are telling me to run, to hide, never to trust anyone again, but my eyes glance down at Luke and the choice is easy, really.

"I'm here," I call out, moving from behind the tree.

There are three of them. They turn as one to face me. There's golden light saturating the world. Within it they approach.

The girl is the oldest—she looks about eighteen. She has a shaved head and huge blue eyes. Through her nose is a silver bolt. To her right is a large boy with blond hair cut into a mohawk. He is covered in tattoos. Last is a smaller boy, wiry and no older than fifteen. He shares the look of his companions though—all three are grizzly and scarred and staring at me with a mixture of distaste and curiosity. They are also heavily armed with machine guns and dressed in camouflage clothing.

"Who the fuck are you?" the girl barks.

It takes me by surprise, and my lip curls without my permission. I am a flame of fury—I always have been. "Watch your mouth," I tell her softly. "I'm not in the mood for lip from a group of kids."

There is silence.

"Holy shit," the youngest boy breathes. "She's not a drone!"

"And I think I love her," the blond boy announces.

The girl strides forward. "Do you even know why you're here?"

I close my eyes, swaying on my feet. I'm too tired for this. I can't work any of it out. "Who *are* you?" I demand.

The blond boy catches me under the arm. I'm so weak that I let him leave his hand there—without it I'll probably eat the dirt.

The girl moves right up close to my face, and I realize her eyes are an amazing shade of bluish purple. "You're uncured," she tells me. "You knew the code. So we're here to welcome you to the resistance. Forget everything you thought you knew about fury. In the West we'll show you what it really means."

www.ingramcontent.com/pod-product-compliance
Lightning Source LLC
Chambersburg PA
CBHW020245200626
46816CB00001BA/130